to

MW01275509

Thank you [ ])
interest &
encouRagement!

TERRY

AN
INCOMING
TIDE

t wilton dale

 FriesenPress

One Printers Way
Altona, MB R0G 0B0
Canada

www.friesenpress.com

ISBN
978-1-03-911953-6 (Hardcover)
978-1-03-911952-9 (Paperback)
978-1-03-911954-3 (eBook)

1. FIC019000 FICTION / LITERARY
2. FIC022000 FICTION / MYSTERY & DETECTIVE / GENERAL

Distributed to the trade by The Ingram Book Company

This novel is dedicated to Mary.
In addition to being my wife and companion for more than forty-five years,
Mary has been a dedicated beta-reader for this novel,
enduring several reorganizations and innumerable edits.
Thank you, Mary, for such sustaining support.

It takes a community to raise an author.
Thank you to my many beta-readers who have tolerated, encouraged,
and helped me bump along the way to get this novel out there.

TABLE OF CONTENTS

CHAPTER ONE

Twenty-five years ago

They fought.

Even in that place of iconic beauty, the place where the waves of the Pacific break onto the shore of rock and tree, even there they fought. Their force against each other was their words, words deliberately crafted with minds intent on emotional vengeance—crafted first and then impulsively flung to settle into the inward spaces of the other, spaces where the viscera of ego and fear dwell. They fought as only married couples can.

K'adsii Kabins. Selected to be a retreat, not a skirmish. He had picked it for the view of the beach. She consented, given the coziness of the cabin rustically constructed of skinned logs of pine and fir. For him, it had windows that looked out over the ocean. For her, a fireplace. She brought her wine in a case of twenty-four bottles, mostly reds but a few whites and a single bottle of a bubbly rose just in case there might be something to celebrate. For him, there was sufficient beach to run and a sheltered veranda on which to stretch.

An incomplete game of Scrabble sat on a low table. It was the deluxe set, with a rigid board and thin bevels of plastic to hold the tiles in place. A Scrabble dictionary rested where it had been thrown, half open and overturned so that its pages warped under the weight of the binding and cover.

They'd come to get away from the kids, to get away from the crucible of chaos the emergent demands of children created in their marriage. She'd readily passed over to his sister the daily tasks of responsible parenthood—the driving to dance lessons and soccer practices, the sitting with homework assignments resentfully and reluctantly undertaken, the management of diets, and the endless interfaces with grim principals and teachers worn out by classroom disrespect.

He'd obtained a locum to cover his family medicine practice so they could get away.

But in their words spoken at each other they'd brought their children with them—brought their disparate, desperate opinions of what is healthy and necessary. This was their ordnance against the other in the marital battle. They fired the children at each other. She'd be glad to be done with them. He wished that their oldest daughter had come to this beautiful place with him instead of his drunk wife.

A gust of wind shuddered the windows on the west wall, blasting in under the veranda roof, sending a spray of sand against the already pitted glass.

Exhausted from his refrains and her own retorts, dulled by the second or third glass of red wine, she retreated to lie down.

He retrieved her half-full glass of wine and selected one of the pill bottles she had brought with her, pills prescribed by his colleague on his recommendation. Selecting a saucer from the cupboard and a knife from the drawer, he pulverized several of the pills and swept the fine powder into her wine glass. At first, it floated on the surface. Then, as the liquid absorbed into the binding agents, the powder settled and suspended in the dark liquid. As she slept, a sleep of snorts and sighs, he carefully titrated the tranquilizer into the wine until the liquid held its maximum. He then decanted the concoction from one glass to another until it was clear of sediment at the bottom, leaving the drugged wine in the glass with the smear of her lipstick on the rim.

Into the saturated wine he poured the bitterness of how she challenged his authority—a family doctor's authority, for God's sake!—challenged it in the confines of his own home. He stirred in every offence he'd taken from her alcohol-uninhibited rants. Into the liquid he poured his fear—fear that she knew, fear that in a lapse of her judgment and loyalty she'd make known what could never be made known.

Once the concoction was mixed came the exhilaration. He was doing it. Over the last few days he had fantasized the plan. The more he went over it, the more inevitable it became. The prospect of getting her drunk and drugged and then drowned in the ocean focused him. It was as exciting as sexual foreplay.

He checked the schedule of high and low tides printed off by the manager of the cabins on a dot-matrix printer. Then he slipped into his wet suit and put his hiking clothes back on to cover it.

Awakening her he told her it was the time for the walk on the beach, that they'd just walk. He feigned being sorry for what he'd said and that they would try talking again tomorrow.

She was disoriented, wondering how long she had slept. Groggy, she picked up her wine glass and walked to the window to see the ocean. She drank. Deeply, desperately, she drank. Confused, she asked if the tide was going out. He replied that he'd checked the tide chart and they needed to leave soon. She drained the glass and quickly dressed for the damp wind of the beach.

On the other side of Snapper's Point was a deep and narrow cove, a half kilometre or so wide. The bay had two names. At low tide it was called Delectable, a sloping tidal flat interrupted generously by large rocks. Calm pools formed there with sand dollars and other sea life imprisoned in the shallow water. The bay was ringed around the back by the dense rainforest and a secure bastion of rock. Delectable Bay cradled walkers with a sense of peace and shelter.

At high tide it was re-named—Devilish Bay. Underwater rock formations and the claustrophobic sides of the bay funnelled the relentless ocean into an increasingly narrow gap. Wave heights grew taller. Wave speed grew faster. Undertow strength increased as the beach exhaled back into the sea.

There were no other beach walkers that day as they rounded Snapper's Point, picking their way between boulders with feet on the gravelly beach. The tide was partway. In the haze of the red wine, with its unexpected grogginess, she assumed the tide was ebbing. Mellow, she looked forward to the beauty of Delectable. Determined and clear of mind, he knew the tide was coming in.

The sound of the sea was too overpowering for him to hear the manager of K'adsii Kabins trying to warn them it was the wrong time of day to go walking. And even if he had heard the warning, he was too far gone to even consider paying heed.

He returned alone two hours later, his clothing soaked but his body warm within the neoprene suit he wore underneath. Frantically, he sounded the alarm that she'd been swept away by a wave. The panicky manager called the Coast Guard.

Back home, a thousand or so kilometres away, Aunt Leanne took care of their three kids—Annalise, age twelve, nine-year-old GJ, and little Stella, who was only four.

CHAPTER TWO

On a Monday last June

Leanne stands at the far end of the Denny Armann Gallery on Calgary's 11th Avenue as Estelle arrives with Tim's.

"No Jemma?" Leanne pulls the no-spill tab on the takeout cup and smells the brew.

"I dropped her off at your house on the way over. Gordon will take her to school."

"It's good she's getting some time in with him now. Pretty soon his summer gigs will take him away from us. He's playing side for so many solo artists coming through Calgary—blues, jazz, even some country." Leanne takes a sip of the coffee. "Jemma must be just about done school, eh?"

"Her last two weeks of grade one. When I went over to the house to drop her off, I thought I might be able to pick you up and bring you here."

"Oh, I've been here for hours. The gallery opens at ten. Lots to do in getting this all hung. Denny has the big ideas and then leaves me to do the work." She sips again. "So are Gordon and Jemma are happily ensconced in his music studio?"

"Of course, he greeted her at the door with his pan flutes. She gave him one of her instant hugs and then took the instrument from him and, blowing on it immediately went back to his music room."

"I hope they remember she has to go to school eventually."

Estelle looks at the painting resting on an easel behind Leanne. "Oh, you've that one up for the show, too. For the longest time, I didn't know that you were the one who'd painted it, you just doing portraits and all. Saw it over at Father's office. I thought the show was just the family portraits."

"Yeah, I painted this one for Jax's opening a few years back."

Estelle's brow furrows slightly, her voice drops. "It's nice."

"So, let me be the psychologist for the minute now and ask you, how does it make you feel?"

Estelle smiles at the turn-about of profession. "I don't know. It's a peaceful scene but somehow unsettling."

"Jax wanted a painting of the coast. He even had the interior designer for his office dictate the colour palette I had to use. At first he wasn't excited about the totem poles, but I insisted, thought it would give it that West Coast feel. Anyway, once I got started on it, I had fun with it."

"How so?"

"So, this was to be a painting for his waiting room, right?"

"Yeah."

"How do people feel sitting in a psychiatrist's waiting room? You should know this, being a psychologist and all."

"Depressed, anxious?"

"Yeah, and . . ."

"Nervous." Estelle takes a drink of her coffee, then flips the safety tab back on. "That's what it makes me feel, nervous. How'd you do that?"

"So, a person is going to a psychiatrist. What might they be afraid of?"

"That he can't help."

"Yeah, that too. What about being judged?"

"I'd hope not. But that's true, that the psychiatrist will be listening to everything they say, judging it. Watching facial expressions and body language."

"So look at the painting again."

"It makes me feel nervous because somehow it seems as though the painting is watching me. Judging me. How did you do that?"

"Come over close to it. Look at the brush strokes."

Estelle looks intently. Suddenly, appearing in the lush green vegetation, painted in the same hues of green and black, eyes stare back at her—piercing eyes with angry furrowed brows, grim mouths. "Yuck. Oh my God, Auntie. Creepy."

"So, look at the totem poles. They have the spirit animals and birds watching over from above—such a hopeful, protective, spiritual presence. Then, when I did the trees and the bushes, I used the brush strokes and slight changes in colour to add in human facial features—scary ones, not fully formed, like peering out while hidden in the trees. If you step back, they disappear, but they are still there."

Estelle takes a step back and then goes back in to take a closer look. "It's enough to make you a bit paranoid."

"Perfect for a psychiatrist's office, eh?"

"With your portraits I've always felt that the people in the painting are looking at me, like we're in the middle of a conversation."

"That's what I'm going for. Everyone thinks that they look at paintings, not that the paintings look back at them. I make it go both ways."

"You have labelled this one *Looking Back*. That kind of gives it away."

"Not too many people get it. You have to get up real close to see it, but it's there."

"We call it subliminal. I see the title there on the card, *Looking Back*—looking at it makes me remember the times that I went to the coast with Father. Those memories, well, they're pretty grim too, like the faces in the painting."

"Well, *Looking Back* is the name for the whole show, the seven family portraits. A way of looking back over the history of our family. When I told Denny about this one, he insisted we had to have it for the show. We put it out here to set the stage before the patrons go into the rest of the show in the back. It's all about going forward while looking back."

Estelle steps away from the painting and peers into an opening in the back wall leading to a darker space. The walls there are in a deep charcoal, the light is dim.

"So the portraits are in the back. Denny built a series of partitions back there, like little alcoves for each portrait, displaying one at a time. It's a maze, one dark maze that pulls the patrons farther in. Let's go and take a look."

Leanne stands aside allowing her niece to enter. Estelle hesitates, taking a deep breath before she enters the darkened space.

Lit by an overhead spotlight, the first portrait depicts Estelle's childhood family formally seated and standing as if arranged by a professional photographer.

The facial expressions are frozen at an awkward moment. Everyone appears to be waiting for the completion of the photographer's final few equipment adjustments. A moment suspended in time.

The parents are central in the image. Izzy is seated, Jackson standing. Izzy is perched on a high stool—one foot angled into the low crossbar, the other hanging down. She's dressed in a sophisticated denim and plaid outfit. Several gold chains hang down toward her breasts and the top button of the collar is fastened. Her skin is powdered, her mouth slightly puckered in a peeved sort of way. Her eyes look glassy. GJ, perhaps at eight or nine years of age, stands to her right. He has tucked himself into her right shoulder as her arm circles his torso. Her hand pulls him in close. In these moments before the photographer asks for GJ's readiness, his head is tilted toward his mom, eyes deflected upward. His mouth is open as if he's speaking to her.

She holds a glass of red wine in her left hand and her eyes have taken a momentary glance downward toward it. The deep crimson tones of the wine are luminous.

Jackson is to her left. He wears a physician's white coat with the name *Dr. Horvath* in a blue patch on his breast pocket. The stethoscope around his neck suggests he has just rushed in for the sitting. His facial expression is presentable but disconnected. There is space between his right arm and her left shoulder. Distinct and impenetrable, an invisible wall exists there. On the other side of him stands a girl of eleven or twelve years, Annalise. The back of his left hand brushes the back of her right.

Completing the image is a young girl seated cross-legged on a cushioned chair—Stella. A hardcovered children's book rests on her lap, tilted upward as she concentrates on it. Stella's forehead, furrowed in concentration, shows above the top of the book. The shape of her golden curls, dead centre in the portrait, is repeated in a set of drapes behind the family. The curtains meeting in the top centre of the portrait provide further symmetry—odd and stultifying.

"I've no memories of what my mom looked like. I guess this painting is going to be it. The way I remember her—a mom with a wine glass in her hand."

"She died when you were four. After she died your father insisted that all the pictures of her were to be boxed up, put away. His way of grieving, I guess."

"Or, not grieving." Estelle's lips clench into a hard line. Leanne reaches a hand around Estelle's waist, pulls her in.

"You know, even before she drowned she was not a happy woman. The pregnancies and births were hard on her. She had to go into hospital with depression—three times it happened, after each of you were born. Then the drinking started. I'm afraid she never paid you much mind. I was there when she went into hospital, took care of you quite a bit even when she did come home."

"Yeah, I know. When I was in graduate school, we had to do family diagrams and timelines. I tried to talk to Father about it, and he wouldn't tell me anything other than she drowned in the tide. I called you to get the details, remember?"

"Yes. I remember."

There's a slight tremor to Estelle's body. Leanne holds onto her more tightly.

"So, back then, I had this plan to become a portrait artist. I was already getting commissions. My career was off to a good start. I'd thought I'd do families, so I blocked this out while Jax and Izzy were away. I could sketch you kids while you were around and I was taking care of you. I blocked it out in a very traditional way. It was to be a sample to show prospective customers.

"I'd taken a bunch of Polaroids to work from." Leanne motions Estelle over to a side table. A Polaroid SX-70 rests there, surrounded by scattered photos of the family members. Now, with the passing years, the images have discoloured to more sickening hues, the detail has gone soft.

"I found the old camera and the box of Polaroids. We're displaying the work-up materials with each of the paintings for the show. Denny insisted. It makes a lot more work in setting it all up, but I guess it adds to the effect."

Sketches from a coil book are mounted on the wall above the table, the little flags of paper still attached at the holes from when they were torn out. The paper is yellowed, now twenty-five years old. There is one brilliantly white sheet of paper with colour swatches establishing the palette for the painting.

"I did lots of drawings of you, but in every one your nose was in a book. Imagine, back when you were just four-years-old, not even in school yet, you were already a reader. Figured it out on your own."

"Really, that young? Jemma didn't start to read that early."

"I made a lot of notes back then when I was drawing someone. I went back to read those notes as I was selecting the sketches to display here. They brought back so many memories for me. I wrote down that you parroted lines from your picture books into every conversation—how cute that was, how it made me laugh. But I also wrote about the way you taught yourself to read so young. You weren't just memorizing the stories. You were figuring out the words—every book was an adventure, every page, every new word. If you needed help with a word, you'd come to me, but then go back and keep working on the next one yourself. Such an independent little soul you were. You had your favourite books but always wanted a new one, just so you would have new words to figure out."

Leanne takes another sip of her coffee. "Then there was this long note, written on the day your mother died. We were reading *Love You Forever*, that Robert Munsch story. You asked me if I would love you forever. I wrote that down. It really touched me."

"And you have." Estelle looks at her aunt. "You always have."

"Best that I could."

Estelle picks up a few of the Polaroids, holding them by their white plastic cases. She looks intently—tries to retrieve her older sister and brother. In the shots of her as little Stella, she either has her head in a book or is looking up at the camera with the artificial smile that a four-year-old thinks is expected when a picture is taken.

"Anyway. I'd just done the sketches and the blocking for this painting when I got word that Izzy had died. Put it away. It was all hell to pay when Jax got back from the coast. He drank heavily, was violent toward GJ. I had time when you kids were in school to go back to the painting and decided that I'd paint it as the family was, or at least had been, not what would be attractive for a prospective commission. I thought it would be a tribute to Izzy, to paint her as I remembered her with her family. But I couldn't put smiles on anybody's face. I was trying to work everything out in my mind, I guess. Eventually, I just put it away again."

Estelle goes back to the painting. Wipes a tear.

"Look who is touching who," Leanne suggests.

"Well, Father and Mother aren't touching. But look at Father's hand, touching Annalise. And Mother is pulling GJ in close. Oh my God, Auntie. We studied this in Family Dynamics and Development class in graduate school. A cross-generational, cross-gender pattern of family alliances. How did you know?"

"I didn't know what it was. It's just what I observed. Jax was so close with Anna, too close, probably. And Izzy had GJ."

"And no one had me." There is a tremor in Estelle's voice.

"*I* had you. Back then you were my Bookish Stella."

Estelle lingers long. Her cup of Tim's dangles awkwardly from her hand. Leanne lets her just stand. After a few moments Leanne nods to suggest they head around the corner, into the next alcove to see the next painting.

The second portrait hangs decidedly askew, deliberately at an odd angle.

The portrait contains four figures. Of course, Izzy is gone—but Jackson is too.

GJ is in the foreground, taking up most of the canvas. The image catches the moment he kicks over the empty stool on which his mother had sat in the first portrait. He is off balance, arms in motion. His face is in three-quarter profile—the eyebrows descending, the mouth in a short firm line. The stool is in the process of toppling, two legs still on the ground and the seat emptying toward it. GJ is larger than in the first portrait, grown as a middle-school boy grows. Substantial. Kinetic. Fury full.

Anna stands behind. Her body has emerged into adolescent curves, sensually emphasized by the jazz dance leotard she wears. White dance sneakers are tied together by their laces and slung around her neck. Her hands are on her hips. The pose oozes disgust as she looks at her brother. Anna's face is largely hidden by the makeup she wears, garish both in the way of teens and stage performers.

The scene takes place in the same room as the first portrait, its view rotated a quarter turn to show the corner of the room. The horizontals and verticals of the painting are at an angle of five or ten degrees from its frame.

The first portrait hangs on the side wall in the background, retreating from the viewer. The light of a portrait lamp on top of it has gone out—its cord scrambles out the bottom, dangling toward an electrical plug on the wall. The painting just hangs there crooked—bumped, and no one has bothered to right it.

The third figure, partly hidden by GJ's moving body, is Stella. She is draped over a wing-backed armchair, sitting sideways. Her back is supported by one arm of the chair, her legs bent at the knee over the other. The chair itself is rotated to be looking out of the space of the room. She is wearing a hoodie of muted orange, her golden curls slipping out the sides. She is reading a chapter book, not looking at the violent movement of her brother just inches away.

The drape over the window hangs at its own odd angle, leaving part of the window revealed. The blackness of outside is hard-pressed to the top corner of the portrait. Leanne is faintly reflected in the window. She is standing at her easel—paint smock on, brush in hand, a horrified look on her face as she takes in the scene.

"Oh my God, Auntie. Look at GJ."

Leanne sighs. "Yes, look at GJ."

"Was it really that bad?"

"What do you think?"

Estelle tilts her head, trying to take in the unsettling arrangement of angles. She goes to straighten the painting on the wall.

"Don't. I want it hung that way."

Estelle steps back, takes a deep breath. "You're going to have to fill this in for me. I have no memories of this time in my childhood. How old would I be in there? Six maybe? Seven?"

"Yeah, about that. Maybe it's best that you don't remember."

"I look pretty checked out, looking away from what GJ is doing."

"Okay. Let me fill you in. First, GJ was really violent in the years after your mother died. A whole lot of anger bursting out of a boy's body. He was rude and crude to you especially. And Jax wasn't much good. He was off to rehab for his drinking—but even when he came back, he left the parenting to me. It was all so much out of control. And when Jax came over, it got even worse."

Leanne pauses the story. Estelle looks over at her. Grim determination has set in as the artist stares at her painting.

"He kept taking you three to the coast, the same cabin where your mother died. I tried to tell him not to. Thought it was traumatizing on you as children. Traumatizing . . . is that the right word, Dr. Estelle Caylie, clinical psychologist?"

Estelle is biting her lower lip. There is another tear to wipe, but she is paralyzed standing there and just lets it course down her cheek. She doesn't even nod to her auntie's question.

Leanne sighs.

"So I adopted you three . . . well, you and GJ. Anna wouldn't have it. She was almost fifteen and so close with your father. The lawyer told me not to push it with her. But I adopted the other two of you. That's when I changed all our names to Caylie."

Estelle remains silent, staring at the portrait.

"The Caylie name goes back to your grandmother, my mom. She was a Caylie. She was making a name for herself as photographer and so when she married she took the hyphenated name Caylie-Horvath. I picked that up from her, used her hyphenated name for myself. But your father, Jackson, he went with just Horvath like his own father. When I adopted you I was really disgusted with Jax and that arrogant, workaholic line of doctors he was a part of. So I changed my surname to just Caylie, and for you and GJ as well. Anna is still a Horvath, I guess, wherever she is."

Still no look of connection from Estelle.

"Back then most of my time was spent trying to corral GJ. He kept getting sent home from school because of his behaviour. Finally, the school told me he had to be on medication. Jax stepped up and got that for him. What do you call it? When a kid needs medication to control his behaviour?"

Leanne implores Estelle with the question but Estelle just stands staring blankly, her body at the angle to match the crooked painting on the wall. Leanne waits. After a moment or two Estelle shudders and rights herself, connects back. She looks surprised at the coffee cup in her hand, pulls back the tab on top and takes a drink of the now tepid brew.

"So, what do you call it? A kid whose behaviour is really violent, out of control?" Leanne asks again.

"Oh, you mean GJ? For boys in the middle grades, that would be ADHD probably, or oppositional defiant disorder."

"I remember it now. It's funny."

Estelle looks at her—a look of curiosity, engagement.

"The psychologist said he was odd. I will never forget that. This guy with all the briefcases and zigzag graphs said he was *odd*. I still have the picture of it in my mind, him and his artificial smile. I must have sketched him when I got home, probably back in one of the sketchbooks up on the third floor."

"Odd?"

"Wouldn't say the word directly, just spelled it out for me. O-D-D. Later I found out it was what you said, that oppositional thing."

"Did they put him on meds?"

"Yeah, most of the time it worked, I guess. He was really secretive about it, wouldn't let me watch him take it, said he was doing it himself. I don't think he was a lot of the time."

Estelle goes over to look at the display of sketches mounted on the wall perpendicular to the painting. There are photo prints of the room, of the stool. Leanne has displayed them on a small table, turned on an angle with the eventual sides of the portrait frame drawn in. A large sketch blocks out the final composition with the angles transferred onto it.

"So, anyway, I guess that's where Jimmy came in."

"Jimmy?"

"Anna's boyfriend. Jimmy. I never trusted him. He had an old farm truck, an F-150. I remember sketching him with it. He was older than Anna, like by a couple of years at least. She said that Jimmy had been on the same medication, would talk with GJ about it."

"Wow, look at Anna. She was quite a looker, eh?"

"Looked a lot like her mother. Had a dancer's body, the way that she moved. Far beyond her years though. But, she and Jimmy...I didn't think he was any good for her, but what could I do? Anna was getting more and more out of control. I couldn't discipline her—she was so tight with Jax. And Jax, when he was around, he really undermined whatever I tried to do with her. Between him and Jimmy..."

"So what's happened with GJ? Do you ever hear from him?" Estelle is still staring at the figure of the boy so out of control at the centre of the portrait.

"Not for years now. I think the last time was when he was charged for the third time, drugs and dealing. Jax intervened and got him out of it. Apparently, they got him to give up the drug dealer further up the chain from him. After that, I have no idea."

Estelle goes back over to the sketches, back and forth between them and the painting. She looks closely at the many sketches Auntie had done of her back those years ago. Some show her face—but it is a strained face, empty even. When it finally came to the portrait, Leanne had hidden her, hidden in the hoodie, hidden in the wing-backed chair with legs dangling over one of the arms.

"I'm completely checked out."

"You were. Except for your books."

Estelle stands, now upright, now with her psychologist mind engaged. "Why, Auntie? Why?"

"Heavens, I don't know, Estelle. I did my best. But with GJ the way he was, and Anna the way she was, I guess I was just content that you were there reading your books, not causing any trouble." Leanne sighs. "I did my best."

"You did. You were my rock. That's what I always say, 'Auntie is my rock.'"

Leanne alerts to the sound of someone else coming into the gallery, rustling in the back office. She goes to check. Estelle stands absorbed into the golden curls straggling out around a dull orange hoodie, legs dangling over one arm of the chair. There are distant voices.

Coming back in Leanne comments, "Just Denny. He's going to work on the wiring for the fifth portrait. We aren't there yet."

Estelle doesn't respond.

Leanne goes back to her niece's side, to her adopted daughter who never called her *Mom*.

"My mother was dead, and Father isn't in the picture."

"No, he wasn't there when I needed him the most. When he came around . . . between him and GJ, GJ really needing a father. . . well, Jax just made matters worse."

"Let's go on, get away from this one. As much as I can't see me, the way that you've painted me there, I feel me. It is not a good feeling."

They go around the corner into the next darkened space.

15

The room angle of the third portrait has been rotated again. The back window is no longer visible but the kitchen is now seen through an archway.

GJ has grown in height and has the faint film of facial whiskers. He wears a black hoodie and stands behind a large dining table. He's looking out of the frame, not making eye contact, staring down the hall toward the front door of the house.

Auntie Leanne and Stella are sitting at a dining room table, Auntie on the short side of it. On the long side of the table Stella has her back to the archway. She's no longer a child but somehow not yet quite an adolescent. Stella's face is propped up on her hands, elbows down astride a hardcover book resting on the table. The book looks to be a substantial work of fiction. It is likely a Dickens or an Austen—a book too heavy for such a slight girl to hold. Her aunt is reaching out to her, her left hand touching Stella's right forearm.

The fourth figure is of Jackson Horvath. He stands in the kitchen holding a coffee, no longer wearing the white lab coat and stethoscope. Jackson's eyes are focused on Stella's back as she sits to read.

Behind Auntie Leanne, to the side of GJ, are the other two portraits. They rest on easels nestled together, set at an angle.

Jackson, the table, and the walls are painted to appear solid, substantial. The other three figures are not; they seem fragile.

As Estelle draws in closer to the painting, she sees GJ, Auntie Leanne, and Stella were rendered with fine fracture lines. Portraitist Caylie has painted these figures rife with splinters. The fine lines and slight discontinuity of tone and colour convey the same effect as a shattered mirror, with each fragment reflecting at a slightly different angle.

No, not a mirror, more like a bone once broken and not properly reset—a bone fused again slightly off, functional but painful. Even likely to give way when put under stress.

"You and your books." Leanne sets her coffee down on a side table that now holds a bulky digital SLR camera. The sketches are scattered around it, not yet mounted on the wall above.

"By grade three, you had read your way through the entire library at Earl Grey Elementary School. So it was trips downtown to the library, once a week at least. More if you ran out of books because you got panicky then."

Estelle stays close to the painting, not bothering with the bigger picture, studying the fractured renderings. She hovers a finger just a centimetre above the surface, as if she is trying to smooth out the cracks. Leanne leans one shoulder into the wall beside the painting, studies the flow of muscle changes on Estelle's face. She notices Estelle's cup is starting to tip, is in danger of spilling on the floor. Leanne takes it from her and sets it on the side table with her own.

"So you see Jax is back in the picture now," Leanne comments.

Estelle's eyes don't go to her father, still fixed on her own profile as her face emerges from the fingers of her left hand propping her head above the book she is reading there.

"When he got home from rehab, and he went two or three more times at least while you were at Earl Grey, when he came home he was sanctimoniously sober for a few months. Every Saturday he would pick you up, take you to the Chapters over on MacLeod Trail, do the Starbucks there with you. Then back here to sit on the veranda and read.

"Then, without warning, the drinking would start again. You'd sit out there on the wicker loveseat, watching for him to come, and he wouldn't. And you'd get cold or tired and come back in and ask me to take you."

Estelle's finger still hovers. It is now tracing the look of concern on Auntie's face, a face seemingly broken but holding itself together.

"And then a year or so later he'd be back from rehab again, all clean and sober, haughty about it, too. That man has no shame, no shame at all. It's like he is entitled to our forgetting..."

Estelle looks from the auntie in the portrait to the auntie beside her.

As if in a sudden reset, Leanne smiles. "Do you remember *Stella's Way to Read Club* that you started at the school?"

Estelle smiles, a sweet, almost childish smile. "And grade eight, I got the senior student of the year award."

"You'd started with the reluctant readers when you were in grade two, the kids from grade one who hadn't started to read yet. You took them aside to that corner of the library and taught them your way to read. And it worked. You must have taught dozens of kids to read over all the years you were there in Earl Grey. More than dozens, I bet. And when they announced you were senior student of the year, they all stood up and chanted '*Stella, Stella, Stella*' like you were the hero of the school."

"And Father was there. He came to the front with me, with you and me, when Mr. Bagatti gave me the award. He was there then."

"Yes, he was there then. So let's move on."

Leanne retrieves their coffees from the side table and they head around the corner to the next room in the maze of partitions.

Stella!

Looking up from a haphazard collection of open books in front of her on the dining room table, Stella stares directly out from the centre of the fourth portrait. It is the first time Caylie has painted her face-on. Like that of a prey animal, Stella's face bears the vigilance of having just come to full height, aware of danger—out of the burrow, into the perilous world.

Her countenance is startling as much as it is startled. Gone are the long golden curls that had once framed her face. Her hair is now cropped short, straightened spiky. Her eyes are wide. Her mouth set grimly.

The books in front of her are substantial—not the gracious books of literature but the stark texts of a university.

There are three other figures in the portrait. Stella is most brightly lit. Auntie Leanne stands directly behind Stella, off to the left. Beside her is Gordon—a balding man, middle-aged, holding a harmonica in front of the lower third of his face. Far to the right, Jackson has entered the room.

The four figures are luminous. The room behind them is dark, almost black.

The fracture lines are gone—smoothed over, buried.

Auntie's hand is on Stella's upper arm. The look of concern so evident from the previous portrait remains. It seems less acute; her facial features now just morphed into chronic worry. She's older now, a lifetime spent raising this girl to the point that she suddenly, shockingly views the world around her.

Gordon has kind eyes, eyes looking at Leanne as she looks at Stella. There is love in those eyes. Not the disoriented, dutiful, desperate love that Aunt Leanne holds toward the girl, but the discovering and delighting love a secure man can have for a woman.

Jackson, off to the right, is another story. His gaze is engaged but somehow clinical—as if he is observing, judging.

"It's Kimmi," Estelle says.

"Kimmi?"

"Kimmi from grade nine. When I look at me in the painting, it's Kimmi I see."

"She came to the house. I sketched her, didn't I? Now that you say her name, I remember her face. Don't remember her, though."

"He/she was trans. We didn't use the word trans back then, or the indefinite pronouns. But that's what Kimmi was. She was bullied by the other girls, teased for her looks. And beaten up by the boys, beaten up when they discovered his body didn't add up with her behaviour. Kimmi committed suicide because they couldn't be. That look, the look you have on my face in the portrait, that is how I saw Kimmi."

Estelle pauses. "I loved Kimmi."

"I remember it all now. She hung herself, himself, out at the back entrance to the high school. I was afraid you'd never go back to school yourself. You were so devastated."

Estelle sits on one corner of a side table in the room lit only by the spotlight on the painting. Leanne stands at the other end. On the table rests a metal palette with bursts of oil paints haphazardly strewn over its surface, a brush to the side.

"I went back but didn't go to class—or went as little as I could get away with. The guidance counsellor found a back corner of the library for me to hide in. I did every high school module that existed. When I had to be in classes, I just went for the quizzes and exams. Pretty quickly I ran out of high school and got in books from the university."

The sound of a harmonica wafts in around them—melancholy, eerie, rich. Leanne looks back to the portrait. She warms to Gordon's eye there. Then the burst of sound stops.

Estelle continues, not having even noticed. "It was because of Kimmi I went into psychology. It's why I am who I am today. Kimmi's suicide pulled me out of literature to read everything I could on sexuality and gender, on discrimination and homophobia. I loved Kimmi. I had to understand what happened and why, so it would never happen again, never again to someone I knew or loved."

"But you, too, I was so afraid for you. You seemed so young going into high school having skipped grade three. So small, so slight. Then after leaving elementary school on such a high, you crashed. I worried about you, your mom having depression and drinking and all. I worried you were going the same route."

"The books saved me, and a kind guidance counsellor, and my motivation to help others who were having trouble just like I did with those in the reading club at Earl Grey. But I needed to understand, know the science of it all and how to do it properly. That's what got me started. It wasn't like reading—that I did naturally. With what happened to Kimmi, I needed to dig in, to really know why something like that would happen."

"I thought it was Jax, him specializing in psychiatry—that was why you wanted to become a psychologist."

"Not at all. And please Auntie, even though I run the agency that he got funded, follow the model he set up, that's not why I decided to become a psychologist, not to follow in his footsteps. Heavens no!"

"But didn't he give you that book? When I was looking back through my sketchbooks, I found the drawing I made of you with that really old book that he gave you."

"Book? Oh, that one. After graduation from high school, the graduation he never bothered to attend, he made it up by taking us out to the golf course for lunch. And gave me the book, a first-edition Jung. That was long after I started to read psychology, to seriously read."

Estelle pauses, smiles. "Do you remember the golf clubs, the ones on that day when he took us out to lunch?"

"Golf clubs? No."

"So there we were, probably after my grade twelve finals, standing in the foyer of his golf club, waiting to go into the restaurant for the reservation he made. He was late, like always, and came through the lobby with this old leather golf bag over his shoulder. He walked right by us into the pro shop. It turned out that they were antique clubs he got from a colleague when he was doing his residency. Throughout the lunch, he talked about how they had come from Scotland or some such place. Well, it turned out that the club didn't want them for a display, so he set them on the chair at the table while we had lunch. Eventually, he took them back to his office to display the ugly things there. I still see them when I go over to his office, always remember that they were at the table when we had lunch in the golf club years ago."

Estelle pivots to look at the array of drawings mounted on the wall above the table. She immediately orients to many workings of Anna, of GJ, and of her distant, forgotten mother.

"What's with these? They aren't in the portrait, but you spent so much time sketching them and have put them up here."

"What do you mean, they're not in the painting? Look closely."

Looking back at the portrait, Estelle first sees Anna. She is barely perceptible, standing just behind Jackson. Estelle steps to the side of the painting to catch the texture of the brush strokes by the light reflected off the surface. The brush strokes have the slightest hint of Winsor Violet rounding her features. Auntie Leanne has used the same technique in painting Anna as she had in the *Looking Back* painting out in the main gallery.

And GJ appears now, similarly rendered in the dark background, he with a slight definition of indigo.

And Izzy floats above, barely discernible. Her brush strokes are less evident, as if she has faded far back in history. And the colour defining her features—it is the deep crimson of a pinot noir.

Denny rounds the corner. "Ah, Stella. How marvellous that you are here. Your aunt has told me all about you."

"It's Estelle," Estelle asserts limply.

Leanne jumps in. "Stella calls herself Estelle now. When I did the first portraits and all the work-up drawings, she was Stella back then."

"Then it's Estelle, the grown-up Stella, here in the flesh. How marvellous."

Denny turns back to Leanne. "Have you prepared the studio upstairs to receive the patrons after they have gone through the show? You know, the whole reason we are mounting this exhibition is to get commissions through the gallery for you to paint other families."

"Not yet. I'm getting there. There's a lot to do just getting the work-up material properly displayed here with the paintings."

"What about the self-portrait, the one I asked you to paint for upstairs in your studio?"

"I'm still working on it. I'm rendering it with a palette knife and lots of jarring colours."

"Will it be ready by the end of the week? The reporters from the newspapers and arts magazines are coming Friday."

Leanne sighs.

"So you are expecting commissions based on these portraits?" Estelle asks.

"Yes, these portraits display a really wide variety of technique. That's why I wanted Leanne to do up herself in yet a different style for upstairs. Patrons can see the range of things that Leanne Caylie can do when they are considering commissioning her for their own family."

Estelle swallows down a catch in her throat. "These really are far too real. I'm not sure I'd want my family represented with this degree of emotional realism hanging on my living room wall."

Leanne looks over at Estelle. Her eyes question.

"Ah, well. We will see!" Denny exclaims and turns back to Leanne. "I have the electrical all working in the fifth space. I'm so excited. You have to come."

"Well, we're finished here and working our way through. The fifth space is our next."

"Hold on. I'll get it ready and call you." Denny heads back around the corner, out of sight.

"So when did you paint all these?" Estelle asks.

"Oh, some of them were completed back at the time. I guess I kept going back to them, working on them. I remember one or other of them would be on the easel for months. For others, what eventually would become a canvas was just a bunch of preliminary sketches and blocking. In the last couple of months, I went back to those."

"They look so real, so what was happening back then. I feel it when I look."

"I took a lot of photos. It really annoyed GJ and Anna. You didn't seem to mind."

"I don't remember that."

"As well as the sketches, I made a lot of notes on family life in my journals."

"I never knew that."

"I kept that all to myself, up in my studio. Spent the time there when I wasn't chasing you kids."

"You always kept your studio locked."

"It was my sanctuary. Like you and your books."

Breaking the spell between them, Denny calls. "Ready. Walk in."

The space is completely dark as Estelle and Leanne round the corner. When they pass a sensor two spotlights come on from the ceiling. One of them shines on the front of a gauzy curtain on the opposite wall where the fifth painting would be hung. The other lights a panel of three switches on the adjoining wall. Leanne heads over to the switches, flips the first.

The light on the front of the curtain goes out. Behind the curtain, hidden by it, another spotlight is lit. Now visible through the gauzy fabric is a tall, vertical panel to the left. The painted panel shows Gordon and Auntie Leanne sitting on the front veranda of the family home at 113 Durham Lane. Gordon is, of course, playing the harmonica. With the lighting of the first panel, a small audio speaker is also activated—a harmonica plays a repeating, bluesy riff. The same riff floated in on the conversation while Estelle and Leanne were in the previous alcove, looking at the painting where Gordon first appears. In this vertical panel, Auntie Leanne sits beside Gordon, a sketchbook on her lap. She is looking off to her left, out of the panel's frame, toward the middle of the space. A blinder of black metal, perpendicular to the wall and reaching forward to the curtain, prevents the light from leaking from this panel onto one presumed to be to the right of it. The viewer doesn't know who Auntie Leanne is looking at.

Leanne flips the second light switch.

The light above the first panel and the harmonica riff turn off. A spotlight hidden behind the curtain lights a second vertical panel. Stella is coming down stairs that centre the front of the house. Her hair is cut in a jagged, angular fashion and striped in intense shades of green and violet. She is dressed provocatively. Her tight top displays the upper surface of her breasts, trussed up to be more than they are. Her belly button shows below. She wears faded jeans strategically cut and frayed to reveal bare legs. Gone are the hidden looks of her childhood and early teen years. Gone is the frightened prey look of the previous portrait. Her face is too mature for the provocative look of her clothing, too old in years, and too determined in expression. She is propelling herself down the steps, taking them two at a time and unbalanced in doing so. She is also looking off to her left, into the dark space still to the right behind the curtain.

Heavy metal guitar plays, all caught up in itself—primal, chaotic.

Leanne flips the third switch. The light over the central panel goes out. The music stops.

On the final panel, now visible through the gauzy curtain, a cowboy stands with his back to the viewer. He is looking in the direction of the two other now-darkened panels. All that shows of his skin is the weathered back of his neck between the plaid shirt collar and the back of his cowboy hat. His upper back is muscular. The viewer is drawn to the scalloped yoke of the shirt across the broad shoulder blades, the fabric drawn taut to contain the bulk of him.

A country ballad plays, the steel guitar and crooning male vocal in counterpoint. Lyrics intermingle pickup trucks, a faithful dog, and making love in the moonlight.

Denny goes over to the panel, flips the switches in order. Gordon and Leanne, then Stella, then the cowboy—four individuals disengaged by the flicker of time, but by circumstance stuck together.

"It works," Denny proclaims.

"Beautifully." Leanne smiles her encouragement at the technological feat the gallery owner has perfected.

"I suppose." Estelle sounds less confident. "Flip back to the middle one."

Denny does. "So, Stella-Estelle. There's a story here. I'd love to hear it."

Estelle collects herself. The story is all too real, too present within her.

"So, I got sent home from school. No mean feat, that. Graduate school in California to become a clinical psychologist was costing my father tens of thousands of dollars. And, I got sent home. Initially, I was to be expelled, but one of my friends and one of the profs intervened with the dean to make it a leave of absence. I was told to go home and grow up."

"How so?" Denny asks.

"You knew I was a reader, right?"

"Perfectly obvious from the portraits."

"Well, I read ahead, ahead of the other students. I was always bringing in material that was further ahead than the assigned readings for the class. I guess it got annoying to everyone else.

"And rather than just accepting what we were being taught, I questioned it. Brought forward perspectives that weren't politically correct. I guess I came across as a smart-ass teenager even though I was just into my twenties. I was still pretty young to be in graduate school; all the other students were older, more mature, I guess. To be sure, what I was saying was valid enough. But it was ways of thinking that'd fallen out of favour, not what the school wanted us to be learning.

"And the other students . . . well, they went from amused to annoyed to hostile. Banded against me, all of them except for Dodi."

"Dodi?" Denny asks.

Leanne breaks in. "She's the black woman in the next portrait."

"So, Dodi intervened, and I got put on leave of absence to come home."

Estelle pauses. She looks at Denny as if she is wondering how much of the story to tell. "I'd never had a boyfriend, not interested in that at all. But from what happened down there, I realized I couldn't just have my head in the books, realized that I had to get out into the real world. The dean said I had to grow up—socially, emotionally. So that's what I did."

Estelle goes over to the panel of light switches. She flips the third.

"And that is where Everett comes in. In the process of growing up, I got myself pregnant."

Leanne turns to Estelle. "So, we have Everett in this one and in the next. Have you been able to get his consent for us to display his image?"

"Oh, Everett is Everett. Everything is a deal. I had to loosen up a bit on visitation this summer for him with Jemma in exchange for him coming down here to take a look and decide. He did his typical, 'Well, maybe I will, maybe I won't.' That said, in the end I always get my way with him, after him having his way with me got all this going between us."

Leanne turns back to Denny. "That brings us back to the whole issue of the consent. Anna and GJ are the problem. We don't know where they are.

Jackson is okay. When I picked up the painting from his waiting room, I left the consent with Joan. She said that she would make sure he signs it and will fax it back over here. Apparently, he is all wrapped up in a paper that he is presenting at a conference this week."

Estelle breaks in. "Yeah, I know about him and his paper. It's all he can focus on right now." Pausing, she takes a sip of her coffee. "I'll get Nikki to come down and give her consent when she is back here on her days off from Fort Mac. But that's not until next week."

"Nikki?" Denny asks.

"Last portrait." Leanne answers, then turns to Estelle. "What about Dodi?"

"Oh, no problem with Dodi. I FaceTime with her every so often. I told her all about the show. She's thrilled to be a part of the process."

"And you can give consent for Jemma. That's it. All except for Anna and GJ." Leanne pauses, takes on the look of an artist pondering a part of a canvas that she has no idea how to paint. "Anna and GJ." She sighs.

"You don't know where they are, eh? They don't keep in touch at all?" Estelle asks.

"Not at all."

"Well, there is potential liability for the gallery here." Denny shifts from his effusiveness as the gallery owner with a dynamic show to his businessman persona as someone who could be sued. "I don't like the risk of displaying the image of an identifiable someone without their consent."

"What's the likelihood they'd ever know?" Estelle asks. "GJ is probably lost into the world of drugs and crime. And Anna. She's probably not even still in Calgary."

"We could wait to see if they turn up. Deal with it then," Leanne suggests.

"Between the three of us, we could reason with them. In graduate school, I did a couple of units on the mediation process, coming to a mutually respectful course of action . . ."

"The show certainly wouldn't be complete without them. GJ especially. He's the central focus of the second portrait. But there's no telling what sort of crime world he might've gotten himself caught up in."

"I don't like the risk," Denny says. He peers off, deeper into the gallery space.

Estelle goes over to the sketches lying on the floor, arranged there but not yet mounted on the wall beside the light switches.

"Look at this, Auntie. Your work-up sketch of your facial expression. It's like you knew Everett was a creep right from the beginning."

"Yes, I did. But there was no dealing with you, how determined you were that you had to do this, this *growing up* as you called it. But then . . ."

"But then, before very long, I was puking out the night's drinking and looking at the vaginal thermometer to realize that I was ovulating, and then . . ."

"And then our dear sweet Jemma. Shall we go forward to the next portrait?"

A phone rings. Denny orients to it and exits through the younger years of Stella, back toward the front of the gallery.

The sixth portrait is painted in a classical style—a *tableau vivant*.

A hospital bed centres the portrait, the chrome panel behind with the call cord dangling toward the bed, the monitor on a swivel off to the side.

On the bed is a pale but smiling Estelle, holding a tiny baby. Sitting beside her is a youthful but substantial woman, beaming through her dark skin. She has one loving eye on Estelle and the other on the new little person who has come into their lives.

There is a picture of the California countryside on the wall above the bed, one of those cliché images intended to create a sense of peace. Warm lighting bathes the bed from above, golden in its haze. It creates an aura around the three.

But the energy of the painting is drawn to the left, to another trio of figures. Jackson and Everett are in profile doing pokey chest, facing each other with looks of absolute fury. Everett stands taller. He has a dishevelled look about him, his face flushed red. Jackson is back on his heels from the strength of the other man. A doctor is rushing into the room, stereotypical in a white lab coat and stethoscope. His eyes are set resolutely on other two men. The three men are lit by the stark, sterile, white light of the hospital corridor.

The seventh figure is Auntie, prone on a sofa off to the side. Daylight oozes from an unseen window just beyond the edge of the painting. She lies there exhausted, staring toward the ceiling.

A tear courses down Estelle's cheek. "Is it wrong to miss her so?"

"Dodi?" Leanne asks.

Estelle nods.

The two women stand.

Leanne breaks the silence. "When I went down to California, just before Jemma was born, and stayed with you and Dodi . . . well, it was the happiest I'd ever seen you. You were focused, had made the adjustment back into school, done everything ahead you could possibly do—everything except putting the crib together, which was still in the IKEA boxes in the spare room—but ready to devote yourself to Jemma after she was born. And Dodi, she held you both, held you in such love. She . . ."

"Do you remember—before Jemma was born, when you came—how we danced? You and Dodi and me as big as a whale. And Jemma danced inside of me while you and Dodi danced me around. Oh, how we laughed. And you took pictures. Do you still have those pictures, Auntie?"

"Somewhere."

"But you painted this, this instead. Everett and my father going at it right in my hospital room."

"Yes, I painted this."

"I miss Dodi, how I miss her. It was so hard to part ways when our graduate school days were over. She had to go back to St. Louis to fulfill her commitment to the Health Management Organization that sponsored her doctorate. I had to come back to Canada to work here because I only had a student visa to be in the States. How I wish we could've just gone somewhere together to live and work with each other."

"But you still keep in touch, don't you?"

"We FaceTime, usually when I'm at work, sometimes from home when Nikki is north. Dodi wants to see Jemma, so I put her on. I don't think Jemma remembers. She was only two when we came back after I got my doctorate. But I hope so. I hope she remembers somewhere deep inside of her how much Dodi loved her, loved me."

Estelle stops, a look of terror crosses her face.

"We can't let Nikki see this. She'd be so jealous, jealous that it was Dodi with me when Jemma was born, that she wasn't there. Someone else held

Jemma when she came out of me."

"I don't know how we can prevent it. This painting has to be in the series. Denny loves it for the style. I don't know how I could . . ."

"We've got time. I'll have to prepare Nikki. If I let her know ahead, let her get her rant out about it being Dodi and not her back at Jemma's birth, she'll be okay. We can plan a fun day for her and Jemma and me, make her feel secure. Then bring her here. If I prepare her . . ."

"I do need to get her permission for her image in the final portrait. Let's go and see it. I hope she will be okay with how I have rendered her."

Estelle doesn't move. "Can I just stay here a moment longer?"

Leanne nods.

They hear voices. Then the riffs from the fifth portrait filter in. Denny must be showing it to someone who has come in—the melancholy of the harmonica, the chaos of the shredding guitar, the croon of the country ballad.

As Estelle prepares to walk around the last partition to view the final portrait, there is a grim look—a wistful leaving behind the scene that surrounds the birth of her daughter and the love that held her there.

It is an echo, an echo across the chasm of a generation. Leanne has recreated the first portrait's formal photographer's setting in this final one. Now it is Jemma—four-year-old Jemma, bursting from her mother's lap on the wingback chair—Jemma centres the portrait. Her eyes are bright. Her smile infectious.

Behind her, Estelle sits on the same chair where she had sat twenty-five years ago. She looks lovingly bemused at her daughter in the process of bounding into the big wide world. Estelle's smile bears the contented look of a woman who is made more complete by having a girl child of her own. There's a faint weariness there, too.

Nikki stands behind Estelle and Jemma, just to the left. She bears stress in her eyes. Caylie has captured those eyes staring forward, having just darted there. Nikki wears a western shirt, her leg, descending beside the chair, is clad in worn denim. Her hand rests on Estelle's shoulder, her knuckles and nail beds pale. There is strength to her grasp there.

To the right of the tidy little family, Leanne sits on the stool—behind her, Gordon. They bear the roundness and generosity of grandparents. Both of their eyes are deflected downward to the granddaughter. A smile sneaks in to deflect the corners of Gordon's mouth. His eyes are aglitter with the delight of looking at the bursting Jemma.

Jackson stands on the other side. He wears a tailored sports jacket, under it a knit turtleneck that picks up one of the colours in the muted tweed. Jackson's body has slimmed out, an athletic bearing to his posture. His face is hollowed out in the way of runners burning off excess fat. It bears a rugged, windburned quality. His eyes are creased around by a forced, habitual look of kindness and concern—his way of working his trade.

When Estelle slowly walked in to view the final portrait, Leanne lagged behind to let her look. Still standing there, Leanne observes, "Your back tensed up."

"What?"

"And your right shoulder dropped, dropped under the pressure of Nikki's hand on it."

"In the painting?"

"Well, both. You in the painting and you looking at Nikki's hand on your shoulder in the painting."

"I guess I do tense up sometimes when I'm with her."

"We portraitists notice those things. Paint them in. The photographer might suggest *Sit up a bit straighter* or *Can you just turn slightly this way and raise your chin?* that sort of thing. But real bodies in real life aren't like that. Like the way when someone has a hand on the shoulder of another person then the person's body adapts—accepts that energy, mounts pressure to resist it or caves into it."

"I've always felt Nikki's energy as protective, but holding me down too, I guess. Like, *Be careful here, this might be dangerous,* or *Let me fight this battle for you.*"

Leanne lets out a knowing "um-hmm," with a little nod of the head.

Estelle looks at her. "Now you are really being the psychologist."

"It's just what I see. I hope what I see and convey makes my portraits more than just nice paintings."

Estelle continues to study the painting, looking now for the nuances that her auntie had included.

"With Jemma, every time I come back to her in the painting she seems to have jumped a bit farther off my lap, into the space between me in the painting and me looking at the painting."

Leanne just smiles.

"How did you do that?"

Leanne smiles again. "Trade secret."

"I think Nikki will be okay with it. She'll be captivated by Jemma's energy in the painting. I don't think she'll notice the way she's standing there keeping watch over us as if she has to defend us against some improbable foe."

"I really debated in my mind how I would draw her. I'd wondered about conveying the playful energy that develops when she is with Jemma, the fun they have together. But then, I wanted this particular arrangement, like the first portrait of the series, coming back around again."

Estelle's eyes are doing the circuit of the figures in the painting.

"I look at Father. He's in the painting but doesn't seem to belong. You and Gordon, though, you are there for us. And Gordon's absolute delight in Jemma, it comes through in the way that you've painted his eyes, his mouth."

"I love that face of his. All of him."

"Do you have work-up sketches? Can I see how you arrived at the facial expressions?"

"Yeah, they are over here. I have them in this folder."

Estelle takes the sheaf of drawings. In going through them, she focuses on a half-dozen or so of Nikki—looks from them back to the painting.

"In the final rendering you've been generous to Nikki. A lot of the negative energy, that protective *I will fight your battles for you* sort of energy, that *holding me down* energy . . . that's what's in the sketches. But on the painting, you've toned it down. You put just the slightest of smiles on her face. It softens it."

"I struggled with that. Knowing that she would be coming to view it, I didn't want the wrong thing to come across. I wanted to paint her as strong because she would want that to come across. But with the slight smile, I thought she'd be okay."

"Well, she'll be home next week. I'll bring her in and see how she reacts."

A chime comes from Estelle's phone as it rests in an outside pocket of her purse.

"Do you need to get that?"

"Probably just work. What time is it?" Estelle looks at her watch. "Oh my God, I've got to get going. I told Merrill I'd likely be late. He'll get everyone in. Get them settled. But this is supposed to be his supervision time with me. I didn't have any idea it would take this long."

"Sorry."

"No, it's okay. It's my whole life. I shouldn't just rush through. You've brought back a lot of memories for me."

Estelle pulls out her phone to look. "Well, that solves one problem."

"What?" Leanne looks at her curiously.

"The chime was on Messenger. Believe it or not, it's from GJ. Somehow he found me on Facebook, wants to get together sometime if I am willing to, maybe go for coffee."

"Gosh, that's sure good timing. We can get his permission for displaying his image as part of the family, if he'll give it. Then again, maybe he won't. When I painted him, I never even thought that he might see it, might be . . . what was that word? Oppositional?"

"I guess we'll know soon enough."

Estelle pulls herself together, begins to walk back through the maze of her younger years, out to the front of the gallery.

"Thanks, Auntie. Thanks for everything. Like, I mean for all you did to help me grow up . . . But for the show, well . . ." She smiles back at her aunt as she leaves.

CHAPTER THREE

Tuesday

Nali enters the police station dressed in a thin halter top and scant, fraying, blue-jean shorts. Goosebumps immediately raise on her arms. The temperature in the air-conditioned facility is already well below the temperature outside. It's not even ten a.m., but the Calgary sun has already been above the horizon for nearly six hours. Uncomfortably hot at this time, by afternoon, it will be a scorcher.

"Can I help you?" a uniformed constable greets her. His shirt lies smoothly over a protective vest beneath, his belt heavy with various equipment in leather and black metal. Not waiting for an answer, he asks, "your name?"

"Nali, Nali Freeman."

The constable briefly glances down at the countertop, picking up a wooden clipboard with a large silver clasp. As his eyes rise, he scans the shocking image of the lithe, middle-aged woman standing in front of him. Slowly, deliberately, he takes in the vivid tattoo of a large snake as it loops across her torso below her pierced navel, following it as it comes back above her bellybutton to be briefly hidden by her halter top and then re-emerges ascending her collar bone and curling around the left side of her neck. His eyes deflect to focus on the head of the snake as it appears on the other side of her neck, just below her right jawbone.

"Nali?"

"Yes, Nali, as in the country Bali, only with an N."

"Do you have a driver's licence or some other form of government identification, ma'am?"

Nali has a small clasp purse hung by a thin shoulder strap on her left hip. As she turns to get it, the officer catches sight of her lower back. The tail of the snake is curled over her sacrum. Needing two hands to get her ID card out, she lays a manila envelope on the counter. She hands the ID to the constable.

"Thank you." He takes the government-issued photo ID card from her, looks at it, and without looking up, says, "Nice tattoo."

"Thank you. I got it for work."

"You must do interesting work then." The constable's voice is dry, but there is a slight smile on his lips. Then looking at her name on her licence, he asks, "So how do you get 'Nali' out of that?"

"Drop the first two letters, A N, and then the last two, S E, and . . . Nali is in the middle."

"Okay. How can I help you?"

"I'm being harassed. I want to make a statement."

He hands the clipboard to her. A Bic pen dangles by a string tied to the clasp. There are several pages of a printed form on the clipboard. "So how about you write out what you want to say, bring it back to me, and I'll go over it with you?"

She takes the clipboard and turns to go.

"By the way, just what type of work do you do that would need a tattoo like that—in a reptile and exotic pet store?"

"Something like that. I'm an exotic dancer."

"Alrighty then," he says, smiling. His eyebrows raise in amusement. "If you don't mind, I'm going to hold on to your ID and give it back to you when you finish writing out your statement."

There's a row of metal chairs against the far wall of the station reception area. Nali sits and arranges herself with the clipboard and the papers she brought with her. Cold air blows from a vent in the ceiling. A shiver spasms through her, causing the snake to tremble on her abdomen and between her breasts, the tattooed image in subtle animation.

It takes Nali fifteen minutes to write out her statement. Just as she puts the pen down and places the papers back into her envelope, the constable reappears with a detective.

The constable hands her ID back to her. "I've asked Detective Irwin to go over your statement with you. Thank you for coming in today, ma'am."

Nali looks from the uniformed officer to the plainclothes detective. A bit of greying has crept in at the temples of his jet-black hair. The detective's eyes are resolute on hers, as if to look down to fully take in the curves of the snake would violate proper conduct.

"So you go by Nali, do you, Ms. Freeman?"

"Yes."

"We also have you in the system as an . . ." he pauses, "an *Ansa Jewel*."

"That's how I'm known to customers where I work, at the Emerald Grove Gentlemen's Club."

"What do you do at the . . ." The detective pauses to speak in a way that would be politically correct, " . . . at the gentlemen's club?"

"I coordinate the dancers and the floor girls. When we're short, I fill in as a dancer—but most of the time, I manage the adult entertainment services there."

"You're a working girl, then?"

"No, a manager and a dancer."

"I see."

"Sir, I'm not here about my work. I want to lodge a personal complaint, to have you investigate."

"Yes, I understand. Can I see your statement?"

The detective takes the clipboard. While he looks at it, Nali places her ID card back in her purse.

"So, I understand that you've been receiving text messages you don't want. And he has sent you pictures."

"Yes, there were seventeen text messages last night alone. He sent pictures of my apartment zooming in through my bedroom window."

"You've attached a printout of the text messages to your written statement. Let me take a look."

Nali shivers. It is warmer in the interview room but she's now been in the refrigerated police station for long enough that her body is thoroughly chilled. "Can I get a cup of coffee or something? I'm cold."

Not looking up the detective says, "You won't be here much longer. You'll warm up when you go back outside."

Nali's skin has grown pale, her blood pooling in her guts to conserve heat. The cobra now languishes on snow.

The detective looks up at her. His gaze latches onto the cobra tattoo writhing there. "So do you think this guy is one of your customers from the strip club?"

"No, I'm sure it's someone else who has been bothering me for years. I think he lives off and on here in Calgary. The texts just came in as a number, not a name, but I think it's him. I don't know how he got my new number. On my statement I've written down who I think it is, the cell number he is using now."

"I see."

Nali shifts in the chair, leans forward as if she might become more aggressive. The cobra takes on more animation with her movement.

"Okay then. Settle down."

"I'm cold."

"Yes, you said that." Detective Irwin manages his dismissiveness with a tone of authority—as if he can't be bothered, has more important things to do than to deal with a working girl making a complaint about a man. When he looks up from her written statement, Nali watches him eye the head of her snake, then again follow its body down from her neckline through her halter top, toward her stomach. The cold has made her nipples stand hard against the white cotton of her halter top.

"You better keep your eyes where they belong, sir. Can we get on with this?"

The detective looks at one of the pictures Nali had printed out from her text message feed. It shows her in her apartment, barely discernible but fully dressed. The picture had been well timed—the curtain on the open window blown open by the breeze revealing the view into the apartment.

"You're more modestly attired in this peeping tom photo than you are here with me now."

"That's not the point. That's my private apartment. He took those pictures of me without my consent."

"Look, miss. From what I've seen of the text messages he's not threatening you. If anything, he wants to protect you, take care of you, has your well-being in mind. Sure, there's a lot of them, and you were clear in texting back that you didn't want to receive them. If you were undressed in the photo, I could make a case for him being a peeping tom. If he threatened you rather than promising to take care of you, I could make a case for him uttering threats. Maybe you should just change your number again. Our records show that you've been in before and we've gone out to speak to this guy about it. That's about all we can do."

"Really? So, if you're not going to actually *do* something to get him to stop, like charging him, I'm out of here." Nali shoves the chair back from the table, gathers her papers.

Catching up to her as she leaves, the detective puts his hand on her elbow, guiding her along the corridor toward the front of the station. Nali pulls away.

Walking through the station's front door, Nali is embraced by the warm sun and hot, dry air that is already rising off the surface of the sidewalk. The bus stop is just a block or so away. Standing there, she's aware of the other pedestrians walking by, watches their expressions as she stands with most of the snake exposed, her skin still pale from the chill of the police station.

A woman stares with disdain. Some of the men are oblivious, absorbed into the Beats headphones that bracket their heads. Others leer. She's accustomed to the sexualized stare, knows how to dismiss it when she needs to do so. It is a power thing for her. She can get the men to stare and then reduce them with a *fuck you* stare back of her own.

But there is another sight that chills her—a black Dodge Challenger with tinted windows. She takes it all in—the year, the trim package. She needs to know but doesn't think it is—doesn't think it is the same one whose driver accosted her the previous week with probing questions about her father.

A handful of businessmen sit around a board table in the comfortable cool of a conference room. Name cards identifying pharmaceutical companies sit in front of each place at the table. Burrard Inlet, Vancouver, is visible through the windows.

Near one end of the table sits an empty chair. There's no padded writing tablet, no glass of water at that place. A man enters. He is neatly put out in business attire—dressed down to look casual, not a thread out of place. The Chair motions him toward the empty end of the table.

"I've asked Mr. Pierre Bolton to brief us on a situation that has arisen, what he has done so far, and what the plan is from here." The voice of the Chair is empty of all but formality.

"Gentleman, thank you for the opportunity to speak to you," Pierre begins. "As you may be aware, we have reason to believe that a paper to be presented tomorrow is of great concern to your companies. It is a minor paper for sure but one that will go on the record of this year's Congress.

"Several weeks ago, when it became clear to the executive that this was happening, I was asked to come before you. I had already been onto this issue, had already started to investigate.

"Concern began with the keen awareness of a sales representative from one of your companies. He encountered resistance and received rude treatment on one of his calls. He immediately referred the matter to his manager. In taking this anecdote, that manager rightfully recognized there might be a systemic problem to investigate.

"When I was assigned to look into the situation, I got in touch with representatives from each of your companies. I received full cooperation from managers in your marketing and sales departments, cooperation with suitable safeguards in place that none of your individual companies' proprietary intelligence would be compromised.

"I aggregated sales data using a complex vectoring program. Looking at classes of drugs and location of sales, I found that the original suspicions were borne out.

"Recognizing that psychotropic medications comprise the largest portion of revenue for each of your companies, and that much effort has gone into establishing consistent prescribing patterns for them and sustaining prescriber loyalty, the results of the data analysis are disturbing. Your tablet computers display a series of graphs and a map that illustrate this problem."

Bolton pauses as the tablet computers are activated and the executives around the table open the delivered material.

"You'll see that in contrast to all other prescription medications, a discernible decline in most classes of antidepressant, novel antipsychotics, and anxiolytic drugs has taken place in a Calgary quadrant. While I recognize that this is a very small problem in terms of total revenue for Canada-wide sales, it is significant in a pinpoint locale."

Pierre stops to make sure that each man at the table has had sufficient opportunity to grasp the detail on the graphs.

The Chair urges him on. "Cut to the chase, Bolton—we don't have all day."

"So, this is what I found—and, I have to acknowledge that the permission I had to speak to the individual sales reps for your companies helped me to narrow this down. What I found was this. There's a group psychiatry practice on the North Hill in Calgary that has begun a program to divert patients away from pharmaceutical treatment of common mental disorders."

The Chair breaks in. "Name names, please."

Pierre pauses for effect. "Dr. Jackson Horvath and his associates."

A few of the executives look up.

"The numbers I see here are very small. Why are we being troubled? It is barely a blip." The voice has a slight French accent and comes from the other end of the table.

"The executive wanted you to be aware that this blip could become a bigger problem based on what is going to happen here in Vancouver tomorrow. Horvath is presenting a paper outlining what he sees as the benefits of his different approach to community psychiatry."

Pierre pauses in such an obvious way that all eyes lift to look at him.

"If this is not discredited and stopped, the ramifications for future sales might become significant."

"So can we cancel his presentation tomorrow?" the Chair queries.

"I'm not sure that would be the best approach. Let's let him present. Get a grilling in the question period. Then, based on that contrary reaction, it might be possible to get his paper withdrawn from the Proceeds of the Congress."

Another pause for effect. Once Pierre is assured he has the careful attention of all, he continues. "I also think I can get him to back down."

"How so?" The Chair looks up.

"In the last few weeks, I've done some research regarding Horvath. I've found a number of things that might be used as leverage. He has—what might we say?—an interesting personal background and significant family problems. I've recently returned from a week of investigations in Calgary and have compiled a rather significant dossier."

The Chair stands, a signal that this needs to be over.

"No dirty business for sure, here, Mr. Bolton. Thank you for your excellent research and detective work. The Consortium will track this carefully. You've certainly shown us the foundation for . . ." The Chair shifts uncomfortably on his feet. "For continued vigilance. No dirty business."

Pierre detects a wink. Wonders what the records will show.

"For sure, sir. Thank you for having me come. No dirty business for sure. I'll keep you informed of any developments."

Dr. Jackson Horvath sits in the waiting room of the Nose Hill Depression and Anxiety Clinic. It's been a long day with more patients than usual. The clinic is now closed for the rest of the week. All the doctors except for him have already left for the conference on the coast.

The conference could well be the crowning glory of Jackson's career. His paper was accepted. Tomorrow he will speak to psychiatrists from coast to coast, assembled in Vancouver for the annual conference of community psychiatry. True enough it is an elective session, but maybe next year he could be a keynote. Jackson shakes his head to dispel the unreasonable fantasy.

Joan speaks from behind the reception desk. "I've finished the revision on the paper that Dr. Eigner recommended, the way we reported on the statistics."

"Did he water it down too much? These academics, they are so . . ." Jackson reaches for the word. "Petty, or should I say *particular*, about stats and conclusions."

"Not too much. You won't be reading those sections anyway when you do the presentation."

"Thank you, Joan. You've really worked hard today."

"It's been a long day. The airport limo will be here soon, then I'll go home." Joan goes to the file room to do the locking up.

Jackson reflects on the role Joan plays in his life and practice. She knows him probably better than any other person, has stayed with him through it all—putting him back together after Izzy drowned, his many trips to rehab, and then the shift to a specialty practice. Ever since she first came in as a medical secretary for his family practice, she's stood by him.

Joan rolls his suitcase out from the file room and sets it beside him. She extends the telescoping handle and places his leather messenger bag on top. "Do you want me to stay and set the alarm after locking up?"

"No need, Joan."

"Will you call me when you arrive in Vancouver? Call or text. Let me know you got there safely."

Her comment seems faintly motherly. Jackson replies limply, "Will do. And thanks again."

As Joan leaves, Jackson locks the door, locking himself in.

It's been a satisfying enough day but he is tired. It is a Tuesday. The protocols have him listening, nudging, encouraging. Patients are doing well enough—more so when they were *doing well*, doing the wellness tasks and habits that he prescribes.

Now with Estelle on board, Tuesdays and Thursdays are not nearly as taxing. Many of his patients in the Tuesday/Thursday protocols have utilized her program, the one he designed and set up. She's hitting her stride and his patients love her for her freshness and life. And, she's putting them through. She's taken the program and made it her own, added on the mentoring and alumni support phases, making it much more than he had initially envisioned when he set the program up three years before.

But it is still his idea—his vision, his innovation.

Feeling impatient with the wait for the limo Jackson gets up and walks around the waiting room, a place he has always just walked through. He sees the empty place on the wall where his sister's painting had hung. It is disorienting, the empty wall there. He remembers Leanne being in, leaving something to sign. What was it now? Joan was dealing with it. *That's right, something about a show his sister was mounting in a gallery, needing my consent.*

For some reason the empty space brings back memories of Izzy—her drowning. He can't bring to mind the painting itself—but in its emptiness there, he feels queasy, a quickening of his heart, a dampening of his upper lip, a trembling of the hands. A shudder slices through him. *That place on the coast. What was it called? Took the kids there, too.*

Aware of the rise of anxiety, conscious of the compact protocols that he teaches his patients, Jackson decides to do the *doctor, heal thyself* thing. With a few deep breaths he feels his sympathetic nervous system response fade, the circulating levels of cortisol and adrenalin gradually dissipating through the discipline of his mind and the gentle instructions he makes to his body.

Then it shivers through him again. A haunting.

Jackson picks up the messenger bag and extracts the paper: *The Gift of Health. Paper presented at the 47th Canadian Congress of Community Psychiatry, Vancouver, Canada.* Mentally he reviews what he will say in his presentation—the research design containing two protocols of vastly different approaches to community psychiatry, both protocols provided by the same four psychiatrists, dramatic differences then seen in patient outcomes. It is tight. Tight and provocative. Poking a finger in the eye. A shifter of paradigm.

Jackson reflects on leaving today, a Tuesday. Yesterday, he and the other three spent the day practising on the Monday/Wednesday protocol. How weary he gets titrating cocktails of psychotropic drugs, counteracting side effects with the addition of yet another pharmaceutical. How hypocritical it now seems to give the false words of reassurance that yet a different mixture of pills will somehow correct the problem. But today he's been wound up in the goodness of the Tuesday/Thursday protocol with its emphasis on meditation, yoga, journaling, and exercise. It's felt good. Clean, hopeful.

His cellphone chirps out a personal ringtone. The name Dr. Estelle Caylie appears on the phone's display, beneath it in smaller letters the agency she directs—ReClaiming Ourselves Inc. He feels himself tighten a bit. His mind races to find a different footing. *She's my daughter, for God's sake. Why does she make me feel tense, inadequate?*

"Hello." There's a hard edge of formality to his greeting.

"Hello," Estelle replies. "Are you gone yet?"

"Just leaving for the airport now."

"Cutting it close."

"Should be fine."

"All good here. We'll take good care of your patients while you're gone."

"Thanks."

"But when you're back, we may have something interesting to talk about."

"What?"

"I've heard from GJ."

Jackson goes silent. His mouth sets grimly, his brow firms down over his eyes. There's no way he wants to give a second thought to his son at this point in his life.

Acquiescing, he mumbles, "Maybe Sunday," and says, "I've got to go."

CHAPTER FOUR

Wednesday

Estelle wakes very early with the morning sun.

Estelle and Nikki had selected an easterly facing condo—those on the west side of the building with the mountain view were $50,000 more. Aside from June and its neighbouring months, the morning sun dawns through their windows conveniently. On this day, it's way too early.

Nikki will be calling in that scant few minutes between waking in the camp and riding the bus to the mine site. It is more than halfway through the two weeks Nikki spends in the north working as a heavy haul driver in the mines of Fort McMurray. Time to check in with each other.

They had blackened Jemma's room with blinds and curtains so she wouldn't wake with the rising sun. Estelle makes her way to their daughter's window to release the darkening slightly. After the call from Nikki, she'll do so a bit more, letting the day fall upon the six-year-old gradually. Jemma had fallen asleep reading again. Her favourite hardcovered book, clutched within a blanket, nestles under her child body. It looks awkward and uncomfortable there, but Jemma is in a deep sleep. It is a book that Jemma has treasured for years. Estelle pulls it out—*Bookish Stella*. Jemma rolls over to her other side, not yet awakening. An indentation of the bound edge of the book creases her cheek.

Bookish Stella. Estelle smooths her hand over the tattered dust cover. While Jemma slept, she'd drooled. The well-worn dustcover bulges with the moisture.

Bookish Stella—written and illustrated by Leanne Caylie. On the cover illustration, her eyes, Estelle's own Stella-child eyes, hover over a hardcovered children's book depicted there. Her hands, her slender Stella-child hands, hold the edges of the book in the illustration. Her locks, her golden curly locks, frame the furrowed Stella-child forehead.

Bookish Stella—written and illustrated about Estelle's own five-year-old self by her aunt. Now, it is Estelle's gift to her very own not-so-bookish girl, a peaceful fragment of her own childhood given forward into the next generation.

Looking at it, Estelle still can hear the echo of her Aunt Leanne's words, an echo that travels over a generation of time—*Are you hiding in there, Stella?*

And for much of her five-year-old self—her six-, seven-, and eight-year-old selves—Stella was.

Estelle doesn't have time or space to hide in books any longer. Life is too complicated.

The MacBook on the kitchen table rings with the FaceTime beckon. Estelle rushes to see Nikki's face, to hear her croaky voice—her lover and partner. With a "Mornin' luv," they greet each other.

"Jemma up yet?"

"Not yet. I've opened the blinds a little. She fell asleep reading again."

"She's like you. I bet she'll have read her way through the school library before she's out of grade one at the rate she is going!"

"Well, our dear Jemma will have to hurry, just over a week left in grade one. You sleep okay?"

"Blackout blinds on the window, thankfully. At least it's dark inside. I was out on the patio at the camp last night. Still full daylight when I went in at ten. It's worse up here, the light. Hard to turn my brain off. You?"

"Not so well. Lots on my mind."

"Work?"

"No, it was the time I spent with Leanne on Monday. We went through the show she is having down at the gallery, the family portraits."

"How does it look? Did the picture of me turn out okay?"

"Yeah, she did really well. I think you'll like it. You look very strong in the picture. She has me sitting on a chair with Jemma. Jemma is kind of leaping out, like she's going to run off someplace. Auntie painted it as Jemma was a couple of years ago, right when you and I first starting living together. In the portrait, Leanne has you standing behind us, hand on my shoulder. You'll see it next week when you come down. It is the last portrait in the show."

"How many total?"

"Seven." Estelle pauses. "I was in them all. It was like the story of my life. Brought back a lot of memories. I think that's why I couldn't sleep."

"You never talk about your family growing up. Now your auntie paints a bunch of pictures about it to bring it all back. You had a brother and sister, right? You never talk about them."

"Well, they're not a part of my life, haven't been for a long time. And now suddenly I'm seeing pictures of them. Annalise and GJ."

"So what happened to them? Where are they now?"

"That's the thing. Auntie painted them like they were back when we were kids, but she's lost touch with them both. Doesn't know where they are now."

"Some family you got, eh? Auntie is alright, and Gordon, too. Your father, I can do without, but he's never around, anyway. Your mom died when you were young. A brother and sister, long gone. Not much of a family."

"The strangest thing happened though, happened while I was looking at the portraits for Auntie's show."

"What?"

"Well, Auntie has to get consent from all the people she painted, consent for their images to be part of the show. She'll get yours next week when you're back here. So, we figure it's going to be okay with just about everyone. Everett might be a bit tricky. But then it comes down to Anna and GJ—we don't know where they are to get their consent. Auntie said that she hasn't seen Anna in years. The last she saw of GJ, he was up on charges for drugs and dealing. Father got him off—got a good lawyer, I guess—but he disappeared after that."

"What? Your brother is a drug dealer?"

Estelle alerts to Nikki's image on the screen as it takes on the characteristic expression of her protective instincts—the tendons at the sides of her neck becoming more pronounced, the set of her jaw harsher. Estelle sighs. "Yeah, I guess."

"Some screwed-up family," Nikki declares.

"But wait, Nikki. While I was standing there with Auntie looking at the paintings, I get this message on my phone. And it's GJ. He found me on

Facebook and sent me a message on Messenger. Right there, we'd just said we didn't know where to find him, and then the message from him comes through. So, he wants to meet with me. We're going for coffee this morning, before I take Jemma to school."

"Hey, wait a minute. What?" There's an edge now to Nikki's voice.

"GJ wants to meet me at a Starbucks across town, early this morning, before I go to work."

"You're not going to go, are you?"

"I was."

"Look, 'Stelle. He's a drug dealer, you just said. You have no reason to spend time with him. He probably wants to hit you up for money or something."

Nikki pauses, her eyes having shifted from angry concern to sparkle with delight. "Good morning, Jemma-Sweet. I see you hiding in behind your Momma-Stelle."

Surprised that Jemma has come into the room, Estelle turns to pull her daughter into where the iPad camera will catch her sleepy look. Jemma rubs her eyes. "Mornin' Momma-Nik." She turns to Estelle. "Momma-Stelle, I can't find my favourite book."

Estelle smooths her daughter's tangled curls. "I put it on the table by your bed. You were sleeping on it when I went in to open your blinds. Go, find it there. I'll come, and we'll read it together after I finish the call with your Momma-Nik."

"Bye, Momma-Nik." Jemma saunters off.

"I don't like this at all, not at all—you getting together with your long-lost brother."

"It's just in a Starbucks. It should be okay."

"Well, it's not okay with me—and you said going before you take Jemma to school. Are you taking her to meet your drug dealing, criminal brother? And I'm not there. Wait until I'm home at least, then just you and I can go together."

Nikki moves closer to the camera on her phone, looms there slightly off centre, takes a breath to come across more forcibly. "No, 'Stelle. I don't want my darling little Jemma exposed to a drug dealer, even if he is family."

"It's just in a Starbucks. It'll be alright. I'll get her a strawberry frappuccino and have her with earbuds and a book. And I can use getting her to school on time as an excuse not to stay long."

"She's so happy, so normal, so perfect. You have no business taking her to where he is."

"Nikki, let's not fight. I can keep her safe. And we don't know what GJ is like now. From what I saw of him on his Facebook page, he's a family guy now—working, trying to do right."

"And you trust Facebook?"

"I trust my gut."

The two stare at each other for a few minutes, caught in that limbo time when they fight. There will be no convincing—someone will have to cave.

"Well, you are the shrink." Nikki is the one this time.

"Don't call me that."

"Gotta go. The bus will be here in a few minutes."

"Nikki. Please trust me with this."

"I don't have much choice, do I?"

Estelle stares at the image on the FaceTime screen. She hates this edge to Nikki, now a little clearer with what Auntie Leanne had artistically depicted. True enough, it is Nikki's way of loving her by protecting her, by cherishing her and their daughter. She looks up at the framed wedding photo of them on the wall, the one that has the meme *Choose Love* inscribed as a halo around their heads.

Estelle swallows and says, "Choose love."

Nikki's tone softens. "Alright. We choose love. In love, I guess I have to trust you with this. I don't like it, and I wish I were there to watch over you. But do what you want."

"Thanks. I better go and spend time with Jemma."

"You both be safe now."

"You, too."

And simultaneously, timed by the look in each other's eyes, they end the call with "I love you."

"Read it, Momma-Stelle."

"You can read it yourself."

"I know. But I want you to." As Estelle sits on her daughter's bed, Jemma creeps onto her lap. Sleep has long left her but a desire for a morning cuddle is not yet satisfied. Tenderness overtakes them.

Opening to the first page, Momma-Stelle begins.

Has anyone seen my bookish daughter?
 Her eyes so blue. Her hair pure gold.
 She'll be hiding behind hard covers.
 E'en though she's five years old.
Up in the attic? 'Mongst boxes and dust?
 Or down the stairs in the dark cella?
 A book she'll have, 'cause reading's a must,
 And she is mine, my Bookish Stella.
And just what colour will her jumpsuit be?
 Pinkle or bluey, greenish or yella?
 To know the colour will surely help me.
 Oh, help me find my bookish Stella.
Her daddy is gone, grouchy sister's gone too,
 And her brother, that pesky fella.
 Today we're home, with reading to do.
 'Cause she is mine, my Bookish Stella.

"I'm going to wear my blue shorts today. And my purple top." Jemma slips off Momma-Stelle's lap, the cuddle done.

"Okay."

Bookish Stella is open to the page where Aunt Leanne has drawn four identical images of Stella sitting cross-legged, holding a large book. In each drawing, the book hides almost all the child body except for the eyes and forehead in intense concentration. In each of the four images what little can be seen of Stella's pyjamas and the covers of the book are painted a different colour—pink, then blue, green, then yellow.

"Momma-Stelle, who is GJ?" Jemma breaks the trance.

"GJ is your uncle."

"I have an uncle? Like in the book *Family Ways*?"

"Yes, you have an uncle."

"And why were you and Momma-Nik fighting about my uncle?"

"I'm sorry you heard that, Jemma. And we weren't fighting."

Jemma sighs, reaches over to the pile of books on her bedside table. "Okay, Momma-Stelle, I want to read for a while."

"That's okay. I'm going to have a shower. You go to the bathroom first. Then you can read."

A few minutes later, as Estelle goes toward the bathroom, she looks in on Jemma in her room. Years before, as if by magic, when this little person was just a few cells in Estelle's womb, she turned Estelle into an adult. Now, as a curious, connecting, caring, and cuddly young girl, she is Estelle's reason to keep a laser focus on being that adult, responsible and functional.

Jemma-girl has climbed into a book, fully into it, as if her body had ceased to exist. Just her eyes and furrowed brow are visible as she sits cross-legged on her bed. Her posture is identical to the image Aunt Leanne painted a generation ago. Estelle knows what that is like, knows it deep in the core of her, deep in body memory and in the very organization of her mind. She knows it and wonders why her own daughter needs to do that too.

April appears from the bedroom with little prince Harry on her left hip. The toddler's eyes, still crusted in sleep, blink into tentative wakefulness then close again. His cheeks are flushed, his hair sweaty and askew. In a moment of brief looking, he sees his father sitting at the kitchen table dressed in the blue polo shirt and tan khakis of his workplace. Little prince Harry blinks his eyes shut, open again, and then retreats farther into the softness of his mother's neck and shoulder. His pudgy leg stretches across her belly.

Nate rises, greets April with a kiss, and strokes his son's back. The next look from the toddler prince gives Nate a brief smile. Then with eyes opened wider, he reaches to be held by his father's grasp.

"Long night," Nate observes.

"Yeah. He's teething again. When I changed him, his bum cheeks were red too."

"Poor little guy." Nate holds his son so they can be face-to-face. "Hang in there, buddy. There are wonderful things you can chew with those teeth once they are all in."

Harry pulls back from the intensity of being directly spoken to. His face contorts toward a cry. Nate eases him back onto his shoulder, rubbing his back.

"You have both binders out," April observes.

"Yuppers, I was reading over the handouts from rehab on Step 9."

"Oh, that right. That's today."

"Well, probably not today. Today I'm going to have coffee with Stella at Starbucks and ask if she's willing. If she is, we'll plan to meet again when there's sufficient time."

"Nervous?"

"You bet. This is going to be the hardest one of all. I'm going to do Stella first, then Aunt Leanne. I want to be able to tell Aunt Leanne that I've already reached out to Stella to make amends."

As much as Nate dreads the exercise he hopes to do with his sister, he anticipates the relief, the cleanness and clarity he expects will come after.

April goes over and lays the two binders side by side on the kitchen table. She designed the cover of the second binder for Nate, a tree with roots showing underground and a lush crown of branches and leaves. He'd entitled it, *My tree of recovery has many branches.*

"When do you have to leave?" April asks, taking Harry from him and installing the child into a highchair with Cheerios on the tray. From the refrigerator, she retrieves a handful of berries for her little prince.

"I'm meeting Stella at quarter to eight. It's a fifteen-minute walk over there. I want to get there early, so I will probably go in about fifteen minutes."

With a few excited flailings of arms and hands, Cheerios hit the floor and blueberries smear the flushed cheeks of the suddenly animated child.

Nate looks at the cover of the other binder, reflecting. On the cover are his old initials, inked there in the stylized version he had doodled over and over again starting in high school art class—GJ. The stroke of the J descends below the bottom of the G, sharing the little line. The bottom of the J forms a fishhook. In the countless in-school suspensions he had as a teen, that hook dangled many images and swear words in speech bubbles. GJ had been his identity—the way he had signed his name, the moniker that had labelled him in many dealings. It was still his name when he went into rehab.

Various AA sayings are now inked on the binder cover—*Easy does it, One day at a time, Let go and let God* and *First things first.* Meeting his sister today certainly isn't a *First thing*. In fact, he's left it to be just about his last in the list he formed in rehab. Over the last few weeks, he's been diligently reworking the steps to get up the courage to do it, be serene in the midst of the doing.

Opening the rehab binder, he flips through the pages until he comes to the amends letter he has prepared for Stella. He reads it through again, tears up for what it truthfully acknowledges, and fuels himself with resolve for the next hour.

"Are you taking that with you?" April asks.

"No, I'll give it to her later."

Harry shrieks a sudden, piercing distress—one of his leg's little folds of pudginess has gotten caught in the crack between parts of his highchair.

As Nate leaves the quadruplex he worries about how April and Harry will pass the day. It's hot. The quadraplex cooled a bit overnight with the fan in the window but the day promises to be hot, dry, and windy again. The fifteen-minute walk over to the strip mall where he will meet Stella is pleasant enough now—it will be scorching this afternoon when he returns home from work.

Stella.

The worry about April and Harry morphs into anxiety as he anticipates seeing his kid sister again, this after fifteen years, maybe more. He was delighted when she agreed, delighted and determined. He has to do this. Then on her Facebook page, he saw there is now *Dr.* in front of her name. Maybe she is following the family tradition of doctoring. Like his dad. He chokes on the word dad.

It is the next sober day.

Like every other day, but even more needed today, Nate recites the mantra that Rachel, his counsellor at Addiction Services, developed with him. It got long and complicated, but he cherishes every line.

Deep inside of me is a self that craves and can achieve a healthy, responsible life. . . (breathe) . . . Even though that self was dented by what happened in my childhood . . . (breathe) . . . by my father's abuse . . . (breathe) . . . by my own harmful behaviours . . . (breathe) . . . tarnished by the grime and crime of my addictions . . . (breathe) . . . that self is now being revealed . . . (breathe) . . . It is beautiful in my recovery . . . (breathe) . . . Sobriety allows that healthy, responsible life within me to be my life now . . . (breathe) . . . That healthiness, that drive for a sober life is innate within me. Fundamental goodness. In Nate.

GJ changed his name after that. He and Rachel found *Nate* inside his second name of *Jonathan,* right there in the middle of it all, at his core. He could claim that.

And there is the Starbucks now.

Breathe.

Estelle and Jemma have to leave the condo fully an hour before their usual time. It sets their routine off. Jemma dawdles. They're late leaving.

Then Estelle has to navigate rush-hour traffic across the city to the distant Starbucks. Because it'd been tense getting out the door, it's tense in the car. Jemma wants to play *I Spy,* but Estelle says that she has to concentrate on driving. Estelle wants to play calming music on the car stereo, but Jemma shrieks and asks for Katy Perry. Finally, they settle into a silent truce, Jemma reading one of the books they keep beside her car seat.

"Momma-Stelle, why are we going this way? This isn't the way to my school."

"Remember? I'm buying you a strawberry frappuccino at Starbucks."

"Yay! There it is!" Jemma points out a Starbucks they'd just passed.

"That's not the right one, Jemma."

"It doesn't have strawberry frappuccino?"

"Probably does but doesn't have GJ."

"What is GJ?"

"Your uncle."

"Oh, him." Jemma's voice falls.

Estelle wants to say *You'll like your Uncle GJ.* It's a reflex whenever she takes Jemma to meet someone new. Jemma wins the hearts of strangers with her perky smile. She brings out the best in people.

But Estelle holds back. The possibility of GJ being likeable is weird for her. She never remembered liking him at all, not even a little bit, ever. When they grew up, she always had to be on her guard.

Now, in the car, Estelle finds herself retreating to the practices of her psychologist's profession as she thinks of her brother—culture neutrality, take others at face value, don't make hasty judgments, believe the best of most.

Somehow that doesn't fit for family. Somehow *GJ* is wired into some scary part of her brain.

"When does Momma-Nik come home?"

"What do you remember from the calendar this morning, Jemma? We counted out the days."

"I remember I hate counting. I hate numbers."

"Sleeps, then. Name the days, if you don't like numbers. She comes home next Monday."

Jemma settles silently, a defiant look on her brow.

Estelle needs to break the tension. With eyes flitting from rear-view mirror to the impatient traffic in front of her, she tries a different conversation. "So, Jemma, tell me more about the class trip to Drumheller you had yesterday."

Jemma sighs and then begins. "We went on a bus. When we got there, a bunch of older kids were just coming out. Like it was weird . . . that the museum was just opening, but kids were already coming out."

"I think they have sleepovers for kids in the higher grades. Right in where all the dinosaurs are."

"That's creepy."

"So, what did you see?"

"I saw Billy Watkins grabbing his penis through his shorts as soon as we got off the bus because he had to go pee so bad. We all laughed at him."

"Jemma!" There's an edge to Estelle's voice, one that suggests disapproval.

"It was funny. And in grade one, they teach us the names of all our body parts, even the boy ones."

"So, did you see the dinosaurs?"

"Of course. They were just bones. But some had skin. They all looked old."

"Of course, old."

"Old like Gran-MomMom. When do I go to Gran-MomMom's place?"

"This weekend."

"Will Daddy be there?"

"I don't know, love. But you always have a good time with Gran-MomMom and Papa."

The traffic has built up. The Deerfoot is madness. Estelle checks the electronic signs that identify how long it will take to get to the interchanges to the north. It might as well say *forever*. Estelle feels the tension rise in her—tension about cars packed too close, tension about being late. Tension about her brother.

"Why don't you know?"

"Jemma!" The frustration rising within Estelle has edged out her better self. Jemma begins to pout. Estelle reverberates with the tension of the stop-and-go traffic. The tone of her daughter's name spoken in anger vibrates the long silence between them.

Estelle eases her way onto an off-ramp heading to the Starbucks that GJ had identified for her. Getting off the packed freeway, there's a bit of relief. She checks the rear-view mirror to catch tears in her daughter's eyes. Estelle reaches for a kinder self, an apologetic self. She can't find it. There's something more going on—more than traffic, more than the struggle with Jemma's weekends at her father's house with a father who can't be counted on to be there.

"I just don't know, Jemma," Estelle speaks with exasperation. She's trying to find her way in a different part of the city. She's trying to find a different way to have this conversation with her daughter. She's lost. "Can we leave it this way for now, Jemma? I'm driving. Can you read a book for a minute? I don't know how to get through this traffic, where my turn is."

Estelle reaches down and switches the car stereo to the CD player, and hits button five. Katy Perry fills the car.

Estelle's throat had caught with Jemma's question. *Will Daddy be there?* Seven years ago Estelle was desperate to have a man father a child within her. What she got in Everett along with the pregnancy was a whole lot of toxic masculinity. In the end, Jemma did come out of it and Jemma is her gem. Now Estelle faces the chaos of having saddled her sweet daughter with that man as her father—and how Jemma craves seeing him.

But that is not all that catches her. Churning away deeper inside of her is the memory of Estelle's own historic, six-year-old Stella craving a father in her young life too.

Nate settles at a high table in Starbucks at the front window. His feet dangle, finding the low sill of the plate-glass window. It is 7:43. He looks for Stella, then checks his phone for pictures of her from her Facebook page.

Directly in front of the coffee shop, a 2009 Cadillac Escalade backs aggressively away from the parking bumper. Halfway across the parking lot from the Starbucks it stops and begins to accelerate forward, directly toward where Nate sits. It picks up speed rapidly, its V8 engine and high-performance powertrain pushed to its max.

Engrossed in the photos on his phone, Nate marvels at his barely recognizable kid sister, now grown into a professional-looking young woman. He doesn't hear the gasp coming from behind him.

The front tires of the Escalade hit the curb, propelling it upward. Its high centre of gravity and the high ground clearance carry the Caddy forward, crashing through the window. Nate's table tumbles over backwards, pinning Nate under the car's front end. Amid the screams of the other patrons comes the gentle sound of the glass falling. Heating vents in the ceiling fall off their moorings to dangle, dispelling dust over the scene. Suspended lights swing.

The driver's door of the Escalade opens, and a thin man in a hoodie gingerly picks his way through the debris to run off with a limp.

A blue and white handicapped placard swings from the rear-view mirror behind the shattered windshield.

As Estelle pulls into the parking lot, the target Starbucks in sight, she notices a disorderliness. Cars are askew. People are running. She looks down at the dashboard clock as if, for some reason, it would be important for her to know what time it is, whether she is late. 7:48. Pulling around the line of stores, she catches sight of the bulky SUV halfway through the front window of the Starbucks.

Estelle hits the brakes hard. Jemma jerks in her car seat.

"Ouch! Momma!"

Estelle feels her gut grab. She's fully stopped, looking at the scene in front of her. Bits of the building are still falling on top of the car penetrating the plate-glass window. People are running out of the Starbucks. None of them look like the picture of GJ on his Nate Facebook page. Sensing her mother's panic, Jemma starts to cry in the back seat. Katy Perry is asking if they are ready for a perfect storm. Car horns behind her are honking as Estelle blocks the way into the parking lot.

She throws the gearshift into park as if there is nowhere to go.

Dr. Jackson Horvath stands at the entrance to The Outlandish Cafe on the main floor of the downtown Vancouver hotel. He doesn't see his colleagues. Then, almost immediately, Monica emerges from one of the side rooms and waves to him. She mouths the words *over here.*

As he enters the small private room he's greeted by the three of them— Monica, Eric, and Amir. They stand and clap an enthusiastic, but sparse, applause. Following behind him as previously arranged, a waiter enters carrying a tray holding a large plate carefully stacked with a half-dozen buttermilk pancakes. Atop the pancakes is a lit sparkler sending off clicks and blips of fragmented light.

"Oh, guys. No! Sit down! You shouldn't have."

"Jackson, this is your day. Your presentation to the Congress." Monica beams in pride at her colleague's accomplishment.

"All of your names are on that paper with mine. It's a day for all of us."

"But you get to stand up in front and present the paper." A sly smile emerges on Amir's face. "And we can hide in the back."

Jackson receives hugs from his three colleagues. Here at the hotel, an easier camaraderie breaks out amongst the four of them. In the group practice back in Calgary they often see little of each other, their schedules deliberately staggered so there is never more than one patient in the waiting room. Back there, when they meet in the mornings, it's all business—Mondays and Wednesdays one way, Tuesdays and Thursdays the other. Protocols are carefully reviewed, and the progress of difficult patients is tracked amongst them.

"Are you nervous?" Monica asks. Then, not waiting for an answer, she smiles. "I'm so glad it is you up there and not me."

"Our data is good. The write-up clear. Amir did a great job on the PowerPoint. We should be fine."

The sparkler goes out. Fine grey ash, almost too small to see in the dim light, settles over the top pancake. They allow the server to take orders and refill coffee mugs.

Eric rises, his hands behind his back. Monica and Amir start to chant, "Speech, speech, speech."

"Jackson, I thought you were crazy when you brought your big idea to the group practice four years ago. Crazy as a personal judgment—no, clinically crazy. And as you know, I am a psychiatrist able to be a good judge of that." He pauses and smiles. "What you've done has made a new man of me, and I think of all of us, except for Monica, of course.

"You've transformed our practices, made them ultimately more satisfying and successful for our patients. Personally, I don't know if I would still be in practice if it weren't for the change that your crazy idea has created for me.

"Jackson, thank you!"

Monica and Amir give muted fake applause and chant again, "Speech, speech, speech."

Jackson remains seated, his eyes diverting quickly from one to another. He watches the coffee being discreetly poured into his cup by the server.

Eric passes a gift across the table to Jackson and Jackson unwraps it. Inside is a hardback, leather-covered version of the paper he is to present in just six hours. He looks at the gold leaf printing on the spine of the book: *The Gift of Health. Paper presented at the 47th Canadian Congress of Community Psychiatry, Vancouver, Canada.*

Jackson opens the book, a book insanely luxurious to the touch. He flips to the dedication page.

This paper is dedicated to our courageous patients who, despite living lives of suffering and despair, took control. In that control, they found they could grasp the health that had so long eluded them.

This paper is further dedicated to our dear colleague, Dr. Marc Morrissette. Marc tragically took his own life three painful weeks after the death by suicide of one of his patients. Marc believed in what we were discovering but ended up a casualty of the science of this grassroots trial of innovative psychiatry.

And finally, with deepest sadness and respect, this paper is dedicated to Patient PP38, Marc's patient, tragically lost. To the family of PP38 go our continued

t wilton dale

condolences. We, too, suffer together with you in his loss.

Jackson tears up briefly. These are his words, now presented formally. Still, they are words that move him.

Monica, Eric, and Amir respectfully wait.

Amir breaks the silence. "Do you remember when the pharmaceutical rep came on a Tuesday?"

Sly snickers break out amongst the three of them as they remember. The rep had come into the morning meeting, tugging a catalogue case full of free samples into their small lounge at the back of the group practice. The rep smelled of sweat laden with an NSRI antidepressant seeping from his pores, the sign of too heavy a dose being dispelled by the body.

Amir continues, "I'll never forget the look on his face when you told him to come back tomorrow, that none of our patients today needed what he was selling.

"And when he went to give you samples, you got up. You took the offered drugs and returned them to his hand, suggesting that perhaps he needed them more than we did."

More reminiscence chuckles pass contagiously between them. Monica speaks. "I'll never forget how he turned tail and left, his wheeled case behind him."

The server returns with a tray of fluted glasses of orange juice and opens a bottle of champagne. Jackson Horvath's three colleagues add the sparkling wine to their glasses. Jackson patiently waits for them to be ready, lifts his unadulterated glass of orange juice, and proposes the toast. "To our patients, and to our . . . our too often misguided profession."

The air fills with sound—the sound of Jemma screaming in the back seat, the sound of horns honking, the sound of some man swearing at Estelle. There's a stench coming through the air conditioning vents of Estelle's car, blowing at her. Her knuckles are white as she clenches the steering wheel. The sun is far too bright, coming down at her from the open sunroof.

Then Estelle's mind goes peacefully, eerily, quiet. Colours become saturated and dense—primary colours, rich yellows and greens, a blue so beautifully pale that she could reach out her finger to touch it. Animals and people move around her in happy ways, discovering the world, rhyming their words. Then, there is GJ, annoying GJ, at her again.

"Ma'am, ma'am." There's an insistence at the window beside her.

Go away, she says in her head, then stronger, *Go away. GJ, stop bothering me.* Then, *Auntie! Auntie!* Auntie Leanne is shaking her, telling her that she is there. Her child body feels the book hugged all around her, keeping her safe.

"Ma'am. Ma'am, I have to ask you to move your car."

The tapping on the driver's side window shifts from the police officer's knuckles to a harsh metallic sound, a sound that could break a window if it became strong enough. *Go away. Let me be. Auntie Lee, Auntie Lee!* Stella is angry now, so angry.

Estelle is hugging her arms around the steering wheel of the car, drawing it into her, her protection. The officer at the window is more insistently tapping. Behind her, the honking car horn again.

Breaking through it all, Estelle hears Jemma screaming, a panicky shrill scream.

"Ma'am. Please. We need to get the fire truck in here. You're blocking the entrance. We need you to move your car."

"Shut up!" Estelle yells back at her child in the back seat, yells in that angry voice of her father. Then the crying erupts. Six-year-old Stella tears mix in with six-year-old Jemma tears.

"Ma'am!" The officer's voice is more forceful, an authoritative, commanding presence.

She catches sight of the police officer, seeing him for the first time. A startle runs through her, jerking up from her legs and tummy. It throws her hands to her face. Estelle hears the honking horns now, the increasingly loud taps of metal on her driver's side window. She turns to the officer, a sick feeling in her stomach. Catching his insistent gesture she shifts the gearshift from park to drive, moves her right foot from the brake. Her car slowly rolls forward, as if a child was driving.

The smell becomes stronger. It's a smell more remembered than sensed. The sun is so bright. A car alarm honks rhythmically somewhere in the distance.

Across from the strip mall entrance, Estelle backs into a parking space on the other side of the lot, facing the chaotic scene before her. Several police cars are parked strategically around, the officers moving back the curious lookie-loos who have gathered. Firefighters in bunker gear check the car, examine the damage to the building, usher the remaining customers and staff out of the shattered coffeeshop. A second firetruck comes on the scene, discharging more firefighters who begin pulling out equipment. The scenario takes on a sense of more purposeful chaos, of people doing their job, doing it quickly, alerting each other to this or that.

Estelle closes the sunroof of her car—the sun was shining right into the eyes of sobbing Jemma. The air coming through the air conditioning vents is now clean and cool. She reaches a juice box from the centre console back to Jemma in the back. She says, "It's alright now, hon."

Responsible and functional. It's what Estelle needs to be.

"Strawberry frappuccino?" Jemma asks through shattering sobs.

"Oh, little one. I'm so sorry. We can't do that today, not here. Something awful has happened."

Jemma struggles to pull the straw off the outside of the juice box and push its pointy end through the little silver hole. The concentration of the task settles her cries.

"What Momma-Stelle? What?"

"That car . . . that car crashed into the front of the Starbucks."

"Why?"

"Don't know. But maybe people are hurt. The police officers and firefighters are here to help."

Jemma squirms in the booster seat in the back of the vehicle to look out the front.

A *Global News* van pulls up, blocking Estelle and Jemma's view of the scene before them.

"Why Momma-Stelle?" Jemma asks again.

Estelle focuses on her phone. The only contact information that she has for GJ is through Facebook Messenger. She confirms the old message. This is the Starbucks he mentioned. This is the day—Wednesday. She is to meet him at quarter to eight. It's now five to. He must be in there. Maybe he's been hurt. She'll have to get out to see. As Estelle unbuckles her seat belt there is a light tapping on her window. A woman is there, with a microphone in her hand and a cameraman standing behind her. Estelle lowers the pane.

"Excuse me, ma'am. Did you see what happened here?" The young woman's voice is soft, silky.

"Not really. I came in just after it happened."

The young woman glances in the backseat and sees Jemma there, Jemma now with a juice box and book.

"Would you go on camera? Let our viewers know what you did see?"

"No, I don't think I would have anything to say. And I have my little girl here."

"Momma-Stelle, am I going to school?"

"Thanks." The young woman walks away, approaching yet another onlooker.

Estelle secures her purse into the compartment in the centre console, making sure she has the key fob in her hand, turns to Jemma and says, "Soon, hon. Soon. I'm going out to look at what's going on. I'm going to lock the car but I'm leaving it running, so the air conditioning is on. Don't let anyone else in if they come to the car. I'll be right back. I can get back in with my key fob."

Estelle gets out. Her stomach is queasy again. She looks around and skirts the back of the *Global News* van to take in the scene in front of her.

Firefighters now surround the bulky SUV protruding into the front of the Starbucks. Equipment is in place to stabilize the vehicle. They deploy airbags under the front of the vehicle to slowly lift it.

Paramedics with a stretcher rush in to extricate a body pinned underneath. After assessing the prone figure, their movements cease being urgent, their faces become grim.

Silence surrounds the scene as all collectively gasp.

Estelle watches as the stretcher emerges. There are so many people around. She strains to catch a glance. She doesn't see the face. She sees the blue polo shirt and tan khaki pants.

An hour later, after leaving the Starbucks parking lot and battling traffic back through the Calgary rush hour, Estelle pulls up to Auntie Leanne's house—Estelle's own childhood home, 113 Durham Lane.

As far as Estelle can tell, Jemma was only upset about the failed promise of the strawberry frappuccino. That was an easy fix—a promise of another strawberry frappuccino at the end of the day. Estelle gentles herself with the thought that she'd been able to shield her daughter from the horrific scene at the front of the Starbucks. Tears and confusion had greeted a query to Jemma to find out if she wanted to miss the day at school. Estelle relented—the grade one class at Earl Grey School is a place of safety and delight for her daughter. It would be the best place for her today. By the time she'd called the school to speak to Ms. Gliddenhurst, Jemma had settled into headphones and a book in the back seat. Ms. Gliddenhurst, gracious in the special way of grade one teachers, had promised to call Estelle if Jemma had any difficulties in school that day.

Finally, Estelle contacted her office. She directed Merrill to stand in her stead for the tasks of the day.

Harmonica music plays through the open front door of the Durham Lane house.

"This is a surprise." Auntie Leanne greets Estelle on the front porch. Then, "Oh my God, girl, what's happened?" Estelle breaks into tears. Leanne wraps an arm around her and brings her into the home.

Gordon retreats to his sound studio, escaping the female emotion erupting in the hall. Once there, the notes from his harmonica convey the incredible sadness he witnessed. It sounds corny.

Leanne ushers Estelle through the kitchen and out onto the back veranda. They sit on the two-person swing, Leanne patiently waiting as Estelle cries.

The sound of birds mixes with the blues riffs, the birdsong out of tune but in dialogue with the mournful musical instrument. Estelle's mind vibrates back and forth between her adult self and that of young Stella. Rude GJ bothers her and then lies deathly still on a stretcher in his blue polo and tan khakis. Fierce anger rises in Stella and then falls away into Estelle's blankness. Estelle's adult body takes on child postures, rocking. At one moment, she is Estelle and Leanne is Leanne—then in the next, she is Stella and Leanne is Auntie again. Back and forth. Minutes pass.

Estelle makes a final, firm climb back into her own adulthood. "You remember GJ?"

"How could I forget?"

"I was to coffee with him this morning . . ." Tears come again, but she controls them this time. She looks pleadingly at her aunt.

"Okay, Estelle. Now, start from the beginning. Tell me what happened when you had coffee with GJ."

The story spills. The harmonica plays. Surely he, Stella's brother GJ, could not have survived. He must be dead.

After the halting story, the story told with gaps of disengagement and panic, Leanne calls Gordon to join them on the veranda. She briefs him on what has happened. Gordon's eyes convey his deep concern, but he stands to the side to allow Leanne and Estelle to figure out what to do.

Estelle tells them what she had learned about GJ from his Facebook page—that he has taken the name Nate, has had a child, seems to have settled down, sobered up. The enormous tragedy settles between them.

"I should call Father. Let him know. GJ is his son."

Leanne looks back at Estelle, doubt in her eyes.

Estelle's call goes to voice mail. She leaves the message asking him to call back right away—lets him know it's about GJ.

Estelle opens GJ's Facebook page on her phone and shares the images of April and toddler Harry with Aunt Leanne. Leanne looks closely at Harry with her eye for the human figure and says, "Oh my!"

"What?" Estelle asks.

"It's like I've seen that face before, that pudgy little body."

"Really?"

"Yes, really, but not in your generation, in a generation back. That little guy looks just like your father when he was that age. I'm sure."

"Oh my God. Really? Are there any pictures?"

"There is a box of them in the third-floor storage—old family photos in albums from when Jax and I were small. I'll go and find them."

As she turns to go back into the house, Gordon holds out his phone for the others to see. "Watch this. *Global News* is carrying the story."

The announcer's voice comes on. "Over to Breanne Gibson, at the scene. Breanne, so tell us—what happened there at the Starbucks this morning?"

Breanne begins reporting, the same soft silky voice that had come to

Estelle's window when she was parked there. Behind her, a tow truck slowly extracts the damaged vehicle from the shattered store front.

"A car travelling at high speed crashed through the front window of this Starbucks, killing one person, injuring three, and frightening others as they got their morning coffee. Police and firefighters rushed to the scene. EMS had hoped to resuscitate a young man who had been sitting in the front window where the car struck. Sadly, he was pronounced dead at the scene. The victim is unnamed at this time, pending notification of the family."

"Is there any explanation as to why this has happened?" the announcer asks.

"The police are not saying much. The driver of the vehicle fled on foot before the police arrived. The police traced the vehicle to a Calgary resident living nearby. Apparently, that person has been admitted to Foothills due to a medical episode and is under observation. The police are not releasing that name, either."

"Thank you, Breanne."

"Back to you."

The young reporter looks grim as the news broadcast goes to a commercial break.

"You can see by this graph, at the six- and twelve-month periods, we had twice the number of crossovers from the traditional treatment cohort to the low-pharm cohort."

Dr. Jackson Horvath allows the participants in Salon D of the conference centre to think through the graph. A haze settles over the group—the haze of early afternoon, the slackness of twenty minutes after indulging at a carbohydrate-laden smorgasbord.

Dr. Samuel Smithson rises to his feet, draws himself up circumspectly, and clears his throat. "Jackson, I'm not so sure I understand here. You permitted the subjects to switch treatment groups?"

"Yes, but only at the six-month or the one-year interval."

"And this was available for both treatment cohorts?"

"Yes."

"Did you then identify to each of the subjects that they'd been participants in a study with alternate treatment protocols? How did they react to that news?" Dr. Smithson puts an edge on the question, as if he is catching Dr. Horvath's experimental design in some sort of ethical *faux pas*.

"Actually, we'd briefed each of the subjects when they entered the study that there were two protocols. You'll find the briefing we gave to all participants in Appendix D of the documentation package. Both treatment approaches were outlined in positive terms when their consent was requested. We gave the individual patients the right to switch cohorts upon intake from the one to which they had been randomly assigned. With the way the two treatment protocols were outlined, emphasizing the potential advantages of each, no one decided to switch at the outset of their participation. And then, at the six-month and twelve-month time frames, we outlined the two treatment protocols again and gave them the choice again."

"So neither the patient, er . . . subject . . . nor the psychiatrist treating them was blind to the treatment manipulation?"

"That's correct. The rigour of treatment blindness is impossible to achieve in any study that involves psychotherapeutic intervention."

Dr. Smithson continues curiously. "Now you show many more subjects in the traditional treatment switching to the low-pharm treatment at the six-month and twelve-month time points? Hmm, let me make sure I understand. Very few in the low-pharm group switched to the traditional treatment group?"

"Yes."

"But at the end of the study, after two years, you again have roughly equal numbers in both of the treatment protocols."

"Actually, quite a lot fewer in the low-pharm group."

"Oh yes, I see. How could that be if more people switched into it rather than vice versa?"

"As you will see in the next slide, most of the subjects in the low-pharm group ended treatment prior to the full two years."

"Dropped out, eh?" There is a smug tone to Dr. Smithson's voice, as if he has caught the flaw that reveals the research finding is not as positive as it seems.

"No, actually. They ended treatment by mutual consent." Dr. Horvath pulls himself to full height and declares, "They got better."

The room seizes itself into alertness.

"How do you know they didn't go somewhere else to get *proper* treatment rather than what you'd given them?"

"We had exit interviews conducted by an independent researcher on all who left. Additionally, we had prior consent to do follow-up with the patient and the patient's family doctor post-treatment, at both six- and twelve-month intervals again. The participants in the low-pharm—which for most of them actually became *no-pharm*—were doing considerably better."

"Better than?"

"Better than at the outset of treatment, even better than when treatment was ended by mutual consent, and certainly better than those in the traditional treatment cohort."

Alert now, with Dr. Smithson's questions and Dr. Horvath's replies, others in the room shift uncomfortably in their chairs.

Later that afternoon, the speakers' hospitality suite is as hospitable as a small gathering of psychiatrists could hope it to be. Most are being careful with the wine, aware of its synergistic effect with the various pharmaceuticals they too take. There are the requisite trays of hors d'oeuvres, cold cuts, and cheeses.

Peers exchange pleasantries. Most other psychiatrists are dutiful with Jackson—thanking him for his presentation, carefully avoiding any mention of its content. Those who know him well ask about his daughter. Those who do not shift awkwardly on their feet. When they can, they become distracted by how hungry they are and how they need to get some free food. In parting, they wish him luck.

"Dr. Horvath." The middle-aged man approaching Jackson does not bear either the dishevelled look of some psychiatrists, nor the distracted bearing of others. He's not awkward in the space, but purposeful.

"Yes."

"I am intrigued by your presentation at the conference today. Might we discuss it?"

Dr. Horvath looks suspiciously at him, has a sense that something is amiss.

"Pierre, Pierre Bolton, of the Consortium. Can I call you Jackson?"

"If you wish."

Dr. Jackson Horvath immediately feels defensive. The label *Consortium* belongs to an umbrella group of pharmaceutical companies. Typically, they are executives or science types at these conferences, not smooth operators like the man in front of him.

"Your findings are intriguing, to say the least. Certainly, though, not at all in keeping with the body of evidence that has been developed by the gold standard methodology the Consortium advocates."

"Yes." Distrust coats Jackson's single word. His eyebrows descend, his lips harden.

"Jackson, we don't want to be in conflict here."

"My findings are in direct contradiction to yours."

"That's why I'm approaching you. I've spoken to directors within the Consortium. We would like to attempt a replication of your findings, to do so with greater rigour than you can achieve as a practitioner in the field."

"I doubt that."

"Sir." Pierre Bolton takes on a more assertive stance. "We're on the same side, here. We at the Consortium want to further effective treatment for mental health patients, the same as you."

"I'm well aware of your organization, of what it considers 'fundamental to effective treatment.' I disagree. That's why I conducted my study. Your consortium has vested interest—"

"Your findings will have no weight of serious scientific consideration if they're not replicable."

"I'm sure they will replicate. But, perhaps not by your group."

With these words, spoken in soft, sinewy intensity, the hospitality suite becomes silent, takes on a chill. The few other conference participants stand at a distance, listening.

"If they are valid, not biased by your lack of blindness to subject assignment, they will replicate. If they don't, your results will be revealed for what they are."

"Which you believe is?"

"Oh, let's not get ahead of ourselves. I'm prepared to offer you funding to be a consultant to us in the research design of another study if you withdraw your paper from print for this Congress."

"I don't want your money."

Pierre Bolton shifts on his feet, transitioning from a stance intended to set a tone of collegiality to one more aggressive.

"We will do the study regardless of your participation."

"Very well."

"We are convinced that your findings will not stand up. But we want to give you an out here, to ease your way back into respectability, if it doesn't replicate."

"So you enter the replication study with a bias as to what it will show."

"As you must have held before your study. To even think of the violation of ethics your little experiment entailed . . ."

"My data speak for themselves."

"Your data are tainted by bias."

"We are done here." Jackson Horvath turns to leave.

"I don't think so, sir. If you participate with us, there are options available to us that we will not need to pursue."

"Options?"

"Let us say," Pierre Bolton pauses, "we really don't want to walk forward with an ethics complaint we feel could be filed with your licensing college."

"Really?" There is a sarcastic tone to Jackson's retort. Within, however, he battles down an incipient dread.

"And we are aware of other issues that you would not like to have brought forward. Issues of your own mental stability. Family issues. We recognize that these are deeply personal matters, personal matters with a painful history for you."

"Are you threatening me?"

"Oh, no. Why would you think that? Rather, we're giving you an out."

"Thanks, but no thanks."

"For now, all we ask is you withdraw the article you prepared for the *Journal*—that and consider coming on board with us."

Pierre Bolton smiles, smiles an unfortunate, ominous sort of smile. "There's more at stake here, Dr. Horvath, more than just your reputation. There's your daughter, too, to consider, the one you have finagled a cushy funded job for. In fact, Dr. Horvath, we know about all of your children, where they are. And your wife. Well, we know all about that, too . . ."

Pierre Bolton lets the sentence die with strong innuendo. He flips a business card in the direction of the psychiatrist. Pierre Bolton turns on the heel of his well-polished dress shoe and walks out.

Dread pounds in Jackson Horvath's ears. Even he doesn't know where all his children are.

CHAPTER FIVE

Thursday

Estelle sits in her car outside the quadraplex.

As soon as she had fully grasped the tragedy of her brother's death, she sent April a friend request on Facebook Messenger. The wait for her reply seemed interminable—Estelle kept going back to check. When she repeatedly looked at April and GJ's Facebook pages, she felt a kinship with little Harry. Then April accepted the connection and chatted back with her through Messenger. Estelle detected reticence in those hastily typed messages from her sister-in-law. Finally, April relented, accepting that Estelle could come over. They voice chatted for April to give her address and phone number. Estelle searched for nuances in April's voice—obvious grief, definite apprehension, but self-reliant determination, too. In the Facebook photos, April seemed soft and round. Estelle sensed another April.

The summer sun drenches the front of the quadraplex. Heavy cardboard covers the living room window from behind, placed to keep out the heating, beating sun. The grass outside is brittle brown. Shrubbery languishes unattended, barely holding on.

April greets Estelle at the door with the toddler on her hip. Estelle hands her newfound sister-in-law a bud vase with a yellow rose in it, a rose surrounded by several sprigs of tiny white flowers. April says, "Thank you," and tears up, turning away. Harry presses his face into his mother's neck.

Inside the home, the smell of a toddler bum greets Estelle—little Harry's disposables bound tightly and placed in a diaper bin but still giving off the heavy scent of baby powder.

April places the bud vase on a dinette table behind a couple of loose-leaf binders, out of Harry's reach. Immediately Estelle notices how out of place the gift of flowers is. There are few adult touches in the home. The only breaks in the interior's drabness are infant and toddler toys in bright primary colours, just a scattering of them on the floor. A fresh flower there seems bizarre.

"Thanks," April says flatly.

"I'm so sorry." Estelle feels the words deeply, hopes they express a tentative kinship for the young mother.

"Thanks," April repeats, the word eking out what little spare energy she has. "Can I help?"

April sits holding Harry close, crying softly.

Estelle senses a question in April, a question that would take too much strength to even ask—*What am I going to do?*

Finally, April says, "The flower is nice."

She opens the card, reads that it is from Estelle, Nikki, and Jemma. She then takes in the reality of the gift credit card also contained in the envelope.

"It's for Safeway. Some money for groceries or whatever you need—$200."

April's tears flow again. Estelle sees her try to shuffle them off to the side. Is it pride on her face? Did the gift card insult her? Is it shame?

"I'll use it someday. Thanks again."

Estelle looks around the quadraplex. It is sparse, so full of need.

"Do you want us to go today, get some things?"

"The Safeway is too far away for me to walk. We shop at the Save-On-Foods. We don't have a car." *We—Nate and me.* April wipes a tear.

"We can go in my car."

"I don't have a car seat for Harry. Just a stroller."

"Oh," Estelle says. The desperate lack of resources for April and Harry is becoming clearer. Estelle realizes the things she takes for granted—an SUV and a booster seat the right size for Jemma, two incomes from Nikki and herself. Not only are there fresh flowers on their dinner table, but dark chocolate in the cupboard for after.

"I've Jemma's seat in the back of my car."

"Is it the right size? He squirms a lot."

"No, I don't think so. Jemma is six."

"Yeah, well, I won't put him somewhere that isn't safe."

The two women sit. Mothers. Harry had grown comfortable enough to look at Estelle. Then he slides off April's lap. She holds his hands as he feels his feet under him. He toddles over to the blanket on the floor with each hand holding one of April's fingers and sits down heavily. There are blocks there and a ball. He bangs things together while he sits, secure on his bum.

"Do you have any help, April? Anyone to support you?"

"No." After a long pause, she says the unsayable. "I don't know what I'm going to do."

"Do you have parents to help out?" Estelle asks.

"No. That's another story. It's just Nate and me. We are . . . were . . . determined to raise Harry right, on our own. Not like my family or his." Suddenly April looks scared, like she's worried she offended her guest.

"Well, I don't know about your family, April, but I know about GJ's. It was a mix, both good and . . . well, not so good. My auntie raised us. Our dad provided for us financially. But it was screwed up."

"Nate told me." April inhales and then pauses a long time, as if there is something she wants to say and doesn't know how to do so. Estelle waits.

"Can I ask you something?" April asks.

"Ask away."

"Nate straightened his life out, went to rehab. He works hard to give us the best life he can. But . . . but before that, way back when he was growing up, what was he like? You were his baby sister, right? What was he like to you?"

Estelle pauses. There is a socially correct answer begging to be off-loaded as a means of avoiding the truth. She looks at the strength in April to have asked the question. She realizes that only an honest answer would do. "April, to be honest, it wasn't good. He was mean. He did cruel things."

"Yeah, what I figured, what I know. I'd hoped it wasn't as bad as all that."

"You know?"

April looks at the binders on the table.

"Yes, I know."

"April, what about your family?"

"My parents have divorced me. Their pastor told them to. He said I was living in sin, and they shouldn't do anything to help if I didn't come back and live with them and go to church again. They won't give me money as long as I stay with Nate. Dad was very clear about it. We could really use the help, but I guess we are managing without it. Still, every week they phone and ask to take Harry to church with them. But I don't want Harry growing up like the men in that church, so I won't let them take him. I know too much about the men there, what they are like. All respectable and holy on the outside—selfish and entitled, arrogant more like, in their personal life. I don't want Harry to stupidly look up to them, to end up like them."

Estelle fills with awe at the young mother, the strength she has, then cringes at how desperate her situation is. She senses her brother—the grown Nate, not the crude and cruel brother GJ—still anchors April's world. A good man. And now, in harsh reality, April's Nate is gone. Gone, and yet she still speaks of him in the present tense.

"They've threatened to have Harry taken away from us so they can raise him. Said that they had a lawyer. Estelle, how do I fight that?"

Estelle's mind brings back the problem solving that is a part of her work as a psychologist. She could be full of advice, and maybe will be so for April at some time. For now, though, she just sits with April—is a presence. Finally, she whispers, a wistful confidence. "There'll be a way. I'll help however I can . . . to figure it out . . . if you want me to."

Within the hour they are at the Save-On-Foods. Estelle figures Nikki would probably be mad about it, but she takes April shopping anyway. April insists the Safeway gift card go back to Estelle, so Estelle can use it to buy her own groceries. Estelle insists on paying for whatever goes in April's cart today at Save-On.

When April puts in an economy-sized package of disposable diapers for Harry, Estelle, behind her back, puts in two more. April protests, saying Harry has just about grown out of that size and puts the extras back. Estelle picks out two packages of the next size up and puts them in the cart. Cheerios and blueberries. Then Estelle puts in another box of Cheerios. Bananas, peaches, and watermelon, too. Cheese, eggs, homogenized milk, and two boxes of Goldfish crackers. They argue about the dark chocolate, but Estelle insists April needs it for herself; that, and some microwavable frozen dinners. Coffee, too. April nervously puts some soup and packages of KD in the basket.

Throughout the shopping, Estelle anticipates what Aunt Leanne would say. Auntie would tell her to go for it, buy whatever this young family needs. It is an easier thought than the argument she would have with Nikki.

They can't do Starbucks; it's closed with police tape all around it. They do Yugo-Freeze. It is a delight for Harry.

"What about the funeral?"

"I don't know. The funeral home put me in touch with Welfare. But we've never gone to Welfare, so they have to open a file." April pauses. "Mom called and said that her pastor would do the service."

"That might be okay." Estelle looks hopeful. Perhaps this might be a bridge of support for her sister-in-law.

"I said, 'No bloody way!'"

"Why?"

"I was at a funeral there, all church folk. But it must not have been for one of them, 'cause the minister talked about how sad he was that the dead person was going to hell because he didn't believe. What a shame, eh?"

Estelle gasps.

April looks up, her eyes flashing with anger. "And, all those old men there said, 'Amen.'"

When Estelle let her father know by text the day before that she needed to talk to him about his son, he didn't respond. She soon realized if she'd indicated she needed to connect about a patient, one of his patients downloaded to the day program she runs, he would have replied right away. But about GJ? No, that is family. In her grief, in its confusion and paralysis, anger at his nonresponse edged to outrage, then her outrage lapsed into resignation.

But now the call comes in.

"So . . . what?" Jackson Horvath's voice emerges from Estelle's iPad as it rests on the kitchen table in her condo.

Estelle hears annoyance in her father's voice, impatience. She takes in a deep breath. "It's about GJ."

"Yeah, you said it was about him in your text. So . . . what about GJ?" Jackson speaks his son's name with disdain.

Estelle looks down at the iPad. Tears well up. Her head fills with images of toddler Harry on the hip of his grieving mother, of an oversized SUV piercing a plate-glass window, of her crying Jemma in the backseat. She blinks through her tears and sees the screen image of her father staring back at her.

In the way of FaceTime, he is looking down on her, his eyes downcast as he has placed his iPad on a tabletop while hovering above it. As he looks at her image in the centre of his screen, the tablet camera off to the side, his gaze appears to be deflected.

It seems so like him—looking down on her, his gaze going past.

Finally, after a long, dead still pause, Estelle says, "GJ is dead."

Starkness shudders through the space between them. Estelle's eyes fill with tears. Jackson's eyes stare back blankly.

It's a long time before the father speaks. "GJ has been dead to me for a long time."

"Not that way dead. Dead dead."

"Dead dead?"

"Hit by a car."

Jackson gradually shifts to the look of a psychiatrist whom a patient has told of a distant, impactful tragedy. "What happened? When? How do you know?"

"I was there. It was when I was supposed to meet him for coffee. A car went out of control, drove through the front window of a Starbucks. It hit right where he sat."

Jackson sits silently, staring. A hint of compassion for the daughter he still has left in his life dawns into his eyes.

"Oh my God! If I hadn't been five minutes late, it would've been me, too. Me and Jemma." Estelle convulses with the sudden realization.

"Tell me again. A car drove into a Starbucks?"

"Yeah and hit right where GJ was sitting. He asked me to meet him there. I was late. Thank God I was late."

"And it was GJ? You're sure?"

"Yes, GJ. He calls himself, called himself, Nate now. But it was our GJ."

"When did this happen?"

"Yesterday, yesterday morning."

"And you were going to meet him?"

"Yes. He and I had connected on Facebook. He had reached out to me, had found me. Said he wanted to meet. Then before I got there, this happens."

"Thank heavens you weren't there when the car hit. Estelle, that sounds awful, awful for you to be there to see it. I'm so sorry this has happened to you."

Warmth has crept into the father's voice. It is so unlike his usual demeanour toward her, the obligatory transactional relationship they had developed as interdependent professionals. Now he speaks to her as family, as a father for the moment. His tone disorients her, then she figures this is just probably his therapy voice reflexive to her sadness.

"Yeah, I'm okay. But shaken. Jemma was in the car with me."

"Is she okay?"

"She was upset. But she wanted to go to school right after, like normal. She was okay through the day yesterday and at Auntie Leanne's after school."

"Kids are resilient," Jackson, the psychiatrist, asserts.

"Some kids," Estelle, the psychologist, counters.

"So."

"So, I went and saw GJ's wife today, and their little guy, just a toddler, Harry."

"Yes."

"We need to help them. You need to help them. They're really poor."

"Wait a minute. Suddenly, this is about money, is it?" Jackson's demeanour instantly reverts to the defensive.

Estelle lapses into silence on her end, her heart touched by April and Harry. She is touched by the disparity between the lifestyles—her lofty condo and their stiflingly hot quadraplex, her SUV and their stroller, her chocolate-covered blueberries all decadent and sweet and Harry's Cheerios and blueberries on a highchair tray. She glances at the screen, sees her father's resentment at the prospect of giving financial help from the money he makes being compassionate to others.

"I'm afraid it needs to be. I bought them groceries today. GJ was working to provide for his family, but now he's gone."

"Working? Dealing drugs?"

"He's sober, went to rehab, was turning his life around."

"So it's up to me now? My son doesn't give me the time of day for fifteen years, and now I have to support his wife and kid?"

"You don't have to do anything. I'm just telling you. If you don't find it in your heart to help them, I will."

"I'm tired of all this."

Estelle pauses. She gives it one more try.

"Father, I want you to look at two pictures. I'm going to hold them up to the camera."

The first one, printed off Nate's Facebook page, is an image of a very proud young man holding a son. The toddler sits on the dad's hip, one leg around the front, the other around the back. A pudgy hand reaches up and touches the father's hair. And, as if caught by a sudden call from the person holding the camera, the young child has turned to look full on. A brilliant smile beams from the toddler's face.

Estelle takes out the second picture. It's black and white, printed with the scalloped border around the edge—an image of a very proud young man holding a son. The toddler sits on the dad's hip, one leg around the front and the other leg around the back. A pudgy hand reaches up and touches the father's hair. And, as if caught by a sudden call from the person holding the camera, the young face has turned to look full on. A brilliant smile beams from the child's face.

The black-and-white photo was from the box of old family photos. Aunt Leanne found it. It depicts her brother, young Jackson, being held by their father. The resemblance between the two toddlers, grandfather and grandson, is unmistakable. Harry bears the face of his grandfather.

Jackson shows a moment of recognition. He sighs. "I'll see to it when I get back. I fly back Saturday."

The FaceTime call has gone on too long. It has strained the tolerance in the discussion of family matters for both Jackson and Estelle.

Finally, Jackson says, "I want you to look at something." He holds up to the tablet camera a business card. "Can you read it?"

"Yes, it says 'Pierre Bolton, Consortium of Pharmaceutical Treatment and Research Initiatives.'"

"Have you had anything to do with him?"

"Never heard of him."

"Let me know if you do."

As Estelle walks into the family home at 113 Durham Lane, her eyes draw immediately to Jemma. Jemma sits on a padded stool beside Gordon, the two of them at a bank of keyboards and sound equipment. There is energy between them, one of delight as Jemma stares intently at her Uncle Gordo while he explains this and that of technical music production. The mournful riff of a track he has just recorded is coming from the monitors. The sound morphs subtly as Jemma's fingers twirl the knobs on the soundboard. Estelle barely notices the differences in sound quality, but she sees fascination in her daughter's face at the impact of her child fingers there.

There is even a greater delight on Gordon's face. It is the delight of a being with a child—the pure and clean delight in the sweetness and simplicity of human companionship.

"She's in her inner sanctum, the studio upstairs." Gordon throws off the comment to Estelle in such a way that doesn't break the magic between him and Jemma. Estelle cannot forego a hug and kiss for her daughter before she goes up to see her aunt. She cherishes Jemma's wayward curls as she tucks them behind her ear, then she cherishes even more the distracted but grateful adaptation of child body to adult embrace. Impatient with the affection, Jemma stares at Momma-Stelle, "I'm busy, Momma-Stelle. Go away 'til I'm done."

Estelle trudges upstairs and knocks at the door to the studio. Leanne waves her in, a rag wiping solvent from brushes in her hand.

Catching sight of what her aunt is painting, Estelle exclaims, "That is stunning."

"Do you like it?"

"I'm not sure."

The painting is a cacophony of hard edges, clashing colours, irregular shapes. It has the coarse texture of thick paint applied with a palette knife, angled in all directions—a shocking departure from the carefully constructed, delicately articulated paintings that are usually Caylie's style.

Estelle stands, her jaw dropped slightly. It's a painting one cannot look away from.

"Here, I see your eye wandering all over. Look here, at this small area of white."

Estelle does.

"Keep staring, just at that one spot."

With a sudden shift of gestalt, Estelle sees her aunt's image emerge from the chaos. What had been seemingly random patches of blue or violet suddenly become eyes, eyes as warm and welcoming as a lingering hug. A sudden beaming smile emerges, then her full face, then her shoulders, pivoted as if she is suddenly looking over.

"That's you!"

"That's me. Denny wanted a self-portrait for the studio space we are developing upstairs from the gallery. After going through the seven rooms of the exhibit, patrons are to trudge up the backstairs where I will greet them. Denny's daughter, Kaitlin, will be up there to sell commission contracts." Leanne pauses. "Do you think it is too much? Too self-important, too flattering?"

"No. It's you. You are important." Estelle takes another moment to look. "Do you know what it reminds me of? When I was sent home from graduate school, I was a mess. Life seemed to be over—that I'd failed, and Father would be so mad at all the money he spent. But amid all that, you greeted me on the porch. In the midst of it all, you were there. I guess that's how I've seen you all along in my life, suddenly appearing out of the chaos to take care of me."

"Brings back memories, eh?"

"It's beautiful." The image captures Estelle, holds her.

"I'm afraid most people will just see the colours and lines, not be able to find much beauty in it."

"It's beautiful because it tells the truth."

"Well, you might be interested in this one, too." Leanne goes over and pulls a canvas from behind the easel, holds it for Estelle to see.

Immediately Estelle recognizes the familiar cover of *Bookish Stella*, painted in childlike simplicity—a cross-legged child with a picture book, the cover of the book bearing the image of the same child holding the same picture book, the echoed image growing smaller and smaller. However, the eyes peering over the top of the book in this painting are not the Stella-child eyes but adult Estelle eyes. The hands are not pudgy fingered but gracefully manicured adult hands. The brow is not furrowed by the task of reading but the challenge of living.

"Oh my God, Auntie. It's me. It's the grown-up me holding the book."

"It's you."

Leanne stands there, holding the Stella-Estelle in her hands.

They both breathe.

"Did you talk to him?" Leanne asks, breaking the spell.

"Who?"

"Jax."

"Oh, yes, I reached him by FaceTime just an hour or so ago."

"What did he say?"

"That GJ was dead to him already."

Leanne puts the brushes down. She turns full on to be with her niece.

"I think he'll help. He was hard, bitter at first. But I showed him the picture you found in Grandma's photo box. His eyes softened as he saw the resemblance between him from years ago and little Harry being held by GJ. Anyway, he's going to be home the day after tomorrow. I'm pretty sure I can get him to help financially, help with the funeral, maybe even . . ." Estelle's voice trails off.

"He's a hard man—hard about family, anyway." Leanne speaks with resignation.

"I see such a different side of him with his patients. He's warm, hopeful. His heart is in it, and his patients love him."

"Just like his dad, like our father." Leanne's eyes flash with successive emotions. Estelle tries to decode them.

"From the way he treats his patients, I think I can get him to have the same compassion toward April in her grief, in her terrible situation."

"Well, if he believes he has an obligation, he meets it. I guess he was generous with money for me to raise you—you, Anna, and GJ. But it was like he was trying to buy me off, buy off something anyway."

Decades ago, when Leanne returned to live in her childhood home so she could take care of Jax's kids, she converted the balcony above the back veranda into a three seasons room, commandeered it for her studio space. Over the years, the studio gradually expanded to overtake what had been the master bedroom in the house.

Now, with the balcony doors and windows open, a warm summer breeze wafts in. On it comes the sound of a ukulele and the encouraging instruction that Gordon gives Jemma. Soon there is a gentle Hawaiian plunking—first one chord and then another. Jemma is getting it. She takes the required time to move the fingers of her left hand from one chord to another, but when she is there, her right hand strums the rhythm clearly, correctly. And once Jemma has found her own way, moving fingers and making music, her emerging confidence meets the short, sweet notes of Gordon's harmonica. He's accompanying her, accompanying her with all the attentiveness and respect he would give to a recording artist touring through the clubs—the consummate sideman. His harmonica mimics the sounds of songbirds.

The breeze feels less dry than a typical Calgary summer afternoon, almost oceanic—the music moistens it, makes it magic.

Estelle shifts, looks directly at her aunt. "We're going to have a funeral, a funeral for my brother. Anna is his sister, too. We should let her know."

Leanne stares back with a mixture of confusion and hardness. "I think she's long gone."

"I've no idea where she is either, whether she's still in Calgary even. I think we should try to find her."

"Why? She wants nothing to do with us."

"Still, she grew up with GJ. They were closer in age than either was to me. We were taught in graduate school about the bonds of family, that there would always be a yearning to know about the other, a yearning for reconnection. Anna might feel that, want to know."

"Wait, wait." Aunt Leanne shows a sudden awareness.

"What?"

"She came by here, back to the house. Oh, a long time ago. A year maybe, maybe even more. She didn't look herself. She looked hard, like it was a hard life. Looked older than I could ever imagine her to be." Aunt Leanne's eyes turn upward as if she was sorting through an archive of memories buried somewhere in her mind.

"I remember. She was on about something, about someone. Was scared. What was it?"

Leanne puts the brushes down, moves toward the door. Estelle lets her by, gets ready to follow.

Then Leanne turns. "I remember looking at her, not recognizing her. She was dressed funny. A high scarf around her neck. I remember thinking, *Have you been sick, girl?* Like there was something wrong with her throat. It's coming back now. A scar there, or something, like she had surgery on her thyroid, and she was trying to hide the scar. There was terror there too, terror in her eyes." Leanne looks over at the portrait of Stella-Estelle on the easel. "That's it. She was afraid that someone was coming after her. She came to ask if the person had come to the house."

Leanne rushes out of the studio, down the stairs, toward the kitchen.

A desk sits between the window and the door out onto the back veranda. It's cluttered with family life—mail and stuff. There's a corkboard there with Post-it notes and pictures. Successive years of calendars are stuck on it with a thumbtack, one on top of the other. It's Leanne's archive of what and when. She pulls off the calendars and starts going through the pages. There are notes in the squares for each date, doctor's appointments and the like, and Post-it notes stuck to it too. Leanne flips back, more and more deliberate. There is something to find there.

"Here it is," she proclaims. She's on a page from August three years back.

"She said someone was harassing her. Asked if he came here looking for her. Did she say a name? . . . No way I'd remember if she did. Wanted me to get in touch with her if anyone came by asking about her. She said I could reach her at this number."

Leanne holds out a note, a Calgary phone number with instructions—*Leave a message with Lenny, tell him to have Nali call you back. Leave your number.*

Estelle pulls her phone out of her purse, puts it on speaker, and makes the call.

"Lenny here."

"Hi Lenny. My name is Estelle Caylie. My sister, Anna . . . er," Estelle looks at the Post-it note from Aunt Leanne's calendar, ". . . Nali, said she could be reached at this number. Can I speak with her?"

There's a long pause on the other end of the call. "Nali? Nali who?" Lenny's voice has a manufactured perplexity to it, as if he wants not to give away any information about any Nali he might know.

"Nali . . . Nali Caylie. I'm her sister, and there's a family emergency."

Leanne interrupts Estelle. "Horvath, her surname is Horvath, not Caylie."

"Sorry, her last name is Horvath, not Caylie. Anna Horvath, but apparently she goes by Nali now."

"A Nali *Horvath*, or *Caylie* or whatever, you say? Hmm. I don't know any Nali *Caylie,* or *Horvath* either. Maybe you have the wrong number."

Estelle reads out the number she'd called.

"Okay, then. Well, I guess I can check with the regulars, see if anyone knows about a *Horvath* or a *Caylie.*"

Estelle hears glasses and the bleeping of electronic gaming machines in the background. "I really need to get in touch with her."

"If I find out anything, I'll call you back. Your name and number?"

"Estelle. Anna, Nali, would know me by the name of Stella, Stella Caylie. Or she could call her Aunt Leanne."

Estelle gives the numbers.

"No promises, eh? Don't know anyone by the name *Caylie or Horvath.* If I find out anything, I'll call back."

Estelle looks over at Aunt Leanne. She's at the kitchen sink scrubbing the infant car seat that Estelle had picked up at The Children's Place second-hand store—one in the size she thought would fit her new nephew, Harry.

"So," she says to her aunt, "I guess we'll wait. He said he'd call back. Said he didn't know any Nali Horvath. But I sort of figure that maybe he knows a *Nali* by the way he said it, maybe a different last name. How many Nalis could there be?"

And just outside the kitchen, beyond the open screen door, Jemma is making the two-person swing on the veranda move in time with the music. Gordon has installed his harmonica on a neck holder and is playing the uke and the harmonica together. It's sweet, bluesy, a ballad. Simple really.

CHAPTER SIX

Friday

ReClaiming Ourselves Inc. is the innovative program Estelle heads as executive director. It assists those on sick leave with depression and anxiety, its fifteen or so clients attending daily for eight weeks. The basics of establishing and sustaining good mental health are taught and prac-tised. Clients also learn strategies to reintegrate successfully back into work, maintaining good self-care to make it through the stress of re-entry.

Estelle's program takes her father's natural mental health approach further than he had first imagined. Mindfulness is not just taught as a practice but integrated into activities as a way of staying present and responsive. Clients learn to spot potential toxic interpersonal behaviours and respectfully keep safe from being drawn in. A core element to the program has clients master reading their own flux of emotions, acknowledge what is inside them, and then make healthy choices for their behaviour in response to those emotions.

Together with Merrill, a graduate student on practicum placement with the program, Estelle has just incorporated a unit they call Triple T-YN— Take The Time You Need. The benefits of taking mental-health days off work when needed are identified. Clients are encouraged to include these in their return-to-work plans and coached to be honest and proactive with employers about what they need to keep healthy and on the job for the long term. Roleplaying activities are included in the program to deal with nosy questions from co-workers when a client needs to take a mental-health day. Clients learn to spot and use co-workers and supervisors who will be kind and supportive. Most importantly, they learn to be assertive rather than aggressive or collapsing in response to unreasonable demands that would compromise their ability to cope.

When Estelle contacted Merrill on Tuesday and said that she needed a couple of personal days, he immediately took on her role in the program. He found a way to use her absence as an example of good mental health.

For Estelle, the last few days were as distant from good mental health as anyone could possibly imagine. There was the flood of memories triggered by her auntie's portraits. Some of those memories still reverberate with wordless nausea and sudden gasping breath. Then came the tense FaceTime call with Nikki—the quarrel and then the cave. A few hours later, she watched as her brother was run over while sipping his morning coffee. Then, a day after that, the call with her father who has no interest in stepping up for his son, or his grandson. Estelle's nights have been filled with nightmares of cars going out of control—sometimes she is in them, sometimes she is just watching it happen. Sometimes it happens in the ocean.

Mental-health days? Hardly.

But now it is Friday.

Fridays are special at ReClaiming Ourselves Inc.—TGIF. The Monday to Thursday psychoeducational lectures, interpersonal roleplays, individual counselling sessions, and guest speakers are replaced by board games, movies with socially constructive themes, and lively music. Sometimes line-dancing breaks out for those so inclined. Clients are encouraged to socialize informally, supporting and encouraging each other.

Estelle decides she can return for this end to her week. Maybe it will help lift her spirits, distract her from all that is rumbling around inside.

But on the other hand, Estelle feels she has to. When she and Merrill encourage clients to take necessary personal days, it is never more than two in a row—any more can morph into an inability to return to work at all.

Clients greet Estelle warmly when she comes in. As they have been trained to do, they carefully watch for signs of whether she wants to talk about what is going on in her life—which she doesn't. Several of them kindly say that if she needs to talk, they are there for her. Estelle smiles, and says "Thanks, but I'm okay." Which she isn't. Clients seek to include her in what they are doing, a kind and generous way of making her feel a part of the group again. Merrill has gone over all this with them—they take up the task as a good application of their training, almost as if Dr. Estelle Caylie's sudden absence was all a part of the lesson plan. And it works—for a couple of hours Estelle forgets the chaos that is unsettling her from inside, has her spirits lifted by those she is supposed to be helping.

Agency policy specifies participants in the program are to stay all day, going home at 4:30, just like a usual workday. But come mid-afternoon on this TGIF, Estelle has to leave. On the phone when Lenny called her back he told her to come to The Rooke Neighbourhood Pub at 3:30.

When she arrives, Estelle notices The Rooke has seen better days. Years ago, its initial design placed stuffed ravens on small shelves set into the walls. Their iridescent feathers are now covered with dust. The lighting is dim, and there are but few patrons there. It has that stale beer smell.

When Estelle enters, she immediately wishes she'd dressed differently. She'd worn business casual—tan culottes with a pressed crease down the front, a pale blue blouse and sheer scarf. Blue jeans, T-shirt, and a baseball cap would have fit in better at The Rooke.

"Howdy! You Stella?" Stan greets her enthusiastically, as though he relishes his assigned task.

Estelle immediately likes him—the slight Maritime accent, the sense he gives of *folk-help-folk*. He reaches a gnarly, swollen hand to her. Immediately, she sees the bulging joints of his arthritis. As she takes his hand, she glances around the small pub, trying to catch sight of her sister.

"Yes, are you Lenny?"

"No, Stan. Lenny's over there." Stan nods his head in the bar's direction.

"Is Nali here? Nali is my sister."

"Well, maybe . . ." Stan blinks back the twinkle that has come to his eye. "Buy a round?"

There are three or four of them there, a couple at one table, including a large woman in a wheelchair. There are few empty glasses on the table, as if there is more socializing happening than drinking. A guy is over at the VLTs, his back to them all. Lenny looks over, Estelle makes a circle gesture with her hand to have him dispense another beer to all assembled. She throws a twenty on bar to pay for it.

"So, Nali's sister, eh? Thought Nali was my kid sister, and kiddo, I've never met you!" Bernice rolls over toward Estelle in her wheelchair, offering her hand, grasping Estelle's a bit too tightly. "But we meet now. Hi, I'm Bernice."

"Actually, I'm Anna's, oops sorry . . . Nali's . . . *kid* sister."

"Well, I guess we're family then!" Bernice releases her grip on Estelle's hand. As Estelle pulls her hand away, Bernice extends hers toward Estelle's body, grasps the thin scarf tucked discreetly into the top of her blouse, and pulls.

"Just checking!" Bernice says, waving the scarf overhead as if it is a victory flag and she is celebrating an outrageous win. Bernice infectiously cackles, and the others in The Rooke reflexively join in with her. Stan walks over. From a scolding posture toward Bernice, he retrieves the scarf and hands it back to Estelle.

"In-joke," Stan explains. "Sorry about that. I guess you're one of us now, eh?" There's warmth in his eyes. Estelle takes the scarf and self-consciously tucks it back around her neck and into her blouse. She is caught between being offended, being made fun of, and perhaps, just perhaps, having been offered an immediate acceptance.

Lenny breaks in from behind the bar. "So, Estelle Caylie. Do you know a Jimmy Murphy?" His tone is serious.

Estelle looks over at him. "Jimmy Murphy? No, I don't think I do."

Lenny is looking directly at her as if trying to detect prevarication. Then, satisfied, his face relaxes. "Just being careful . . . for Nali."

And so, a barrage of questions comes—*Where did you and Nali grow up? Other brothers and sisters? Oldest? Youngest? Did she always dance as a kid? Was she prissy or a tomboy or a vixen?*

Estelle is taken aback but senses the interest is benign—interest in the way of curiosity about someone loved, a chance to get the goods that could be used for future teasing. She senses her answers are heard and accepted at face value. Estelle likes these people. They are people who are real, people who bear their wounds differently than the clients at work or even her colleagues in the mental health profession. But she also has an eerie sense, the sense of the one not in the room—the one apart, watching.

Back behind the wall of the bar, Lenny set up a little office for himself at The Rooke. The desk is piled with unopened mail. Nali sits there, her eyes fixed on the images from the closed-circuit video cameras Lenny installed to monitor the activity out front. Lenny had put in a high-quality system the last time that Nali was being harassed by Jimmy Murphy, a year or so ago. It was what Lenny could do to help Nali feel safe.

Nali watches with fascination the confident young woman who has come into The Rooke. She strains to see the remnant of a younger sister she hasn't seen in about twenty years. In her line of work, Nali has learned to read and trust body language and facial expressions—those always prove more reliable than what is said. Could this woman be her kid sister, Stella? She looks for her in the body, in the face. Nali had asked Lenny to ask the Jimmy Murphy question, to ask it when this supposed-Stella was facing right into the camera. In response to the question came the puzzled, nonrecognition on this maybe-Stella's face. Could it be the echo of the face of the little kid sister she used to know? Nali watches with fascination as Bernice pulls off the scarf—an impromptu, serendipitous act but one that leads to a look of sudden panic playing out on the visitor, like the look of a little girl caught in a whirlwind of something she can't understand.

Maybe it is. Likely even. Still, Nali has to be sure.

Nali watches the monitor as the possible-probable Stella extracts something from a tote bag. It appears to be a large binder. With Lenny, Stan, Bernice, and now even Trevor gathered around the table, Nali has trouble seeing it despite the multiple cameras. Then she recognizes it as an old-fashioned photo album, the kind containing snapshots in plastic sleeves. Gales of laughter triggered by the pictures penetrate to the backroom. It's a laughter that knows her, relates the Nali she is now to what are apparently the images of the Annalise she had been as a child.

Nali can contain herself no longer.

The doorway between the bar and the back consists of two swinging half doors with eye-level windows. Nali looks through one of those windows. Given how they are all standing, she can't get a good sight of the visitor. She edges her way silently between the doors to stand in front.

Estelle, in looking from one to the other—Stan to Lenny, Lenny to

Bernice—catches sight of her sister standing there. The sudden change in her renders the laughter silent. Estelle takes in the full look of Anna-become-Nali.

Nali is dressed in such a way that much of the cobra is on display. She watches her kid sister take it in, watches with the silent analysis of how the other is reacting. She watches for the facial expression of disgust that so often greets her when another woman sees the tattoo. She watches for the look of curiosity, even celebration that some achieve after a moment or two. What she sees on the face of the now most-certainly Stella is absolute disorientation.

Nali stands waiting for Stella to recognize her as her sister. Now she sees in the woman the meekness, the fear, that had been her kid sister those years ago in their home at 113 Durham Lane. The disorientation lasts a few seconds, seems like longer, and then comes a look of recognition. Of acceptance. Of compassion.

"Anna. Annalise. What's happened to you?" Estelle leaves behind the gaggle around the photo album and rushes toward her sister, arms outstretched.

They hug a moment or two, Nali's gazelle-like body going rigid. Then Estelle pulls back. She stares into the stress-wrinkled eyes of her older sister. Then with clear intention Estelle follows the tattoo of the snake from the throat, around the neck and then down to Anna's torso. Finally, she reaches both of her hands to hold both hands of her sister.

It's too much for Nali. And yet it's not enough, could never be enough. There is a strange sense of relief, seeing her sister standing there. And then a wave of impenetrable guilt. Nali's mind swims. She remembers little Stella, bookish Stella, as fragile—mousy in a withdrawn sort of way. This woman before her looks so professional, so put together. No longer the little kid Stella, the one she was supposed to love and protect—the one she failed to protect.

"Stella?" Nali asks.

"Yes, Anna. It's me. Can I call you Anna still?"

"Yes . . . I guess . . . for now."

The vulnerability of holding hands so close together grows cloying. Nali spots the photo album on the table and walks over to see it.

"Wait, Anna. I've something to tell you. Something difficult."

Nali turns to her.

"GJ is dead."

Nali's face goes blank, as if she is the one disoriented now. Stan comes over to her, Bernice looks up from her wheelchair. Turning to them she says, "So GJ. That's my brother . . . or was . . . I guess."

Nali closes the photo album.

Estelle asks, "Is there somewhere we can go to talk?"

"Yah, I've got to get to work eventually. Let's walk over there. We can talk while we walk."

The sidewalk blisters in late afternoon sun. Estelle fills Nali in on the Starbucks, how GJ had reached out to meet with her, the funeral upcoming.

Nali takes it in, doesn't interrupt, lets Estelle say her piece.

"Well, Stella, I have a different life now. I suppose I will go, go to the funeral. But I'm not Anna, not even a Horvath any longer."

Estelle lets the silence of their footfalls on the sidewalk surround them. Then, making an attempt to connect again, asks, "So, that guy, back at the pub—Stan was it?—and Bernice in the wheelchair. Why did she pull my scarf off?"

Estelle feels the tension in Nali release.

"Oh, that's a story. It all started years ago on a winter day. I'd dropped into The Rooke on my walk between where I got off the bus and the club where I work. It was bitterly cold, a three-block walk. I was just going to warm up, but when I went in, there was something about the place. You saw. The people there.

"Anyway, I kept going in, every day before work. Stan became like a dad to me. Bernice, a mom. They are both misfits, but they took me in. I already had the tattoo, but I could dress with turtlenecks and scarves so it didn't show because it was winter. The more I got attached to Stan and Bernice, the more I was hesitant to let them see the tattoo, like they would disapprove. Well, one day, my scarf slipped. Bernice caught sight of the head of the cobra, there on my neck. She pulled off the scarf and waved it over her head, just like she did today with yours. I was mortified. Stan came over and got it back for me, just like he did today with you. But you'll never believe what happened next."

"What?"

"So Bernice breaks the tension by saying, 'There, there girl. Don't give a mind. You should see what I have tattooed on my ass.' The whole room broke into laughter."

Nali checks for Estelle's smile.

"What she did today was to test you. I'd asked them to do something while I watched, to catch you off guard, to have you react to something, just so I would know it was you."

Estelle beams respect toward her sister. "That was strategic." She pauses. "So, you mentioned something about a club."

"There it is now." Nali gestures toward the Emerald Grove Gentleman's Club just ahead. "We go in around the back."

"You work there?"

"For the last fifteen years, anyway. I'm a manager now. Fill in as a dancer when I need to."

Estelle goes silent. The two stand while Estelle's mind swims. Her training as a psychologist begs her to take her time with this—*Don't make hasty judgments. Take people at face value whenever you can. Accept others in their struggles as doing the best they can under the circumstances they face.* But there is another part of her—the part that isn't a psychologist, that is a sister, a little kid sister with a teenaged sister all made-up and looking so grown-up but into who-knows-what.

"So that's what I do. What do you do?" Nali asks.

Blinking back into the present, Estelle responds to her sister's question. "Oh, a psychologist. I run an agency for people off work with depression and anxiety. Mostly middle-class folk."

Nali turns, speaks assertively. "You are going to meet my staff. Don't you dare mention to them that you are a shrink. Some of them have seen shrinks and felt judged, belittled."

Nali presses four numbers into the combination lock on the back door and they go in. Reaching a second-floor staff lounge, Nali goes about straightening the space. Finally, she glances down toward the parking lot at the back of the building.

"I expect Kristine will be in soon. She's going through a rough time with her grandma in hospital. It was her grandma who raised her. Now she's had a stroke. Kristine's been feeling guilty that it happened when no one else was around. They didn't get Grandma to the hospital soon enough, so the stroke has left permanent damage. It breaks Kristine's heart."

"That's sad."

"Everyone is sad. This is a sad business. All smiles and winks out front. Heartache back here."

"So tell me, Anna. How did you end up here?"

"Long story." Nali turns, eyes both wary and pleading.

"Can you start, start to tell it?" Estelle hopes their relationship is secure enough for the telling.

"Are you sure?"

"I'm sure."

"So, back when I left . . . well, I wasn't going to stay with bitch Leanne, she was all rules and responsibilities, and I was fifteen. I'd been staying at Dad's condo. When he told me he was going away because of his drinking, he said I could stay on my own in the condo . . . stay there as long as I was going to school. But I refused to go back to Western Canada High—the tomb! So we looked up where else I could go. Shaganappi Point Charter Academy for the Performing Arts, aptly named the Shag, had just opened. They had a program in dance. Dad had always wanted me to continue to dance, and so that was what we decided. Right away, before he left for the treatment centre in Ontario, he enrolled me. So, promising to be a good girl, I went."

"Going to a charter school and living on your own in a luxury condo, what a sweet deal."

"Yeah, I guess." Nali's voice takes a sad dip.

"Within a few weeks, they discovered I was living on my own, without an adult. Dad had to fly back from Ontario to meet with the headmaster and Child Welfare Services. I don't know how it got resolved, but I was almost sixteen and I stayed in the condo. I was assigned staff, called success mentors, who were to keep track of me—the dance instructors, Ivan and Katya. They were married, stormily married, from Russia. Anyway, I spent a lot of time in the studio with them, and they took me back to their home when I got too lonely in the condo . . ."

Nali pauses. "Stormily married. Did you catch that?"

Estelle nods.

"Before long, Katya was resenting me, and Ivan was calling me *second wife*. It went downhill from there."

"What do you mean?"

"So, nowadays, we call it sexual abuse. Back then, it's what I did to survive. Actually, in the academy, it was something I did to thrive."

"Oh, Anna. No!"

"It was not so bad. After all . . ." Nali walks over toward the window. "Dad had already got me started on all that."

Estelle chokes. Her face goes blank. Nali stands with her, lets her think.

In taking in the reality of the tattoo and the club, Estelle had reflexively thought sexual abuse might have been a part of her sister's life. Estelle had been in the mental health business long enough to realize maybe something like that would explain her sister's sensual tattoo, her choice of work. But with Father? The shock triggers her psychologist mind to spin its explanatory magic. There were risk factors in her family. She can name them all—substance abuse, a sense of male entitlement, highly gendered roles and power structure, the loss of a mother and the oldest child a female.

Nali again looks out the window. Her timing is perfect as she sees a car drive in. "Yup, she's here. Stella, is it okay that I spend time with her? It'll probably be a while, what she's going through."

"Sure, I guess. That's a bombshell you just dropped."

"Well, for you, maybe. But I'm at work now. I've someone I have to take care of. You're the shrink. You deal with it."

Estelle collects herself. "Okay, do what you need to do. I should move my car, anyway. It's in a two-hour parking zone on the residential street. My laptop is in it. If I bring it back here, I can catch up on what has been happening at work. Can I connect to wi-fi?"

"Yeah, I have the current password on my desk. Good idea to move your car. I can't believe that you left a laptop in your car in this neighbourhood. Silly girl. Park around the back when you get here. Our parking lot is monitored by security cameras."

Estelle feels like a little sister again, chided. "Is the back door open?"

"You saw me put in the combination. Strange enough, the number I chose was the last four digits of Aunt Leanne's phone number . . . 3376. You should be able to remember that, eh?"

"I'll put back the photo album."

"No, leave it. I'm sure that Kristine and the other girls will want to see what I looked like when I was a kid."

"I hope we can talk some more."

"Yeah. Once everyone is in, once I have hustled them down to the green room to get ready, there'll be lots of time."

As she leaves the air-conditioned club into the stifling Calgary summer air, Estelle is relieved to have the time alone—the time it takes to air out a car left in the hot sun and then to move it in behind a strip club. But most of all, she needs the time it takes to get her footing again after the seismic shift that has occurred in what she thought of as her family.

"So, where did we leave off?" Nali asks.

Estelle had interacted first politely, and then teasingly, with the women who'd come into the lounge to seek her older sister's ministrations. They accepted her when she identified herself as their boss's kid sister. There was no mention of her being a psychologist. Estelle watched the ease and grace of Anna's attention to them. In the lounge with Anna, all the 'girls' had seemed like ordinary women, not sex trade workers. In a way, Estelle realized Anna was doing what she herself does, does in the socially sanctioned, mental-health-funded space of ReClaiming Ourselves Inc.—listening, validating, encouraging.

Now, again, they are two sisters. They are two sisters, standing at an interior window, looking down from the second floor onto the floor of a gentlemen's club. The ordinary women they had talked with upstairs are now dressed seductively, mingling with the men. Estelle processes the sight before her, the change in the women out there, what the business requires.

"Where did we leave off?" Nali asks again.

"Oh, you were at the charter school. Ivan and Katya. Then you talked about your relationship with Father."

"Does it shock you?"

"Yes. No. I guess so."

"Did he do it with you?" Nali turns to look full on at her kid sister.

"Father? No."

"It's what worried me in the years after I left. I know he visited you when he came back from treatment. I worried he was doing it when you were the same age as he started with me."

"Which was?" Estelle immediately regrets the way she asked the question. It sounds clinical, like she is interviewing a client.

"Ten or eleven, I guess. It'd started before Mom died, started already. They were already fighting a lot. And drinking. I guess, like with Ivan, I became a second wife."

"Oh, Anna."

"Apparently, Mom never got over the depressions. Dad told me she had it after each of us was born. He treated it with drugs, but she never really got back on her feet. Then she started to drink. It went downhill from there. He told me all this when I was still just a kid, as if he was justifying the way he was with me, how close we were. I was Dad's confidante. Then, also . . ."

"How long for?"

"Years, I guess. It eventually stopped. Dad kept relapsing with the alcohol— had to keep going for treatment. The last time he came back he said he wouldn't do it again. Said he was sorry, I guess."

"Oh, Anna."

Nali looks sternly at her sister. "Anna is what *he* called me. I'm Nali now."

Estella realizes that all this time she was still calling her sister by her sister's child name, *Anna*.

"I remember when I was a kid, before Mom died, she called me Lise and Dad called me Anna. When it came to us kids, they could never agree on anything, eh? After I finished at the Shag, started to dance professionally at clubs, I changed my name to Nali. That's who I am now, except on stage, I am Ansa Jewel. Stella, don't call me Anna anymore; call me Nali."

Estelle smiles. "So, I'm Estelle now, not Stella. And Father is Father to me, but Dad to you. And GJ. He changed his name to Nate."

"Weird, eh?"

"Family trait, I guess."

"Dad wouldn't have anything to do with me after I got the tattoo, not directly, anyway. I had to get it. I was a good dancer but needed to have an edge to make it in the adult entertainment world. The tattoo was expensive and painful. But it established me, gave me a reputation, got men in the door. A few years ago, I started saving to have it removed, but the tattoo parlour said it would be too disfiguring. So I keep getting it touched up because I still have to dance sometimes. Now when I need to be out in public, as much as I can, I cover myself."

"Regrets?"

"Yeah, but not the dancing. When I dance, somehow I lose the pain of it all, even in front of the men. When I'm up there, I'm in charge. I'm manipulating them, toying with them, exploiting them financially. I don't do any of the sex favours anymore. I'm in management. They can leer all they want. It's me turning the tables now. Since I went into management, I realize the more money out of their pockets, the more into mine. And the women here—Kristine, Chloe, Tasha, and the others—they're the ones I care about now."

Nali pauses. A look of sadness clouds her eyes. "Stella . . . Estelle, do you ever hear from Dad?"

"We actually work together."

"Really. Is he still a doctor?"

"A psychiatrist now. Somewhere back when I was growing up, he took a residency in psychiatry."

"Oh my God. Our screwed-up family—now with two shrinks."

"I pick him up at the airport tomorrow."

The twinge of a sick feeling catches Estelle, like a memory, a memory without an anchor or a trigger, just a sense of something, something sickening inside.

CHAPTER SEVEN

Saturday

Estelle wanders the condo unable to sleep. It is 3:45 a.m. Dawn light is already slipping onto the eastern horizon. It's still an hour and a half before she will have her FaceTime call with Nikki. She'd hoped she would get some more sleep before entering the emotional jeopardy she expects the call will entail. She has not.

Normally, they wouldn't FaceTime this close to when Nikki is due home. By this point in Nikki's two weeks of work she's pretty tired, too grumpy for a FaceTime call in the early morning before her work at the mine. Estelle reckons it'll go better for them when Nikki gets home if she gives her a heads-up on all that has happened. She'd texted Nikki the day before to set up the time.

If Jemma were here Estelle would take solace in watching her sleep. Estelle's breathing would hook up with Jemma's peaceful breath. Her mind would borrow some of the naivety and delight of her daughter's mind. But Jemma isn't there. Yesterday, after supper, Estelle had taken Jemma to Everett's parents' place, to her Gran-MomMom and Papa, for her access visit weekend.

Sighing, sitting at the dining table where her iPad awaits the FaceTime call, Estelle feels anxious about what she needs to say. Nikki will be pissed when she hears.

It's Estelle's world that is being rocked by the realizations about her child-hood family. But it will be Nikki who will be pissed, pissed about this thing that isn't Estelle's fault, but pissed with Estelle all the same. And Estelle accepts that. That's her Nikki, and she needs and loves her Nikki. Estelle feels more secure in the world with Nikki's protective energy around her, even when it comes across in anger. Estelle values that it is Nikki parenting with her, making this girl child from Estelle's womb her own, and keeping them all safe. The love that Estelle and Nikki share is what makes Jemma's home complete, each Momma playing out her love differently.

She stares at the black screen. Fatigue burdens her despite a mind so starkly alert.

Estelle's mind takes to going down rabbit holes. For some reason, she wonders what life would have been like if Jemma wasn't a girl but had been born a boy. It's just a coin flip of nature: boy or girl. Would Nikki have fallen in love with her if it was a preschooler boy who graced Estelle's life when they met? Nikki has a distaste for most everything that is male. If Jemma was a James, would that have changed Nikki? Would she have welcomed that change? And if Jemma had been a James, would the worries all be different now? Would he have grown into a GJ? What little she remembers of her brother from her childhood was that he was a bully and irresponsible. He'd turned out okay, though, or so it seems. Would James have grown into a Jackson, distant and entitled? Incestuous? A shudder runs through her. Would her father be more involved with a grandson than with a granddaughter? Would he pressure the grandson to take the family heritage of doctoring?

And knowing what she now knows of her father and Anna, should she be worried about Jemma with him now, at age six? The revulsion of the thought seizes her.

Then come the rabbit holes of a brief excursion into REM sleep. Cheerios and blueberries fed to her by her father at La Bonne Baguette during their obligatory weekly lunch together. Blueberries as some sort of bribe or buy off—she has no idea why but eats them sweetly.

"So, what's this all about?" Nikki's words come across brusquely. Then, seeing Estelle's face, her voice softens. "Love."

Estelle had fallen asleep at the table awaiting the call, her forehead resting on her hands. An indentation of her engagement and wedding rings have dented her brow. She accepts the FaceTime call with the disoriented mind of being abruptly awakened. "Morning, luv. Sorry to have you call this late in your fourteen in."

"Yeah, okay. I'm exhausted and got up early to talk. Has something happened?"

"A lot."

"Your brother?"

"Yes, it's about GJ. He's dead."

"Dead?"

"Dead." Estelle had not cried since she told Aunt Leanne three days ago. Then it'd been from being overwhelmed, the tears of disorientation and helplessness. This time tears bear the weight of grief—the grief of sudden, bizarre loss.

Nikki, the fuck-the-world Nikki, immediately softens into the sadness she sees in her love's eyes. "When? . . . did you meet him like planned?"

"He was killed that morning, Wednesday, just before I arrived where we were to have coffee."

"Oh my God! How?"

"A car crashed into where he was sitting at the window in Starbucks."

"That was him? Oh, my God. That was GJ, your brother, killed in the Starbucks? I can't believe it! I saw it on the news. Him, your brother! Wow."

Estelle waits for it to sink in. Nikki is not as angry as she expected her to be. Still, there's a lot more to tell. Sadness is tinged with fear.

"There's a lot to this, Nikki. Please understand. A lot has happened since we spoke. I wanted to tell you before you got here. Give you a chance to get your head around it."

"Right, my head around it. Okay. What else?"

"Well, we have a nephew. Harry. He's cute, a toddler. But, his mom, April . . . Well, they, GJ and April, are really poor. I went over to see her. I've ended up helping her with groceries and stuff."

"And stuff?"

"They have nothing, really. GJ was just getting back on his feet. They were living hand to mouth. Now, he's gone."

"So we are taking them in, right?" Frustration is obvious in Nikki's voice.

Estelle immediately senses her partner's frustration. So often, they've argued about money, about how expensive it is to live in Calgary, about the cost of Jemma. In fear, Estelle doesn't want this call to go there, can't let it go there. "No, we're not taking them in. Don't worry. I just helped with a couple of hundred dollars in groceries for now. I talked with Father . . ."

"Oh, so he knows?"

"Yes, and I've found my sister, Anna, too."

"Okay. So, fucking Caylie-Horvath family reunion time. Jackson and Anna, too."

"Nikki . . ." Estelle's voice pleads.

Nikki softens again. "Sorry."

"Nikki, I need your support. These last few days have been really hard—helping April, little Harry's mom, telling my father, finding Anna."

"Okay . . . okay."

The two go silent for a few moments.

Nikki comes back in, softer yet. "So, your brother died in the Starbucks. You were supposed to meet him there with Jemma." Then her voice hardens again. "You were going to meet him with Jemma. Were you in the Starbucks, too? Were you hurt? Was Jemma hurt?"

"No, we hadn't got there yet. We pulled into the parking lot just after it happened."

"And Jemma, did Jemma see it?"

"I don't think she saw much of anything. She was more upset that she didn't get the strawberry frappuccino, the one I had promised her when we got to Starbucks. I gave her a juice box and drove her to school. That's what she wanted, to go to school. Talked to the teacher when I dropped her off. By the afternoon, when I got over to Aunt Leanne's, she was just fine. Like nothing happened."

"As long as she didn't see it, see dead bodies or anything."

"I talked to her so she'd know that something had happened. I was pretty upset, and so she got upset because I was upset. I told her that something bad had happened, but she was okay, and I was okay." Estelle pauses, catches her strength again. "She's so loved, our Jemma is so loved, so secure that she . . . She's fine."

"Look, I've got to go soon. The shuttle bus is going to be here. I want to get some breakfast before I go. Just two more days, and then I'll be home."

"One other thing, Nikki. Real quick."

"What?"

"I found Anna."

"Yes, you said. And?"

"Anna is a dancer in a strip club."

"You gotta be kidding. What did I marry into?"

"You married me, Nikki. Me."

Nikki paused, her rage deflating a bit. "Yeah, choose love, right?"

"Choose love."

"Okay. Gotta go. Send me an email with more of the story so I can get my head around it before I get home."

"No, Nikki. Don't go. I have to tell you something else. Something really big."

"Make it fast, then."

Estelle screws up her courage, switches from diplomacy to blurt. "Father sexually abused Anna. Treated her as a second wife, back even before my mom died."

Nikki goes silent on the other end. There's a long, breathless pause. Finally, she speaks, not with an impetus of anger, but one of resolve. "I'm going to kill him. That's what I'm going to do. I'm going to kill him."

Estelle, on her end, can no longer be shocked, can no longer react. She just sits.

"Bye," Nikki says bluntly, then her FaceTime video image goes black. The iPad display shows the reflection of Estelle's face looking into the screen. Her hair is a mess, her forehead red, her eyes swollen.

There are expressive totem poles in the concourse of the Vancouver International Airport. Jackson finds his eyes coursing up them, taking in the iconic representations by the Coastal People, their animals and birds.

Looking up is difficult. More naturally, on this day, his eyes crave being downcast. His spirits lift briefly with his eyes. The totems with their spirit animals and other sculptures are compelling. Then both eyes and spirits fall again.

There in the airport, a massive emptiness sucks Jackson energy away. His sense of future has vanished. As a matter of mental health, he knows to expect an emotional letdown after a high point such as the presentation. So much effort had been spent generating the right words, written and spoken. So much excitement had been tied up in the provocativeness and rebellion of the content he would present. It had focused him for months. It had given special meaning to his daily work. He had indulged in daydreamed scenarios of being recognized, being esteemed even, for his innovation and shocking findings.

And now it is done. In the days after his presentation, participants were commenting on what they had just heard—heard not from Jackson, but heard in the sessions they had attended after his. All too quickly, he became old news.

The wings of an eagle atop the pole soar over him, oblivious to his insignificance below.

A shiver of panic flashes through him as his eyes descend the pole. At its base stands that Pierre Bolton staring penetratingly into the crowd, seeing all. His presence is unsettling. Jackson moves away to stand behind a pillar. When he sees Bolton look in the other direction, he raises his cellphone and snaps a picture, catching the man in profile. It bothers him that he is there. Bothers . . . *No.* Terrifies. That comment he made, made about Jackson's kids, that he knew where they were. Why would he know that?

As Jackson walks away from Bolton's line of sight, he contains his terror through distraction, touring the impressive entrance hall. He moves amongst the various pieces of West Coast art, art of the Salish people. The *Jade Canoe* captivates him. He walks around the massive sculpture, touching the smooth surfaces. At its centre is a Person of the Salish, a study in stoicism—focused on being in the present, looking into the future. Around the Salish Person is a cacophony of characters. Animal spirits and mythical monsters are a tumult of presences.

Practical, functional Jackson feels a sense of unease as he takes in the sculpture. He is disturbed not to know what all those presences are, what he's to make of them there. This piece is much more a Leanne than a Jackson. Leanne is the one who dabbles in the emotional world, paints intense emotions leaking from the faces in her portraits. He, the psychiatrist, stays stoic above the emotion of others.

Staring at the sculpture, Jackson sees within the chaos of spirits emotions he works so hard to suppress, emotions that persist in bubbling up from the depths of his subconscious—fear, inadequacy, impotence, anger, violence. Throughout his life, he denied those emotions whenever they arose. When tears leaked out, they frustrated and embarrassed him but he wouldn't openly acknowledge them. If anger erupted, it was always someone else's fault. He's invested so much to be the strong one, endeavouring to remain unperturbed by what roars and threatens from deep within. Not always successful in doing so. Here, with both stoicism and spirits done up in smooth surfaces and rich deep colours of green and amber, emotions are depicted as a natural part of the world. On the surface, it is a scene of man and nature. On a deeper level, it is a depiction of human nature.

He moves away from the *Jade Canoe*, discomforted. His walk takes him to stand in front of *The Great Wave*, up on a high concourse. Lit from behind by the window, the glass wall depicts a giant wave, a wave strong and poised to break over him. Even though it is static there, just an arrangement of thin strips of coloured glass, his mind sees it in perpetual motion—always breaking, always pulling him under. Within that depiction of the wild Pacific Ocean, Jackson sees Izzy—Izzy constantly being swept away but perpetually present.

Jackson settles into the aircraft with 131 others. He'd not slept well the night before in the hotel and looks forward to a brief nap on the flight. Most other passengers absorb themselves into screens. His own cramped space affords him the view out a window. He puts in noise-cancelling earbuds to stifle the roar of the jet engine just a few metres away on the wing. In the muffled silence of the earbuds plugged into the aircraft's entertainment system, the safety instruction intrudes to irritate him.

Takeoff takes the plane directly out over the Strait of Georgia, an expanse of water with waves pushed by strong northwesterly winds. With enough elevation gain, enough distance from the airport, one wing dips and the plane banks steeply to the north. Out the window, all Jackson can see is the sea, a rhythmic expanse of parallel whitecaps. He closes his eyes, resisting the G-force that presses him away from the window, pressing his thigh into the thigh of the large gentleman sitting beside him.

REM comes quickly. It comes with images of Pierre Bolton standing and staring at him from two rows behind and one seat over. It comes with the terrifying image of the escape door over the wing malfunctioning and opening in flight. He is sucked out of his seat, down an inflated slide, off the wing, into the waves of the sea. Estelle is there to greet him, somehow hovering above the waves. And Jemma, too. They wave at him, drawing him into the foaming salt water. Quickly, he is lost to them. He watches them sigh and turn to leave.

And then REM passes, and Jackson is left in a numbed state, not even responding to a cabin steward offering him tea, coffee, or a soft drink with a packaged cookie.

Arriving at the airport, Estelle settles into the cellphone parking lot to wait. She texts her father, asking him to let her know when he has retrieved his suitcase from the luggage carousel, which door to go to.

There's a part of this that she's just not going to process, can't process yet. The man destined to get into her car is a child molester, an incestuous father. Not incestuous with her, at least not that she remembers with her, but with her sister. All of her professional understanding about families and abuse is gone from her mind. This is about vile betrayal, vile betrayal of her own childhood. No, this is not about some other family, some other fucked-up guy diddling his kids. All the protocols of mental health professionalism are just bizarre now. What she knows sickens her.

Yet still he, her father, is a man on whom she is professionally dependent, a man whom obligation has insinuated into her continuing life. She just has to put the other fucked-up stuff away. There are practicalities that need to be managed—get him home, get him hooked into doing the right thing for April and Harry. That's all for now. The other stuff must be for later.

He calls. She drives to the door where he stands.

"No, Jemma?" Jackson asks as he puts his suitcase and messenger bag into the back of Estelle's SUV.

"No, this is her weekend with her Gran-MomMom."

Estelle looks at her father and immediately detects tiredness there, as if he's emotionally beaten up. "How did it go?"

"Well . . . it was well received."

"And?" Estelle encourages him to say more.

"Well received. Probably nothing more will come of it."

She's heading out on Airport Road toward Barlow. The traffic seems impatient with itself, requires more concentration than she wants to give. Estelle is picking up a vibe off him, exhaustion. But there's more there than just exhaustion—fear, fear that has grown fetid. Her father has never shown fear. He's always been authoritatively confident, entitled of respect and submission, dismissive of others not aligned. But now she senses fear, fear bizarrely there in the passenger seat beside her. And as powerfully as she senses it, he is her father and she could never ask. Back-burner that, too.

Estelle picks up the dialogue, not missing a beat. "Well, I believe in what you're doing, what we're doing together."

"My patients? Any crises while I was away?" He's oblivious to her, to what's happening in the emotion-scape of their relationship.

"Nope. All good."

They lapse into silence. Estelle feigns that she needs to concentrate on the surrounding traffic. By the time they make it onto Deerfoot the traffic eases, most of it heading north rather than south. She turns south toward his condo in the city centre.

"We need to talk about GJ, about the funeral, about your daughter-in-law and grandson."

He doesn't answer.

"I was over to see them today before I came to the airport. She's coping, can't do much else with a toddler in tow. I've taken her out for groceries twice now because they didn't have much in. She went to Welfare about the funeral yesterday."

"I'll cover the costs of the funeral. Which funeral home?" Jackson speaks with a sense of resignation as though this is his fatherly, his grandfatherly, duty.

"Heritage."

"I will pay, whatever the cost, but let's keep it simple. There might be issues, issues with her family, with whatever the seedy crowd GJ ran with."

"We do need to be careful. April is a proud woman. If we're going to pay, we'll need to be discreet in how we do it. And I don't think that the *seedy crowd*, as you called it, will be a problem. GJ was in recovery, turning his life around."

The conversation goes silent.

"He was your son. And now he is dead." Estelle glances over at this man who is, who should be, her father. A man who seems impervious to what is family, to the family grief.

Jackson pulls out his phone. Within a moment, he is holding it over for her to see, shows a picture of a man standing in an airport looking away. He asks her to look, to say whether or not she recognizes him.

"No, doesn't look familiar," Estelle says, quickly returning her attention to the traffic and the ramp onto Memorial Drive.

Pierre Bolton has a ritual of settling himself and his accoutrements upon arrival in a hotel room. First he completely strips the bed, scanning for bed bugs. If none are found, he remakes the bed as precisely as would an award-winning chambermaid. Then he lifts his suitcase onto the foot of the bed to unpack.

He splits open his 25-inch Delsey titanium clamshell. Atop, in the right-hand compartment, are a silk dressing robe, silk boxer shorts, and a pair of slippers with thin leather soles and silk uppers. Immediately, he extracts those items, laying them on the bed. Quickly, he strips off his travel clothing, placing it in a bag for the concierge to pick up from his room for laundering—there is no telling what contaminants have absorbed into that clothing on airplanes and in the car he rented at the airport. He showers and then dresses in the silks. Pierre Bolton always makes prior arrangements with his hotel that a garment steamer be left in his room. He extracts all of his clothing from the suitcase, de-wrinkles it with the steamer, then hangs or folds it precisely.

Pierre travels with three levels of attire. There's a blazer and dress pants, ties, dress shirts, dress shoes, and socks for semi-formal wear. Then, several changes of business casual wear—wrinkle-free khakis and button-down sport shirts with cotton sweaters. And finally, he extracts his Tai Chi uniform and gym clothing brought so he can maintain his fitness routine. All items have their predetermined places in the two-sided clamshell. Once extracted, they are placed in the standard furnishings of a better-class hotel room. It settles him to find his clothes securely in place when he opens his suitcase and then to hang them in an orderly fashion when he installs himself in yet another city.

All this complete, Pierre establishes his workspace on the hotel room desk. He installs power cords and rechargers for his devices. His smart phone and laptop computer are arranged with edges perpendicular to the edge of the desktop. Set in behind are the other pieces of equipment needed in his trade—a compact camera with a powerful zoom and binoculars.

Pierre went through this routine when he stayed in the Radisson Hotel in Vancouver during the Congress of Community Psychiatry. Now he goes through it again here in the Hilton Garden Inn, Downtown Calgary. He has come with a copy of Horvath's paper, *The Gift of Health*. One task this week is to trace the human stories behind the death of Dr. Marc Morrissette and find the family of his patient who died three weeks before the psychiatrist's own suicide. Perhaps within that tragedy there will be some way of furthering the goal of ensuring Dr. Jackson Horvath and his insurgent research are stopped.

And it must be stopped by whatever means available.

It's a messy world that Pierre engages in his line of work. It's full of disgusting people and things. He can manage his place within it, but only if he has his personal spaces orderly as he goes about his business.

As compulsively squared away as his arrangement of devices is, the display on the computer screen is organic—confusing at first glance. It displays the huge amount of data he has inputted into the concept vectoring app. In the centre of the screen is a professional photo of Dr. Jackson Horvath. The photographer has done an excellent job with lighting and posing. In glancing quickly at the photo, the viewer might consider a personality profile of wise and kind. Quite a different persona is emerging in the detect and dig venture that Pierre pursues.

With a ballet of finger sweeps and taps, Pierre walks about within the massive terrain of data that he has assembled on the man and his family. Much of the data was collected on a several-day trip to Calgary a couple of weeks before. The database has been configured to provide him with three distinct views. There is a timeline with its origins in Jackson Horvath's own childhood family. There are geographical maps of Calgary and Western Canada. On the Calgary map are the locations of Nose Hill Depression and Anxiety Clinic, ReClaiming Ourselves Inc., 113 Durham Lane, the 6th Ave SW condo building in which Jackson lives, the Emerald Grove Gentleman's Club, and all the

Best Buy outlets in Calgary. On the Western Canada map, Vancouver and an isolated beach on the west coast of Vancouver Island are flagged. The final display is a myriad of items linked by lines and colours. There are text bubbles, icons leading to websites and stored documents, photographs. Some of the photographs are quite old, including cellphone shots of high school yearbook student portraits and elementary school class photos. The other photos are sharp but sometimes poorly lit—surveillance shots from his own camera.

Pierre walks through the landscape of data, always in the same order. He starts with an obituary—*Isabelle Claire Horvath, nee Lamsbreth. Known to family and friends as Izzy, this dearly loved wife, mother, daughter, and aunt was tragically lost to a rogue wave in Devilish Bay, Vancouver Island. She is survived by her husband of 15 years, Dr. Jackson Horvath, a family physician, and their three children, Annalise, Gerald Jonathan, and Stella. She will be missed as an active member of the Optimist Club and Kinettes. Donations in memoriam can be made to those charities or one's own charity of choice.*

Linked to the obit are jpeg images of articles from the *Times Colonist* and the *Nanaimo News Bulletin*, documenting the retrieval of Izzy's body once it had washed ashore.

Beside the obituary, Pierre has placed the names of the three children—Annalise, Gerald Jonathan, and Stella. Hiving off from those names are various lines leading to photos and documents. Each item is dated so that they link into the timeline. Relevant information is extracted onto cue cards. A single tap brings those cards and their information onto the screen.

Pierre has a fairly complete picture of childhood and early adolescence for two of the three children.

The youngest, Stella Caylie, was the easiest to trace from early childhood to the present. Records of her graduations were readily available through institutional databases. There was a wonderful item in the Life Section of the *Calgary Herald* on her same-sex marriage to Nikki Blaser. Little Jemma, preschooler flower girl, is the epitome of cuteness in the photo. A glum Jackson Horvath stands behind, just a little out of focus. According to the article, Stella now goes by the name Estelle.

The story of Annalise was significantly more complicated. The librarian at Western Canada High had been helpful as far as she could go. Her grade ten yearbook had Annalise's picture as a spritely teen dancing in the halls—lithe and provocative. Then she disappeared. By following her apparent love of dance, Pierre found her again in the archives of the Shaganappi Charter School for the Creative Arts. Then he lost her again. Finally, from Vital Statistics Canada, he was able to locate the record of the marriage of Annalise Horvath to Patrick Marlowe Freeman. There was no write-up in the *Calgary Herald* of their wedding, but Pierre found that Patrick Freeman was a gifted tattoo artist still in business in Calgary. On his visit to see Patrick, Pierre was more than adequately informed about the marriage. It happened after Patrick had completed a complex body tattoo on the beautiful, sexy eighteen-year-old. He produced a photograph of the young woman with the tattoo, showing it proudly to Pierre. The marriage lasted only a couple of years. There was still a sense of delight in Patrick as he talked about that particular tattoo and how, to the best of his knowledge, one could still see it on the body of an exotic dancer at the Emerald Grove Gentlemen's Club. And oh, by the way, she goes by the name Nali now.

Details about Gerald Jonathan were sparse. School yearbook photos went up to grade eleven. In them, he was identified by the nickname GJ. Then he disappeared. Queries at the courthouse for public records on criminal convictions found three for him as an adult. The charges were minor—petty theft, public disturbance, possession of a controlled substance. Nothing violent. Nothing resulting in incarceration.

The breakthrough on GJ came just last week. Pierre had been creeping Facebook, starting with Estelle Caylie's page. He had won her friendship by posing as one of her teachers from years ago, delighted to find her again and asking if she still kept up her reading. From her page, he crept onto that of GJ, under the Facebook alias of Itz Innate, and then onto that of his spouse April, who held their toddler son on her hip in a family photo. Pierre saw the Best Buy logo on the polo shirt GJ, now named Nate, wore in one of the photos. Getting closer.

All this is leverage—leverage to motivate Dr. Jackson Horvath to make a wise choice, a choice not to pursue his amateur research on alternatives to pharmaceutical interventions for the common mental health symptoms of depression and anxiety. The organization contracting Pierre requires him to ensure that this comes to an end. The corporate entities forming that organization have billions of dollars invested in a business that makes lifelong customers of a large segment of the population. Any challenge to the well-worn trope of a chemical imbalance causing mental illness must be stopped before momentum can be gained. True enough, there is limited ground scientifically to disprove what Horvath is reporting to have found. Further, the addictive potential of some mental health pharmaceuticals, the negative side effects of others, and the long patterns of dependency to avoid the destabilizing effects of withdrawal from all of them should never become widely known. Horvath was directly asked to desist and turned down the opportunity. If Jackson Horvath is to be stopped, it will be through other motivational means—by threats to his professional legitimacy or personal attacks on him and his family through revealing family secrets.

It is a messy world, fortunately full of disgusting things.

Pierre's tasks for the next day are easy enough. He has the approximate date of the death of Dr. Marc Morrissette. Obituaries from the weeks prior can be searched for the name and family connections of Patient PP38, as referenced in the dedication of the paper Horvath presented at conference. The age at the time of death and suggested directions for charitable donations should help Pierre pick out the mental health-related death from all the others in the obituaries. From there, pressure on grieving family members could mobilize residual anger and loss into a complaint of professional misconduct against Horvath. With the bereaved, Pierre could paint Horvath as a contributing cause to the tragic death by virtue of the unethical and irresponsible research he was conducting. Even a brief suspension of clinical and research practices during an ethics investigation could slow the progress of what had to be stopped, perhaps discredit it all.

A couple of days' work it is, that's all! Horvath's own mistake, the gracious dedication of his paper, would be his downfall. Of course, one cannot always count on Plan B. Plan C has to be at the ready, too.

Typically, when settling into a new city, Pierre asks for the local newspaper to be delivered to his room. While international and national news are irrelevant to his work, the local news stories and lifestyle fluff could always help him blend in with the cultural context.

He checks the crime report.

A short article catches his eye—*The young man killed in the Starbucks incident of last Wednesday can now be named: Gerald Jonathan Caylie of Calgary, Alberta. Police indicate that the matter is still under investigation and expect charges to be laid.*

With his phone, Pierre snaps a photo of the notice and wirelessly delivers it to the computer to be included in his complex family database. Pierre then searches the websites of all funeral homes in Calgary to find the one providing services to the family of Gerald Jonathan Caylie. He muses about the upcoming funeral for the young man.

April answers the door to find Greg there, Nate's rehab and AA buddy. Greg, dressed in khaki pants and a Best Buy polo shirt, is carrying a large box.

"Oh, hi Greg." Her voice lacks life. Harry squirms on her hip, burying his face in her neck.

"Hi, April. How ya doing?" He awkwardly passes through the door with the bulky item, always the klutz. He takes the sympathy card from the top of the box and hands it to April.

April sets it aside.

"We took up a collection, at the store, like. We knew that Nate really wanted to get this portable room air conditioner for here. He'd even set aside the tip money when we did a home installation . . . really . . ." Greg pauses for emphasis. "Really wanted to get it for you and Harry before it got too hot. But . . ."

Harry squiggles his way off his mother's hip, trying to claw his way around to April's front.

"Nate was really careful with his money, so we knew it was really thin for you guys, you two not having any family support and all. Anyway, he was so well-liked . . ." Now Greg chokes up a bit. "We each put in some so we could get it for you. It's so hot today. Everyone figured that even though the store was really busy, I should just bring it over."

April and Harry settle at the dinette table and Harry clambers to nurse. Greg goes about unpacking the box to install the air conditioner. The air is thick in the living room, a room dark with windows covered in cardboard to keep out the sun.

Within ten minutes, Greg has it installed, vented out one of the front windows in the place where Nate had put a small fan. A slither of cold air creeps across the floor. Greg adjusts the vents, and the whole room starts to cool. April has opened the card, has set it on the table. There are two other cards there too, standing behind the binders beside a flower in a vase.

"Everyone at the store, at the AA group, is wondering about the funeral. Do you know when it is?"

"Wednesday. At Heritage on the south side."

"I'll tell them." Greg goes to leave.

"Stay. Can you stay a while?" April begins to cry softly.

"Sure." Greg sits awkwardly.

"Nate sure appreciates, appreciated you, Greg. Going with him to AA and all."

"It should be the other way around. Nate did so much for me. After we met in rehab and came back to Calgary together . . . I'm sure that if it wasn't for Nate, I wouldn't have made it. Nate was so determined and kept me living that one sober day at a time."

"You were good for each other." April says the word *were* with a slight pause before and after it, as if she was determined to get the verb tense correct.

"Absolutely. He got me the job at Best Buy. Nate broke the ice with Don—he's our manager, he's in AA, too—then Nate got me in to work there, too."

April sits silently. The air has cooled enough that Harry feels more comfortable, wants to get down on the floor to play. April sets him down. The sweat from holding him had soaked the front of the nursing top she wore. She rearranges herself modestly.

"The funeral, is there going to be many people there?" Greg asks.

"No one from my family, for sure."

"What about Nate's family?"

"His sister Estelle has been by a lot. Brought me lots of stuff . . . seems kind. She has a kid, and a partner. I'm sure they'll be there."

"Nate talked about his sister in rehab. He had two, didn't he?"

"Yeah, there's another one, too." April reaches for one of the binders, the one with the GJ initials on the front.

"Rehab binder. I keep mine on the kitchen table too. There should be a family diagram in it. We all had to do one."

April opens to the page and turns it toward Greg.

"Yes. Anna. Did she ever connect to Nate?"

"Anna, no. None of them, really. He was completely on his own. Wanted it that way."

Greg continues to look at the family diagram. "He talked about his father. In rehab, he talked about him a lot—that he had disowned Nate, that he could never go back to him."

"That's about it."

"We saw him, you know. About three months ago, in an AA meeting."

"He never told me. I think that whole father piece of his life ... there was always so much shame for Nate."

"I'll never forget that night. I brought him home. He was really mad ... *really mad*."

"I remember that night, him coming in mad. He didn't speak to me, and I think he was up all night. When I got up with Harry at two-thirty to change and nurse him, Nate was just sitting in the living room. Never said anything about what happened. The next morning, he had that look of determination on his face—it was another day ahead to stay sober."

April retrieves a block Harry had thrown out of his reach, gives it back to him. She looks at Greg. "What happened at the meeting?"

Greg sits, bringing it back in his mind, wanting to tell the whole story so it would make sense. What he remembers most clearly was how Nate had stiffened, went pale when he recognized his father's voice.

"So, we were in the middle of our thirty meetings in thirty days. We used the AA website to find open meetings. Some of them were really, really good, like welcoming and all. I remember we were on the lookout for sponsors, and when we walked into the meeting that night—it was up here on the north side—when we walked in, it was all older men. And, we thought, *Well, good*.

"But the meeting wasn't that friendly. It was like we were intruders. All sorts of in-jokes and drunk-a-logs, like they were trying to impress us."

April picks up Harry to smell the back of his diaper, seeing if he needed to be changed.

"Well, anyway, all night long, this one guy, dressed like a catalogue page for Ralph Lauren, kept checking me out. Felt creepy a bit. Anyway, I think he zeroed in on me more than on Nate—the way we were sitting, he was kind of behind some of the others. Maybe he couldn't see Nate. He said nothing when the stories were told, just sat there looking like he was above it all.

"So the leader of the meeting asked him to read in the Big Book. I don't remember what he read, but as soon as he started, that's when I felt Nate stiffen, like a bolt of electricity went through him.

"Nate rushed out of the meeting as fast he could, like not polite at all, not like Nate. When I went after him, he said it was his dad, *that his dad didn't even recognize his own son!*"

Greg had been so matter of fact in the telling. Now there's a sudden rush of emotion. He craves a drink, that familiar feeling like his head is going to explode. For a moment it's all he can think about, getting out of there and going and getting drunk, getting high. He cries, cries for Nate. All the rush at the store to figure out what had happened to Nate—all the *ain't-it-awfuls*, and the *why-hims*? and the *what-should-we-dos*?, the collection to get enough money to buy the air conditioner at cost, the covering Nate's shifts—all that had kept him busy, always on the edge. Now he feels the loss. He craves running, going blotto, but now he just sits and cries for his friend.

April reaches out to him, puts her hand on his as he cries.

Finally, Greg speaks. "I was so angry that day, that day that Nate's father didn't even recognize his own son. I remember what Nate, GJ back then, I guess, had said in group back in rehab, how abusive his father was. And I'd just sat across the room from the man. He was acting so superior, reading from the Big Book as if he knew all about recovery. When Nate told me it was him, I wanted to kill him."

The air in the living room had grown artificial, too cool, almost clammy. Greg collects himself and gets up to go over to the unit, adjusts the push of the fan and the set of the thermostat on top. Harry looks bewildered at him as he does so. April gets up too and takes some of the cardboard off the front window. The room floods with light. Greg can see that she had been crying too.

April breaks the silence. "This makes a big difference. Nate had talked about getting one. It was just that we couldn't, not yet."

"It was one of the things we can," Greg says.

April looks at him, puzzled.

"The Serenity Prayer."

CHAPTER EIGHT

Sunday

"April, I'd like you to meet our other sister, Nali."
Estelle had thought her words through before they arrived at the quadraplex, the words *our other sister*. She wants to wrap a sense of family around April.

"Glad to meet you." April speaks with the dry emptiness of someone wrung out.

Harry stares up from the floor, catching sight of the tattoo on Nali's neck. After a brief, paralyzing few seconds, he contorts his face into fearful tears. He turns to his mom. With outstretched hands he asks to be picked up and hides his face in April's neck.

"And you, too, April," Nali chimes back. Then, seeing Harry's reaction, she says, "Sorry about the tattoo. I think it scared your little guy."

"Oh, he's pretty scared, anyway. Don't worry. These days have been tough for him. He keeps looking for his daddy." April is beyond tears at this point. She just states it as fact.

"Nice air conditioner. Makes a big difference. It's good to get some light in here, too," Estelle comments.

"Greg, Nate's friend from rehab and AA, brought it. A gift from Best Buy."

"We brought some stuff for you. Can I put it in the fridge?" Estelle asks.

"Sure, go ahead."

"So now I have two sisters. You look alike, but you sure are different," April comments, trying to be social.

"Well, I'm not sure that Estelle would think so! About us looking alike."

"I've never had sisters."

"Well, you've got two now." Nali is warming to her. "I'm so sorry about GJ."

"Yeah."

Estelle comes over, having put food away in the kitchen. "I wanted to bring Nali over to meet you. Make sure you had stuff in."

"Thanks. It's getting lonely here. Harry is good if I'm giving him my undivided attention. We cuddle and play toys. But it's a long day with Nate gone."

The three women stand awkwardly.

"Nate said that his family was really fucked up, excuse the expression, but here you are together helping me when you don't even know me."

"To tell you the truth, April, Nali and I haven't seen each other in years. We just reconnected. And you can say *fucked up*. We haven't been much of a family to each other. When GJ died, I thought I better tell big sister here and found her still living in Calgary."

Harry emerges from his mom's neck as he hears footsteps coming up the stairs to the front door. The doorbell rings. April moves past the others to answer it.

"April Needham?" the visitor asks. She's a neatly dressed middle-aged woman. Kind face. She's holding a Pyrex baking dish containing a cake.

"Yes, I'm April."

"My name is Dana Miller. I'm a Victim Services volunteer."

"There was someone else from Victim Services here last week. I don't remember her name."

"That would've been Laura. I asked Laura if it would be okay if I came to see you today, to bring this cake."

"Sure. It's kind of crowded in here, but come in."

"This cake was baked for you by the lady out in the car."

Dana hands the cake to April but April is hands full with Harry who squirms toward the visitor, catching the smell of chocolate. Estelle moves in to receive the cake for her. It's one of those old-fashioned dark chocolate cakes with the gooey coconut icing on the top.

"I'll take it and put it in the kitchen," Estelle offers.

"Would it be okay for the lady out in the car to come in?" Dana asks.

"Who is she?" April asks.

"That's Mrs. Waleski. She has something she wants to say to you. Is it okay?"

"I guess."

Dana leaves and opens the car door. An older woman emerges stiffly from the car and walks up the walk. She is plain and big-boned, a hard-working look about her, dressed like forty years ago.

The five women assemble themselves, too close together in the small space.

"I want to say how sorry I am about your husband. Really sorry. You see, it was our car that hit him—my husband's Caddy. We got it when we moved off the farm because after having a farm truck all those years, he didn't want anything smaller than that Caddy Escalade. Anyway, we were home at the time, Wednesday morning. We didn't even know that the Caddy was gone. Harold left the keys in it. He's getting the Alzheimer's, you know. When we lived out on the farm, we'd always just left the keys in the vehicles in the yard. As he's getting, you know, like more forgetful, he was leaving them there again. We were just getting breakfast when it happened.

"So I wanted to do something for you. Baked the cake. Family recipe, from the old country."

April, Nali, and Estelle stare at her, speechless.

"So, we're just going over to the hospital to see him. Dana here is taking me.

"When the police came about the car and told us, Harold turned on me, all of a sudden like. I think he thought I'd be mad, and he started to get mad at me first. Well, he fell. He fell right there in the front hall. He hit his head and he's in the hospital now. We're just going to see him. But I wanted to bring you the cake. To say how sorry I am."

Mrs. Waleski receives soft-spoken thanks and wishes for her husband to be okay. She turns and walks back toward the car, Dana in behind.

The hot, dry weather of the previous few days has just started to cool slightly, but the winds have come up. Estelle suggests they go to Prince's Island Park. There's a playground there for Harry and a place they can enjoy ice cream and sit amongst the trees.

Down by the river, it's cooler still. As Estelle and Nali talk, April finally begins to relax. They take turns with Harry—rolling him about in his stroller, pushing him on the baby swings.

Nali, discovering that she also has a niece, asks about Jemma. Estelle regales her with stories and pictures. Even though April is largely left out of the conversation, she listens with interest. Jemma is her niece, too.

They go for ice cream.

Estelle takes a turn pushing Harry on the baby swing. Nali asks about April's family, finds out the conditions that are placed on help they would give to April and Harry—help *if only* . . .

One of the benches in the park comes free and they commandeer it. It's in the shade.

Nali wants to know from Estelle all about Nikki—how they got together, where she works, what she is like.

As excited as he has been with the swings and spring-loaded rocking horses, Harry suddenly gets fussy and tired. He lays his head on April's shoulder. Sweaty and limp, he goes to sleep.

Nali asks Estelle about Dad. Estelle talks about the close working relationship they have, how he got the grants that allowed ReClaiming Ourselves Inc. to function, and then about their regular contact with each other in treating the same patients. Estelle talks about the research, the paper he just presented at a national conference.

April listens too, getting the goods on this family that has embraced her. When a gap comes into the conversation between Nali and Estelle, April breaks in. "Well, Nate ran into your father at an AA meeting not so long ago. Apparently, this father who is a great psychiatrist wouldn't acknowledge, didn't even recognize, his own son—"

"Hey, you." A determined looking man with an angry face has intruded on the conversation. He has pointed his intrusion right at Nali.

"What?"

"Get off this playground. Your tattoo is bothering the children here. They're scared of it. This is a playground for little kids, not a place for you to flaunt your body."

"Fuck you!" Nali responds.

Harry awakens with a start at the emotional intensity crackling around them.

Estelle intervenes. "It's okay, Nali. We can go. We're pretty much done here."

Nali immediately pushes against her kid sister's nudge. Then, as she makes eye contact with Estelle, she starts gathering the things to stuff into the carry-all on the back of Harry's stroller. April holds her crying son.

Estelle walks away with the man. Nali can't hear what is said but reads the calming and redirecting body language her kid sister is doing.

Pierre Bolton had arisen late on that Sunday with a vow not to work on the day.

The day before had turned out peevish. Settling his stuff in the room had helped, that and arranging the workstation on the desk. Still, the way the day had gone to that point had left him feeling as though he wasn't as much in control as he needed to be. He goes over it in his mind, still not able to leave it behind.

True enough, a certain amount of good luck had gone into the travel arrangements from Vancouver to Calgary. He'd picked the same flight as his prey. What were the odds? While he didn't get a seat in business class as he would typically fly, he'd been successful in the bump he negotiated at the gate, getting a seat a couple of rows back and off to the side from where Horvath was seated. Perfect haunting distance, worth the cramped conditions and annoying three-year-old flying beside him.

It fell apart when they arrived in Calgary.

He had been successful in placing himself at the baggage carousel in such a way that Horvath would notice him. Pierre hadn't wanted to be too obvious about it but had probably erred on the side of being too blatant. Then, on the apron outside the terminal, he'd spotted Jackson getting into a car with stick figures in the back window—two females and a child. Pierre remembered the wedding photo in the *Herald* for Jackson's daughter, the one with the cute flower girl.

But that's when it fell apart. Pierre wasn't able to hail a taxi fast enough to follow. All he could do was note the licence plate on the Honda CR-V and vow to catch up with it later.

The last straw had been the inability of the rental car company to supply him with an Impala or Buick Lacrosse, sending him away with a cramped and pedestrian Malibu.

Despite Pierre's vow not to work this Sunday, the discipline of his profession reverberates within. Always know where you are. Constantly mentally rehearse your last several moves to find the momentum for what you need to do next. Finally, while you keep your eye on your objective, be aware of alternate side routes you might take. Emerging possibilities are more subtle and adapted to the terrain you've come to inhabit.

Nagging him is the obstinance of this Horvath guy. All things considered, Horvath should have caved, caved the night of his presentation of the paper in the hospitality suite. It's always a judgment call with threats, how explicit to be. Ultimately, you can only be sure you made the right choice if it works. For this one, it hadn't. And that brought him back to Calgary. When he was here a couple of weeks ago, it was to gather intelligence. Now the time has come to act.

To still his mind Pierre retrieves his Tai Chi uniform and uses the garment steamer to free it of wrinkles. Fashioning himself in the unbleached cotton tunic and trousers, he briefly admires his strength and form in the floor length mirror of his hotel room.

Pierre settles his feet into a thinly soled pair of leather sandals and decides to walk the ten blocks or so to do his Tai Chi in the public space of a park, a park pleasantly set beside the Bow River. It'd be cool down there. He needs the movements of this martial art—its deliberate controlled strength, its balance, and its focus.

Once he has situated himself on the crest of a grassy hill, his disciplined body slowly negotiating the strength-filled movements, he glances down toward the river where the families of Calgary gradually accumulate. They find their places in the shade, they push their annoying children on swing sets, and they position their chairs to catch a bit of the breeze.

Pierre Bolton watches, and in watching, smiles at what he is seeing. Perhaps his luck is changing. He recognizes the tattoo. There could only be one like that in Calgary.

CHAPTER NINE

Monday

It's Monday. Estelle, in going back to work, has to prepare herself for . . . *everyone just loves Dr. Jackson Horvath.*

Clients speak of him in the many conversational spaces designed into the floor plan of ReClaiming Ourselves Inc. *He is so kind. He takes time with you. He listens. And so down to earth! He's practical. The things he suggests work if you work them. Simple things that are hard things, but hard things that make a difference.*

Even though her father rarely visits the unique agency, Estelle always has a sense of him haunting the place. He creeps into every corner—the clients, the budget, the liaison with granting agencies and funding.

Today Estelle returns to her clients to provide individual and group sessions of psychotherapy. She comes with a heavy heart. Her brother is dead. Her sister has revealed the depth of dysfunction that persisted in her childhood home.

And while clients speak of Dr. Jackson Horvath as if he is a saviour, Estelle knows the other side of him. It is increasingly difficult to reconcile the two. She always struggled with their awkward lunches together in La Bonne Baguette—breaking the bread of obligation. She and her father started the weekly ritual back when she worked at the Street Level Mental Health Clinic downtown. They were worlds apart—he with the depressed and anxious middle class, she with the addicted and indigent. The lunches continued after he pulled her into the job in the agency he created. Estelle tolerates her time with her father and then goes back to the office to be regaled with stories of how personable and pleasant Dr. Jackson Horvath is. When he works with patients, his encouragement seems to set them free, to allow them to become who they could become. When he is with her, Estelle feels powerless against his efforts to confine her into the job he rustled her into—not free but trapped.

Today, it's even more difficult. She comes now with the explicit knowledge of the incestuous relationship that took place years ago between her father and her sister. The obligatory relationship between Estelle and her father now carries the taint of revulsion.

Last week, Estelle left Merrill in charge while she dealt with her family issues. Even though Merrill is just a graduate student, he's a natural for this line of work. It is amazing the way he works the floor. He engages with clients deeply and gently in his casual, yet comprehensive, style of connecting. Today would start with Merrill's supervision as required within his master's level practicum for his degree program at Athabasca University. It's an easing in for Estelle, easier than dealing with clients directly.

There are only two closable offices in the physical layout for the ReClaiming Ourselves Inc. innovative program. One office serves as a file room and book-keeper space. There's another large office with Estelle's name on the door—big enough for small groups, with an intimate place for confidential interviews. She had a brass door plate made—*Dr. Estelle Caylie, Registered Psychologist, Executive Director*. Then she had a frosted plexiglass cut to lie over it. In her handwriting, her first name *Estelle* overrides her official title. It's like that at ReClaiming Ourselves Inc. At its foundation, the program is professionally and clinically valid. In its interface with its clientele it's relaxed, on a first name only basis. But even behind the closed door of her office, a place where she is most surely *Estelle,* the raves about Dr. Jackson Horvath often take centre stage.

The rest of the space for ReClaiming Ourselves Inc. is open plan. There's a series of bays where clients can gather for the various components. Arts, crafts, and journaling are in one area. A meditative space in another has floor cushions, yoga mats, and an incense burner. When there is no formal medita-tion or yoga going on, introverts can retreat there and have their solitude respected. Finally, a lecture space with a digital projection system is in the third. Throughout the layout are many conversational spaces—two and three chairs clutched in close to each other to allow emotional intimacy of sorrow sharing, consoling, and support. There's a large open kitchen where a Red Seal chef comes every noon hour to teach clients about cooking healthily for oneself and family. His recipes and flair for presentation make the essentials of nutrition tasty and compelling.

During Merrill's supervision time, when both Estelle and Merrill are cloistered together, Rami does an hour of yoga and meditation. All the clients are required to participate in this sacred hour with him. Already, incense and strains of Eastern music are drifting from the yoga bay. Estelle senses the peace that Rami's aura emits through the agency, feels it ease some of the negative energies within her. It's a gentle way for the clients to leave behind the chaos of their lives outside the centre to focus on the work of healthy living they will do for the week.

Despite the careful grooming that Estelle has done to present herself today—the choice of clothing, the care of hair and complexion, the ensuring of a positive time of play and reading with Jemma before dropping her off at school—she looks like hell. Merrill picks up on it. Once the banalities of greetings have been exchanged, Merrill looks at her with concern.

"Ah, Estelle . . ." he stutters a bit, as if uncertain whether he should make the comment, "I sense something is wrong, seriously wrong."

Fuck, you are too damn perceptive! Then Estelle gives in, sits heavily into one of the chairs. "You can tell?"

"Yes. So sorry about your brother. We didn't talk about it when you were in Friday, just got through the day. Do you want to talk?"

"That was so weird. So awful. It's not that we were close, hadn't seen him in fifteen years at least."

"But still . . ."

"But still." Estelle's voice wisps off. Should she tell him? Should she go into the bigger story, the story of Annalise turned Nali? No, she shouldn't. There's another character in that story, and he has to work with him in this agency.

"Is there going to be a funeral?"

"Wednesday."

"I'll make sure I cover everything here. We did fine last week. You've trained me well."

Estelle smiles a half smile. *Typical Merrill—giving away the credit.*

A brief awkward silence hangs between them.

"Merrill, there's more, more to what happened last week. I'll tell you sometime, but not now. Let's get down to business."

Merrill updates on the clients he is counselling, focusing on those still struggling the most.

"And who's on my schedule for today?" Estelle asks.

"I've set it up for you. Of course, this afternoon is your re-enactment group. I've pulled the notes from last week and your intention for today. This morning I've put in two sessions for you. The first is Carissa Efron, a new client but coming in mid-cycle on special request of her union. I've done the initial comprehensive on her. She knows that she's meeting you today. There are some things that she'll likely want to go into in more depth. Then after her is Charlie. Charlie is having a really rough time as her lover screws up more and more the healthier she gets. She's discouraged, and the thoughts of suicide keep coming for her."

"Merrill . . ." Estelle pauses. "Thanks for how well you've handled it all here. I couldn't have got through these last few days if I had been worried about back here. But I knew you could cover it."

"Nothing much happened other than the regular programming. On Thursday, even though your family was going through a lot, your aunt had a fabulous art therapy group. She did that class on cartooning. It'll be interesting to see the client journals now! I've been in on her doing that class a couple of times already, but I'm always so impressed with the way she brings in the psychology side. She has such a fun way to teach about facial expressions displaying affect, how they can be exaggerated in cartoons to convey emotions. Some just did adult colouring books, protesting that they couldn't draw. But they listened. It's really neat to be in the room with her. All right-brain sort of stuff."

"She's really amazing. I'm glad we have her." Estelle takes on a deliberate look. "Okay then, Merrill, I guess I have to get to see . . ." Estelle looks at the clinical file, having forgotten the name. "Carissa, Carissa Efron. It's just about time."

A series of text messages have come in on Estelle's phone. They are from Nikki. The first one is just the letters JGIOT—their acronym for *Just Getting*

It Out There. Estelle prepares herself for a rant. Nikki is on the Red Arrow bus, making the long trip down from Fort Mac to Calgary. It'll take the entire day. Estelle can expect that throughout the day Nikki will vent through text messages, rants about Estelle's father and Nali's disclosure that Estelle had shared with her. Estelle steels herself for the vehemence of protective energy that Nikki will work out with frantic thumbs on her phone as she travels. Perhaps Nikki will have all the negative energy gone by the time she gets home this evening.

"Carissa. Come in. I'm so glad you're here. We have some time to get to know each other." Estelle greets the worn and tired-looking thirty-something woman who has been hovering outside her door.

"Thank you, Dr. Caylie. I'm glad I'm here too, I guess. This is quite the place."

"Yeah. Estelle, call me Estelle. Did you do the yoga and meditation this morning?"

"I sat in, couldn't get my mind around it. Rami was good about it, though. He made a space for me where I could just sit comfortably. Last week, when I was first in, Merrill went over the whole program. I guess that for now, I'm to be here all day, every day."

"Yeah, that's how we work."

They head into Estelle's office, and she pulls the door closed behind her.

"Well, I've been off work now for seven months. Stress leave. I'm a social worker, working for the provincial mental health service. I've been off so long now that they transferred me from general medical leave to short-term disability. The caseworker said that I had to decide if I was going back to work or not. If there isn't any progress in terms of my health, it will go to long-term disability. They don't pay much on it. I don't know how I'll manage financially if I can't get over this thing. As much as I hate working where I work, I'm not ready to give up my career."

"Let's not get ahead of ourselves. So what's happening with your health, your mental health?"

"My old doctor just gave me medication. It didn't seem to work, and he kept upping it. I wasn't getting the thoughts of suicide like I had, but I just felt like I didn't have any life left in me."

"Yah, that sometimes happens. The drugs can suppress strong feelings but leave a person feeling rather empty."

"Anyway, I've transferred over to Dr. Horvath, and he's getting me off the medication, sending me here."

Estelle looks at the tragedy that sits in front of her. "You've been through a lot. You said you were a clinical social worker?"

"Well, I was. Now, I feel like I'm just a clinical mess. For years, it was my patients that struggled with this. Now it's me."

"It could be any of us." Memories of the Street Level Clinic ooze into Estelle's mind, the tough time she had there, especially at the end when the clinic was abruptly closed down.

"I never thought it would be me."

Carissa falls silent. A visible wave of depression descends from the top of her head, courses across her forehead, tears up her eyes, and drops the corners of her mouth. Estelle watches, feels the sorrow there. She pushes away awareness that Merrill had seen the same in her just an hour before.

"At work . . . well, I guess you could say that it's father issues. I've made that connection. My manager is just like my dad—pushing me, judging me, second-guessing everything that I do. It came to a head when I was pushed to close files last fall. I didn't think I was done with those clients, that they still needed the help that I could give them. But Bruce—that's my manager, Bruce—kept pushing, showing me the data reports on closures for the unit, making me do what needed to be done to get his numbers right. He had to do it, and I had to help him do it."

"That sounds awful." Estelle leans forward in her chair, modelling for Carissa an actively engaged posture rather than a resigned, victimized one, the one that her body was naturally falling into. Then another Estelle intrudes in her mind. *You think you have father issues? Let me tell you . . .*

And with that, Estelle's mind leaves the room. She's back with her own family and the complex of relationships there. Aware and unable to stop it, psychologist Estelle loses track of time. She doesn't know if the silence that exists between them has been just a few seconds or a few minutes. The panicky realization of it comes over her, and she clambers for whatever mental strength she can summon, jerking herself into interaction with the client in the room with her.

Carissa continues to eke out her story. "And I realize that there was something about my father's pushing. I could only be acceptable to him if I was successful. And . . ." Carissa silently tumbles back into her own memory.

"I sense that it's hard to stay here, to process this," Estelle asserts.

"Yes, when I think about work, and what happened in my childhood, try to put it together, my mind just kind of shortcuts and I shut down."

Estelle is painfully aware that what is happening for her client is also happening in her—mixing the past and present into a chaotic soup of the mind. "So let's go back there, back to childhood for you. Can you tell me some stories?"

Psychologist Estelle makes a determined effort to engage. The skill of her training, the naturalness of her style of relating casually but meaningfully, clicks in. She knows just the right timing, just the right inflection of her voice to let Carissa bring her story, her struggle, into the room. She dances the dance of compassion and curiosity that validates the importance of all that Carissa is saying. Estelle has made the space safe for her. There is a place in her mind that knows how to do all this.

But Stella is in there, too. She occupies another place within Estelle's mind, a place filled with all the emotions of being at sea—the bleakness of the horizon, the seasickness feeling in her stomach as if she needs to vomit. There's that something else, too. That something that doesn't have words, images, or sounds—just a feeling of too much all mixed together.

We have to do it. I need you to help me do it. The phrase echoes relentlessly in the Stella-Estelle mind.

The capable Registered Psychologist, Executive Director of ReClaiming Ourselves Inc., vacillates between doing her job and dissociating into the confusion of little Stella, Bookish Stella who could always find a place to hide but has emerged right now. Estelle has the powerful awareness that there is something else, something tucked away into a book somewhere that she hasn't opened yet. Emotions are flooding in. She struggles to determine if those emotions are being projected off Carissa or are her own—her own coming from some deep, seeping sewer within her.

Eventually the interview is over, but Estelle has lost the sense of time that typically regulates her. Carissa's story has been spoken, and she is grateful, says she will look forward to the next session. She doesn't let on if she even noticed that Estelle spaced out on her in the middle of their time together.

Leaving her office, Estelle doesn't remember much of what actually happened between them in the session. She can't even be sure if it is Estelle who is walking out of the room or Stella.

Stella just can't be Stella anymore. Stella has to be Estelle, and maybe even Estelle has to be Dr. Caylie as she emerges into the common area of the agency.

She checks her phone. There are half a dozen or so long JGIOT messages from Nikki.

Whether it was the Tai Chi, or the unexpected sighting of the cobra tattoo, or the quick trip in the Malibu that Pierre made to Banff on the previous afternoon, on Monday he awakens keen to the tasks before him.

Dressed in the navy blazer, an open-necked buttoned-down blue shirt, and khaki pants, he stands at the door of Colleen Brett, widow of Jeremy Brett, patient PP38.

"Pierre Bolton," he introduces himself. "Mrs. Brett, may I come in? I'm doing a follow-up on the tragic death of Jeremy and would like to ask a few questions."

She looks suspiciously at him. When he presents a professional-looking business card she appears to relax a bit, perhaps confident that the visit is on the up-and-up.

"And how are you, Ms. Brett? Can I call you Colleen?"

"Well, alright, I guess. It's a couple of years, that Jerry died. I'm getting on."

"That's good. I'm here on behalf of the pharmaceutical company for the medications that Mr. Brett was taking. We are slow at following up on this adverse outcome but interested in whatever you can tell us. We want to ensure that this sort of tragedy doesn't happen again. Can I come in?"

It takes only a slight change of the way Pierre balances his weight on his feet to get the woman to retreat toward the kitchen. They sit at a small table with a window looking out over the backyard.

"Well, yes . . . yes, he was on medication. It didn't seem to do much for him, though. The doctor kept pushing it up, adding this and trying that. I could see him going downhill. Not for lack of trying, the psychiatrist, I'm sure that he tried everything he could."

"Yes, we've reviewed the records, have a sense of the therapeutic manoeuvres and the . . ." Pierre reaches for the right words, "the suffering that your husband endured."

"It was difficult. How he changed. He wasn't himself at the end."

"Did you know he was enrolled in a trial? That he was receiving one of two different treatments?"

"No, I didn't know that. Jerry probably did. He didn't tell me much about going there, to that clinic up on the Nose Hill. Said it was a good place, and they were doing everything they could for him, that he just wasn't responding as he should. He didn't say anything about it being a trial, like him being a guinea pig or anything."

Pierre muses at her use of the term *guinea pig*. "Well, now that you know this, are you still thinking he got the best possible care?"

"Oh, I guess. Seemed so at the time, just didn't seem to work for him."

"We are looking into this, looking at the conduct of the clinic where he was treated. We don't like the pharmaceuticals that we provide being used in this way. There was another doctor there, a Dr. Jackson Horvath. He was running this trial. We want to make sure that everyone was properly treated."

"I remember him. He came to see me—the week after the funeral he came. Said how sorry he was. Nicest man."

Pierre pauses, wondering where to go with this. Then Mrs. Brett breaks in again.

"It was hard on our son, Colin. He really thought that his father was so overmedicated. Won't talk about it anymore when I try to bring it up."

"Do you think he might talk to me about it?"

"No, I don't think so, not with you being with the drug company and all. He's still pretty mad, mad at that place where his dad went. Don't tell him about that other psychiatrist, the one doing the . . . what did you call it?"

"Trial." Pierre pauses again. "But it's okay with you if I approach him?"

"We are all adults here. You can do what you want. But he's pretty mad about it. I think he has some of his dad in him, you know."

Pierre leaves the home with another lead, perhaps more promising for his purposes.

On the third visit to an outlet of Best Buy, Pierre finds the one with a memorial donation box receiving donations for the family of Nate Caylie. He puts in a hundred dollars, doing so when he is observed. Using kind words and acting as though he is a friend of the family, Pierre wins the confidence of one of the staff. Quickly the blue-polo-shirted employee goes off to get Nate's street address, just so Pierre could have some flowers sent there. Pierre marvels at the naivety of some people, is glad as it makes his job easier.

He goes to Nate's place. April lets him in. Immediately, Pierre recognizes her from Nate's Facebook page and the little family gathering in the park on the previous day.

"We, all of us who are friends of the family, are so sad for you and want to help ... "

"Okay." She looks weary of this succession of Caylie folk beating a path to her door—this one with an Edible Arrangement basket of decorative fruit.

". . . help in any way we can." Pierre has a sense that he might be losing her. It could just be weariness or grief. Then maybe she wasn't buying his line. "Oh, someone brought a cake. Gosh, I'm famished. Could I have a piece? It looks like the kind grandma used to make."

The gambit works. In doing something for him, in managing Harry on her hip and the heavy knife in the Pyrex pan, in putting the slice on a plate, the suspicion eases on April's face. The old trick—get someone to do something for you and then up the ask, little by little.

"Oh my goodness, thanks. Tastes good."

Harry is fussing. April manages him. Pierre eyes the two binders on the table and the flower in a vase behind them.

"You said you would do something for me. Could you take the cake pan back?"

"Oh sure, to who? Who brought it?"

"The Victim Services lady, but it was made by the wife, wife of the guy who ... oh, it's complicated." April stops, wondering how to explain it. "She's the wife of the guy who owns the car that hit Nate. Her husband didn't do it, but it was their car. Her address is taped on the bottom of the pan. I don't have a car to take it back to her."

"I'll take care of that for you." Pierre picks up the pan and holds it over his head to read the address there.

"Look, if there is anything else I can do, just let me know. I'll leave my card." Reaching into his pocket, he pulls out a card with his name and phone number, careful not to use the one that identifies the pharmaceutical company.

Mrs. Waleski looks delighted when Pierre Bolton brings back the washed Pyrex cake pan. She welcomes him into her home. Of course, Pierre is gracious. Feigning curiosity, he looks at the many small, framed photographs that adorn the walls and tables in their home. When she mentions her husband's name is Harold, Pierre picks up on it and speaks of him warmly, working the first name into the questions he asks. Once she starts talking, it all comes out—their forty-four years together and how difficult it is now that he has the Alzheimer's, and *so young!* She's glad they'd decided to move off the farm and proudly shows the aerial photograph taken twenty years before where you can see everything—the equipment shed, the grain bins (but they got a lot more since that picture was taken) and a patch of deeper green that was her half-acre garden. Pierre asks about how Harold is doing now. She sighs. The fall has set him back. He's more confused. She hopes she can bring him home again, but then . . .

Pierre picks up a business card from the table—*Golden Years Home Aide Services.* The phone number is in extra-large print. He asks about it. Within just a few minutes of conversation, Pierre has a list of first and last names of the aides who had come into the home for personal care, aides that let Mrs. Waleski get out to the Ladies Auxiliary at the Catholic Church. There are three of them. They would know that Harold was prone to leave the keys in the Caddy in the driveway, just like he did on the farm.

Driving the black Malibu, Pierre attempts to intercept Nali as she goes into work at the gentlemen's club. He immediately recognizes her as she walks across the parking lot at the back of the building toward the door—the tattoo is vivid in the afternoon sunlight. As he hustles toward her, she quickly codes the sequence of numbers into the door and scurries inside.

The door slams shut between her and him. As he stands there, rebuffed, he has that creepy feeling of being watched. He spots a Camaro, a vintage '90s model in need of bodywork, parked inconspicuously off to the side. The driver is taking his picture.

The Red Arrow bus trip from Fort Mac to Calgary takes more than eight hours, including a stopover in Edmonton. For all the time Nikki spends in large vehicles with massive engines, the bus trip home is a relief. Nikki settles into a window seat. She installs a very obvious pair of earphones to discourage anyone sitting beside her from attempting to engage in conversation. Not that she isn't terribly lonely. It's just that the person riding beside her has a ninety-percent chance of being male.

Nikki alternates between listening to audiobooks on her earphones, texting to Estelle, and sleeping. She figures she will never run out of Stephen King novels to accompany her journeys.

And even though it's a long journey, it's a million times more preferable to Nikki than the gut-in-a-knot feeling that she has in an airplane, that thin metal tube of humanity suspended in the sky. Not that she's afraid of heights. Nikki climbs a long, steep, narrow stairway on the front of her heavy haul truck to get into its cab six metres above ground. It's just that she can barely tolerate being held up in the air by some means she can neither see nor touch.

When she's tired of the audiobook, when she has texted about all the JGIOT messages to Estelle she can text, when she's ready to drift into sleep or just emerging from it, she looks at pictures of Jemma on her phone. There are dozens of them there, dozens to cycle through and smile, and then cycle through again. She closes her eyes and imagines it's Jemma there beside her, Jemma rather than a 250-pound man smelling of clothes desperately in need of a washing machine. She imagines Jemma's giggle as she reads through a funny book, the rhythmic movement of her six-year-old body as she listens to music, the pokes into Nikki's side to get her to laugh when she is bored.

The daylong ride transitions Nikki between the work world to family life in a Calgary condo. The world she's been in for the last two weeks is one of numbing vibration arising from the massive engine beneath her seat in the cab, the deafening sounds that disappear when Nikki puts on her ear protectors—the ones that make you think that after all the aural assault you have experienced you now have finally gone completely deaf—and the jaw-dropping shudder of the massive vehicle when a bucketful is dropped into the hopper.

But it's also a world largely of men—men who grow increasingly irritable the longer they are into their rotation, men who see her as a person who must immediately want to hear their tale of frustration and betrayal simply because she's female and somehow wired up to take care of them, men who have no energy to be on the prowl but pathetically don't know how else to relate to her as a person.

While Nikki immediately reacts to all men with vigilant distrust, she realizes that some are actually decent human beings—Gordon is a good example. Some want to look out for her against the assholes. Clearly, they don't realize Nikki is well capable of keeping herself safe, doesn't need protection.

Nikki has developed a classification system for assholes. There are the assholes who have a fantasy of getting rich and by getting rich, magically getting attractive at the same time. Then there are the assholes who, for some reason, happen to be on their fourth or fifth marriage. Even though they have had bad luck with women until now, they think that she, our Nikki, will be different if she would just give them a chance. And of course, there are the other assholes who find a way of mentioning that they have some cocaine and are ready to party. Nikki takes care of herself by not trusting, never trusting.

But looking at the pictures, Nikki knows that in Jemma she escapes the world of smelly and creepy men. Jemma she can trust—trust to be totally, completely real. Jemma pokes for fun, cuddles for security and giggles just because the world is funny.

Jemma always awaits when the Red Arrow pulls up at the terminus in North Calgary. Always.

As Nikki prepares for her reconnection with Jemma and Estelle, she looks back on the series of text messages she has sent over the day. They are all about that bombshell a couple of days ago in the early morning FaceTime call. As she mellows with the late-day sun coming into the window at her side, having made the transfer at the Edmonton terminal to the Calgary bus, she thinks that maybe her JGIOT messages might have come across too strongly, at least at first. But then, Estelle will understand. She's a shrink and deals with that sort of stuff all day, anyway. And, as horrible as it is—this business of Estelle's stripper sister and asshole, abusive father—it seems a bit more tolerable because she has put out there how she feels.

In her mind, Estelle and Jemma await, refreshed and eager to see her. Now Nikki has five days off work before she has to climb on the bus and head back north to be gone from their lives again.

Pulling into the Calgary terminal, she sees it isn't Estelle and Jemma there when she arrives. It's Aunt Leanne and Jemma.

Nikki smiles out the window as she watches Jemma run toward the bus as it pulls in. Running wild and crazy, with arms flailing and legs driving raw energy into the ground, Jemma holds herself up safely on the sidewalk. Bouncing there, she is bursting with delight, barely able to contain an enormous hug she has been saving up for the last two weeks. As soon as Nikki steps down from the bus, she receives that Jemma hug—it just about knocks her off her feet.

"Luv you, Momma-Nik!"

"Luv you more, Jemma-girl."

"Welcome home," Aunt Leanne says.

"Thanks, Leanne. I'm glad to be back. Where's Estelle?"

"She had to stay late at work. Some crisis with a client, a crisis apparently only she could handle."

"Typical."

"Momma-Nik, Momma-Nik, you gotta hear me and Uncle Gordo. We play a duet together. He's teaching me the uka...ukie...uk-e-le-le!"

"Sure. But not tonight. Let's just go home."

"Please," Jemma begs, "we've been practising. I want to."

Aunt Leanne intervenes. "If you have the energy for it, let's go back to our place. Gordon is there, and it's really nice and cool on the back veranda. Estelle suggested you wait there. She should be getting back there soon after we do."

Nikki is too tired to disagree. She has been in a dry camp for two weeks. Gordon will offer her a beer.

Jackson sits in his Lexus outside of the quadraplex.

He was twenty minutes late arriving, late from the time Estelle had arranged to meet him there. It wasn't his fault. He just got tied up at the clinic, hesitant to leave, thinking that something there was not yet done—a Monday day, a dreaded Monday day after being away. Alas, he had checked his watch and decided he had to go, not having completed that whatever it was.

And now Estelle isn't here when he arrives. It isn't like her.

Jackson checks the address she had sent to him by text. It confirms with the nailed letters and numbers beside the door. He checks the GPS map on his phone. It assures him that he is in the right place. He grows impatient. He texts her.

Finally, he decides to go to the door. Alone.

April answers, toddler Harry clutched to her torso. "Yes?"

"Are you April?"

"Yes," her *yeses* are getting less affirming.

"I'm Jackson, GJ's father."

She looks at him askance. "Really?"

"I wanted to come to meet you. My daughter Estelle was supposed to be here, too, now, but she must have got tied up at work or something. Anyway, I'm glad to meet you and . . ." he pauses, looking at the child.

"Harry."

"And . . . Harry." Jackson smiles at the youngster. "I got in touch with the funeral home earlier this evening. Paid the costs in full."

"Welfare is supposed to cover it."

"Yes, that was what was on the books. When I offered to cover the cost, the funeral director said they would notify Welfare, let them know that family had stepped up."

"Okay."

April grows more awkward with every word that Jackson says. But Harry, Harry is not. Harry is lurching forward, asking to be handed over. The face of the toddler is absolutely beaming, looking toward the man at the door. April watches what is happening with her child, and then a look of understanding crosses her face. "Oh, it's your voice. You sound just like Nate. Harry here thinks that it's his father's voice he hears."

"Oh my!" Jackson relaxes into the delight of the young child and the borrowed familiarity he now enjoys. Harry wiggles to slip off his mother's hip. A giggle escapes him.

"There's no doubt whose grandson he is. Look at you two."

Picking up the toddler, Jackson turns toward a mirror on the wall of the quadraplex entryway. He takes in the faces of his grandson and himself. It's as though look-alike had skipped a generation. The toddler delight has given way to curiosity as he touches a face that's like that of his dad but isn't.

"So what's with this paying for stuff?" April asks.

"He is my son, was my son. I have the means. I feel responsible."

April stares at him.

"Whatever you need," Jackson says. Harry has brought a warmth to his voice.

April cries a meek, embarrassed sort of cry. They each go silent awhile—both lost in their own thoughts, their own different worlds.

"It's getting close to his bedtime. Can I take him from you and settle him? If I don't put him down on time, he gets wired and then won't go to sleep."

"Sure." Jackson hands over the toddler. Sleepiness pulls at Harry's eyelids. A switch has gone off inside. As the arms of mother and son entwine, a thumb goes into his mouth.

Jackson is left in the living room. He sits awkwardly on one of the chairs there, surrounded by a floor littered with toys and occasional Cheerios scattered about as if they had been tossed like confetti. The portable air conditioner seems out of place.

He and Izzy, despite all their troubles, had never raised kids like this, like this with so little. Even early in his career, with university loans to pay off, they lived decently. 113 Durham Lane, his childhood family home, had been a gift to them from his father. They didn't drink back in those days, he and Izzy. They'd put all their extra money from his billings as a newly minted family doctor into making the home into something they could be proud of, added the touches that would be theirs. He and Izzy bought good pieces, pieces that have lasted, pieces that are likely still back in there in the home his sister now occupies.

But this. GJ had always been a screw-up. Right from the word *go*. And this, this is such a sad excuse for a family home, for his grandson's childhood home. He searches for the word of it—sad, pathetic.

He hears the soft cooing of the lullaby that April sings in the bedroom. The whole world relaxes as Harry goes limp.

Leanne watches the two partners throw their words at each other.

"I got your texts," Estelle says.

"So you know where I stand on this."

"I know. I'll handle it."

"It's about Jemma, you know."

"She's safe. I never let her alone with him."

"You better not. Hell to pay if you do."

"I won't."

"I'll kill him if he ever."

Estelle's phone signals a text coming in. She ignores it. "It's just that it's not as easy as all that."

"It's really simple, Estelle. We don't need him in our lives."

"But at work, he's the reason we get our grants."

"Get another job."

"It's not like that."

"Can be, if it is important enough to you ... to us ..."

"Don't force me." But with that statement, as strong as it seems to be, Estelle collapses. Her shoulders let down. Weariness pulls at the corners of her mouth.

Nikki knows it's always this way in her fights with Estelle. Just as she is getting up a head of steam, proving her point, generating the energy of protection for the family that is her love—without conceding, Estelle exhausts all the energy out of the argument, like air escaping an untied balloon.

And as always, Nikki softens when she sees the collapse in Estelle. They stand silently for a few moments.

"Let's go home," Estelle says.

They collect Jemma from Gordon's music studio, where she has been peacefully strumming the ukulele under his watchful eye.

Monday is done.

They are a family again.

"How are you doing?" Jackson asks when April comes back into the living room.

"Getting by. Had a nice day with Estelle and Nali yesterday. Went to the park, Prince's Island. Harry had a good time. Me, too. Estelle has brought lots of groceries for us. I don't think our fridge has ever been so full."

"I'm glad. April, do you have family?"

"Not really."

"Not really?"

"That's a long story."

Jackson finds himself shifting into the gentleness he cultures when meeting a patient for the first time. Asking how they are, being empathic and kind. It's a different voice from him. "Tell me."

April looks at him. A sequence of emotions crosses her face. "Maybe. Not tonight. Do you want a piece of cake?" She goes to the kitchen and retrieves the plate that she had put the rest of the cake on after giving the pan to Pierre Bolton to return.

"Okay." Jackson accepts. It would be a slight to decline.

"Funny thing, this cake. An older lady brought it, brought it with someone from the Victims Services. Said it was her husband's car that had driven into the Starbucks, the car that killed Nate. So, okay," she pauses. "I never had a cake like this. It was good. Just a couple of pieces left now after I gave some to Estelle and Nali.

"Then, this afternoon, this guy came. I told him about the lady, why she brought me a cake. Anyway, I wondered about the cake pan, how to get it back, like back to the old woman. She had taped her name and address to the bottom of the pan. But I don't have a car.

"Anyway, this guy said that he would take it to her. So I took out the last pieces and washed out the pan to give it to him to take."

Jackson looks at her curiously, suspiciously. "So who was this guy, anyway?"

"Don't know. It was kind of creepy, what he was doing here. He said he was a friend of the family, but it didn't seem like it. Maybe he was a detective or something, from the police. But he never said."

Jackson is starting to dig into the cake. It had dried out on the edges, gone sort of crusty.

"Oh, he left a card. Told me I could call him." April goes over to the fridge, scans the collection of magnets holding papers there.

"Here it is. Pierre Bolton. Doesn't give anything except his name and phone number."

The cake goes dry in Jackson's mouth.

CHAPTER TEN

Tuesday

Estelle awakens sitting bolt upright in bed, caught in a sudden, gasping, terrorized paralysis.

Nikki is asleep in the bed beside her, a dead-to-the-world sleep. In Estelle's disorientation, she sees her as a stranger, an interloper. Estelle can't figure where this sleeping figure beside her belongs.

Forcing herself to get up, Estelle stumbles into the living room of the condo. It is dark, a transient June dark that has not yet given way to the grey of dawn that will creep in on the eastern horizon. Her dark-adapted eyes find the glare of city lights off-putting, as though they don't belong either.

Estelle's ears are ringing with taunting, sadistic laughter. There's the smell of salt water propelled by the roar of displaced waves. There's the sickening smell of boozy breath. Neither the smells nor the sound has any right to be there. The psychologist self within Estelle, a self desperately trying to get awake, puzzles over their hallucination and then gives in to them unreservedly. The sounds and those smells are too real to deny. From within, or without—too real to deny.

That damn, taunting, sadistic laughter.

Estelle clicks on the bathroom light and throws water on her face. She realizes she has not been breathing. Looking at herself in the mirror with steely determination, she commands herself to breathe. At first, the breaths come jerkily, her diaphragm plunging toward her belly button and then rebounding into the rib cage. She wills it to slow down. The shaking won't stop. She takes another breath, slowly following the summer midnight air entering her nostrils, her belly accepting it deep and then giving it back. The shakes become shudders. Her back aches. Her fingers are numb. She sits heavily on the closed lid of the toilet and makes herself breathe ten deliberate breaths. She counts them. Each time she breathes in, her head goes dizzy. Each time she breathes out, it stops its spinning. She's suddenly cold.

Estelle goes back to the bedroom, retrieves a robe from the closet, ties its belt tight around her waist. She returns to the living room and accepts the haze of artificial light that makes its way to her. Pinpoint lights, the streetlights and car headlights, fight with her dank subconscious to take prominence in her conscious mind.

Estelle retrieves a bound journal from the side pocket of her briefcase. The first dozen or so pages of the journal are a valiant attempt to write three things each day for which she feels grateful. For some reason, that good idea died out on November 28. The last entry was *1. Jemma's careful diction. 2. Cut flowers in Safeway. 3. This gratitude journal.* Her last entry was most definitely lame, a good reason to stop. Estelle flips the book over, opens it upside down from the back cover, and writes.

Tuesday, June 20.

Nightmare. Smell of salt water, sound of waves, sound of evil laughter, can't get my breath.

She feels better. Not well. Just better.

For eight minutes, Estelle practices deliberate, slow breaths. Her psychologist mind is increasingly regaining control. She knows that her bloodstream has been flooded with adrenalin and cortisol. It will take time for those panic chemicals to stop ringing the alarm bell of hyperalert. She can do this. She can calm. She still feels the nausea, is tempted to go back to the bathroom to see if she can vomit, but she sits with her breath. She is believing, believing with all the will inside of her, *I can do this.*

She does it.

Once calmed, Estelle circles back to her bedroom and Jemma's bedroom. She checks on those she loves. Both are deeply asleep, caught within their night dreams and the dead stillness of non-REM sleep.

Estelle searches for the antecedent to her nightmare. She steps backwards through the day. The edginess with Nikki—there was tension there, but she felt no emotional hangover from it. Charlie was there too, back in for a second session on the same day, emergency Charlie and her thoughts of suicide. Estelle feels continuing concern for the agency's client— the risk variables for suicide are so high. But there was nothing from their emergency evening session that would trigger the particular emotional earthquake that had set off the tsunami of her dreams.

Her workday had started roughly after taking two personal days last week. By the time of the re-enactment group of her afternoon, she had hit her stride again, was the capable and confident Estelle. Or at least, so she thought. Then her memory of the afternoon group process becomes hazy, loses its sense of narrative. Estelle struggles to rebuild it. Cheryl was the focus. Estelle had Cheryl pose other group members into a tableau to depict the way she perceives her work colleagues. Cheryl had chosen Joe to play the role of her micromanaging boss—his emotions running unchecked, his anxiety extruding as anger. Others were requisitioned into being her co-workers. Cheryl chose Dawn to play her own role. It was a perfect choice as Dawn within the group had typically come across as vulnerable, unassertive. Once Cheryl had set up the tableau, Estelle directed her to coach the volunteers how to play out their parts. Cheryl's awareness would deepen as she appreciated the emotional processes of each in the drama. She'd begin to see others as not just reacting to her but as engaged in their own emotional battles.

Then Cheryl, sitting in the director's chair, yelled, *Action*. The coached words were said.

And the scene goes blank.

Estelle's mind swims dizzily, intermingling what she can remember with what Merrill had told her in the debriefing afterwards.

Merrill had ended up coaching the re-enactment, her own mind floating up toward the ceiling, looking back down on what was taking place. The psychodrama scenario was repeated and refined, this under Merrill's guidance. Over and over it was re-enacted until it lost its power over Cheryl. Each time through, Dawn, as she portrayed the workplace Cheryl, was surrounded with empowerment, acceptance, and validation by those who witnessed the tableau. Then they all debriefed. Those in the acting roles had jeopardies of their own personality exposed by their roleplay—Joe in how uncertainty turns to fear and fear turns to rage, Dawn recognizing how collapse invites others to overpower her. All of them felt better, felt insightful.

Midnight Estelle is getting sleepy again, a discomforted sleepy. She commands herself to come back to her competent self, to readdress the memories of the powerful psychodrama she'd created. She had started it, had set it up well. Even if Merrill had taken over—*well, that too is good.* A sense of pride emerges in how well Cheryl and Dawn and Joe had done. It confirms her. And how well Merrill, her student and protégé, had done! Estelle's skill, both as a re-enactment therapist and a supervisor, brings a sense of reassurance—as if the world is unfolding as it should.

She pushes away the distaste, the disgust, of her dissociation.

The remnants of the nightmare have dissipated from her mind. But the journal still open on her desk bears witness to the smell of salt water, the sounds of waves and evil laughter, the sense of not being able to get her breath.

And all of that, whatever it was, goes back into that sealed-off place within Estelle's mind.

At 7:45 a.m., Merrill sits outside of Estelle's condo building, nursing a ton of concern. Last night when he'd left, he'd noticed Estelle becoming increasingly chaotic—at one moment lost and childlike, at another suddenly silent and detached, and then back to her confident mental health professional self who could say just the right thing at the right time. He'd watched clients respond with their own confusion to her varied states.

In the afternoon she'd been at her absolute best, at least at the start. The re-enactment group is her forte, getting clients to act out their interpersonal stressors and interior emotional complexes using psychodrama. She'd set it all up beautifully. It was as though she was a director managing a particularly powerful stage play. But then there was that moment, that moment when Joe was convincing in his portrayal of the angry boss—Estelle had gone away into her mind. A storm of emotions leaked out of her face, and she stopped speaking. Noticing her confusion, her lostness, he had to step in to encourage the clients to follow through on the scene. Following the protocol, he then had them go back through it again, choosing different courses of action. Estelle had taught him the process well—he felt competent taking over. The clients were into it and the debriefing went naturally.

Now in remembering it, Merrill realizes that he'd suddenly been completely on his own, Estelle obviously triggered and disengaged. Gone.

Initially, as they debriefed, Estelle hadn't remembered it at all—that he had stepped in, what he had done, and how the clients had responded. Merrill had to tell her, and in his telling it all came back to her. In a flash, once he had done so, Estelle was back to her competent, professional self. She spoke as if there was nothing at all wrong with the whole situation, congratulating him on how well he did.

Then there was the chaos at the end of the day. He knew that last evening Estelle's partner, Nikki, would be coming in on the bus from Fort Mac. Estelle had always treasured those nights. The Red Arrow station was the only place she would be. But as he was leaving she said that she was going over to see April, her newfound sister-in-law, with her dad. It didn't make sense. The call from Charlie came in just then, too—she was in crisis again. Estelle took the call and was promising she would stick around to talk her down if she came in.

Estelle would never do that—would never double book, triple book, herself that way.

He sits, wondering how Estelle had done with it all. Merrill wishes he hadn't left her the way she was at the end of the day, that he'd stayed to do the crisis work with Charlie. But she had insisted that she was fine, told him to go. Now he wishes he'd talked to Estelle about that something more, the something more that he sensed was going on for her. He didn't. But he's here this morning. When Nikki is home Estelle likes to leave her the car. Merrill had texted her to say that he would pick her up.

Estelle is a whirlwind as she gets in. They exchange their *good mornings* and he pulls into traffic.

"I've been thinking about today. I have a plan," Merrill starts.

"Okay."

"I think we should hold a meeting with all the clients at the start and tell them about your brother dying."

Estelle looks at him. He keeps his eyes on his driving.

"You were away those days last week. Will be gone tomorrow for the funeral. We'd just said to the group that you were taking some personal days, didn't say what it was about. I think we should let them know."

"I think you are probably right. I can do that."

"Then I'm thinking that we can use the rest of the day to get everyone into small group discussions on loss—losses they've had, losses they're facing now. If we do it in the counselling office, do three small groups with six clients at a time, run for about an hour for each, then we can give good attention to how it hits for everybody. Let's do it together. If it gets too heavy for you, I can do the small group myself and you can mix with the others on the floor."

Estelle sits silent. Merrill wonders how she's taking it, if she's even hearing it.

"We have Nancy Gretz, from Disability Management Services, scheduled to be in all day with us. I'll set her up in the arts and writing room. She can do her work on personal goal setting with clients when they're not in small group with us. We can also assign videos to watch and reading or workbooks for clients to do on their own. I'm sure that Travis will arrange as many others as he can to go over to the fitness centre with him. Perhaps, at the end of the day, we can come back together again, do a final check in."

After a long pause, Estelle finally says, "Sounds like a plan."

Midmorning, Pierre drives the rented Malibu to the Salvation Army Family Thrift Store off Macleod Trail. Its shiny paint and middle-class appearance definitely look out of place in front of the cinder-block building. He needs to do something about that; there are times when it just doesn't pay to look so conspicuous.

Once inside, he selects a pair of jeans, a Calgary Flames cap, and finds a graphic T-shirt with a Tragically Hip logo on the front. The well-pierced teen doing community service hours at the till says that the T-shirt is a *real find*—everyone is holding on to anything with the Tragically Hip logo on it since the death of Gord Downie. Pierre asks if the clothing has been washed. She says it has, as far as she knows. The colour of the red maple leaf on the shirt matches the red of the Flames cap. The three items cost him $13.50. He gets a receipt for his expense account.

Returning to the hotel he sends the jeans and T-shirt to the hotel laundry service, says that he needs them back right away, attaches a generous tip to ensure they will be ready for the afternoon. The tip is more than he paid for them to begin with. Carefully, he inspects the cap for head lice and steams it well with the garment steamer.

About the car, Pierre Bolton decides to call Calgary Rent-a-Wreck. For an extra fee a driver will deliver the car to the Hilton. Querying their inventory, Pierre selects a ten-year-old Subaru Impreza and asks that they don't wash it before bringing it to him. The indifferent employee tells him that if he likes it, it's for sale at a good price.

The Impreza turns out to be better than he anticipated. It has tinted windows, and its once-metallic silver paint has gone to a dull grey.

As the late afternoon blisters its sun on the Calgary landscape, he drives to the parking lot behind the Emerald Grove Gentlemen's Club. There's a smell of uncollected garbage where he parks. In contrast to the brand-new black Chevy Malibu he rented at the airport, in his rented wreck he has to keep banging on the dashboard with his fist to coax continuous functionality out of the car's air conditioning system.

He waits.

Today, he returns to watch for he who had watched him. He settles the brim of his Calgary Flame cap down low over his eyes.

About 4:15, the Camaro arrives in the parking lot. It parks in the same place as the day before. A few minutes later, Nali walks toward the back door of the building. Again, the driver of the Camaro has a small camera, now focused on the door rather than on him. Pierre watches. As soon as Nali is fully into the building, the Camaro drives off, the burden of an obnoxious subwoofer fading into the distance with its departure.

Pierre follows in his unimpressive Impreza.

It's the end of the day. Estelle and Merrill sit. The clients have left ReClaiming Ourselves Inc., most in a sombre mood. Estelle looks exhausted.

"Despite it all, the day went well, I think," Merrill observes.

"I was really impressed with how you stepped up today, Merrill."

"Thanks. You're really struggling, I can tell."

Estelle looks at him, doesn't respond.

"But everyone came through. Travis was great in ferrying others to the gym. I hear he even got Ellie onto the treadmill. Joe told me he was cheering her on like the coach on his kid's soccer team. And between groups, when I went out and got together who'd next come into group, clients were talking. One-on-one, they were talking. Supporting each other. Caring for each other . . . And the way everyone talked about losses in the groups. It's everyone's issue. Either depressed at what they've lost, or anxious about what they will."

Merrill hopes Estelle will congratulate him on the theme, the one he'd cultured through the day. He had a profound attachment to it as it emerged and strengthened through the discussions. All the theories from his textbooks were suddenly coming to life in front of him.

Estelle doesn't respond. She just sits. Emotion plays at the muscles around the corners of her mouth, eyes, and forehead. Merrill sits with her, reaches a hand to touch her knee—a reminder that he's there. It's a practised move, done carefully, just the way she'd shown him.

"Merrill, I shouldn't have been here today. It was wrong."

"It seemed awfully rough on you. Hearing what everyone said."

"That's it. I didn't hear. I would catch someone's story, and then I would get lost. I shouldn't have been here."

"I think it was good for them, for everyone, to see you struggling. They cared."

"I know. But it shouldn't be them caring for me, it should be the other way around. I got lots of condolences, whatever that means, means for me and GJ." Estelle stares at him desperately. "I don't know what any of this means."

Merrill knows that the thing to do is to just sit, to tune in, to reassure her of his presence but not interfere with her thoughts. He knows that from his training and her supervision of him. He also knows it's wrong to do a therapy thing with his supervisor and mentor. It catches him up, the dilemma of it. He remembers what she's said to him in the past—*typically, the right thing to do therapeutically is the right thing to do humanly*. Humanly he wants to comfort her. She looks so small—like a child, like a confused and scared child—not the confident and skilled Dr. Caylie who is supervising his practicum.

Merrill's mind spins from theory, to ethics, to feelings. He's glad, proud even, that he could manage such a difficult day at the agency. When he talks with his faculty adviser about all this, she will be impressed at how much confidence he has gained. Right now though, with Estelle, confidence is the last thing he feels. In contagion from her he is feeling scared. Sorrowful.

"Merrill . . ." Estelle looks up, desperation on her face. "Merrill, I am so bloody angry I don't know what I'm going to do. I don't know why. I just am. The anger, it's been building all day, and I've been fighting it. Pushing it down. Then it yells at me in my mind. I don't know what it's saying. It's just yelling."

Merrill pulls his chair over beside hers. While she sits, he awkwardly initiates a hug. It's really uncomfortable because the arm of the chair is between them. She collapses into him and sobs. He thinks about what anger does when it's pushed down inside. It goes into rage. When rage then erupts, it destroys.

The Pig 'n Poke is a pizza pub on the seedy side of downtown. Pierre sits beside Jimmy at the bar having followed the Camaro there. He sees no recognition by Jimmy that he's the one in the Malibu from the day before. He keeps his cap on, pulled down low over his eyes. As they greet each other, Pierre recognizes the name Jimmy Murphy from the list of aides that Mrs. Waleski had given him. More than a few beers go in—Jimmy enjoying Pierre's generosity. Then Jimmy, with a wink and a nod, brags about driving the car into the Starbucks. He goes on to tell the long story of him and GJ, a story going back to selling GJ's pills as a teenager and progressing through to doing GJ's time in jail years later as GJ had ratted him out.

It's more than Pierre could ever have hoped to know.

Typically, the Tuesday night after Nikki returns from the north is family night.

Nikki and Jemma come by the agency about 5:30 to pick up Estelle from work. Nikki went back to bed after taking Jemma to school and rested most of the morning. She then awoke, thoroughly refreshed. Gordon had walked Jemma back from school in the afternoon and gave his favourite little girl another music lesson. By the time Nikki picked her up to go and get Momma-Stelle, everyone was singing. As they come hand in hand into ReClaiming Ourselves Inc., Jemma is bouncing and twirling. Seeing her other mom, she breaks away and runs to Estelle.

"Wow, Jemma, you're getting better and better at hugs. I really needed that!" With the contact with her daughter, a wave of relief washes over Estelle.

Nikki joins the hug and engages in a loving kiss with Estelle.

"Where for dinner? Nikki's choice, she's just back home," Estelle asks.

They playfully go through a list of possibilities, with Jemma reacting with a headshake or fake gag until they settle on Montana's. As they walk back out to the car, Jemma excitedly talks about the very last spelling test that she'll ever have and how she got a 10 out of 10 on it. Tomorrow is the second last day of school for grade one. It's going to be a fun day, and everyone is invited, Momma-Stelle and Momma-Nik, too.

Estelle feels more and more normal the more her daughter babbles on. The incredible waves of sadness and rage retreat.

"I'm not going to go."

"Nikki, please, can you go? For me, can you go?"

Estelle and Nikki take their place on the balcony, Jemma contentedly off to bed. The sun's setting in the west and has lit the clouds of the eastern sky with bright hues of coral and orange. Nikki is on her third beer.

"To the funeral? Nope. I'm thinking of going to Jemma's fun day at school instead."

"Gordon's got that covered for us. He signed up as a parent volunteer." Estelle orients herself to Nikki, makes eye contact. "Nikki-luv, can you do this for me? Please. I don't want to go to that funeral alone."

"Who all is going to be there?" Nikki asks.

"I have no idea. April. Nali probably. I doubt if anyone else. Maybe some of April's family, I don't know."

"Will he be there?"

Estelle looks at her lover. She knows who Nikki is referring to. "Father? Yes, I expect so."

"How can you call him that?"

"As much as you're horrified about what he did to Nali, he's still our father.

His son has died. It's his son's funeral. He has a right to be there."

"Men who sexually frig up their daughters have no right to their family."

"Nikki. This isn't about him. It's about GJ, to show respect for another human being. And if you can't go for GJ, then go for me."

"Who is GJ to me, anyway? I never knew him. From what you said, I'm glad I didn't too." Nikki drinks hard back on the beer bottle.

"You are so black and white, Nikki. You make up your mind and don't think anyone should ever think differently than you do."

"So, this is about me, then, is it? It's about what's wrong with me."

"No, Nikki. That's not it."

Both of their voices are edged with tension.

"So your father can diddle his daughter, and you accept him. I have an issue with it, and you make that a problem between us."

Estelle looks over at Jemma's window. It's open, letting in the breeze. If voices get raised, they will wake her. A deliberate evenness of tone comes over Estelle as she pushes back the frustration. "Nikki, I need you now. I need to have your support. It was hell at work today. You and Jemma came in dancing and singing, and that was the very best part of my day, but all day long . . ."

Resigned to her fate, but without a tone of giving in, Nikki replies. "Okay, I will go. I will stay at your side. Won't talk to anyone. I'm sure you don't want me saying what I think. But I will be with you."

"Be polite. Be civil, please."

"I'll try. But you better hold on to me. When I see your father, I just might strangle him."

CHAPTER ELEVEN

Wednesday

At 10:30 a.m., Estelle pulls up in front of the Heritage Funeral Home with April and Harry.

April had nothing to wear. On the way, Estelle took her to her own favourite clothing store, got her a black dress. April was too sad to protest.

Arriving at the funeral home, they plan. April doesn't want Estelle to go into the funeral home with her. She has some things she wants to say to the funeral home director and the chaplain meeting her there. She can say those things just fine on her own. Estelle offers to take Harry to the park—Stanley Park is close by. She can push him in the stroller on the path by the river; maybe there will be baby swings.

After April has had her time at the funeral home, they will go out for an early lunch. It will need to be a quick one because Estelle has to go back to the condo to pick up Nikki, and then swing over to get Nali, too.

April heads into the funeral home, clutching her purse and Nate's two binders from the kitchen table.

At 1:30, the four sisters arrive back at the funeral home. Harry hasn't slept. It's his usual nap time, if he can be settled to take one—it's better if he does. If he doesn't, he gets grouchy. April settles him into his stroller and rocks him back and forth in the vestibule. Seeing this, Nikki goes over and offers to take care of him for a while, mimicking the same rocking motion. She has the touch. Within a few minutes, he's asleep. April stands awkwardly.

The funeral home has put out about twenty chairs in a partitioned off section of the chapel. Estelle thinks it's too many, but then figures that it doesn't matter. There's an empty table awaiting a picture, several baskets of flowers on it. The flowers are too showy a display. The casket is closed, a plain one without adornments or brass.

Dr. Jackson Horvath arrives wearing a suit.

Immediately, his eyes settle on Nali.

Nali is stunningly overdressed. She has an outfit she wears to more formal occasions that completely hides the tattoo—a long, slimming white jacket with a stiff collar that ascends to her ears. A white blouse covers her bosom; over it is a vividly coloured silk scarf. She has tied the scarf so that it covers the head of the cobra. She wears heels and a skirt that goes to midcalf.

"Anna." Jackson's voice crackles with emotion.

"Dad." Her voice is flat.

"It's good to see you."

"Lousy circumstances, though."

And that's all that is said between them.

Three people from the Best Buy come in, all wearing blue polo shirts and tan khaki pants. An older man walks up to Estelle and asks if she is April. Estelle says, "No," and walks him over to April, who is standing awkwardly off to the side. He produces an 8x10 photo in a black metal frame. It was Nate's work photo. He was encouraged to smile for the photograph, and he looks so proud in it. April says, "Thanks," and places the photo on the table beside the flowers. She stands there, her back to the others, weeping. Estelle goes over and places a hand on her shoulder.

The Rooke gang come in—Bernice in her wheelchair, Stan behind pushing her. Trevor too, looking lost. Nali goes over to them.

A man makes several entries with flat boxes and coffee urns. He commandeers a table off to the side and puts out trays of fancy pastries. He proudly displays the sign *Edelweiss Imports and Bakery* beside his work. Jackson goes over to him, slips a bill in his hand, and they exchange a brief hug.

Aunt Leanne and Gordon come. On Leanne's insistence, Gordon has begged off being parent volunteer at Jemma's fun day. Leanne sets a painting on the easel that Gordon has lugged in behind her. In the portrait she has captured a happy glint in Nate's eye and a soft smile. She has lit the painting from the right with hues of yellow and gold lacing the beams of white. Nate is slightly turned in that direction, the dark of indigo, violet, and crimson behind him.

Estelle goes over to her, recognizes the likeness of Nate from the Facebook photos, touches her aunt's arm to say *thank you* for a most meaningful gift. Leanne nods her acceptance of the thanks with a tear to the eye.

Estelle collects Nali and April, bringing them both over to join her with Leanne. She introduces April to Leanne. Nali stands awkwardly by. Leanne gives April a hug and says her condolences then turns to Nali and waves her over for a hug too—once they have embraced Leanne steps back to get a good look at Nali, then she puts her arm around her wayward niece's waist. The three stand looking at the painting.

Gordon gives a CD of music he had compiled to the funeral director. He had no clue what Nate would've wanted. He went back twenty years to check what was on the lists of the most popular rock music when Nate was a teenager, picking songs he hoped Nate would've liked.

Four well-dressed, middle-aged men come in. Immediately, they go over to Jackson, shake his hand, offer their condolences.

"Are you going to get Jemma after school?" Leanne asks Estelle.

"I talked with the teacher, told her we had a funeral today. She's going to stay with Jemma at the school until we can come for her if this goes long. It's fun day. She'll be outside all day playing."

A loud clap of thunder shakes the building. Rain has blown up. Heavy.

"Or maybe not."

Harry cries, scared at the crack of the thunder overhead. Nikki had taken him down the hall in the stroller. April leaves the clutch around the portrait and rushes to him, Nali trailing along with her.

Under the canopy out front, a van pulls up with *Mountain Recovery and Treatment Centre* on the side. Three staff members step out and come in. They stand in a little huddle.

More come, men and women both, all looking awkward. Estelle goes over to April.

"Do you know these people?"

"No."

"I'm curious. I'm going over to them."

She does.

"Hi, I'm Estelle, GJ's sister."

"I'm Greg, and this is Tom and Kent. We're in AA with Nate. His sponsor, Tony, is supposed to come, too. I think a bunch are coming from the Tuesday evening group."

More come in. A couple of them have cameras, notebooks.

And then a middle-aged man comes dressed in that navy blazer, open-necked button-down ivory shirt, and grey flannel slacks. He has a slight military bearing about him. With him is a scruffier fellow. He looks awkward in a collared shirt and khakis. Within a moment, the better-dressed man sees the painting and goes over to it. The other man pulls a cigarette from his pocket and motions that he is going to go back outside.

Standing in front of the painting, the man wearing the blue blazer is approached by Leanne. Immediately, they engage in conversation about the painting. Leanne pulls a business card from her purse and hands it to him.

The two funeral directors add a dozen or more chairs—an extra row behind and an extra chair at each end of the rows.

The drumbeat of Green Day's *Longview* begins to play. Almost imperceptibly rhythmic movements begin amongst several of the people standing there. When the drums come in heavily, smiles emerge on the faces of some, others frown and look perplexed. Gordon grins. The funeral directors look on stoically, watching the faces and movements of those gathering. In hearing the music April is amused—the first positive emotion to sneak across her face since she arrived.

More people come. Some stand alone. Others join the existing groupings—young AA, older and middle-aged AA. The room is filling up. Several more wearing Best Buy outfits come in, join with the others. There is an odd feeling in the room. The music is discomforting, agitating.

Estelle remembers it, remembers GJ playing it in his room.

The funeral director opens one of the side partitions, revealing an adjacent parlour. Quickly they rearrange the banks of seats and add more.

It is five to two.

Thirty or forty people, or more, most certainly more. Estelle can't see around those standing to those coming in. Gradually, the crowd edges over toward the chairs to make room for the newcomers.

Merrill comes in with a group from the agency.

Suddenly the music changes. Queen's *Bohemian Rhapsody*. Its bizarre melody and juxtaposition of forms sound sacred in the funeral chapel—worldly, but sacred too.

Everyone sits down, April between her two newfound sisters in the front row. A hush settles over. Nikki comes to sit beside Estelle, pulling up a chair to add to the end of the row. Harry is beside her, asleep in his stroller. As Nikki leans over to say, "I'm here." Estelle smells alcohol on her breath.

Then, after listening through the Queen's epic, it's Led Zeppelin, *Stairway to Heaven*.

There's a rustling at the back and a breeze laden with the moist air of the summer storm blows across the floor. More people are there, standing at the back.

All are still. The incredible riffs of Jimmy Page waft over those assembled. All are stunned with the beauty of it, with the violence of it. With the grace of it.

Then the room goes completely silent.

"Good afternoon. I am Rev. Alex Reeves. I've been asked by the family to perform this service of remembrance.

"April, Nate's wife, has asked that there be no references to any religion in this service. Confessing that there is a *Reverend* in front of my name, a title given to me by the Anglican Church of Canada, I will let that be it. Today, we set aside religion. But you will feel in the room today a Higher Power will indeed be present. I've had the privilege to say grace at AA Roundups, and have repeated the Serenity Prayer holding hands with some of you who are here. We honour the Higher Power's role in the life of Gerald Jonathan Caylie, someone known to many of you as Nate, to others as GJ. I honour the role that the Higher Power has played in the life of many gathered today in remembrance."

Rev. Reeves pauses, shifts from his sombre tone to one more affirmative.

"And, I honour the role the Higher Power has also played in my own recovery."

He stops, shuffles papers on the lectern at the front of the parlour.

"April has asked me to say thank you on her behalf to several people who have contributed—to the staff here at Heritage Funeral Home; to those who sent flowers; to Gordon Heist, who prepared a great CD of music for us; to her newfound sisters Estelle and Nali, who have supported her over the last few days; to both Estelle and Dr. Jackson Horvath, who have helped her financially at this difficult time.

"I never met Nate. I wish I had. This morning April shared with me two binders. One was Nate's personal workbook when he was in treatment at Mountain Recovery and Treatment Centre. The other was one he kept in the last few months of his life after his discharge. From what I read there, I believe Nate was fundamentally a very fine man once he got his life in order, got it in order through a dedicated process of recovery.

"There's much in those binders that is very personal. I've asked April if I could read one section of it today as we are gathered to honour Nate. She agreed, said that's what she'd hoped I would do.

"What follows is a letter that Nate wrote in his final days at the treatment centre. It's a deeply personal letter to his son. His son—his pride and joy, Harry—is here with us today."

The reverend pauses, looks over in the stroller's direction, tries to catch an eye. Then, with great timing, "But he is asleep."

A chuckle reverberates through the room, a nervous one at that, a breaking of the incredible sadness that unites them all.

"The depth and love of this letter are so much more than any child could ever grasp. April has promised me that she will keep this letter and read it to Harry when he gets older. But for today, it tells best, it tells the best, of Nate."

Dear Harry,

You are too young to get this letter, my little prince. Your mom and I are keeping this letter safe until you get older.

I want you to know that I love you. I have loved you from the day you were born. I will love you until the day that I die.

But there is something else you need to know, too. For many years, your dad was a screw-up. But then his life changed.

You, Harry, will screw up sometimes. I hope you never screw up as badly as I have. When you screw up, maybe you can read this letter because this letter is about what comes after screwing up.

Before you were born, I screwed up so bad that my life was completely out of control. I couldn't manage it anymore. I hope your life never gets that far out of control, but if it does, I want you to know that there is a way back.

I learned that when your life is out of control you need to stop trying to control your life by controlling the other people around you. You can learn to control your thoughts, your behaviours, and your emotions instead. If you do that, your life will fall into line. Controlling your thoughts means that you will not spend the time thinking about getting revenge or screwing someone else to get ahead. At least, that is what it meant for me. Controlling your behaviours means that you will stop and think about what you do, think whether it is respectful of your body, of those you love, of the people around you. And controlling your emotions . . . well, that is hard. Controlling your emotions means that you will accept every feeling you have, let it be, then decide whether or not to act on it or to sit with it until it goes away.

These were hard lessons for me. I had great help in learning them. I had to go away from life for a while to stop what I was doing that was trying to control my life. I hope you will never have to go away like I did. But if you do, if you have to go to a place like rehab, I hope you will have the courage to do so. It does a guy a lot of good.

Not only did I need rehab, but I also needed to give my life over to a Higher Power because I went so far down the wrong road in life. I am still learning about my Higher Power. I don't even have a name for it yet, so I just call it HP for now. But it is real.

You see, Harry. I am an alcoholic. I am a drug addict. I will always be those things, but I hope you will never see me take a drink or do drugs. I hope when you read this, you will say . . . What? You? NO! I want you to know the truth about your dad, as much of the truth as can help you. I am in recovery. I will always be until the day that I die. Knowing that means that I will live a better life. I hope it is a long one. I want to watch you grow up, see everything that you accomplish.

Now, I want to speak to you about being a male. You come from a long line of men who are addicts. It runs in our family. You know from this letter about your dad being an addict. I had a dad, too. I haven't seen my dad in years, but I remember a whole lot of drinking happening when I was young, other stuff too. I know that he went away for treatment. He never much had anything to do with me when he came back. That could have been my fault because I was already starting to go rotten at that point. Anyway, that is your grandfather. I don't know if you will ever know him.

Then there is your great-grandfather. I was told that great is a good word for him. He was a great man, at least that is what my auntie told me when we were growing up. He was a doctor. My auntie said that he worked all the time. Looking back, I think he was probably addicted to his work, put more into that than into being a father or a grandfather.

Harry, I hope you will do great things too. But I hope that the greatest thing you will ever do will be a father. Imagine, you are just a few months old when I write this to you, and I am already thinking about you being a father someday.

I hope you will be a great father because you have had a really, really good one yourself.

That is my goal, to be a really, really good father to you.

I hope when you read this letter, whenever that is, that you will be able to say, "Yes, Dad, you were. You were the greatest."

Love

GJ

There is silence, silence punctuated by snuffles and a noisy nose blow or two.

Rev. Reeves asks if anyone would like to say anything.

Nobody does.

A lit candle flickers beside Gerald Jonathan Caylie's picture on the table. With grace, Rev. Reeves snuffs the candle, and a thin line of smoke escapes the end of the wick, the delicate scent of the wax wafting over the room. The sound of the rain on the roof of the chapel has stopped.

It is finished.

As the room slowly animates, one turning to another to acknowledge the communal feeling of profound sadness, Jackson stands and surveys the room. The act of seeing this collection of people there for his son lifts him out of the memories flooding in of family funerals past—his grandfather first, then his mom, and then Izzy. Memories that had taken him away from much of what had just been said regarding his son.

Other folks are standing now, too. Someone has found the guest book, and there's movement in that direction. A queue forms there. Jackson looks around, scanning for familiar faces. What had been deadening grief on his face suddenly turns to outrage. He moves to the side aisle and members of his AA group join him there. Harsh whispers are shared between them with glances over at Pierre Bolton who stands off to the side, farther back. Jackson whispers into the ear of one, and others nod in agreement. He then approaches the man, his AA buddies trailing behind.

"You have no business here," Jackson says. His words are soft but veiled in authority, in threat even.

"It's a public event. I saw no sign restricting who could pay respects." Pierre matches Jackson's tone.

"Be decent. This is my family."

"Oh?" There is mockery in Pierre Bolton's tone.

"Just leave." Jackson's AA buddies huddle around closer in an attempt to intimidate by outnumbering. Monica, Amir, and Eric press in on the flank as a phalanx of psychiatry.

Someone has come to the side of Pierre Bolton. Pierre turns to him, and together they leave. Jackson doesn't recognize the other man.

Estelle comes up and wraps an arm around her father's waist. Nali stands off to the side. Gordon and Leanne surround April as Rev. Reeves shares words of comfort with her. April responds with a look of appreciation, showing no awareness of what else is happening in the room. Nikki has left, wheeling Harry in his stroller.

There's the smell of coffee. Jackson orients to it, gestures over to the place where it's laid out at the side. Gradually, folk go over as if it will give them something to do with their hands, respite from the heaviness that surrounds them all. Quite a few are leaving after signing the guest book. As the door to the funeral home opens, the air blowing in is cool, fresh.

Estelle walks after Nikki as she pushes Harry's stroller away from the group, slipping her hand into the crook of Nikki's elbow from behind. Nikki turns, stone-faced. Estelle wipes tears before turning back toward the crowd. Nikki spins the stroller to head back. Harry still sleeps. In the slight *pas de deux* they briefly share, Estelle again smells liquor on Nikki's breath. It's somehow stronger.

Seeing her father standing with his psychiatrist colleagues, Estelle takes Nikki over to allow her to give her condolences..

Jackson had attended their wedding, of course, their wedding that had made the social pages of the newspaper. In some strange quirk of family, that's the last time he spoke to Nikki, even though Nikki and Estelle were now two years officially married. Now Nikki knows more about this father-in-law. Estelle feels the crackle of that knowledge with her hand still in the crux of Nikki's elbow. Nikki's body stiffens, her back arches. She emits a coughing sound.

Jackson wipes her spittle off his cheek with a handkerchief he takes from his pocket.

Estelle recoils. Silently, immediately, two funeral home staff members descend on the small family grouping. They step in on either side of Nikki and gently ease her away. There's fire in her eyes. Estelle looks at her with disorientation and disgust.

Nikki extracts herself from the grasp of the funeral directors. She looks at Estelle and says clearly, "I didn't say anything, not a word. Like I promised." And then, she turns and says, "I'm out of here." She leaves Harry, still asleep in his stroller.

The funeral home staff immediately turn to Jackson to check if he's following. He's not. Monica has moved in beside him, a look of both confusion and profound concern on her face.

And Estelle is caught, paralyzed on the spot, watching Nikki leave. Merrill comes in beside her and puts his arm around her shoulder. She grasps her left hand to cover her mouth. Her legs buckle. As Merrill senses her sudden weakness, he reaches for a chair, hustles it to the back of Estelle's legs. She sits heavily, dissolved into tears.

Rev. Reeves comes over and exchanges words quietly with Merrill. He's brought another chair and placed it close to where Estelle sits. Merrill turns from the conversation with the reverend and goes over to the group of agency clients who have accompanied him to the funeral. All have looks of great concern and are asking each other if they'd seen what had happened.

Gradually the gaggle of family and friends—save Estelle, who sits with the reverend—head over to the table where the coffee is out.

Then, getting up suddenly from her conversation with Rev. Reeves, a startled Estelle rushes over to Nali who is standing with Leanne and Gordon.

"Did she take the car?"

"I suppose so, didn't see." Leanne answers.

"It has the car seat for Harry in it."

"Can you call her?"

"I don't think I could civilly speak to her at the moment. I suspect she's gone somewhere to drink."

"Where would she go?"

"Wait. I know." Estelle takes out her phone and taps the Friend Finder app. Quickly, she identifies that Nikki's phone is heading back to their condo.

"She's going home. We need to get the car, for April and Harry. It has Harry's car seat in it."

"I'd like family to come back to our place." Leanne looks around. The crowd has thinned out except for those nursing coffee and plates with strudels, cream puffs, and fruit tarts.

"What time is it? We need to pick up Jemma from school."

Gordon moves in. "We have our car here. How about Leanne drives me over to your condo? I can pick up your car and bring it back here. Then we can go over to our place. I'll walk Jemma home from school."

Estelle hands Gordon her car keys.

"Is there a door code into the underground parking?"

"Wait. I'll get the key card for you." Estelle pauses, roots around in her purse to find it. "Thanks, that'll work. But I'd like to walk with Jemma. I need the walk."

Estelle turns to April who has been overhearing the arrangement, and asks, "Are you comfortable going with Leanne and Gordon when he gets my car back here?"

April nods. "I need to go back home first, need more diapers for Harry if we are somewhere else. I can drop off these binders then, too."

"Okay, that'll work." Estelle has recovered her organizational mind. "Gordon, you bring my car back here and drop me off at Jemma's school, then take April and Harry to their place. We will all meet back at the house."

Jackson moves over to the family conversation, having released members of his AA group and his colleagues. Leanne briefs him on what is happening, invites him over, says who is coming.

As they prepare to leave, Rev. Reeves comes over to Estelle again. He motions to a quiet corner where they can go to talk. Once there, they settle. The others give them space, allowing Estelle, gracious listener and comforter to so many others, to receive for herself. Rising to leave, Rev. Reeves hands her a business card. He puts his hands on her shoulder as if he's giving her a blessing, then ducks his head downward, saying a brief prayer. Estelle eschews a priestly offered handshake to give and receive a hug. She looks at him with a sense of security and relief, a sense of being loved—loved in a kindly, fatherly way. Loved by someone she just met an hour or so ago.

When Estelle picks up Jemma from school, Mrs. Gliddenhurst has a particularly satisfied smile on her face. Jemma is bouncing and talking excitedly, almost too much for the grade one teacher. Warmly, Mrs. Gliddenhurst gives Jemma a big final hug and reminds her that the next day is her last day and she would get her report card. Looking at Estelle, she mouths, *She had a good day*, and then, *How are you doing? I am sorry about your brother.* Estelle just nods.

On the walk from Earl Grey Elementary School to 113 Durham Lane, Estelle hears all about the Olde Fashioned Fun Day. All the grade one students had been matched with a student from grade four, five, or six—with the really good kids. These older students were designated as Honourable Ambassadors for the day and given special VIP badges, badges that they could even take home with them. Jemma got JayLynn-Dawn, who just happens to be the older sister of Jemma's bestest-friend-in-world, Rachael. Jemma talks about how mad she was at JayLynn-Dawn in the three-legged race when they fell right at the start. After that, JayLynn-Dawn called out *left* and *right* for Jemma, and they won!

When Estelle asks about the rain, Jemma, without taking a breath, says they went into the gym. The games continued. They did the egg-and-spoon race and everyone cheered Mr. Braden, the janitor, when he rushed out to clean up broken eggs with paper towels, a wet sponge, and rags to shine the floor again.

"And Momma-Stelle, Momma-Stelle, Ms. Smythe got dunked in a big swimming pool outside. All the boys from grades five and six couldn't hit the target with the sponge to make her fall into the pool, but Mrs. Gliddenhurst did. Down went Ms. Smythe. It was so funny. But it was okay because she had her bathing suit on under her clothes."

And for a moment, Estelle latches onto Jemma's buoyancy. It lifts her above the darkness that wants to take her feet out from under her, that keeps tugging her down. It's just what she needs.

As they walk into the house at 113 Durham Lane, Jemma's stories of fun day begin all over again with Auntie Leanne. Estelle surveys the collection of family. Jackson is in the process of shifting Harry from one hip to the other as the toddler continues to look into his face with puzzlement and acceptance. The incongruity of the pairing strikes her, but she is pleased for both. Nali, April, and Gordon have beers in their hands as they stand, Gordon demonstrating some sort of musical something on the sound equipment he has in his studio space at the back. There is an odd harmony about them that seems distant to Estelle, but hopeful too.

A bowl of tortilla chips sits on the table with Gordon's special five-layer nacho dip beside it—sour cream, guacamole, spicy hot salsa, grated cheddar cheese, and bacon bits on the top. A pitcher of lemonade is there too, and a box of leftover German pastries from the funeral. Aunt Leanne is not much for entertaining and food. She can't be bothered. Folks put together what they can.

"Momma-Stelle," Jemma tugs at Estelle's hand, "where's Momma-Nik?"

A hush settles over the family. It is long and awkward. The happening at the funeral home is not to be talked about. Jackson, with Harry on his hip, turns away, walking toward the entryway.

"Momma-Nik went home. She's not feeling well. We'll go home and see her soon."

Jemma is content, goes over to join her Uncle Gordon, looks up at both Nali and April and bluntly says, "Who are you?" Then, without waiting for an answer, she immediately launches into telling Gordon about Olde Fashioned Fun Day at the school. He sets down his harmonica to listen.

Leanne joins her brother in the front hall. Jackson has knelt down, examining three oil pastels sitting on the floor leaning against the wall. Harry stands with him, pulling himself up by grabbing onto his grandpa's shirt. The pastels are framed under glass.

"I did these when I was raising the kids. Tomorrow I have to take them down to the gallery. Denny wants me to display them in my studio there. At the opening, after patrons have been through the show, they are supposed to come up to my studio and sign contracts for commissions . . ." Leanne's voice trails off, and Jackson wanders away with Harry.

Estelle goes over to her aunt. They stand looking at the pastels, especially the one of GJ, remembering.

"Is she okay?" Leanne asks, turning to Estelle.

"Nikki?" Estelle clarifies.

"Yes, Nikki."

"I don't know. I haven't been in touch. I suspect that she will drink and feel sorry for herself. I've no idea what it'll be like when I take Jemma home. Hopefully, she'll be out on the balcony, will give Jemma a boozy kiss goodnight and not say anything more until we talk tomorrow."

"When does she go back?"

"Sunday. She'll probably be all full of resentment about how GJ's going and dying ruined her week off."

Leanne shakes her head.

"Auntie . . ." Estelle catches Leanne's eye. "How's this for you? You raised GJ, probably loved him more than anyone else."

"Oh, I was glad to hear he turned his life around. He's given us little Harry and April for our family now."

Estelle detects the sadness drooping Leanne's left eyelid.

"Estelle . . ." Nali comes up to join them.

"Yes, Nali."

"I need to get going. I have to get to work for tonight."

"Yeah, right." Estelle looks over at April with Gordon and Jemma, Jackson with Harry. Her father is holding Harry's two fingers, the toddler bouncing lightly on his pudgy legs. Gordon is explaining to Jemma that she is like an older sister now—she and Harry are cousins, but sometimes cousins can be like brother and sister. Jemma gives Harry a big hug. April stands, smiling at the cuteness.

Estelle's eyes catch Nali's. There is a brief smile.

Leanne interjects, "Why don't I take Nali in our car? You stay here with the others."

"No, let me take her. I need some big sister time. I'll come back and take April and Harry when they are ready to go. What's happening here is good."

GJ, in being gone, is bringing everyone closer.

"Estelle. Who was that man?"

Estelle is navigating the late afternoon traffic.

"The guy in the blazer?" It is obvious to both who Nali meant by *that man*.

"Yeah."

"I don't know. Father went over to him. I think he's the one that Father had warned me about. Something happened back at the conference in Vancouver."

"Monday I saw him hanging around outside the club. Sometimes customers will do that—hours before we open, to harass the girls when they are getting in. But I didn't recognize him as a customer. But now that I come to think about it, I remember him from weeks ago. He was asking me questions about Dad."

"That's right. I remember now." Estelle speaks with sudden awareness. "Father showed me a picture of that same man in the Vancouver Airport. That was him."

"So, did you recognize who was with him at the funeral?"

"No. I didn't see anyone with him."

"I did. It was Jimmy Murphy."

"Who?"

"A guy from a long way back. Had a thing for me. But in the last several years, he's been harassing me. I've had to go to the police."

"Oh."

Weariness hits Estelle as she makes the final drive from April's quadraplex back to her condo. Jemma, in the car with her, is tired now too. She flops over asleep in her seat, her head held up by the seat belt.

Finally, Estelle feels a welcome aloneness. The traffic is easing and waves of sadness wash over her. And then, there is the rage. Estelle yells within herself at other drivers—*Back off, will you!* And, *Get off my tail*. It echoes inside of her as if she can never let it out.

Then there's the dread—a dread so deep that it could pull her under. It's dread about Nikki, about the awkward talk they must have about Nikki's drinking and her spitting on Jackson at the funeral.

But the dread goes deeper. It's a wafting dread filled with flashes of memory and sick feelings in her tummy. Somehow it's about GJ, but at the same time, not about GJ.

It's a dread about never being able to hide enough.

Then the rage hits again. She slams on the brakes at an intersection. A particularly aggressive driver has cut her off—he must think he owns the road in his snazzy new Mustang. Jemma wakes with the jerk of it all, crying.

Estelle can't cope. Sadness, dread, rage, disgust, revulsion. Then, back through them all again.

CHAPTER TWELVE

Thursday

Pierre carefully rearranges the desktop in his hotel room. He brings the laptop computer to the front and places the SD card from his camera into its side. A series of images flashes on his screen.

The first is an image of GJ's rehab binder, the one in which he had kept worksheets and journaling pages. Its cover is replete with his ornately drawn initials and AA stickers. The second image is of a piece of flip-chart paper. On it is a large outline of an egg. There are several line drawings inside the egg and notes under different headings scattered around the outside: Family Roles, Family Rules, and Father and Mother.

Pierre zooms in, looking at each of the egg's sketches. There is a wave breaking on the surface of the ocean—curling, rolling over on itself. There is a picture of a wine glass partially full with a bright red liquid, a beer bottle, and a bottle of spirits. There is a hand holding a small collection of prescription pills. Finally, he takes in the drawings of a video game controller, a stethoscope, a hand of playing cards, the bare buttocks of a child.

Pierre progresses to the third image. It shows the tab on a binder section divider—Step 9 Making Amends. Next, from this binder section, is a photo of a handwritten letter to April. Following that is a letter of amends to Stella. The page on which GJ's father was identified is basically blank, just a faint impression of words, words having once been written in pencil but then erased.

He retreats one slide. Reads what GJ wrote to his sister Stella.

Pierre settles back in his chair and stares out the window. He gently rocks.

For some reason, this is hard, this exploration of GJ's rehab binder. He can't figure out why. It's just . . . somehow . . . hard. It's nothing but information, useful information but just information. There's nothing to be emotional about here. This is just a job, a job that just got easier. It's unsettling to Pierre that something else is happening within him. Perhaps it's shame that he feels, shame he must shake off because it will ultimately be counterproductive.

Pierre concludes it must be GJ's shame, shame that had been exploited by some manipulative therapy process eager to achieve a therapeutic goal. Pierre is relieved to understand it that way, that it's not his own shame he feels but that of a sad, pathetic addict, a shame somehow caught by contagion from the writings and drawings of a drunk druggie in rehab. But it bothers him that he would feel this way, feel it now staring out the window of his hotel room at the Calgary street scene below. His discomfort magnifies at the possibility that what he's feeling might be empathy. Pierre knows empathy as an intellectual construct. Empathy has no place in the task he has to do. He thinks back to that other letter, the one read by the priest at the funeral of the previous day, the emotion that it begged from him . . .

Pierre jerks himself out of his reverie. Methodically, he goes about transferring the photo images from the memory card into the concept vectoring act, identifying the linkages to which they belong. There's comfort in the organizational task. He closes the computer, and for a few minutes he repeatedly lines up the edges of the items on the hotel desk so that they are straight and perpendicular to the lip of the desk, carefully spaced so that nothing is touching. Somehow he just can't get it right.

Estelle wakes in a made-up bed on the floor of Jemma's room.

The night before she'd made bedtime into a special treat, a campout-style sleepover for her daughter in her very own room. It was the night before Jemma's big day—graduating from grade one! Estelle said to Jemma the campout sleep was about graduating. She wasn't sure that Jemma had bought it. Probably Jemma had figured out Momma-Stelle camping in her room was because of Momma-Nik. But they had s'mores made in the oven, and Jemma was so happy going off to sleep on the sugar high. Estelle went off to sleep with the grief of her brother's death and her concern about her marriage on her mind.

With morning, Estelle noses into the bedroom where Nikki is still asleep. It reeks of alcohol consumption from the day before. She closes the door and makes breakfast.

Mrs. Gliddenhurst sent a note home to all her students that school will likely be out by 10:30 or 11:00. Estelle texts Gordon to ask him to go and watch Jemma graduate because Estelle needs to be at work. Nikki will be hungover. Better that Jemma goes over to be with Gordon and Auntie for the rest of the day.

Then Estelle texts Dodi, Dodi way down in Missouri. They are one hour later in the day. She asks for a FaceTime call sometime during the day, *If at all possible, please.*

By the time Estelle gets to work, Merrill has already set up the day to be a TGIF—this a day early. Folk are drifting in. The audio speaker is playing the soothing sounds of wind and ocean waves breaking on the shore.

Estelle glares at Merrill. With a demanding edge to her voice, she commands, "Turn that damn noise off." Merrill looks at her in the way of being bewildered, her tone being so unlike her. Today, that particular noise is triggering Estelle to vibrate between rage and immobility. She heads into the office and closes the door.

There are tears.

Soon Merrill is at the door. "Sorry . . . you okay?"

Estelle is not.

Merrill walks in, worry on his face.

"TGIF? Really? It's Thursday." Estelle asks, looking annoyed.

"With what happened yesterday, and the state that you've been in, I didn't think anyone could handle anything heavy. I thought of just cancelling, but then there are so many people to call. So, I've made this to be Friday. We'll see how everyone is—maybe do the same tomorrow, or maybe we could all take tomorrow off and make this to be a long weekend, giving everyone, especially you, a day to recover."

Estelle sits heavily behind her desk, gives unspoken resignation to the plan.

Her phone buzzes with a text. It is from Dodi. *Ten o'clock St. Louis time.* Estelle does the quick calculation: forty-five minutes from now.

"People overheard the way you spoke to me," Merrill stammers out. "Look, I know this is a rough time for you. And everybody here wants so much to be understanding. Me included. But they also need to know whether they can count on you too. You are their therapist, and a hero to many of them. They are out there. They need you."

"Did you turn it off?"

"What?"

"That hideous ocean-sound thing you were playing on the stereo."

"Yes. I put on Israel, the Hawaiian singer with the unpronounceable name, the one who takes us over the rainbow into the wonderful world."

Estelle looks at him. A rapid shift comes across her face, breaking the clouds over her eyes and forehead. She erupts into a chuckle. "Perfect," she says, seeing the irony of it.

They stand silently.

"Merrill, thanks for coming yesterday—and for bringing the group of them."

"Welcome." He pauses. "Estelle, what happened?"

"Nikki happened. I'm still furious with her. She spit on my father. Then she spent the rest of the day drinking. Now she's sleeping it off."

"Yeah, I saw the spit. The drinking, that's not like her . . ." Merrill pauses. "Is it?"

"Sometimes. Not very often. Too often, though, when it does happen . . ." Estelle pauses, not sure how to complete the sentence. "Are you all set up out there?"

"Yup, everyone likes TGIF."

"Except the introverts."

"Except the introverts."

"Is there anything else? I have a call coming in soon."

"One thing."

"What?"

"When I got here this morning, there was a man outside, dressed like a professional person, waiting. He asked when you'd be in. I told him I wasn't sure when but that you'd be busy when you did come in. He left a card, said he would be back at the end of the day. I told him that the clients are usually gone by about 4:30."

Estelle looks at the card, recognizes the name from the card her father showed her over FaceTime from Vancouver. Something else to dread all day.

"Long time, eh?" Dodi's round face enlivens the FaceTime screen, her hair in dreadlocks.

"Too long."

"How is Jemma?"

"Graduates grade one today."

"Whoo-ee! Go, girl. Grade One! She can't be old enough yet for that! Maybe she's precocious like her mom."

"Dodi." Estelle bites her lower lip, draws out her former lover's name, almost pleading it.

"What's wrong?"

"Yesterday, we had the funeral for my brother, GJ."

"Oh, 'Stelle. I'm so sorry." Dodi pauses, "I never knew you had a brother—did I?"

"When you and I were in graduate school together, he was long gone from my life. I understand now where he went—addiction and crime. Then, just a week ago, he found me on Facebook and asked to meet. Before I got to the Starbucks..." Estelle can't finish her sentence as the tears come back again.

Dodi waits. Finally, Estelle looks up at the screen, daubs her eyes with a Kleenex, and blows her nose.

"Do you want me to come up to Canada? I'll leave right away, buy a parka and be there by suppertime."

Estelle laughs. The *buy a parka* is the standing joke between them.

"I'd love you to. You'd better not. You know about Nikki. It's already tough enough with her, you arriving on the scene . . . as much as I'd love that . . ." Estelle's words wistfully fade off.

"Then you come down. Soon. You and Jemma."

"Missouri, in the summer?"

"We're in the middle of tornado season."

"So, it's too hot and humid to move, right?"

"You got that right."

"Still, I think we should meet up. What about California?"

"Hot there too, and the forest fires! I heard on the news the smoke is really bad down in San Diego."

"We could go up the coast."

Estelle lets the conversation die out. Dodi waits.

"Dodi. I'm falling apart."

"Yes, I can tell."

They sit silently together. Estelle longs to talk to Dodi about something other than the weather—about the turmoil that boils inside of her, about every possible emotion she could have running so strong that she loses herself in the mix. Estelle longs to be held again by Dodi, hugged with that enormous hug that reassures every vulnerability that Estelle could ever have. She prepares herself to talk several times, but all that would come out would be words a psychologist would use—words helpful in treatment of a patient in emotional distress but suddenly hollow and horrible as Estelle attaches them to herself. She doesn't bother saying them.

Finally, Dodi speaks.

"Okay, m'luv. I'm coming. I've a family wedding this weekend. Some of the other staff are off next week, through until the fourth of July. I can see if I can—"

"Forget it." Estelle's voice edges into dismissal.

"No. No. I mean it."

"Dodi. I need to get away. Get out. Can I come down? This weekend, next week?" Estelle pauses. "No, I can't do that either."

"We can talk every day, m'luv. FaceTime every day until we can get together."

"Okay."

"You need to talk to someone up there. Is there anyone you can trust?"

"My father is a psychiatrist." Estelle throws it out there, the closest she can get to a joke with her former lover and friend.

"Oh, him. I met him. Remember? No, not him."

Estelle thinks. The last thing she would consider would be to see another psychologist. She's gaining credibility with the only other psychologists in Calgary she feels she can trust, credibility as a young and level-headed professional. Going to one of them as a basket case would blow her reputation.

"Someone."

"Wait." Estelle digs through her purse. She takes out a business card from the day before. *Rev. Alex Reeves, Bereavement and Grief Counselling.* She shows it to Dodi by holding it up to the camera on her MacBook.

"A place to start."

There's a sharp knocking on the door. Merrill opens it and quickly blurts out, "Sorry to bother you—Jack has a knife out here."

The sign on the door identifies the clinic is only open Monday to Thursday.

Nali walks up to the reception desk. "I'd like to see Dr. Horvath."

Joan looks at her, perplexed. "I don't recognize you as one of his patients. Dr. Horvath is only available by referral and appointment."

"I'm his daughter, Annalise Horvath."

The perplexity on Joan's face turns to shock. "Really?" escapes her lips. Then she collects her composure and establishes eye contact away from a reflexive stare at the tattoo. "Does he know to expect you today?"

"No. But I want to see him, to see him now."

Nali looks around the waiting room. Two patients sit there. One is a man, looking gruff—his arms folded across his chest and resting on a generous belly. The other is a female, young and pretty. From the look of her, she could be one of Nali's dancers. She is just that ordinary. But she's not. Both have heard Nali's statement, but are too self-absorbed to attend to the drama unfolding in front of them.

"He's with a patient now. I can't check with him until he comes out. It could be a while."

"I'll wait."

Nali takes a seat with the other two, definitely feeling out of place. It'd taken a great deal of worry and desperation to come. It was against her better judgment. Really against it. But then, with the fitful early morning hours she'd put in not sleeping, she knows she needs to do this. The chance for some future restorative action outweighs her dread.

After about fifteen minutes, a middle-aged woman with a look of relieved sorrow exits through the waiting room. Dr. Jackson Horvath leans down to the receptionist and has a whispered conversation.

"Anna. Come in."

She does.

"Let's make this quick. I've a full slate of patients—re-booked from yesterday to today. I'm already running behind.

They stand awkwardly in Jackson's office.

"What's on my mind . . . well, it's not quick."

"Can we arrange to talk then, maybe tomorrow? I'm off tomorrow."

Nali looks at him. She's not about to be put off. "With GJ's death, the memories are flooding back. Childhood memories."

Jackson doesn't speak. He summons within himself an air of detachment, of judgment.

"It was screwed up. All of it, screwed up. You and me."

He sighs. "Perhaps." Jackson takes an assertive posture. "Anna, this is not the time or place. I'm in the middle of a workday. I can't process this with you now. Please go. You can leave your contact number with Joan at the front. I'll get in touch with you. I promise. Soon."

"I could go out into the waiting room and let your patients know that you'll be delayed a few minutes because the daughter you fucked as a child wants to talk to you about it."

Nali's gambit reverberates between them.

"Let's be reasonable. We're adults here. This is complicated and horrible, I know. I feel badly. But I'm a different man now. We can come to terms with it." Jackson cultures a look of benevolent concern on his face. "Let's give ourselves a better chance to talk than just standing here."

In response to this, Nali sits down.

She begins. "So, about yesterday. And that's the reason that I am here, really. Yesterday. Estelle, my baby sister Stella, she collapsed at the funeral. And as I was going over in my mind who GJ was to me, I'm sure she was going over in her mind how cruel and crude my bratty brother was to her.

"And I'm thinking—how horrible it must be for her, for the memories to come back.

"Then, I'm thinking. In all that she did to find me, in the talks we've had in the last few days, she doesn't talk about what it was like when we were kids." Nali pauses, staring at her father. "So, does she have those memories from her childhood, like the way I do? Does she even remember? I don't think she does. I think it's all just a big blank spot in her life. And damn it all, when I'm going over this in the middle of the night, I realize that I have blank spots too. Anyway, I remember a lot of it and Stella has a right to know, know what happened to her back then."

With a look of resignation, Jackson goes around behind his desk and sits, leaning back in his chair, trying to put a little distance between them.

"I was at work last night. I manage at the Emerald Grove. And it was a quiet night, and the girls on the floor were fine, and I was watching out for them. But it was all okay. And, I'm thinking that . . ."

Nali stops. A look of shame comes over her face. A shudder runs through her.

"I didn't watch out for Stella. Not the way that I should have." She looks again at her father, now with fire in her eyes.

There is no response from him.

With a tic of the cobra tongue, Nali continues. "I was her older sister, and I didn't take care of her because I was taking care of you."

Jackson stands, stands as if to dismiss her.

"It's clearer for me now, memories of how screwed up we were as a family, how what was going on between you and me stole from Stella and GJ. I wasn't there for her. You weren't there for GJ to get him straightened out, not like you should have as a father."

Jackson looks at the door, looks at his watch. "Look, Anna, I apologize for what happened between us. I live with guilt every day . . . " Jackson hesitates, choosing his words carefully, ". . . about the relationship that developed between us. If you wish, we can take the time, go over it together, talk about what happened, and why. It's not going to be easy, painful for both of us."

Nali looks at him as if he is missing the point. "I can live with that. I've sorted that out in my mind. You don't need to do your penance with me."

She pauses.

"What I need to deal with now is my sister, and how we abandoned her to GJ with his violence and insolence. She was his victim. We should've made sure she was okay, Mother being gone and all."

Nali gathers the strength of her cobra, raising herself assertively. "We can't do anything about GJ. He's dead. But Stella. We can at least help Stella deal with all that happened back then; it must impact her now somehow. We can. And if you won't, I will."

"Look, Anna. Estelle is a grown woman now. She's a psychologist. She's strong, resilient. I know. I work with her. Be careful. You might think through the damage you could do by bringing the old stuff up."

Nali rises to leave.

She must do it.

She has to talk to Estelle.

Merrill and Estelle sit at one of the tables in the craft area. The Scrabble games and crib boards have been put away. A faint smell of popcorn lingers in the air. Clients are leaving, some finding excuses not to go right away.

Even though it's a Thursday, it has been a good TGIF. The clients are sad that tomorrow is a day off, but they look at Estelle and realize that she needs it more than they need to come. Estelle, despite her rough start to the day, settled into her gracious, generous, and grateful self with the clients—as if the tumult of her life didn't exist. There were no triggers. With ease, she accepted their many condolences and then made the conversation not about her, but about them. She did well, but by the end of the day her look of emotional exhaustion eclipsed her gracious good will. The edginess came back.

Merrill looks at her. "I was really amazed at the way that you handled Jack."

Estelle pieces together, yet again, a bit of energy to engage. She speaks from her functional skills as a clinical psychologist—that simpler world she inhabits. "I guess I handled it the way we handled weapons and threats at the Street Level Clinic. I figured that at that moment, he needed to have the knife to feel safe, not to feel powerless. He wasn't threatening me with it, so I let him keep it."

"You made some comment about keeping this a safe place."

"Yes, but it needed to be a safe place for him first, as well as for everyone else. In his mind, the knife was keeping him safe. So, I let him keep the knife."

"But you got him away from others."

"Yes, when he knew that I would let him feel safe he could accept that others needed to feel safe too—and that they didn't feel safe when he was with them with a knife. So we went into the office. Right away, when he got there, he put the knife down."

"Wow."

"Merrill. You didn't have to immediately call the police. I'm glad that you met them at the door and headed them off so they didn't come barrelling in. If they had, it would've escalated him. There might be some times that we need their help. But this wasn't one of them."

"How do you know?"

"Do it long enough, have experiences like today, and you get to know."

A stack of TGIF papers litters their table. Everyone is required to complete the form before leaving. It has three questions: *1. What am I grateful for that happened this week? 2. What do I now understand better about myself and my interaction with the world around me?* and, *3. What is my intention of self-care for the coming weekend?* Clients only hand in the top two, tearing off the weekend intention to take home as a reminder. As Estelle and Merrill go over what has been written for the first two questions, they evaluate the progress of clients and the process of the program. Key words and phrases are coded to be entered into the qualitative analysis database they are keeping.

Once they have gone through all the client sheets, Merrill goes and gets two blank copies. He hands one to Estelle and begins to fill out his own. It's their end of the week ritual of debriefing and self-reflection.

Estelle sits silently as Merrill completes his. Waves of emotion pound in her ears again as both questions one and two trigger her. She can't do it, really can't do it. She gets up and goes into the office, takes up her purse, and retrieves her phone. Checking text messages, the look of chaos deepens on her face.

Merrill, having followed her in, asks, "Bad news?"

"Well, for starters, Aunt Leanne texted me that Jemma's father came by the house and picked Jemma up. It's not the weekend for her to go to his family, and it's only Thursday. Nikki is going to want to have family time tomorrow. So after work, I have to go over to his parents' place and wrestle her back."

Merrill nods. "Yeah, bad news. You don't need that after the week that you've had."

"Not at all unexpected. When he wasn't there last weekend for her visit with Gran-MomMom, I figured he'd been delayed in getting back to Calgary, and he'd try to pull it this weekend. He'll give in, argue first, but then give in. He always does."

"Do you have to go right away then?"

"No." Estelle pauses. "But look at this." She holds up her phone for him to read. There's a text message from April—*Broken into yesterday afternoon. Didn't notice until this morning. Feels freaky.*

"Are you going to call?"

Estelle places the voice call to April. She puts the phone to her ear.

"Hi, April. I just got your message. I've been away from my phone all day. What happened? . . . Are you okay? . . . How did you know? . . . Was anything taken? . . . No. That's good . . . Nate's stuff? Just Nate's stuff gone through? . . . Yeah, I'm sure . . . hard to tell . . . Are you sure it wasn't Harry moving things around? He's starting to pull himself up on things . . . The binders? . . . Yeah, I remember . . . on the table . . . moved? That's weird . . . I'm sure . . . Yes . . . Feeling violated . . . Yes, that's understandable . . . "

Estelle looks over at Merrill, exhaustion in her eyes. He smiles back grimly.

"No, I don't think you should call the police. If nothing was taken I don't think they would respond . . . Given GJ's past in dealing drugs, they'd probably think that it was one of the guys he sold to going through his stuff, looking for money, maybe he had tucked it away in the binder . . . or looking for pills . . . No . . . No . . ."

There's a long pause on Estelle's end. She listens through patiently.

"Okay, I can come over tonight. I have to go and pick up Jemma. Jemma and I will come . . . No, I don't think I can tomorrow. I'm sure Nikki needs a family day with me and Jemma and I'm going to take the day off. Nikki and I have to talk about what happened between her and Father at the funeral . . . Okay, will do . . . Bye."

Estelle looks at Merrill, tiredness in her eyes again. She's coming down off the simplicity of her work world in dealing with depressed, anxious, homicidal, and suicidal clients—facing the chaos of her own life again.

Then Pierre Bolton enters the agency.

"Dr. Caylie."

"How can I help you?"

"Perhaps better . . . How can I help you? Help you do the right thing."

"What *right thing* do you have in mind?"

He doesn't reply.

Estelle immediately catches the caginess of the man, is sure that he has an agenda.

As she leads Bolton toward her office, she turns to Merrill and says, loud enough for the visitor to hear, "It's okay, Merrill, you can go." Then, turned away from her visitor, she whispers a request for him to stay.

Once they have settled into Estelle's office, Pierre begins. "I'm concerned for your father. I believe you and he are close. As I share my concern, I'm certain it will become yours, too."

"So what is your concern?" Estelle is remembering him from the funeral, how he was with that guy that Nali knew.

"It's a professional matter. But one that you will understand from the business you have here."

"Yes . . ." Estelle immediately catches herself. *Yes* is the wrong thing to say to a man like this. Men like this turn *yes* into permission to continue. Then they take permission far too far.

"Let's not get too far ahead of ourselves here. First of all, tell me about this place, your program here."

"No, let's not." There's something clicking into place for Estelle—some knowing, some distrust. This man is too smooth.

"You haven't given me your name. If you belong to any organization, you haven't identified it. I suspect that you have a purpose in coming that you are cloaking with supposed concern for my father."

Pierre is looking at her. His opening gambit has been thwarted. "Alright then. My name is Pierre Bolton. I am working for a Consortium that has a goal of getting treatment in place for all with mental illnesses. We support scientifically proven treatments and recognize the barriers to comprehensive care for all who require it. I've researched your program. While you and the Consortium I represent are not on the same page, we share a similar goal. But your father . . ."

"I expect that when you say, 'scientifically proven treatment' you mean drugs."

Pierre shifts on his feet. "Treatment. Efficacious, cost-effective treatment—accessible and scalable."

"Drugs then."

"Your father presented a paper in Vancouver that my Consortium recognizes is flawed. We understand that he's aiming to have it published in a professional journal. If that happens, it will provide credibility to a position that we believe is fundamentally contrary to the—"

"—to the financial juggernaut the pharmaceutical companies hold on mental health research and treatment," Estelle reframes.

Pierre takes a step back, shifts his feet into a more threatening posture.

"We believe it would be better for your father if that paper was not published at this time. If it is, the Consortium will have no choice but to discredit it and discredit your father in the process. We've offered your father funding for a properly designed study that would provide an opportunity for replication of his findings, one that would—"

"—would have the potential of discrediting them as well."

"As it is with scientifically valid research protocols."

Pierre puts a bit of softness into his assertive posture. "We know that you and your father work closely together. Of course, you are family and would have the best interest of each other at heart. We believe that if anyone could convince him not to go ahead with the publication, you could. We're seeking your help in convincing him that this is not the time."

"And what if I believe that this is the time—that what he would publish is long overdue?"

"Well, that's not our view."

"I'm sure that it is not."

"Perhaps you might be interested in this."

Pierre holds a presentation folder in front of him—a funding proposal for ReClaiming Ourselves Inc. from the Consortium. Estelle grabs it and, without looking inside, walks it over to the paper shredder in the corner of her office. She extracts the pages from the cover and shreds them. Once done, she hands the clear plastic cover back to Mr. Bolton.

"Here, you can use this for the next bribe you endeavour to make."

"Well, then. Perhaps you might be interested in this."

Pierre Bolton extracts a photograph from his briefcase. It's of a weathered, wooden sign surrounded by thick rainforest vegetation. It reads *K'adsii Kabins.*

"I know what happened there." Pierre pauses. "*All* of what happened there."

The sick feeling erupts from Estelle's gut. It's the selfsame sick she felt that very morning when she walked into ReClaiming Ourselves Inc. and heard the meditation track that Merrill had selected, wind and waves breaking onto the shore. Her face comes alive with the rapid replay of emotions—disgust, fear, confusion, sadness, anger, and immobility.

"You might remember that place. And as you remember, you might realize that this father of yours, who you must dearly want to protect from the error of his ways has . . ." Pierre pauses for effect, " . . . many errant ways."

Estelle picks up the photograph. Her sweating hands crumble it as she places it in her pocket, hiding it away. She collapses into a chair, wishing that she could remember, remember all that had happened there. Then the rhythm of the emotion emerges again—sadness, dread, rage, disgust. Revulsion.

Pierre leaves—a sense of accomplishment on his face. Merrill rushes in.

CHAPTER THIRTEEN

Friday

Jackson stands on his balcony looking west. The grey peaks of the Rocky Mountains are visible in the distance.

He had purchased high enough in the condo building to ensure the view. Gone from most of the peaks is the white of winter and spring snow. Gone from the sky are the hues of salmon and gold that would have accompanied sunrise. Out on the balcony, there's an in-your-face breeze that plays at him. It's not enough to turn him around to go back inside. It's enough to make it uncomfortable being out there.

He has a coffee—his necessary coffee.

In the plan he concocted for the summer, he'd be now working on two of the chapters for the book he is writing—chapters entitled *Principles* and *Protocols*. Much of the writing of other chapters had been done for the Vancouver conference. What remains is the how-to that would enable other psychiatrists to engage his program, to not have to reinvent the wheel he had already perfected.

But GJ has done-in Jackson's plan for his return from the coast—cost him his focus, with the funeral and such.

The irrationality of that thought appeals to Jackson. He'd never let one of his patients get away with thinking like that. But Jackson isn't one of his own patients. He allows himself the luxury of blaming GJ for dying when, rationally, it wasn't GJ's choice to have done so.

Jackson hasn't slept well the previous nights. He eschews anti-anxiety medications and sleeping pills. Of course, he does. The craving for rye whisky is acknowledged and deflected. For much of the last two nights, he sat in his dark living room, listening to the haunting, dissonant symphonies of Mahler.

Jackson thinks back to the funeral. Clearly, his son had made it to AA. That is good. How he wishes he could've known and supported GJ there. They could've gone to meetings together. Maybe he could've been GJ's sponsor. If only GJ had reached out. As GJ straightened out his life, sobered up, it could've given Jackson a chance to be a father to him. GJ had said something about him in that letter, that letter read at the funeral. What was it? Jackson can't remember.

Regrettable. All of it. Regrettable.

A wave of grief passes over Jackson. He misses his son. Not the son as he had turned out to be—the son GJ could've been . . . had he not been such a screw-up . . . if only . . .

Then there is Anna. Precious Anna. Anna, who had been his refuge. At the funeral, he finally got to speak with her after all these years of disconnection. But it was so formal—and the way that she came into his office yesterday.

Jackson settles into a funk of remembrance. He knows it was wrong, what happened between them. He was her father, for God's sake. But at that time, at the time it seemed . . . she seemed . . . She shouldn't have threatened him with it. Not like she did yesterday—forcing him to talk in his office, threatening that she would announce their past to his patients in the waiting room if he didn't. And with Joan there, too. Has she no respect—for him as her father, for him as a professional man with a reputation to preserve?

She makes tawdry what had been beautiful between them in the innocence of her being his girl, his girl as she grew up.

It all circles back around.

Jackson goes back in. Chilled from the balcony breeze.

Again his mind goes back—something about Stella. But Stella is his success story. There's nothing wrong with Stella. Leanne had stepped in, had raised her better than drunk Izzy ever could. And he got to father Stella after he had sobered up—well, sort of, on Saturdays anyway, with trips to Chapters and Starbucks. He treasures those memories. She was such a reader.

Anna seems like a loose cannon. But why?

Jackson's mind cycles around again. Stella . . . Estelle now, strong and capable Estelle. He'd been frustrated with her choice of psychology rather than medicine, but at least she is helping others. *As I do. As my father did before me.*

Jackson refills his coffee, forces himself out of the family thoughts.

Principles. He already has several of them down. The protocols are all worked out now. He could do them in his sleep—do them so well, no one would even know he was sleeping.

And maybe when he is done the writing, he can get in a round of golf out at the club.

Pierre is disappointed with the view from his hotel room—a streetscape of downtown Calgary.

On the previous day, he found out there was a vacancy in Jackson's condo building. On a call to the listing agent, he feigned wanting to purchase there, arranged a tour. Pierre's personable conversation with the realtor led to finding out which unit in the building was Jackson's and then to view a suite similar to his, just a floor or two above. The vista of the distant mountains was outstanding.

Pierre sits at the breakfast table room service had created in front of his now uninspiring window. He had remade the bed he slept soundly in the night before. It is squared away. He had done so in a manner different than the maid service will do when they come in to clean his room—different so they'll know that it's been slept in and the sheets need to be changed. For him to focus on the work he'll do after breakfast, the room must be neat.

Pierre reflects on the successful days that he has had. He hadn't expected Estelle to cave in to convince her father on the previous afternoon. He hadn't expected his offer of program funding for her agency to work either—indeed, the neatly printed proposal was a ruse, blank pages she had conveniently shredded for him right there in his office. He had expected some version of the emotional collapse upon the triggering of childhood memories. It happened.

So now he knows she has them, the childhood memories that could lead to emotional behaviour. And maybe Jackson Horvath will stop his silliness and take care of his daughter if her emotional condition gets out of hand. Probably not. There are different ways this all might be brought to the end Pierre seeks.

He'll remain flexible, take what emerges. There are still some aces up his sleeve.

The discovery Pierre made in deceased Nate's pathetic quadraplex after the funeral was a genuine buried treasure. Imagine—those binders! Pierre feels delight in the product of GJ's addiction recovery process of writing down thoughts, feelings, and memories. It was a gift to him from beyond the grave. No shame in taking advantage of that. Thank you, Nate!

Then, early yesterday afternoon, he'd visited the gallery, the one identified on the business card Leanne handed him at the funeral. He was disappointed to find the exhibit of family portraits was not yet open to the public. Denny Armann indicated there had been a death in the family, so the opening is delayed. The gallery owner proudly showed the landscape of the Pacific Coast in the main gallery, there tantalizingly beside the entry into the back where the rest of the exhibit is hung. Immediately, Pierre spotted the hidden browed eyes and firm pressed lips. He smiled at its cleverness—a rare, spontaneous, honest smile.

But the treasure of his visit was the oil pastel portraits leaning against the wall. Denny explained that Caylie had just dropped them off earlier in the day. The pastels were stunning. Caylie had captured the demeaning, disgusted look of the young teen Anna—the look reserved for adults who got in her way. Caylie had captured the impatient and intrusive stare of the middle-school GJ—the look that both went through and then past whoever was looking at him. Then Caylie had captured the retreating, myopic look of Stella, hiding behind the book in her hands. A snapshot of family life a generation ago.

When Denny had attended to another customer, Pierre had taken photos of the portraits on his phone.

Now the massive computer database has childhood portrait images as well as Nate's narrative. He's getting to know this family, this family of secrets and pretense, knowing it more thoroughly than he could ever have hoped.

And once the computer work is done, well . . . there are a couple of important calls to make the day interesting. Pierre suspects Jackson will likely head out for a game of golf at his club. He could follow him there once his other work is done, perhaps get the tee time just behind him, haunt him through the entire round.

Nikki and Estelle sit across the breakfast table from each other. Estelle looks worn, like she has aged ten years in the last ten days. Nikki looks at her with worry, worry and love.

On the previous evening, once Estelle got home having retrieved Jemma from Gran-MomMom's house and Everett's self-satisfied grasp, Nikki was ready—ready with an apology for her behaviour at the funeral. Nikki had spent a couple of hours with Leanne and Gordon that afternoon, talking through what happened.

On the way over to the gallery so Nikki could see her portrait and sign her consent, Leanne had given her a fuller account of Estelle's childhood—the story of GJ and Jax. The fuller story didn't make her like her father-in-law any more, but it meant that she could better accept and understand her partner. During the day, Nikki also made some decisions—decisions about working in the north, how hard it is for her to be away. She made some calls.

So it is another day, an unexpected day off together. They sit in uncomfortable silence at the breakfast table—Nikki trying to figure out how to make it up to Estelle, Estelle barely upright. When Jemma awakes, they will go to Calaway Park.

"You didn't sleep, eh?" Nikki queried.

"Must've slept some because I kept waking up in a panic. Nightmares, I guess."

As they sit across from each other, the sun shines in their easterly facing window, lighting hands clasped together on the tabletop. Nikki had reached out to Estelle and is now holding on to her.

"My snoring?"

"No, you weren't. It was me, all this with GJ. With my father."

"I said I was sorry. I mean it, Estelle. I was right out of line. It was a difficult enough situation for you. I made it worse." Nikki pauses, inhales, is on the brink of telling Estelle her other plans, holds her breath as if she's getting ready to speak. Then, she lets it go without saying.

Estelle looks at her, as if expecting her to continue. Finally, Estelle says, "Okay, I accept that. We have dealt with it. Maybe you need to say sorry to my father. But between you and me—I'm good. There's other stuff."

"What?"

Estelle sits a long time, looking at Nikki, then going into a distant stare. When she comes back to eye contact, her face shows that something has passed. Blankly, she says, "Oh, just work stuff."

Jemma comes out of her bedroom, sleep in her eyes. She curls up on Nikki's lap. Nikki's hands slip from Estelle's and hold Jemma close. The three of them speak of Calaway Park, about cotton candy and the rides. Nikki asks that it just be them, not April and Harry, too. Estelle reassures that she has already sorted that out, asked Leanne to go over and support April on the day. It'll just be them three—Nikki, Jemma, and Estelle.

"Good afternoon . . . Mrs. . . . ?" Pierre Bolton stands at the front door of the modest bungalow.

"Fitzgerald, Jean Fitzgerald." The late middle-aged woman answering the door looks at him suspiciously.

"Mrs. Fitzgerald, forgive my intrusion. I'm actually here about Jemma, Jemma Caylie. I'd like to speak to her father."

A gentleman with a bulbous nose, florid complexion, and sparse reddish hair comes to stand in behind the woman at the door. "And you are who?"

"Pierre Bolton. I'm an investigator. I'm here concerning Jemma Caylie."

"Yes, our dear Jemma. Is there anything wrong?" A look of consternation comes to the grandmother's forehead.

"An investigator, you say. Who are you with? The police?" the man in behind asks.

Pierre reaches out his hand to him, a firm, confident handshake. "Pierre Bolton. Yes, I'm an investigator. I'm with an organization called *Safe and Secure Children Canada*. We look into situations where we suspect a child might be at risk." He makes good eye contact. Once his genuineness has won the confidence of the man, he reaches into the breast pocket of the blazer he is wearing and produces a business card. "And you are?"

"Jerry, Jerry Fitzgerald." Jerry looks at the official-looking card. "Are you with the provincial government, then?"

"No, actually not. But if in my investigation I find there is risk to a child, we at SSC will turn over our investigation to them."

A bulky, sleepy-looking man comes up behind the couple. "What's going on?" he asks.

"Everett, this is Mr. Bolton. He's here about Jemma."

"Jemma?" Everett asks, "Is she okay?" Jerry hands the business card over to his stepson.

"Can I come in?" The threesome retreats to a tired living room dominated by a large screen TV, a couple of recliner chairs, and an old sagging sofa. Pierre follows, pushing them forward by placing himself too closely to them. He sees a plastic clothes basket with a collection of dolls and books in the corner of the living room.

"Our dear sweet Jemma. She was just here yesterday but couldn't stay the weekend. We had her last weekend, though."

Pierre was well aware. He'd been watching the Caylie home on Durham Lane when a man drove up the previous afternoon, emerging a few minutes later with the child. Presuming the man to be the child's father, Pierre filled in a gap in the family constellation. Then, after he'd spoken to Estelle at her clinic, he'd followed her back here, to this same house where she had retrieved Jemma for herself.

Now it was time for a follow-up.

Everett is clearly anxious. "Please explain what this is about. The card says *Safe and Secure Children Canada*. Are you thinking that Jemma is not safe? Is this about us? We weren't supposed to have her this weekend but I'd been away and just got back. I wanted to see her."

"Oh, no. It's not that. Don't worry. Just some background checking, really."

"Do you want to see her bedroom?" Jean asks.

"No, no. I need to put your mind at rest. Her visits with you—that's all A-okay." Pierre smiles.

Jerry and Jean take their accustomed places in the living room, Jerry in one of the recliners facing the TV, Jean on the end of the sofa.

"Just a few questions—" Pierre begins.

Everett breaks in, anxiously, "This is about Nikki, Estelle's partner, right?" Everett asks.

"Do you have concerns there?" Pierre focuses on the younger man.

"Nikki doesn't like me. She creates trouble. Really, sir, I'm a loving father.

I don't do any harm. Whatever Nikki might say. Yesterday—that was an honest mistake."

"Oh, I need to reassure you. My visit isn't at all about that." Pierre pauses, makes a show of looking at his file, then looks up at Jean. "So Jemma regularly comes for overnight stays here?"

"Yes, twice a month. She comes on Friday nights and Estelle picks her up on Sundays before supper."

"And could you describe what your granddaughter is like during those visits?"

"She's a happy, well-adjusted child. She's never a bother, although it's hard to keep up with her."

"Any sign of emotional distress? Crying? Temper tantrums? Tummy-aches?"

"No. No. I don't think so. She's a very easy child. Active. If we're in the house, she plays with her dolls and reads. She likes the cat next door, goes over there."

"And next door, do you know those people? Are they safe? Jemma is a cute six-year-old girl."

"Oh, the MacMillans. They're fine people, just fine. He's a retired fireman. We've known them for years."

"And they wouldn't pose any risk to your granddaughter?"

"Certainly not."

"We are tracing the various adults who would've had contact with Jemma. Are there any others when she's visiting with you?"

"No. When she comes, she's our focus. We always watch out for her." Jean is looking very concerned.

"And you, Everett. Are there other adults she's exposed to when you are with her?"

"You're freaking me out, man. What are you suspecting here?"

"Just checking." Pierre is content with the anxiety that he's creating, given the reactions the family are showing. He lets the tension reverberate. "Okay, then. Just a few more questions. What about modesty, is she independent in the bathroom?"

"Oh, yes. She's quite a private and capable girl, with her . . ." Jean hesitates. "With her bathing and all."

"Nightmares?"

"No."

"Unnatural interests?" Pierre looks up, hoping the insinuation is catching.

"No, certainly not."

"All good. I really am relieved. You've been very helpful."

Pierre closes the file folder, prepares to leave. Everett gets up with him.

"Thank you, Mr. and Mrs. Fitzgerald." He shakes their hands, softens his eyes to portray warmth and gratitude. "Everett, would you mind accompanying me to my car? There are a few more questions I would like to ask."

"Sure."

Everett goes to the back of the house, retrieves his cowboy boots, and puts them on at the front door where Pierre Bolton stands. The two leave and end up standing on the sidewalk beside the black Malibu.

"You're freaking me out in there. The questions you were asking. I know what you are getting at. If anyone were ever to touch my daughter—"

"This is quite a sensitive matter. Thanks for talking to me, just us. I don't want to alarm your parents. We're tracing the network of connections, just trying to rule out any other possibilities here before we go ahead."

"Other possibilities? Look, sir, I'm really getting freaked."

"Who else has contact with your daughter?"

"I really don't know. I work out of town, down in a feedlot near Pincher Creek. I don't get to see her very often. Most of her visits are just with my parents. They're good people. They'd never let anyone harm her."

"Yes, I'm sure, but others?"

"You'd have to ask Estelle. Estelle has her most of the time."

"If I can be frank, well . . . I appreciate your cooperation." Pierre lowers his voice, feigning confidentiality. "Before we talk with Estelle . . . we want to make sure . . . before going down that road."

"What road?"

"Well, can you tell me about the grandfather?"

"Gordon?"

"No, not Gordon . . . Gordon is?"

"Leanne's partner. Leanne isn't really a grandmother. She's an aunt. But she raised Estelle. Gordon is her partner. I've only met him a couple of times.

Seems like a decent chap. We got off on the wrong foot, but now I'm getting to know him. Seems okay. A musician, I believe."

"Yes. No, it's not Gordon I'm concerned about."

"Estelle's father, Dr. Horvath then?"

"What do you know about Dr. Horvath? About his relationship with Jemma?"

"Well, he doesn't like me. I think if he could, he'd make sure I never get to see my daughter. It all started when Jemma was born. Really rude. I went all the way down there, down to the States, and he kept me out of the room. I couldn't even see my own daughter on the day she was born."

"Wow. I'm so sorry." Pierre adopts a soft, caring look. Everett's eyes are showing rage.

"Yeah, he got me kicked out of the hospital and all. I had to fight in court to get access. I think he was behind all the expensive lawyers that Estelle got. It would've broken my mom's heart if Jemma couldn't be in our lives."

"So, you and Dr. Horvath . . . you don't get along?"

"I hate the man."

"Look, Everett. Have you ever suspected—hmm, how would I say it?—unnatural interests that the grandfather might have toward the child?"

"Are you asking if he is . . . ?"

"A pedophile? Oh, I really mustn't say. Just wondering if you ever saw any reason to believe that your daughter, Jemma, might be at risk?"

Everett slams his fist down hard on the hood of Pierre Bolton's rental car. With an explosion of anger, he takes his boots to the front fender of the car and then kicks hard at the side mirror. Pierre cringes at the thought of the damage he'll be charged for.

There's an awkward silence. Pierre realizes he has to be careful here. He has lit the fire in Everett. Now it's a matter of how much fuel it needs. The reading of GJ's journal from rehab had disclosed the sexual relationship between Anna and her father. Should he be that forthcoming? How much does he need to insinuate? How direct does he need to be?

Without much help, Everett seems to be drawing his own conclusions.

"I really have said too much. Thanks for your discretion in all this. If anything else comes to mind, you can reach me at this number." He hands Everett another of his cards.

Pierre pulls away from the curb. He has one more job to do today. He's sure that Jimmy will be interested in what he found out from GJ's recovery journals.

And then the golf course, traipsing around behind Jackson Horvath. Pierre just loves his work.

CHAPTER FOURTEEN

Saturday

Estelle wakes midmorning with a migraine. Vaguely, she remembers through the haze of pain and distorted vision that she'd been awake earlier, had talked with Nikki. About what, she can't recall.

Barely coordinated, she takes her migraine medication—at least that's proof that she knows what's going on. She goes to the bathroom and looks in the mirror, only to see a woman much older than herself looking back.

Sitting on the bed, she pressures reflexology points on both of her big toes, between them and their seconds. She does the same on each of her hands. Relief comes, not an erasure of the pain, but a transient relaxing of it—a way of surviving until the medication kicks in. She's running the protocol, doing what she knows will help, getting it under control.

When the pain has sufficiently subsided, she realizes she's had the aura off and on for days. She had been too distracted by the events of those days to take the medication that may have prevented the headache from developing. She could've done, she should've done, she was not present enough in her body to have done. Now she remembers the sudden change in the weather that had happened at GJ's funeral, the downpour that had been the universe crying over his death. She never made the connection, the connection that it could've triggered the migraine process on the surface of her brain.

Estelle just got through the week, did not give a thought to taking care of herself. She had to push through, couldn't stop. Even the day at Calaway Park was a pushing through, something she had to do with Nikki to satisfy

Nikki's need to have a fun family day. Now she remembers the orbs of her aura—glittering, glimmering spheres dancing and blocking her vision while Nikki and Jemma had enjoyed the midway rides. She just didn't connect, connect with the presence of her aura enough to take her meds. Her mind was somewhere else.

But now, the pain is easing, some chemical miracle coursing through her veins.

Estelle stumbles out to the kitchen, finds a note on the table.

Gone shopping for a new outfit. Got Jemma with me. You are in no condition to take care of her. Called into Lammle's to take a midday shift. Stampede busy this weekend. Will drop Jemma off at Auntie's. See you later.

Estelle reads again. *Gone shopping for a new outfit.* Where the hell does that come from?

Then it dawns on Estelle that she is alone. Aside from occasionally in the car while driving, she hasn't been alone for days on end. There was always someone to take care of, something to make turn out all right. Something fucked up. In the middle of all that fuck-up, all she could do was follow her mind away as it left, leaving her body behind. Now, pain easing, she's alone and it feels glorious, sublime even.

Estelle begins to think who she should call. Dodi would be safe now. She could tell Dodi . . . No, Dodi has that family wedding today, she shouldn't bother her.

Maybe April, is April okay? Then her mind goes to Father, from Father to Bolton, and the mess creeps back in.

Within minutes, Estelle has the confidence to stand in the shower. Suddenly her body has something different to focus on, to pleasure in. The meds must be fully clicked in.

She checks her phone. A message is there from Dodi. *I'm off to the wedding now. I'm working on getting flights for tomorrow. Hang in there, love.* Estelle texts back *Great!* sees it was delivered but not immediately read. She wonders how she will deal with Dodi and Nikki together.

She texts April and finds out that Nali has just arrived at her place on the bus. Okay then.

Nikki has left her without the car. Nice. She could call over to Leanne. Gordon would come for her. No, it's too good a day not to walk. Estelle feels the vibrant refreshment of the headache being gone. On the twenty blocks or so, she revels in how well her limbs move, how her arms swing even.

She doesn't even watch for Bolton.

When she goes in, it's pennywhistles and pan flutes. Gordon's eyes dance with Jemma's, and neither of them acknowledges her. Estelle climbs the stairs and finds Leanne in her studio.

"So, we don't have to worry about Dodi's consent. I got a text from her that she's coming up tomorrow."

"That's good news," Leanne replies. "I think you need her here. You haven't been doing well. How did that all happen?"

"I FaceTimed her through the week, told her about GJ. She just texted back that she's going to come to be with me."

Leanne goes over to the Stella-Estelle painting sitting on the easel. "Can you carry the easel? I'm taking this downstairs."

"Wait a minute. Let me look again."

Estelle takes in the look of her own eyes, eyes hooded by a furrowed brow, eyes peering out above the hardcover children's book that bears her image as a naïve, hidden little girl. And she is swimming again, being pulled under by her own mind.

Leanne watches as Estelle's jaw clenches, her eyes dart, her brow collapses into her eye sockets. Then her face goes still, as if a storm has passed.

"What just happened?" Leanne asks.

Estelle looks at her aunt, disoriented, with a *how did I get here* sort of look.

"You left me, just a minute ago. I could see it in your face that you were gone some other place, some scary other place."

Estelle struggles to come back. After a deep breath, she says, "I've had a migraine today, must've just come over me again."

CHAPTER FIFTEEN

Sunday

"Leanne, it's Jax. How about brunch? The club puts on a good spread. I could pick you up in fifteen minutes."

Holding the phone, Leanne sighs. "Gordon is sleeping. He had a gig last night, didn't get home until about three."

"Well, just you then. Brother and sister."

"Thanks, Jax. But I'm working on stuff here."

"Can I come over then?"

"I can make coffee . . . I guess . . ." Leanne checks the cupboard to see if they have enough Keurig pods.

"Coffee will be great. I'll stop by Edelweiss Bakery and pick something up. Oh, it's Sunday. They'll be closed. I'll go through a Tim's. Bagels okay?"

"Really, Jax. I'd rather not."

"I insist. Bagels it is. Half an hour?"

They sit in the screened-in veranda at the back of the home. The Stella-Estelle rests on the easel off to the side.

"Look at that," Jackson exclaims. "Wow, you've really captured Estelle's eyes there."

"Speaking of Estelle. I'm really worried about her. This last week or so has been really rough on her. She was over yesterday, went all space cadet on me for a few minutes."

"I haven't noticed. I think she is still going in to work. She's a strong woman—skilled, capable."

"She has really stepped up for April and Harry, has thrown herself into helping them, but she looks exhausted."

"And that is good, that helping out. That's her character coming through. I think she is more like me than like Izzy. The way she helps others."

Leanne stares back at him.

Jackson turns back to Stella-Estelle on the easel. "The painting, I'd like to have it."

"I've debated in my mind selling it. Maybe give the proceeds to April. Denny wanted me to take it in to the gallery. He wants all the family work that I've done. But this one is really personal for me."

"What about keeping it in the family? I'll buy it, put it up in the condo or in the office; we could hang it there on the opposite wall from the landscape that you painted, like she looked up from her book and saw the beautiful West Coast landscape."

Leanne just stares at him.

"Really, how much would that size canvas sell for?"

"That size is going for $4300, but the gallery gets sixty percent."

"Sold." Jackson smiles. "Let's see. Forty percent of $4300, that would come to about $1700. I'll give you $2000."

Leanne looks at her brother—the one who buys family, always has. "I guess."

"What? You think me cheap? The full $4300 then. Are you going to charge me GST?"

"Jax, it's not that."

"What is it?"

They settle into awkward silence.

"Jax, this week you lost a son. And I . . . a nephew . . . but he was a son to me too, I adopted him, raising him after his mother died."

"Yeah, it's been hitting me. He was so gone from our lives, so gone for so many years."

"Why is that, Jax? You're the psychiatrist."

"Lots of reasons, I guess. His own choices, mainly. Drugs, petty crime."

"But why those?"

"He was very close to his mom. I could never get close to him. She never let me. I had Anna, Izzy had GJ. Then Izzy died and I guess nobody had him."

"You were drinking."

"She was the drunk, really Leanne. She was the drunk. I just . . ."

"Just what?"

Jackson pauses. A brief wave of regret crosses his face. Leanne decodes the expression and looks at him impatiently.

"I was going to say *I just kept up*, but that isn't right. I went at it heavy too, for my own reasons. I realized that after she died and I got treatment. I acknowledge I'm an alcoholic. Thank the Higher Power, sober now seventeen years."

"Jax, that's not right, not the way it happened. You didn't suddenly recognize your drinking and go for treatment. I forced you to. Don't you remember? With what was happening between you and the kids, the way you treated GJ after Izzy died, I felt I had to. You were brutal to him. And all the while, you and Anna had this cozy little relationship. I threatened to call Child Welfare Services on you. You were drinking really heavy. I forced you to go and get treatment. Don't change the story."

"A lot went on back then."

"Right."

Leanne notices a slight vibration of fine muscles around his mouth, around his eyes. She wonders if this arrogant brother of hers, this brother with his inherited sense of entitlement, might yet be able to come to terms with himself. She holds her silence.

Jackson sighs. "And now two of them are gone. Izzy and GJ."

"There's still Estelle. Estelle and Nikki and Jemma. And Nali, too. You and I are connecting." Leanne looks at him. "There's plenty of family here yet."

Jackson reaches over to the table, takes half a bagel, and spreads the cream cheese from the little plastic container that came from Tim's. "Estelle and I work together. We've a good relationship professionally. I regularly get together with her for lunch, once a week or so now, still do, did even when she was back working at the Street Level Clinic."

Jackson's voice dips a bit as he goes on. "I could do more with Jemma, I guess. Nikki, well, since the funeral . . . I don't think Nikki and I . . ." The slight softening that had appeared on Jackson's face hardens.

"What about Nali? Nali is back in our lives now."

"You mean, Anna? She'll always be Anna to me. Perhaps I could rekindle that relationship. I guess that one is complicated, too."

Leanne looks at him, puzzled. He takes his time to chew the tough bagel.

"No, I think it should start with Jemma. Jemma, she's an age where a grandpa will be good for her. Do you remember when I came back from treatment? I would come over here and take Stella. She and I . . ." Jackson smiles. "What was it? The Starbucks at Chapters, that's what it was, the one down on seventh avenue. We would read together."

"I remember."

"Jemma is the same age, roughly the same age as Stella was back then."

"Jemma is a different girl. Stella was so into the books. That's all there was to her. Jemma, she has her books, but she's more active, and musical, too."

"And I am older!" Jackson manages a quick smile, as if he has been the butt of his own self-deprecating humour.

Leanne stares back at him blankly.

"Jax. Be careful. Jemma . . ." Leanne pulls herself up, sits forward in the padded patio chair. "Jax. I'm not sure how to say this, and I don't want you to be offended. I don't think you are a good influence. I know you are a psychiatrist and all. And I'm just a portrait painter. Who am I to judge, right? But you took Anna to yourself when she was a child. And look where she ended up."

Jackson looks startled that someone would dare speak to him that way.

"I am in recovery. I go to meetings. And as a psychiatrist, I know about what children need, need to grow into emotionally stable adults."

"Do you?"

The silence hangs awkwardly.

Leanne's phone buzzes on the glass-topped table between them. They both look at it.

Neither says a word.

The phone buzzes again.

"I'm going to make another coffee." Leanne gets up to leave, taking her phone with her.

As the Keurig heats ten ounces of water, Leanne looks at her phone. There's a text message from Estelle—*Can Dodi stay at your place? She just texted me.*

She's on her way to Calgary now, today! I will explain later. Thanks, Auntie. You're the best.

And then the next message. This one a group text, destined for both her and Dodi—*Hi Dodi. I'm glad that you're coming. I'm falling apart. Have been since GJ died. I need you here. I'll pick you up at the airport. I hope you don't mind but I'm going to have you stay over at Aunt Leanne's. It's awkward here. Nikki and I aren't doing well, and with Jemma, I don't want you staying at my place. It would confuse Jemma and Nikki would be furious.*

Another text message comes through—*What time does your flight come in?*

As Leanne takes one coffee pod from the Keurig and starts another, she looks out through the window onto the veranda. Jackson is standing, looking out at the backyard.

On the phone, there are the pulsing three dots. Another text is being written. Leanne waits for it. When it comes, it's from Dodi, sent to her and Estelle—*I'm in Minneapolis on standby. There's a flight at 2:30 to get into Calgary around six. I told the ticket agent it's urgent, a family emergency. They're bumping someone for me for an extra $200.*

Leanne sighs. She feels like a mom. There's Estelle's old room to air out. She'll need to wash the sheets.

Another group text—*I'll be glad to see Aunt Leanne again. When do I get to see Jemma?*

And another, just to her, from Estelle—*Can I drop Jemma over later? She and I will take Nikki to the Red Arrow to get her bus back north at noon. I think I should go back over to April's place.*

Leanne wonders if the sense of entitlement has made it down to yet another generation.

She looks up to see her brother leave through the side gate.

Estelle has held it together. She's in the car driving from Auntie's where she has dropped Jemma off. Nikki had been dropped off, too, at the Red Arrow bus depot. Like always, there'd been the Jemma crying jag as she waved one of her mommas goodbye.

Estelle and Nikki had a good morning. Jemma had slept in. This had given

Estelle and Nikki time together. Their relationship seems leaky—needing one patch after another. Being in the business, Estelle wonders if all relationships are this way. She sees it often at work; almost all clients struggling with depression and anxiety struggle with their partners, too.

Estelle realizes that being married to a psychologist is tough for Nikki—all this about processing your feelings. Nikki just has them—they're not to be discussed, just blurted out. You have your feelings. You act on them. But Estelle knows feelings are to be processed through by talking, that's what her profession tells her. Nikki—action-oriented, playful, protective Nikki—is bewildered by the process that talking is somehow supposed to change them or make them go away. Estelle recognizes the bewilderment, is always frustrated with it.

But with mornings like this morning, with Nikki satisfied with the last couple of days south, it seems alright. And Nikki seems somehow different, like something is settling inside of her, some secret sort of something that Estelle can't put her finger on.

Still, waves of anger and revulsion threaten to wash over Estelle, wash over her from who knows where. She takes a deep breath. With Nikki there, despite all that Nikki is, Estelle feels that she will be protected. Now Nikki has left to go north.

These spells of emotion trying to take her away—whatever they are, they are not about Nikki, or are they?

No, it's something about GJ being gone. Something.

Estelle feels another one coming on. She feels panicky behind the wheel of the car. She jerks herself out of it, grounds herself in a more present reality. *I'm going over to see April and Harry. I feel good there, like I have another sister, and another kid.*

Estelle's breathing settles.

And Dodi is coming! A smile plays at the corner of Estelle's mouth. Dodi's timing is perfect. Nikki is to be north for two weeks.

Estelle jerks herself back from her self-indulgence, brings to mind the playfulness of Nikki and Jemma at the rides Friday. Like two kids, really. Not one. Nikki can be playful, brings playfulness to their daughter. Jemma needs that. *I need it, too.*

Estelle settles into the traffic flow—it's not too bad heading over to the north side.

I have much to be thankful for. I must write that on the TGIF forms next week!

But the bubble bursts. There's another thought about Dodi—Dodi and Nikki together. The dread comes back inside. As much as Jemma needs Nikki, and Estelle needs Dodi—but Dodi and Nikki? Well, that doesn't mix. Nikki knows about Dodi, but it's about Dodi in the past. She doesn't know about Dodi in the present—the FaceTime calls that Estelle makes with her from work, the sense of confidence, the depth of sisterhood, the depth of love. All this she has with Dodi, has even yet.

Nikki is sure to be jealous. Sure to be furious.

This morning when the text messages came in while she and Jemma and Nikki were watching cartoons, she didn't tell Nikki that it was Dodi. When Nikki asked, Estelle lied. *Just a work thing,* she said.

But she can't ask Jemma to keep a secret. Dodi wants to see Jemma. Nikki will know from Jemma that Dodi is here.

A rude Calgary driver captures Estelle's attention, honking from behind. Despite the *Baby on board* sticker that Estelle has left in the back window, the asshole is tailgating her. He weaves into the lane beside her, accelerates with a roar of power, gives her the finger as he passes. Then he pulls back in front of her, slows right down and waggles his middle finger at her as she looks at him through his back window. She brakes to create more space and checks her rear-view mirror to make sure no one is right behind. *It is a Sunday afternoon, for God's sake.* Then the tears flow.

Dodi. I need you. Hurry that plane along.

"Did you bring Jemma?" April asks.

"I dropped her off at Aunt Leanne's. We just took Nikki to get the Red Arrow."

"Harry is down for his nap. It's just us . . . sister."

"I went to Chopped Leaf, got us lunch. Hope you like this sort of stuff. I got two different ones. You can have your pick. This one has prawns and rice, and this one just salad with chicken."

"Thanks." April wipes the table and they sit.

"How are you doing?"

April is separating off some of the chicken with some of the vegetables for Harry when he gets up. "Oh, okay. You and Nate, you are alike."

"Are we?"

"Kind. After he went to rehab, and I know it was only a few months, but he put every bit of energy he had into Harry and me."

Estelle looks at her.

"Even before, when I first met him . . . like I knew he was dealing and using drugs . . . but when he was with me, he turned it off and made me his focus. It was different than other guys, guys who treat you as a princess until they have you, then they treat you like shit. Nate wasn't like that."

"I'm glad to hear. It's awful that he's gone."

"It is." April pulls over one of the binders, the one from rehab. She opens it to the front page, the Serenity Prayer. "With him gone, it's my turn, my turn to be a healthy me. I read the stuff they gave him at rehab. What he wrote, too. It keeps him alive for me, sort of."

April cries. Estelle reaches a hand across the table to hold April's forearm. After a few minutes April takes one of the napkins that have come with the lunch order, dabs her eyes, and noisily blows her nose.

"When Harry gets up, shall we go out? Get in groceries."

"Oh, we are pretty good, pretty good with what you got us last week."

Estelle gets up, asks, "Can I look?"

"Go ahead."

After checking Estelle sits down at the table, opens the notepad app on her phone and begins to make a list.

"There's something in there for you, in the binder, you know."

"For me?"

"Yeah. Nate wrote you a letter . . . well, it was GJ who wrote it, back when he was still in rehab. He was going to give it to you. When he went to meet you at Starbucks he was checking you out, checking out whether he should give it to you."

"Oh?"

"Let me find it." April takes the binder, looks at a series of tabs on coloured dividers. She pulls on one. Estelle sees the label *Letters of Amends*. April orients the binder back over to sit in front of Estelle for her to read.

A knock comes on the door.

"April Needham?"

"Yes."

"I'm Detective Lars Jonsson, with the Calgary City Police. Can I come in?"

April opens the door wider, Estelle just a step behind her.

"Sorry for your loss, ma'am. I have a few questions for you. Some information has come in regarding the death of your husband." There is no warmth to his eyes. He appears as though he just has a job to do.

Jonsson turns to Estelle. "You are?"

"I'm Estelle Caylie. GJ is my . . . was my brother."

"Glad to meet you, ma'am. You might be able to help with this, too."

The detective looks around the room. There are only two chairs and a sofa that looks too soft to sit on. He chooses to stand, takes out a notebook.

"Do either of you know a James Anton Murphy?"

April looks at him. "No."

"And you?" The officer turns to Estelle.

Estelle pauses. "Maybe, I'm not sure . . ."

The detective stares at her as her words fade off.

Estelle is caught in a mind that can't organize itself. After a few awkward moments with a disengaged gaze, she blinks her return. "I was wondering if there had been any security cameras around the Starbucks, that maybe you could've identified the driver."

The detective looks perplexed by Estelle's non sequitur. He sighs. "No. There was one image, but the guy fleeing the scene was wearing a hoodie so we couldn't see his face. Anyway, from his height and build, we knew it wasn't owner of the vehicle, once we had tracked down the residence of the registered owner. It had been stolen that morning and abandoned after it crashed. But getting back to . . . this James guy . . . A first name and description came in on a tip. Basically, just a conversation overheard in a pub, someone bragging about driving the car into the Starbucks. We traced back through Gerald's criminal records and found that he had informed on a James Anton Murphy. But that was years ago."

Detective Larsen turns to April. "Do you know if there has been any recent contact?"

"Nate didn't ever mention it. He was very careful not to have anything to do with the people from his life before he went to rehab. Back when I first got to know GJ . . . like he was really good to me, but he often seemed scared. It was like he was afraid that some of the people he was dealing with were threatening him. He never would talk about it, though. He never mentioned names to me. If he did, it was so long ago I don't think I would remember."

April pauses, a look of a sudden memory comes over her face. "By the way, I think someone else was in here, going through Nate's stuff. It happened after the funeral on Wednesday."

"Anything taken?"

"Not that I could tell."

"You didn't report it?"

"No."

The detective makes a note in his book

A look of confusion washes over Estelle. The wave of tumult threatens to crash her inside again. Noticing her swaying on her feet, the detective looks up at her, sees her face go pale.

Estelle is caught in successive waves of confusion. They take her feet out from under her. She sits heavily in the chair at the table. *It's there somewhere. Somewhere she heard the name James Anton Murphy. Where? Nali . . . her father . . . the funeral . . . what was it?*

Finally, the detective grows impatient. He pulls two business cards from a case in his shirt pocket. "If either of you remembers anything . . ." He looks over at April. "If you find anything like an old notebook with names and numbers, or an old phone."

April puts his card down on the table by the binders, next to the one Pierre Bolton left there a few days ago.

The detective turns to leave. Estelle suddenly collects herself and rushes out the door after him.

"Sir—" there is urgency in Estelle's voice.

"Yes?"

"I'm a psychologist." Estelle thinks this should impress him, give herself more credibility.

"So?" There is sarcasm in his voice.

Estelle offers the detective the Pierre Bolton card that was sitting on the table. "I want you to have this. This guy has been hanging around. He showed up at my office the other day, putting pressure on me about my father. And he came to see April, saying he was a family friend when he is not."

Detective Jonsson takes the card, looks at the number there. "Thanks. Call if anything else comes to mind."

When Estelle goes back in, April is tending to a crying Harry. He'd been awakened by the sound of the door but didn't awaken calmly. Estelle gives a quick hug to April as April rocks the little one. Picking up GJ's binder, the one that April had offered to her, she whispers—*Can I take this?*

April nods, opening her top so Harry can nurse.

Estelle pulls over into Confederation Park. She finds a place for the car in the shade under some large trees. The smell of barbecue drifts into the open window. She takes the binder, goes to the *Letters of Amends* section, and reads.

Dear Stella.

I don't know when I will ever get this letter to you but I hope I do soon. I don't know how. But I will figure out a way.

I hope you will read this letter and understand.

I am so sorry.

I'm supposed to tell you what I'm sorry about, be specific. I will do that. But first I want you to know that I will never hurt you again. I can't say "I promise" because I can't promise, and people sometimes break their promises. All I can say, is that I don't ever want to hurt you, ever again. If this letter hurts you, I hope you'll get help with the hurt. I have lots of hurts and I'm getting help.

I'm writing to you from Rehab. I've been clean and sober now for 75 days. My mind still gets fuzzed but more and more I am clear.

I'm working on my Step 8 and 9. If you don't know what that is, you can look it up. I am trying to make amends to everyone that I harmed when I was drinking and using drugs. I'm taking this really seriously.

But you didn't know me when I was drinking and using drugs, at least not very long, maybe a little before I left Auntie Leanne's house. What I need to write about is different. Me and my counsellor have talked a lot about this. We're not sure this is a good idea but she said for me to go ahead and write the letter anyway. I'm going to try to meet you when I get out of rehab. I can decide when I meet you whether it would harm you to give it to you.

This is awful. I am so sorry. I feel so ashamed. I'm not writing this so I will feel better but because I think you should know. It's about what I did to you.

I'm not sure if you will remember. I hope you do and hope you don't. When we were kids I was really mean to you. Even though Auntie Leanne did her best to stop me, I was mean all the time. I made fun of you and hurt you by poking you and punching you when no one else was looking. I called you names. I made fun of you. You didn't deserve that. You were always smarter than me but I did everything I could to make you feel stupid.

I'm learning not to blame others for my behaviour. I am trying. But you'll know that things were not good in our family when we grew up, Mom being dead and all. I am not blaming that. It was me who did what I did. I think that the things that were wrong for me in my childhood were probably wrong for you too. But what I did, that was wrong by me. I think it hurt you growing up and you were just a little kid, my kid sister, and I shouldn't have hurt you that way.

And then there is the other thing.

I don't know how to write this. So I just will. When I was about 11, 12 maybe, when we were out at the cabin on the coast. I am so sorry Stella . . .

Estelle tears up. The sound of ocean waves and chimney roar drowns out whatever thoughts could be in her mind. She feels sick. The words on the page go to a blur, a blur that spins on itself. Estelle knows that there's more there, but she can't read it. Her mind won't let her read it. She is hyperventilating, her hands trembling as she holds the letter.

Estelle has no idea how long she sits. When she comes out of it—whatever it was, wherever her mind went—the letter is damp, the damp of tears and sweat. She clears her eyes so they can focus again, but the remaining part of the letter still blurs, illegible. She looks to the bottom of the letter, the place where it's signed.

Little Stella. I love you. I am learning to love. Maybe we can be brother and sister again, in the right way.

Love GJ.

After a listless, lifeless few moments she slams the car into reverse and backs aggressively out of the parking place. She squeals tires as she rushes out of the Confederation Park parking lot, oblivious to the potential of children there.

She has to see Nali. She has to see Nali *now*.

"Auntie Leanne, I'm hungry." Jemma stands at the door to the second-floor studio.

Leanne looks up from the drafting table. She's been working hard at solving the puzzle of composition for her next painting. It's of a gardener, the owner of the Paradise Garden and Patio Centre, Mr. Olgivie. He festooned himself in his Scottish ancestry with tweeds and wools, a tam on his head. The photoshoot had him in his garden, a pitchfork in his hand. Leanne posed him stooped down to the earth, the pitchfork stuck into the soil at an angle. The composition was to have the handle deflect the brim of his tam slightly, at a jaunty angle. She'd got lost in the work.

"Oh my goodness, child. What time is it?"

Jemma shrugs. Leanne looks at her watch—it's going on for seven.

"Didn't Gordon get supper on?"

"He's practising."

"Okay then. Sorry little one, let's go."

They head down to the kitchen. Leanne dips into the freezer drawer at the bottom of the oversized refrigerator. "You like cheese pizza, right? And we have a pepperoni for Gordon." She goes about reading the instructions.

"When's Momma-Stelle coming back?"

"Glory! Now that's a good question. I'd expected her long before this. She was going over to April's. Had she said anything else to you? Shopping? Going into work?"

"Don't think so."

"Okay, let's get the oven on." Leanne goes about extracting the pizzas from their cardboard and plastic. "Gord, get in here. Help us get dinner on." She stoops down to little Jemma and gives her a hug. Her grandniece has been a bit out of sorts today.

"What's up?" Gordon asks.

"It's late. We need to get some supper into this poor little girl. Have you heard from Estelle?"

"No. I've been practising. We want to lay down some of the background tracks this week in the studio."

"Can you call her, please?" Leanne looks over to Gordon.

"Where's my phone?"

"Oh, I'll do it. You put the pizzas in."

When Leanne picks up her phone upstairs, she sees a series of text messages have come in from Dodi—*Aunt Leanne, do you know where Estelle is? She said she would meet me. I've been texting her but she's not replying. I'm through Customs but I can't see her.*

And then another—*She still isn't here. Should I just get a taxi over to your place? What's your address?*

Finally—*This isn't like Estelle. Should I be worried? Did she say anything to you? Is it okay that I've come?*

Quickly, Leanne touches the screen to call back the number.

"Dodi, Leanne here. Has she shown up yet?... I have no idea. I haven't seen her since just after lunch when she dropped Jemma over here... No, it's not like her, she is very responsible... I can try... I probably have more numbers I can call than you do... Yeah, just Estelle's... You were smart to notice that she'd included me on the group text this morning. I'm glad you texted... "

Holding the phone between her ear and shoulder, Leanne wiggles out of her artist's smock.

"Taxis are expensive. I'll come for you. It'll be about half an hour. Is there someplace you can wait?... Of course... Yeah, you're going to come back to stay here anyway... Dodi, I'm sure there's an explanation, but let's get you back here now... Sorry... Goodbye."

Leanne rushes down to the kitchen. "Get the pizza out of the oven. We have to go to the airport."

"What?" Gordon asks.

"I got a call from Dodi. Estelle was to pick her up at the airport. Didn't show up."

"Auntie, where's Momma-Stelle?"

"I'm not sure, honey. Look, Momma-Stelle's friend, Dodi, is at the airport. We need to go and pick her up."

Gordon takes the pizzas out of the oven.

"Let's see. You're here to stay with Jemma while I run out to the airport. No, let's drop you and Jemma off at Estelle's condo. I have a copy of her key card to get in the front. It's going to be a long night for Jemma by the time I go out to the airport and get back here."

"I'm hungry." Jemma is tearing up. "I want Momma-Stelle to come for me."

Gordon leans down and gives her a hug. "It's okay, Jemma-girl. I can take you home and put you to bed."

"But I haven't had supper yet."

Leanne is sliding the pizzas back in their boxes. They are not too hot yet.

"Let's have you warm these up in Estelle's oven, back in the condo. You and Jemma can eat there, and she can go to bed. I'll go and get Dodi. Can you check your phone in case Estelle tried calling you?"

Gordon leaves, shuts down the amps and mixing board, comes back with Jemma's jacket.

"Have you heard from Estelle yet?" Leanne has pulled into the airport arrivals area, popped the trunk, and is climbing out of the car.

"No." Dodi initiates a hug.

"I'm baffled. I've never known Estelle to . . . but then . . . she has been spacing out a lot lately. Her emotions have been all over the place. I've never seen her so . . ."

"I must've sent her a dozen texts, and she hasn't answered any of them. That's not like Estelle."

"The last few days have been really rough. Her brother, GJ, died."

"Yeah, I know. That's why I'm here."

Dodi's suitcase and carry-on stowed, they climb into the car. "She's been all over the place, like she's completely lost, doesn't know where she is, or where she ought to be. One minute she can be the capable and responsible Estelle, then she looks . . ."

They are caught in a line of cars waiting at the stoplight to get onto Barlow. Leanne looks at Dodi, who has tears in her eyes. Seeing them, Leanne tears up as well—tears of confusion, of worry. They ride in silence for a while. As much as Leanne is navigating the traffic, she is also looking for Estelle's car.

Getting her composure back, Leanne tries to reassure her guest. "So, we're going back to our place. I've a bed made up for you. We'll keep trying Estelle. Probably her phone has gone dead. It's an older iPhone. The batteries are getting weak, I guess."

"Where's Jemma? Is she with Nikki?"

"Gordon, that's my partner, he's taken Jemma back over to Estelle's condo. Nikki works up north. Estelle put her on the bus to go back up there at noon."

Pulling into the back parking place of 113 Durham Lane, they get out of the car. The comfort of years ago when Leanne went down at Jemma's birth comes back between the two women. It settles the profound anxiety they both feel. Leanne has been reflecting on the last week, a week when maybe she should have been paying more attention. Estelle has been so fragile, irresponsible even. She takes one look at Dodi, and out the flood comes. Dodi holds her.

"I'm sure it's nothing. She'll check her phone, find the battery dead. She'll plug it in if she can, get a charge into it. She'll call." Leanne isn't convinced by her own words. They head into the kitchen.

As they enter Estelle's eyes peer out over the top of the child's book, staring anxiously at them from the easel set up in the back veranda. Dodi goes over and stands in front of Stella-Estelle. Leanne pulls out some crackers and cheese, puts it on the table with lemonade. Dodi eats slowly.

"Is there anyone else who would've been with Estelle this afternoon, before heading to the airport?" Dodi asks.

"She was going over to April's place, maybe take her for groceries."

"Who's April?"

"GJ's wife. Since he died, Estelle has been helping her out."

"That sounds like my Estelle. Can you call her?"

Leanne reaches for her phone. She finds a text message from April and goes about placing a voice call to her. April tells her that Estelle left hours before, and *No, I don't know where she went.*

Dodi asks, "Estelle's phone, does it have one of those Friend Finder apps?"

"What?"

"It's an iPhone, yes? On the iPhone, you can put numbers into an app, and when you open the app, it will tell you where your friend's phone is."

"I don't have that, do I?"

"If you have an iPhone, you do. Did Estelle ever set it up?"

"No, I don't think so. You can check." Leanne enters her passcode and hands the phone to Dodi.

"That app is empty of any other numbers." Dodi pauses. "If she'd set hers up with anyone else, who would it be with?"

"It would be with Nikki. But if her phone is dead, what good will that do?"

"This is going on a long time. We have to try something. You said Nikki was on a bus. Do you have her number?"

"Yes."

"Let's try calling."

Leanne rings Nikki's phone. No answer.

"Let's try texting her."

"Okay."

Leanne texts—*Nikki, do you know where Estelle is?*

Nikki replies right away—*With you? At home with Jemma? I don't know.*

Leanne texts back—*No, she hasn't come for Jemma after dropping her off this afternoon.*

Nikki replies—*shit*

Leanne—*Can you check to see if her phone is on? We keep trying to text her but she's not answering.*

Nikki—*just a minute.*

After a couple of minutes, Nikki again—*I tried texting her too, no answer. I went into Friend Finder. Her phone is on. It's at this address. 8650 112th Ave, NW.*

Leanne looks at Dodi. "That's Jackson's office, up on the North Hill."

Leanne texts back to Nikki—*Thanks, I'll text you later. I'm going over to see if Estelle is OK. She's with her father and must've lost track of time.*

"Let's go."

There is a sense of urgency as they pile back into Leanne's aging Pontiac.

Jackson's office is in a new development, various professional offices and retail stores. The parking lot is largely empty, it being Sunday evening. Jackson's Lexus is parked in front, Estelle's Honda, too. Leanne confidently goes to the door, pushes on it lightly to find that it's open. She knocks briskly on the glass, announcing they have arrived, not wanting to just walk in on the father-daughter talk.

Dodi pushes past her, opening the door widely.

The smell of blood permeates the air. Acrid but sweet. Metallic.

Dodi reaches her hand back to Leanne, pushing her back out the door. "Let me go in. Something's wrong."

The waiting room is empty.

It is perfectly silent.

Dodi creeps cautiously forward. She calls out, "Estelle." Her voice is hushed, whispery. Terrified.

Only one of the office doors is open, and that just partially. It has Dr. Jackson Horvath's nameplate on it.

As Dodi pushes the door open, the stench of blood almost overcomes her. A west-facing window, its horizontal blinds partially open, casts diagonal slashes of light over the walls of rough plaster and decorative rough-cut fir. As her eyes adjust, she sees the blood splatter. It's lit to golden tones on its scarlet-brown surface.

She calls out again. "Estelle."

The smell in the room tries to expel her. Stalwart, she goes in.

Behind the door, she finds her love, curled into the fetal position on the floor. Estelle is splattered with blood. Dodi crouches down to her, gathers her in her arms. Estelle's body is stiff, resistant. Dodi feels warmth in her body, detects shallow breaths.

From the vantage point behind the door where Estelle was lying, Dodi sees the body of Dr. Jackson Horvath lying face up behind the desk. His face and head are a mass of dried blood, red burnishing to brown. Bizarrely there is a golf club, handle down, plunged into his crotch.

Dodi struggles to pick up Estelle. There's no sign of awareness from her, no helpful adjusting of her rigidly curled body to being carried. Dodi stumbles with the burden of dragging her back into the waiting room. Leanne stands at the door.

"Call an ambulance. Call the police. He's in there. Dead."

CHAPTER SIXTEEN

Twenty-three years ago

The ceiling of the K'adsii cabin is made of rough-cut beams with tongue-and-groove boards between. It holds the grime of smoke and soot from the woodstove.

The mind of six-year-old Stella floats there, in the place beside those rough beams and smooth boards—hovering. The slivers of the beams do not prick her.

For the hovering, floating Stella it is alternately deathly quiet and then deafening—deafening with the roar of the wind, of the sea, of the rush of flames and smoke up the chimney pipe, of the cackling wail of voices. The voices are laughing, laughing in a mean sort of way.

Below the hovering Stella is the child body of Stella. The hovering Stella doesn't feel the coarse hairs of the bearskin rug beneath the child body down below. She doesn't smell the musty scent of the hide. The hovering Stella is cold, cold as if the wind blows right through her. But the coldness doesn't matter.

Her body below is lying on her back, squirming on the rug. Her pyjama bottoms are pulled down.

The woodstove is hot, as if it is burning too many logs, as if it can't contain its fire.

The hovering Stella can hear what's going on when she tries, when she lets the sound through. She listens, wondering what is happening, wondering why. She doesn't understand, so she turns off the sound. Deathly quiet again. Nothing makes any sense to young Stella's mind as it hovers there.

Whatever this is, this that doesn't make any sense, it is somehow both horrible and curious and then horrible again. She can go farther away if she needs to go. But she stays. She could go to the beach. But it is cold and rainy out there.

Hovering Stella looks too long at the child Stella below. She feels hollow. Oh, GJ is there. He looks weird, but she knows it's him.

She's underneath him.

GJ keeps going all blurry. Looking up at him from the bearskin rug, she squirms beneath him because he's so heavy. She sees the tight clench of his teeth. She looks at the ceiling, desperately wants to go there to get away from his ugly face. Then she's up on the ceiling again. Hovering, she sees his bare bottom, his underpants around his feet. When hovering Stella looks too hard to figure out what he is doing, he disappears—first too close and then gone like the sound of the wind and rain.

What are you doing, GJ?

Then she hears the slurred, smelly voice of her father, and then the bossy voice of her sister. But Anna's voice is slurred. It's smelly, too.

Hovering Stella remembers her favourite book—*Pippi Longstocking*. Her mind dances with Pippi, with the long red braids and the striped socks. She loves Pippi, loves that Pippi does what she wants, loves her horse. Hovering is easier if Pippi is here.

She hears the voice of her father as if he is reading her the story, the story that she already knows by heart, reads it with his slurred voice, the smelly one. But he doesn't have the words right. Hovering Stella strains to hear the words. They are all wrong. *Do it, GJ! Oh, you can't do it, can you? Try GJ. Try harder. That's so funny. Make her do it to you. Like me and . . .*

It all goes silent again.

Then GJ whispers to her—*We have to do it. You have to help me do it.*

Then waves. Waves and wind.

Hovering Stella looks down for Stella on the bearskin rug. She can't see her. All she can see is GJ lying there, facing down. His feet try to untangle themselves from his underpants.

That bad breath smell happens again.

Pippi and her horse. Where are Pippi and her horse?

Anna is reading to her, reading the story and getting the words all wrong, too. Doesn't she know? Stella knows the book off by heart, but when Anna reads, she says—*Look, he is so little! GJ, don't you know what to do? Can't you do it? You're pathetic, GJ. Don't you know how?*

Anna! Those aren't the right words to the book. Hovering Stella looks at the pictures and knows the right words. Then the pictures are hard to remember. Hovering Stella tries hard so she can remember. She says the right words to the story, but no one can hear them. They don't care.

The bearskin rug is prickly, but Stella doesn't feel it.

There is no sound. All sound has gone up the chimney. No roar of wind and wave. Hovering Stella is hollow. Where did Pippi go?

GJ is crying. GJ crying? *Why, GJ?*

Her father is there again. He stumbles, trips on the footstool and goes down, says the bad words. Anna goes to him, picks him up. Unsteady, he sits in a chair, giggling and then mad at the footstool. From the hovering, Stella watches all. Anna looks at GJ and tells him to *Get lost! Go to your room.* She tends to Father. They are not laughing at GJ anymore. They're mad at him.

It's okay, GJ. Don't cry.

GJ tries to run to the bedroom in the back of the cabin. Stella can't see it from where she hovers. Stella on the rug looks up and says, *Pull up your pants, GJ. You'll trip.*

Hovering Stella descends to the bearskin rug, to the child Stella. Little Stella is crying now. They both are one. Stella cries. She runs to her room, runs to find Pippi Longstocking, to pull her into bed with her, to look at the pictures and say all the words right—to pull those hardcovers in tight. To be safe again.

CHAPTER SEVENTEEN

Sunday evening

Two police cars and an ambulance are the first to arrive on the scene. A couple of officers go in with weapons drawn for a quick surveillance, others stand at the door. Within a minute or so, the inside officers wave the others to come in. Two stay with Dodi and Estelle who are collapsed on the floor in the waiting room. One crouches close to Dodi, partially shielding the two women with his body. The other stands over them with his Glock drawn. All smell the blood in the air.

The other two officers probe deeper into the clinic, their weapons still drawn. One stands at the open door to Jackson's office, his feet shoulder-width apart, his raised gun clasped in both hands. The other goes in. A half a minute or so later, he comes back out, looking grim.

They try the doors to the other offices. Finding them locked, they shout, "Police!" Getting no response, the bigger officer kicks in each of the doors. With the splinter of wood, each opens quickly. The washroom doors are unlocked. They, too, are clear. The door to the file room doesn't yield. One officer goes to the reception counter, looks from one drawer to the next, finds a ring of keys. After several tries, the file room door opens and reveals its emptiness.

The officer standing watch over Estelle, now satisfied that the other officers have found the unit to be safe, waves in the paramedics.

Even though Estelle is still rigidly clenched in the fetal position, her hand has sensed the hand of Dodi. She grasps it tightly, so tight her knuckles have gone white. Paramedics take the fallen woman's pulse at the neck. They whisper to each other. One of them speaks softly, reassuringly to Dodi.

Leanne stands just outside, a step or two away from the door. An officer goes to her.

"Did you enter the building?"

"Just inside the door. Then Dodi waved me back out when she went in."

"Dodi is?"

"That's Dodi there, with Estelle." Leanne puts her hands to her face—a half gasp, a half wail.

"Come with me, ma'am. Over here by the cars. I need to know what went on here." He leads Leanne away.

An officer briefs dispatch, describing the scene. No officers at risk. One bloody body—dead. Another bloody body—LOC. Clearly a violent struggle. He requests the FCSU and a detective.

The ambulance attendants diligently pull at Dodi to get her off, to get access to the woman on the floor. Dodi struggles to get up, easing the weight of Estelle back down to the floor again. The paramedics pry her hand loose from Estelle's grasp. Dodi brushes herself off. None of the blood has transferred from Estelle's clothing to her own, but a look of revulsion, revulsion and panic, grips Dodi's face. One of the medics leads her outside, leaving her partner with Estelle on the floor of the waiting room. She hands Dodi off to one of the police officers, says a few words in the transfer. The medic then goes back into the clinic with a stretcher.

Two more cruisers arrive, parking to form a barrier around the scene.

The officer who briefed dispatch comes over to Dodi. "You were inside, in the inner office?"

"Yeah, I carried Estelle out."

"I'm going to need you to wait here. A detective will be coming. He'll want to speak with you."

Dodi begins to shiver.

They wait. It seems like hours, but it is only a few minutes. Leanne in front of one of the police cars, and Dodi in front of another five metres or so away, watch as the paramedics carry out Estelle. She is lying on her side in the same self-protective position on the stretcher. The paramedics have attached security straps to her deathly still body. They load her into the back of the ambulance. One of the officers talks with the paramedics. He walks over to Dodi and waves to Leanne to join them.

"Alright. The woman is alive, being transported to hospital."

"I'll go with her. I have to go with her." Dodi looks desperate as she watches Estelle being loaded into the ambulance.

"You are?"

"Dodi Marseilles."

He jots her name down in his notebook. "You better stay with me, both of you. Were you here when this all happened?"

"No, we just got here. I went and found Estelle in there on the floor. And Jackson."

"You know the victims . . . the deceased, the woman?"

"The woman, she's my ex. We're still close. Look, they're taking her. I have to go with them."

"Ex, eh? You better just stay here until I figure this all out."

An unmarked car pulls up, its blues and reds flashing. Detective Lars Jonsson hauls himself out. The officers on the scene describe what they found on arrival. He nods in receiving the information, glances over in Dodi's direction, then gestures for them to lay out yellow crime scene tape. He walks over to Dodi.

"Ms. Dodi Marseilles?"

"Dr. Dodi Marseilles. I'm Estelle's friend, her ex."

"Estelle?"

"Yes, Estelle Caylie."

Jonsson takes on a puzzled look, as if he is trying to place the name. "Okay then, Dr. Marseilles, I understand you arrived after this was all over but went in where the bodies were?"

"Yes. I carried Estelle out."

He looks at her. Sighs.

"Apparently it's a mess in there. I haven't gone in yet. The officers have described it to me. The FSCU is on its way. The coroner will be coming, too, later. I want you to stay to talk to the lead forensics officer. He'll have some questions for you."

Jonsson calls back over one of the uniforms, motions him to stand with Dodi. Then he motions to Leanne to follow him a few steps away. "So, who are you?"

"Leanne Caylie. I'm Estelle's aunt. Mom, really. I adopted her when she was a child." Leanne steps back from him, takes a good look.

Jonsson presses on, his voice functional and dry. "Did you go into where it happened?" His words have taken on a staccato quality, an impatience.

"No."

"Did you see anyone—leaving the scene, hanging around?"

"No."

"And you said you were her aunt?"

"Aunt, yes, but I adopted her when she was six."

"Were you here when all this happened?"

"No. I came later, with Dodi."

"Okay, I'm going get the officer to take your name, address, and phone number. Then you can follow the ambulance to the hospital."

Jonsson looks back over at Dodi, notices her shivering, then says bluntly, "Marseilles, you are not to leave. The officer here will take care of you."

With that, Jonsson walks into the clinic.

The officer retrieves a blanket from the trunk of the police car. He wraps it around Dodi's shoulders. "Is there anyone I can call? A support person for you? This is probably going to take a while."

"The only people I know here in Calgary are Estelle and Leanne. They just left. And Dr. Horvath, too . . . but . . ." Dodi struggles to retain composure.

"Okay then. I'm going to call the Victim Services Unit to have someone stay with you through this. It'll probably take a while before I can let you go."

FCSU arrives about a half-hour later—behind it, news vans from three different stations.

Two forensics officers clad in pale blue coveralls enter the building. They have cameras and a couple of large metal briefcases.

A few minutes later, one of the officers comes out to where Dodi sits with a Victim Services volunteer. The volunteer had brought a thermos of hot, sweet tea. Dodi is sipping it. It calms her tremors.

"Dr. Marseilles, am I pronouncing that right?" the officer, loosening his coveralls, doesn't wait for an answer. "I understand you entered the scene. We're doing a preliminary analysis now, taking some photographs and samples, but I need some information from you. I've made a rough sketch of the room where the body was found. I need you to mark with this pen where you went in the room. Please describe your movements when you were there."

Dodi looks at the sketch. "I looked in but I couldn't see anything at first. Then, noticing the smell of blood was stronger, I looked behind the door and saw Estelle. I went over to her, leaned down to check if she was okay."

"She was on the floor?"

"Yeah, collapsed there, curled into a fetal position." Dodi points to the sketch indicating where she found Estelle.

"Can you mark on the drawing where she was?" He hands her the pen.

Dodi does so.

"Did you touch the door? Move it?"

"Yes, I had to, to get to her. When I got to her, I saw Dr. Horvath."

"You knew who it was?"

"Yes, I met him. Years ago. It was his office. I presume it was him. Looked like him."

"What then?"

"I dragged Estelle out of there."

"Can you mark your route? Use little arrows on the line to show the direction you went."

Dodi does.

"How tall is Estelle Caylie?"

"My height. No, shorter. Five-seven maybe. No, shorter than that, five-six?"

"Weight?"

"She's slender. Maybe 140 pounds."

"Okay then. And the position that you found her in? You said she was lying on the floor?"

"No, she was curled up in a fetal position."

"On her side?"

"Yes."

"Facing out?"

"Facing into the wall."

"Thank you. That's what I needed to know. You can go now."

The shudder runs through Dodi again. The Victim Service volunteer comes over and takes her to her car.

Dodi enters Foothills Hospital's emergency department with Danielle Lefebvre at her side.

Danielle, the Victim Services volunteer who attended the shivering Dodi at the scene, had promised she would stay until Dodi could connect with some form of family support. On the ride over to the hospital, Dodi commented on how thankful she was for the hot, sweet tea. Danielle mused that hot, sweet tea on a warm summer evening in Calgary might not always work the best. If it hadn't been a fit, she also had an ice-cold can of ginger ale in her car as well. The conversation had helped Dodi feel a bit more settled in the midst of the horrendous situation she had stumbled into.

Now, in the hospital, a nurse directs her to Estelle. Dodi looks grimly at her beloved friend and former partner. Estelle is on a gurney, covered in a blanket. She is still curled on her side, her knees brought up close to her chest. The pale green fabric of a hospital gown is around her neck. Her left hand is outside of the blanket. An IV port has been installed on the back of that hand, and a clear plastic tube is dripping fluid into her veins.

Leanne stands off to the side.

A porter comes to wheel Estelle's gurney from the emergency department to another part of the hospital.

A police officer stands guarding the scene.

"The doctor has done a preliminary examination and is admitting her." Leanne speaks flatly and then takes a closer look at Dodi, who looks like hell. "How are you doing?"

"Okay. They kept me waiting for ages out there, asked a few questions, and then said they were done with me. How is she?"

"Oh, the doctor hasn't said much. Said they were going to do some tests. Emergency is really busy, so he's going to turn over care to the hospital ward doctor. Here he is now."

Dodi is touched by the tired warmth in the doctor's eyes. He's dragging a couple of nurses behind him, but he stops and takes in the look of Dodi in front of him.

"How is she, Doctor?" Leanne asks.

The doctor looks over at her, hesitates for a moment, then asks, "And, you are . . . next of kin?"

"I adopted her when she was a child. I've been in contact with her wife, Nikki. Nikki is up in Fort Mac and gave her verbal consent over the phone for me to act on Estelle's behalf until she gets here. The nurse spoke to her."

"Well, your daughter is rather baffling to us at the moment. The results came back from the blood work. All organ functioning is good. Physically, she is stable. She is dehydrated and her blood sugar levels are low. It could be that she just hasn't eaten or had any fluids in a long time."

"Do you know how long she was in this state? We suspect something is going on neurologically. Peripheral reflexes, including eye reactions to light, are present but weak. There is no unilateral paralysis. This state of unconsciousness is a peculiar one. It doesn't present like a stroke. She's incredibly strong in resisting us in trying to straighten her out physically. She resists with all her might and then goes back into the fetal position. We don't know what is going on with that."

"I don't know whether this is helpful or not, Doctor, but she's curled up like she used to curl up when she was a little girl."

"That's interesting. We don't think it is a wilful act now. She doesn't seem to be responsive to any human interaction except resisting us when we try to lie her on her back or straighten out her limbs. She's not speaking to us yet."

"She responded to me when I found her," Dodi interjects.

The ER doctor looks at her. "How so? Who are you?"

"I'm a long-time friend of Estelle. We used to be partners. We're still quite close. When I found her, I think she knew it was me. She held my hand."

"Interesting . . ."

"Well, it was more like a reflex. When my hand touched hers she gripped it tightly, like a baby holding onto the finger of her mother."

"Okay, then." The doctor looks disinterested. "I've transferred her care to Dr. Isaac. Please let him know."

A nurse catches the doctor's focus, and he is off.

Leanne, Dodi, and Danielle follow the gurney behind the police officer as it heads out of the emergency department. There is a sign on both the front and back of the gurney—*CODE WHITE*.

They enter a private room facing out over the Bow River Valley. A nurse does a routine check—temperature, heart rate, blood pressure. Leanne catches her eye.

"How is she?"

"Seems stable. Are you family?"

"Yes. By the way, what does *Code White* mean?"

"That's a hospital code." The nurse looks hesitant. "It's for a violent patient, or a potentially violent patient. She's passed out now, but that's what they put on her in Emerg. Maybe they are concerned she might be violent again when she comes to. I really don't know any of the history. I hope the doctor's notes will be up on the computer soon. I expect that Dr. Isaac will be in soon to assess her."

Leanne, Dodi, and Danielle stand baffled as the door closes behind the departing nurse. The police officer stands dutifully in the room, watching the three women beside the patient in the bed.

"Have you had anything to eat?" Leanne asks Dodi.

"Danielle here gave me some tea. I'm okay. What about you?"

"I could really use something."

Danielle pipes up. "If it's okay with you, Dodi, I'll be on my way. The two of you have each other now. Why don't I take . . ." She looks at Leanne and realizes that she doesn't know her name, ". . . you down to get something to eat on my way out."

"Leanne, I'm Leanne. Estelle's mom. Yes, if you could. I'm starting to feel faint."

Leanne looks at Dodi. "There's a Tim's downstairs. How about I bring something up for you?"

Dodi shakes her head, not having a clue what a Tim's is.

"Are you okay to stay with Estelle while I go for a few minutes?"

Dodi nods.

With the room empty, save now for her dear Estelle and a stone-faced police officer watching every move, Dodi crawls onto the hospital bed. She spoons in behind Estelle's curled body. She reaches her hand into Estelle's and feels the touch of Estelle's fingers around her own. The grip is not so desperate. She feels Estelle's body start to relax.

The clock on the wall of the hospital room reads 10:38. Suddenly, there are several people in the room—the nurse who had checked the vitals, a doctor holding an iPad. Leanne is there, too. And Detective Jonsson. The police officer still stands guard over them all.

The doctor speaks. "I'd like to examine the patient. Can I have the room cleared?"

Within about five minutes, Dr. Isaac emerges from the room. "Who is next of kin?"

Leanne, looking less pale, says, "I am. I'm Leanne Caylie, her aunt, her adoptive mother."

"Dr. Thompson's notes from Emerg indicate he spoke to you. I've done a quick check, and everything seems to be stable, much the same as when she was downstairs. We're providing supportive care. We've put in a catheter because she's not conscious, and as we rehydrate her, we need to provide a means for her bladder to empty. Obviously, we want to have a CT scan done to determine if there's a neurological issue."

"When can she have the scan?"

"We would like it to be right away, but the way her body is rigidly constricted, we can't do it yet. We hope that her body might relax so we can get her into the CT scanner."

"It started to when I was with her," Dodi mentions.

"How so?"

"I cradled her in my arms, held her, spooned with her on the bed. We used to be lovers. We are still very close friends. She responded to me."

"Well, that's a good sign. Maybe you might be our best bet in getting her to respond. You are . . . ?"

"Dodi. Dr. Dodi Marseilles. I'm a clinical psychologist, but I'm also Estelle's ex and . . ." Dodi's voice fades out as she turns to return to the room.

"Ms. Marseilles, can I have a few minutes of your time before you go in?" Detective Jonsson imposes himself.

"For?"

"I need to review your whereabouts for this afternoon and evening. I'm investigating a murder here, and you were in the room."

"You've got to be kidding," Dodi retorts.

"At this stage, everyone is of interest to us. Including you." The detective gestures toward Estelle's hospital room. "And her. She was in the room with the deceased, covered in blood. And then, you were with her. We need to follow up on everything."

Dodi looks shocked. Silently, eyes only, she tells him to *Fuck off.* She heads back to be with Estelle. Leanne intervenes with the detective to see if she can content him with the details of her own whereabouts.

Within a few minutes, Dodi's soft singing voice can be heard through the open door of Estelle's hospital room. She's singing about mockingbirds and rocking cradles, the same songs she and Estelle had sung to infant Jemma.

CHAPTER EIGHTEEN

Monday

Leanne makes the miserable trek home from the hospital shortly after midnight. She'd taken a last, long, lingering look at Estelle and Dodi in the hospital bed. Leanne took comfort in this woman who had returned to them—a woman who had loved Leanne's dear Estelle, had loved Leanne's dear Jemma, loved them as much as she herself had.

The two-and-a-half-storey house on 113 Durham Lane looks like it is grieving. It sits in the sad, summertime darkness that cloaks Calgary for a few impatient hours at the summer solstice. Leanne wanders the empty house with the ghosts of Izzy, GJ, and Jax. Even the paintings are gone, and many of the best sketches with them, gone now to a display in a commercial gallery. Such a sense of loss.

In the morning, she'll retrieve Gordon and Jemma. How she needs them both.

Leanne's mind swims with the happenings of the day. To calm herself, she gathers a large sketchbook, pencils, and a tray of oil pastel crayons, sits at the drafting table in her studio. Soon the nondescript lines of the front door to Jax's office emerge on the page, then police cars with the red and blue lights atop. A yellow tape with black lettering crosses the scene.

Dodi's image comes next—her dark skin, her features darkened further by fear and sorrow. Leanne enlivens her face with whites at the corners of the eyes, the tips of teeth just showing through the hard set to the mouth. Somewhere, somehow, there needs to be a spark of light. If from anywhere, it would be from Dodi.

And then down in the lowest quadrant of the page she sketches the detective, the asker of blunt questions. Into the lines of his face, Leanne etches his worn-out look as he surveyed the scene outside the clinic. She draws the desolation of too often attending the tragic end to a human life. His eyes emerge tarnished by all that they must have seen, eyes overfull of what can never be unseen. Leanne tries to remember the shape and bearing of the detective's body. All she can bring to mind is that it was there, not present, just there. She courses another span of yellow police tape across his chest. The words DO NOT CROSS hides the place where his heart would be.

The drawing done, she can sleep.

At 5:30 a.m., a text message comes in from Nikki—*How is Estelle? Do you need me to come back? Could make it back to Calgary by noon. Can you pick me up at the airport?* Leanne had only talked with Nikki briefly the day before, got her consent to act as next of kin. Then she didn't get back to her. How worried she must be! Leanne quickly texts back—*Yes, come back. Yes, I can.*

Brilliant sunlight streams low through the backseat window—the vibrant gold of a prairie sunrise. It falls full on Nali's face. She's lying there, head pressed hard against the armrest on one backdoor of the car, feet against the other. Her legs are askew.

With the sudden light, she ascends briefly into consciousness. Her eyes endeavour to blink open. When they do, her vision is blurred and she can't unite the disparate images from her two eyes. The blinding light is painful. With consciousness comes the brutal pressure of a headache that has her in a vice grip. Feeling the motion of the car, she needs to vomit but can't coordinate her arms and legs to get up to do so. She rolls to her side and retches into the floor space behind the driver's seat. Her hand goes to her mouth. Now it reeks of bile.

She closes her eyes. She's gone again.

Leanne arrives at the hospital at 6:30. The police officer has taken a position outside of the door to Estelle's room. Leanne has a tray of Tim's with her—coffee with the cream and sugar in little packets, a couple of muffins. Dodi is snoozing in a chair beside Estelle's bed. Estelle has straightened out, is lying corpse-like on the bed, pale, eyes closed. The monitor shows a steady heart rate. A red warning bar with the word BRADYCARDIA flashes there.

As Leanne enters, a rush of cool air moves the curtains. With it, Dodi's eyes blink open. She struggles to her feet, slightly ataxic, a brief look of confusion on her face. Her eyes react with relief as she recognizes Leanne. As Leanne goes over to Estelle's hospital bed, Dodi stands with her, her hand on Leanne's arm. They talk in hushed tones.

"I felt her finally relax about three a.m. I'd been drifting, singing, holding her. Soon after, the nurse came in. She made note of the change in Estelle and took her vitals, suggested that I could leave her to sleep."

"She's okay now?"

"She's starting to speak, but it doesn't seem to make any sense. Before I fell asleep, I recorded on my phone some of her verbalizations. Gibberish with angry words mixed in, angry words I've never heard Estelle utter before. But there were some words."

"I guess this is a good sign."

"I guess. Did you get any sleep?"

"Some. The house felt eerie. Too many family who lived there have died."

Dodi looks at her grimly. There's a reality to this—a reality that can't be expressed, only felt.

"I thought I'd check in here. Then I'm going to get Gordon and Jemma and take them back to the house. I've heard from Nikki. Expects to be here by noon. I'm to pick her up at the airport."

Setting the coffee on Estelle's bed table, Dodi puts in all the packets of sugar and plastic tubs of cream. She takes a small bite of the muffin, chews it slowly, swallows it deliberately, and puts the rest of the muffin back in the bag. "So this is Tim's, is it? Like Dunkin."

A different doctor comes in. The name tag on his white coat reads *Dr. Wesley, Hospitalist.* He introduces himself politely, goes over to Estelle and takes her pulse at the wrist, checks for limb rigidity. Her arm falls limply to the bed. He lifts an eyelid and shines a light into Estelle's eyes, uses his stethoscope on her chest. Standing at the bed, he consults the medical record on the tablet computer he has brought with him. Finally, he sighs and turns toward the two women.

"I'm Dr. Wesley. I'll be taking over Ms. Caylie's care today. I've met with Dr. Isaac, who was on last night. He's reviewed the case with me. I'm pleased to see some progress."

Leanne introduces herself as Estelle's mom. Dodi reaches a hand forward and says, "I'm Dr. Dodi Marseilles. I'm Estelle's friend and former wife. I spent the night beside her."

"Doctor?"

"A psychologist, D. Psych, not medical."

"We're not progressing to psych with her yet. We need to do neuro first."

"I understand. I'm here as a friend, someone she can trust." Dodi pauses. "If she needs to."

"Yes, yes. From the chart, she's been through a shock. The notes say she came into emergency covered with blood. No signs of injury on her body, presumably someone else's blood, then. But LOC."

"Through the night, she relaxed a bit. She'd been in the fetal position. Now, she's straightened out."

"Good, good. They gave her some Diazepam in the IV."

"Dr. Isaac, last night. . . he said something about a CT scan."

"Yes, we can do that now. That'll tell the tale. We'll know then what we are looking at. Maybe then you psychs can have her."

"I'm not registered to practice here in Canada. I'm from Missouri."

Dr. Wesley looks at her. Perhaps for the first time, takes her in. "Oh, that's right. You're just a friend."

"Yeah, just a friend." Dodi sighs.

Leanne interjects. "The police officer outside the room. Is that really necessary?"

"That's not my call. They decide. He doesn't seem to be interfering."

With that, Dr. Wesley leaves.

Pierre woke at his usual 5:09, one minute before his unnecessary alarm would have sounded.

His bathroom ablutions take their accustomed eleven minutes of time.

By 5:25, he was off in the black Malibu to the World Gym. He'd seen spin bikes there and decided he was disgusted with the inadequate cardio equipment at the hotel. With noise-cancelling earbuds in hand and a challenging workout ready on his phone, he headed off to push himself to his very limit.

By 8:00 a.m., he's back in the hotel room, showers.

Pierre had put in the day before in the world-class Chateau at Lake Louise, even walking the path beside the lake in his dress shoes. He had a sense that his work pertaining to Horvath was just about done, that it might be best to be out of town accumulating receipts with dates and times elsewhere. Just allow it all to unfold.

He stuffs his laundry from the gym and the day before in a concierge bag and marks it *urgent*. He hangs it on outside of the door and calls down to the concierge desk.

Just before the local news comes on *Global TV*, there's a review of weather and traffic. Pierre waits it out impatiently.

"Breaking news. We are over to Jason Gilbert up on Nose Hill."

"Thanks, Sam. I'm at the site of Calgary's fifteenth murder of the year, up two compared to this time last year.

"Behind me is the Nose Hill Depression and Anxiety Clinic. Police were called to this scene last evening and found the body of Dr. Jackson Horvath.

"Dr. Horvath was a prominent member of Calgary's psychiatric community. Recently, he presented a paper at a national conference outlining innovative approaches to community mental health. Horvath was a third-generation doctor in a medical family that has dominated the health care scene in Calgary for decades. His father was respected family doctor, Dr. Emmitt Horvath. And before him was Dr. Lionel Horvath, also a family doctor. Our community is sad to see this line of respected physicians come to an end.

"Last night, an ambulance transported another person to hospital from the scene. Police have declined to comment on that person and their involvement in the incident.

"Back to you, Sam. I'll stay on the scene and provide updates to this story as they become available."

Pierre stares at the screen. Robotically, he pulls out the twenty-five-inch titanium clamshell to begin the process of repacking. His work here is done.

Carefully, he plans. He can turn in the Malibu at the downtown Hertz office, settle up for the damages. He can flee the city in the aging Impreza— getting a flight out of Edmonton, abandoning the car in a parking lot there. Quickly, he routes his escape plan—Edmonton to Winnipeg, and then a connector to Minneapolis, Minneapolis to Chicago. It's a milk run of a route but less likely to be traced by the authorities. He will be home in thirty-six hours.

Pierre reclaims the bag of unwashed laundry from outside the door. He tightly closes the plastic bag, and with a grimace, stuffs it into his suitcase.

When Leanne buzzes Estelle's condo, Gordon answers with a cheerful, "Good morning, come on up."

Up in Estelle's kitchen, Gordon has commandeered a small Bluetooth speaker to connect with music files on his phone. Jemma has his emergency harmonica, the one Gordon keeps in the inside pocket of his denim jacket. She's stalwartly blowing notes, out of tune to the music playing in the background. Her face contorts in concentration and consternation.

"How are you two doing?" Leanne asks.

"Fine. She was a bit upset when she woke this morning and neither of her mommas were here. But we found corn flakes and strawberries. She didn't want cartoons but wanted to practice her music because I was here. But no ukulele. So I'm teaching her harmonica. I think she's getting it."

With that, Jemma looks up. "Auntie Leanne!" she exclaims and runs over for a hug.

It's normalizing for Leanne, an antidote to the horror of the last twelve hours.

"How is Estelle?" Gordon asks.

"Momma-Stelle?" Jemma immediately catches the words and the tone of anxiety that accompanied them.

Leanne kneels down to her.

"Jemma-girl. Momma-Stelle is in the hospital. She's very sick, but we hope she'll be getting better today. Dodi is with her."

"Dodi?"

"You remember Dodi, don't you?"

"From FaceTime?"

"Yeah, that Dodi."

"Can I see her? I want my Momma-Stelle." Suddenly, Jemma starts to cry at the strange that this all is.

"We'll see. But you're going to see Momma-Nik today. She's coming back on an airplane. Would you come with me to the airport to pick her up?"

"Yay! Momma-Nik." Jemma's face then falls as if she's just getting it, how sick her Momma-Stelle must be. Momma-Nik just left to go to work yesterday.

Leanne holds her close. The tears that have stored up inside for twelve hours break forth. Gordon stands awkwardly off to the side. He takes the harmonica out of Jemma's hand, wipes the moisture off it, and stuffs it back in his jacket pocket.

"So, are you going back up to the hospital?" Gordon asks.

"I think I'll head back home. Maybe we all can. Wait there until I hear again from Dodi. I didn't get much sleep, and I have to go out to the airport to pick up Nikki at noon."

The rhythm and bass of a blues number still plays from the little Bluetooth speaker in the background.

Nali rouses to the sudden sensation of the car door behind her head being opened. Her eyes, still blurry and doubled, briefly take in a shivering curtain of green leaves. The pounding of her headache is beyond tolerability. She retches again.

"Wakey, wakey," a male voice implores. Whoever he is, he starts to pull her from the vehicle.

Stumbling to her feet, Nali looks at the woods that surround the car. A pair of tire tracks curve behind the vehicle off to the side, through a tunnel opening into the bush.

She feels pain radiating out from the back of her neck at the base of her skull—it is so intense that she clenches her eyes closed, trying to shut it out. She reaches a hand to touch the back of her head and feels the crackle of dried blood.

His hand is in her armpit to lift her, steady her, help her get the wobbles out. Despite the softness of the woods, she hears the sounds of low-flying jets overhead. With it comes the pounding of explosions and the drone of a large aircraft coming in low to land.

"Welcome home . . . well, my home. Maybe yours, too, if you wish."

She blinks her eyes open again, struggles to recognize the man. Then the pain becomes overwhelming, and she closes them again without the blur clearing.

"Rough trip, eh? We'll get you comfortable inside. It's beautiful in there, you'll see." Forcibly, he escorts her from the car.

Once inside, Nali sinks into a chair. She intends a single word—*fuck*. Her mouth doesn't work to speak. She blinks her eyes open to see the inside of an A-frame cabin. A triangle of windows, spanning up to a height of at least seven metres, looks out through a cut of trees. The sky is overpowering in its brightness, the early morning sun streaming in. The pain in her head increases with the light. She covers her eyes with the palms of her hands. She slumps, elbows on her knees.

He opens the fridge, takes out a can of ginger ale, pops the tab, and gives it to her. Then he walks into the bathroom. Coming back, he begins a monologue, one of pride. "Technically, this place belongs to my mom. I live here, though—when I'm not in Calgary working for my aunt. I'm a home health aide now. Who would have ever thought that, eh?

"Dad built this place about fifteen years ago. They rented it out as a B & B, and for weddings and family reunions, too. It never paid for itself, but Mom loved having it, a hobby for her—keeping up the gardens, making the reservations and all. Then Dad's emphysema got a lot worse, and he couldn't farm our section and a half up top. So they sold all that—even the home quarter with all the granaries, corrals, and the big equipment shed. The two of them moved down here."

He sighs. "This was Mom's heaven with the flower gardens and the view of the valley."

The story continues with a hint of sadness. "Dad died with the lung cancer. Five years or so ago now. Within a year, Mom had a stroke. She couldn't live out here on her own. She's in town now, at Points West, a nursing home. Maybe

I'll go and bring her out today from the nursing home so you can meet her."

By this time, Nali is gathering her strength. "Fuck you," she says, looking at her captor, trying to bring him into focus. Then, "Got a Tylenol or something? This headache . . ."

"Yeah, I bet. Sure. I'll get you some right away. You've been out a long time. Figured the headache would be pretty bad when you woke up.

"Last night, when I rescued you, I took you back to my place in Calgary but couldn't get you to wake up. You were really out cold from that blow to your head. And I thought to myself the best place in the world to wake up is here, here in this beautiful cabin in the Battle River Valley. So, I decided I would pack you up in the car and drive through the night so you could wake up here. It's lovely. You see, eh?"

Nali gags as she brings the can of ginger ale to her lips. She realizes how dry her mouth is, how much she craves something to drink. She sips with fear that she will vomit it back up again. Deliberately she takes two of the Extra Strength Tylenol from the bottle, then washes them down with a small swallow of the ginger ale. She settles back into her chair, concentrating on keeping her body still so she can hold the medicine in her stomach long enough to be absorbed into her bloodstream.

He lets her sit.

"Where am I?" she asks.

In response, she hears the patio doors that lead out onto a wooden deck slide open. A cool breeze comes in.

"That, my friend, is the Battle River Trestle bridge near the hamlet of Fabyan. Just over that rise is the town of Wainwright. And that racket you hear, well, get used to it—war games on the army base. That's live fire you hear."

Nali has no idea of Fabyan, Wainwright, or an army base. Wherever it is, the war outside with all the pounding is no match for the war going on inside her head.

Then she connects, connects to the sound of the voice. It's Jimmy Murphy. *The* Jimmy Murphy. He has her. She doesn't know where she is, why she is with him. She has no recollection of how she got here or any sense of how she can get away.

She shivers.

"You're still in shock. I understand. Give it time, time for the Tylenol to kick in, time to get your bearings."

She stumbles to her feet. Seeing the open patio door, she thinks to make a bolt for it—but she can't get across the room without stumbling to her knees. She smells her own reek.

"Easy, girl. Lots of time. Lots of time before we go outside. I'll show you around. You'll love it here. I do."

Nali sits on the floor, trying to keep the shudders and the shivers from making her vomit.

"What day is it?"

"Well, that'd be Monday."

The answer doesn't make sense to her. She has no sense of Sunday. She struggles to bring to mind the last clear thing that she can remember.

He helps her up onto the sofa, sits beside her with a satisfied smile on his face.

Nali opens her eyes, tries to make them focus. "Jimmy. You're Jimmy, right? You brought me here."

"Yup. So you would be safe."

"Safe?"

"Don't you remember? Your dad and everything?"

"I don't remember. Don't remember at all."

"Oh." Jimmy pauses, then smiles with the way he will say it. "I guess you didn't hear it on the news in the car because you were passed out. Came over the Calgary news this morning. Your father was found dead. On my count, that's two members of your family dead in the last couple of weeks. So, I say to myself, *Jimmy, Jimmy, you better get Anna out of Calgary. It is not safe for her there.* So last night, I brought you here, here to Mom and Dad's place. So you'll be safe."

"Dad is dead?" A brief trickle of memory wants to seep back in. As Nali tries to grasp it, it vanishes. Jimmy's story doesn't make any sense.

"Yup. Good thing I came along. Got you out of there. You're here now. You'll like it here."

"Wait a minute. You got me out? Out of where?"

"That was quite a blow you took to your head. No wonder you can't remember."

Nali sits staring at him. He hasn't answered her question.

"Let's get you up, take you for a bit of a walk. I'll show you around." Jimmy stands, hauls her up by the hand. Feeling the Tylenol gradually kick in, Nali is barely able to stand on her own. She steadies herself, teeters toward the open patio door. When she gets out onto a generous balcony, she sees a three-metre drop from the edge of the deck to the bush area below. She feels dizzy as she looks down. Nali breathes the freshness of the air. Her vision comes clearer now, clear for a moment then doubled and blurry. It's still painful to have her eyes open.

"I have to use the bathroom. Where's my purse?"

"I'll get that for you. You had it around your shoulder. It's in the front seat of the Camaro. I'll go and get it for you. Steady now. The bathroom is just over there on the other side of the kitchen."

Nali manages to keep her feet under her. Both hands go to her temples. She holds her head together so it won't blow apart with the pain. While she is on the toilet, Jimmy discreetly opens the door the width of her purse and drops it onto the bathroom floor. It is there for her, but out of her reach.

Her whole body aches.

She checks her purse for her phone. It's not there. She takes out her comb. In trying to make sense of her hair, she feels the sharp tug of the dried blood on the back of her head. She winces. Wetting a washcloth, she dabs at it back there. It comes back with the dull brown speckles of dried blood and the brilliant crimson of fresh blood still seeping from the wound. She tries to wipe it clean, but it is too painful to touch.

Exiting the bathroom, she finds Jimmy on a stool at a high counter. He's cracked open a beer. He slides off the stool and takes her by the hand. "I've something to show you."

They walk over to a large stone fireplace at one of the sides of the A-frame. It has a thick wooden mantle, shoulder height, holding a series of framed photos. Jimmy pulls one from behind and proudly shows it to her. "Do you know who those two are?"

Nali looks. It is her, her and Jimmy, at a prom, twenty years or so ago. Must be longer—she doesn't have the tattoo.

He stops, looks at her with curiosity and eagerness. "That's us, Anna. You,

Anna, and me, Jimmy. That's us.

"Yeah, that was my senior year. I asked you to be my escort to the prom. Down in Western Canada High." Jimmy pauses. A wide grin contorts his face. "You were just a grade niner. But I asked, and you came to the prom with me. You were quite the vixen back in those days, leading me on, then denying me."

Nali can remember that, yes, vaguely.

Jimmy gives the smile of accomplishment, a smile tinged with a sexualized leer. "Well, we're together now. Twenty years later, together. No more games."

She feels the strength going out of her legs. She needs to lie down. There is a slight easing of the headache as the Tylenol is kicking in. But she is so tired. So very tired. She closes her eyes and is out.

On the trip to the airport, Leanne talks to Jemma about what's going to happen and what Auntie Leanne expects of her.

Jemma looks grim. Aunt Leanne is scaring her.

When they arrive at the cellphone waiting area, Leanne texts Nikki to let her know the plan.

As Nikki emerges from the airport, Leanne releases the lock on the back door. Jemma gets out. Very deliberately, very carefully, like Auntie Leanne told her, she walks over to Momma-Nik and gives her a big hug. Nikki receives the hug, then buckles Jemma back in the backseat.

When Nikki gets in the car, she doesn't say anything. She and Auntie Leanne ride in silence until Leanne can pull into the Sobeys parking lot off Country Hills Boulevard. When they stop, Leanne reminds Jemma that she's to put in Uncle Gordon's special earbuds and listen to Uncle Gordon's music on the iPad. Jemma, tears in her eyes, nods and says she will.

Nikki and Leanne get out of the car to talk. Nikki's hands become fists as Leanne briefs her. A foot stamps nervously. Leanne stares deliberately, pleadingly into Nikki's face. She updates her on Estelle's precarious condition in hospital, about Dodi being there. Nikki contains her anger at the mention of Dodi spending the night with Estelle, contains it because Jemma is just a metre or so away in the car behind a closed window, earbuds in. Slowly, the anger that has warped Nikki's face, the nervous energy that has animated her feet and hands, dissipates. Leanne keeps talking, keeps reassuring until it's enough.

When they are done, Nikki opens Jemma's door, unbuckles the car seat. Jemma climbs out. Nikki initiates a big hug. "I'm here now," she says to Jemma, who cries as Nikki holds her.

Back in the city, Leanne drops Nikki off at the hospital. She and Jemma head back to 113 Durham Lane.

As Nikki enters the ward, a doctor and Dodi are standing at Estelle's door. The police officer stands there as well, stoic. The doctor is lightly directing Dodi down the hall.

"Estelle Caylie's room?" Nikki asks.

"Yes, just back there. You are?" the doctor asks.

"I'm her wife. Can I see her?"

"Nikki!" Dodi reaches out a hand and a smile to her.

"Dodi." Nikki's tone is less hospitable.

"You're family then, next of kin?" the doctor asks.

"Yes, I was away. I just made it here. Came as fast as I could."

"I'm Dr. Aaron Marsh, psychiatrist. Dr. Marseilles and I were just going to discuss my findings on examination. Would you join us?"

"I want to see Estelle first."

"Very well, we will wait." Dr. Marsh opens the door to Estelle's room for Nikki.

A few minutes later Nikki emerges, pale of face.

"Shall we go then?" Dr. Marsh leads them down the hall to a doctors' consulting room. Nikki enters, staring daggers at Dodi.

"Alright then, first, there's some really good news. I've the results of the CT scan. A normal brain. No abnormalities. There's no sign of stroke, aneurysm, tumour, or any other physical cause for Estelle's peculiar state. I hope both of you breathe a sigh of relief.

"Secondly, there's more good news. Peripheral reflexes are back, and within normal limits. And physical examination shows no sign of injury anywhere on her body."

Dodi interrupts. "So what's the explanation, Doctor? Why this unresponsive state?"

"Well, we know that she's been through quite a shock. Notes say that she was covered in blood when she was brought in. As she has no injuries, we can only surmise that it was someone else's blood." Dr. Marsh pauses. "She must've been in the presence of extreme violence, even if she herself was not violently harmed."

"So you're considering this simply shock?" Dodi asks. Nikki sits looking numb, overwhelmed.

"It's going on a long time for shock. I'm concerned that something more complex psychiatrically is going on here."

"Such as?"

"It is early . . ."

"You must have a provisional diagnosis, something arising from this consult, a foundation for your medical intervention at this time."

Dr. Marsh looks at her. "You are a psychologist, right? Is that research or clinical?"

"Clinical. I am registered in Missouri. I work at St. Louis University Hospital—acute care inpatient and Emerg."

"Can I speak diagnostically, then?"

"Yes. I'm aware that Nikki is here, too. I can explain the terms to her later, but for now . . ."

"Psychosis. Undifferentiated Catatonia."

Dodi looks shocked. "Your differential?"

"Conversion disorder. She's unresponsive to all human interaction for no apparent cause in terms of neurological condition."

"She's beginning to respond to me. Last night, I stayed with her. She relaxed the rigidity she had when she came in. She held my hand."

"And that's a good sign."

"She looks at me when I speak to her. Sure, it's a faraway look, a thousand-mile stare, so to speak. But, briefly, she orients in my direction."

"I hope you'll spend more time with her. I presume that until this trauma she was well-functioning, that this is a very odd state for her."

"She's a psychologist as well. We were in graduate school together. She was a top student."

"Very well, then. That contributes to a good prognosis. Well, I guess that's all for now. Remember there is good news, good reason to be hopeful." Dr. Marsh leads them out of the room.

Back in the hall, just outside Estelle's door, Detective Jonsson stands with the police officer. He accosts the doctor and introduces himself. "Detective Jonsson. I'm the investigating detective for a murder. I must interview Estelle Caylie regarding the death of her father, Jackson Horvath."

Dr. Marsh looks askance at him. "Good luck," he says sarcastically and walks away.

Detective Jonsson turns to Dodi. "I missed you last night. You were in with Ms. Caylie. I need to ask you a few questions." He turns to Nikki. "And you are?"

"Nikki Blaser. I'm Estelle's wife, *legally* married partner."

Detective Jonsson immediately looks at her suspiciously. "I need to meet with you also, then." He looks around for someplace to talk.

"We were just in a consulting office down the hall. We could meet there," Dodi suggests.

Nikki looks furious. "Look, I've come to be with Estelle. I've only seen her briefly. Let me go in there."

"Alright. First, I'll talk to you, Ms. Marseilles, and then you, Ms. Blaser." He walks off with Dodi.

They settle in the conference room. "First, I need an account of your whereabouts between three p.m. and seven p.m. yesterday."

"On a plane. From Minneapolis to Calgary. I touched down at quarter after six Mountain Time. The flight was about two-and-a-half hours. When I got to Calgary, Leanne picked me up at the airport, and I was with her until we went to where I found Estelle."

"Can anyone vouch for you on that flight?"

"Oh, probably a hundred and fifty people." Dodi replies sarcastically. "Wait." She reaches into her purse, pulls out her phone, flips through her email. "Here's my boarding pass."

Detective Jonsson takes a picture of it with his own phone.

"You were coming to see Ms. Caylie, then?"

"It is Dr. Caylie. She's a psychologist. Yes. I had a call from her Thursday. She was in distress. I came as quickly as I could."

"Distress?"

"Yes, her brother had died."

"Gerald Jonathan Caylie?"

"I guess so. She called him GJ."

"So you didn't see or talk to Estelle at all yesterday before you arrived and went to meet her at her father's office?"

"We texted in the morning. I let her know about my flights."

"Can I see those texts?"

Dodi shows him.

"And how did you know she was at Dr. Horvath's office, know to go and meet her there?"

"Auntie Leanne found out. She raised Estelle. She's also the sister of Dr. Horvath. She'd been in touch with Nikki. Nikki had it on her phone, could see where Estelle's phone was."

Nikki walks in looking shaken. "She doesn't say a word. She just sits and stares." Tears well up. Nikki transforms them into tightening fists.

"I'll catch more of your story later, Ms. Marseilles."

"Dr. Marseilles." Dodi flashes a look of pique at him.

"Now, Ms. . . ." The detective looks at the scribbles on his notepad. "Blaser. Where were you yesterday between three and seven p.m.?"

Nikki looks stunned, as if she didn't expect to be accounting for herself. "Yesterday morning, late morning, I guess, I left on the Red Arrow going north." She stammers a bit. "I have a job up in Fort Mac. But last night I heard Estelle was in hospital, heard from Leanne. So I made it back here today."

"Can anyone attest to this?" Detective Jonsson is making notes.

"As I said, I took the Red Arrow out of Calgary, yesterday about noon. There were dozens of other passengers who may remember me being on the bus with them. Lots of us do that, take the connection through Edmonton to get to Fort Mac."

"Could you excuse me a minute? I just need to check back in with my office." He leaves Dodi and Nikki awkwardly standing there.

In contacting his office, Jonsson asks Joyce to check both women's alibis. He also hears the preliminary forensics report. Apparently, there were at least two other people in the room at the time of the murder. When most of the blows were inflicted one individual was already on the floor, creating a shadow pattern of no splatter. The other one was standing beside the collapsed figure. The amount of blood and the multiple overlapping vectors of the splatter suggest that there were multiple blows, a frenzy of them. Broken golf clubs litter the scene, many of them bloody. Preliminary analysis of the body suggests that in addition to the multiple blows, a substantial knife was used. It was not found at the scene.

When Lars returns to the room, Dodi and Nikki are staring at each other in stony silence.

"Okay then…We initially considered Estelle to be a suspect in the murder of her father. She was found at the scene and covered in blood. I've collected her clothing and spoken to the nurses who attended her in the hospital last night. Our preliminary forensic assessment, though, suggests that she was not the perpetrator but at the time of the killing had already collapsed where you found her, Ms. Marseilles."

"So, for now, we consider Ms. Caylie a witness to a violent murder and believe that she may be at considerable risk herself. Thus, I'm leaving a police officer in place to guard her while she's in such a precarious state."

For the first time in the eighteen hours, an exhausted Dodi breaks into tears. Nikki looks on, disturbed and angry.

As Detective Jonsson leaves the hospital, he gets a quick call back from Joyce down at CGIS.

"So checking with the airline," Joyce says, "the alibi for Dodi Marseilles is confirmed. There was a problem, though, for Nikki Blaser. She did leave on the bus from the Red Arrow terminal in Calgary around noon, but only purchased a ticket to go as far as Red Deer. I had them check other buses north to Edmonton and onto Fort Mac. Nothing. Nothing for her out of Edmonton, either. The agent pulled records and found that every third week she would transfer onto the Fort Mac bus, but not yesterday. So I checked the hotels in Red Deer near the bus terminal. Nikki stayed there on the Sunday night rather than going all the way to her job in the north."

"Oh, that's interesting. She was just an hour or so drive from where Horvath was killed, not all the way at the other end of the province. I wonder why."

"Yeah, I was thinking that."

Concern edges the detective's voice. "And I just left her up there with a very vulnerable partner lying on a hospital bed."

"You think she might be a risk?"

Detective Jonsson doesn't answer.

"There's one other thing. A tip came in on Crime Stoppers this morning, naming Horvath."

"Can you read it to me?"

"I've loaded it up on the computer. You can get it in the car. It's from a couple in the Marlborough area."

"I'll go and check it out. After the craziness of the hospital, I really could use a drive."

An older woman, roundish in a grandmotherly sort of way, answers the door at the modest bungalow. "Hello?"

"Jean Fitzgerald?" he asks. She nods.

"I'm Detective Jonsson, with Calgary General Investigation Services. We received a call from you. I'm just following up."

"Yes, I phoned Crime Stoppers this morning. Didn't know who to call, so I called them."

"Because this is an active investigation, they passed your message onto me. Can I come in?"

Jerry has come behind her. They step toward the living room. Lars stands officially. They motion him to sit. He doesn't.

Jean starts. "This is probably nothing, but when we heard that Dr. Horvath was killed, heard it on *Global News* this morning, we remembered something. Thought we better call."

"I'm glad you did. What did you remember?"

Jean sits up on the edge of her chair, her back straight. She's not used to talking with detectives, especially not about something like this. "On Friday, a couple of days ago, we had a visitor. Nicest man. But he had questions about our granddaughter. He said he was doing an investigation of some sort. Our dear Jemma, we sure wouldn't want anything to happen to her. She's such a dear. Anyway, he gave us a funny feeling, like something was not quite right."

"Was he from Children's Services?"

"Something like that," Jean says hesitantly.

"We don't always know the families they are investigating. Unless there's a chance of a criminal charge, their investigation process is quite separate from us."

"He didn't say anything about a crime ... but—"

Jerry butts in. "He was asking questions about who had contact with Jemma, asking if we noticed she was disturbed in any way." Jerry looks assertively at Detective Jonsson. "He asked our son about her other grandfather, Dr. Horvath. We think that's the man who was murdered. The way he spoke ... well ..."

"Well?"

"Our son—that's Jemma's father, Everett—when he went out to the car to talk to him, it got quite heated out there. When Everett came back in, he was furious. He said that man, this Bolton fellow, implied that Dr. Horvath was a pedophile. You can just imagine—telling a father that his beautiful daughter had been in the hands of a pedophile, right in her own family. And Everett and us, we can't even get custody of her. Just have her on weekends, and even at that ..."

"I'm sure this was shocking for you. I'm so sorry. I am investigating the death of Dr. Horvath. This information will be important, and I thank you for it. Can you tell me more, more about this man—Bolton did you say? I'll want to speak with him."

"He left his card. I have it here." Jean produces it from her hand. It has grown limp from the perspiration of her nervousness.

Jonsson reads the content of the card aloud. "*Pierre Bolton, Investigator. Safe and Secure Children Canada.* Never heard of it. But I have seen that name before."

"He said that they watched for children at some sort of risk. It's a national organization. He said that if he found anything, he would pass the information over to the province, to the social workers to investigate from there."

"This is very helpful. Thank you."

Detective Jonsson asks, "Can I keep this?" He tucks the card into his notebook, not waiting for an answer. "Your son, Everett, you said. Everett Fitzgerald, is it?"

"Oh, no, he's from my first marriage. I was a Smith then. He is Everett Smith."

"You said that he argued with this Pierre Bolton?"

"Out at the road, yes. And Everett was furious when he came back in."

"Is Everett here now? Could I talk to him?"

"No, he left yesterday. He works on a feedlot down by Pincher Creek. Started back today."

"Do you have a phone number?"

"Yes, I'll get it. It's on my phone. He keeps changing his number. I don't even bother to try to remember it, just have him put it there in my phone for me." Jean digs through her purse, pulls out the phone, and shows it to the detective. Lars jots down the number.

"You said he went out yesterday?"

"Yeah, earlier in the day, like about noon. He usually leaves to go back after supper, but he said he wanted to go early, Jemma not being here, like . . ." Jean replies.

Jerry breaks in. "I remember that in the morning he asked whether the guy had left his card—that he wanted to call him, the Pierre Bolton guy. They had words over the phone. Then he packed his stuff up and left. Barely said goodbye to us. But he's like that. He gets into a snit and is gone."

They sit silently for a few minutes.

"I hate to say this," Jerry continues, "but when they were out at the road, it kind of got physical. Everett has a bit of a temper on him."

"Physical?"

"Yes. Everett took his boots to Mr. Bolton's car, all down the side, even knocked the side mirror off."

"You saw that?"

"Yes, from the window, right here. I remember thinking that if that car is a rental, the guy is sure going to be in trouble with the rental company. It was a black Malibu, brand new it looked."

"You know the make and year of the car?" Detective Jonsson looks incredulously at Jerry.

"It was exactly the same as the one we rented in Victoria this spring, when we went to the Butchart Gardens to see the tulips. I remember saying to Jean how much I liked the car. It had navigation and everything. I remember saying that the next car we get, I wanted to get one just like it. Then I look out the front window after Everett went out with him, and there's one sitting right out in front of our house! But boy, did Everett ever dent the fender. Makes you wonder, eh? Wonder how durable it'd be if it dents that easily. But Everett, he's pretty strong."

Detective Jonsson makes a few notes. Jean and Jerry wait. The detective launches back in. "We were talking about Dr. Horvath. Have you met him?"

"No."

"So this business, the suggestion that he's a pedophile, that's news to you?"

Jean answers, taking the floor from Jerry. "Most certainly. I don't think so, really. But that's what the guy kind of said. We know Jemma's mom. She was just over here the other night. Estelle is her name. She seems like a good mom. She keeps us pretty close to the line, about visits, you know. She doesn't seem like the sort of person who would let something bad happen. But you never know . . ."

Jean pauses. Having drawn her breath in, she continues in a softer voice, almost as if she doesn't want to be overheard, "She's a lesbian, you know. That's the sort of home that our granddaughter is being raised in. I don't think it's right. But nowadays, you know . . ."

"I'm certainly going to follow up on this. The information you've given is really important. If you remember anything else, you can be in touch. I'm going to give you my card." Detective Jonsson pauses, thinking there might be something else that he might need to ask. Finally, he goes to the door. He turns back to them. "When do you get to see your granddaughter again?"

"This Friday. This coming weekend is our weekend."

"Very well, then. Take good care of her. She's had a tragedy in her other family."

"Thanks for coming over, Detective," Jean looks at his card, "Jonsson."

When Lars gets back to the car, he leans the soggy business card against the screen on the computer that protrudes from the centre console. It's the second time that he has come across that name. Estelle Caylie had given him a similar card with that name on it. From his recollection, the card from her didn't have an agency name or logo on it, the one for Safe and Secure Children Canada. He would have followed that up.

Lars searches the name *Pierre Bolton* on the database of police contacts. Nothing comes up. He searches name variants and finds some records on three different Peter Boltons from across the country. Worth following up, but probably not relevant to someone who comes posing as a child investigator in Calgary.

Going to the internet, he types into the browser *Safe and Secure Children Canada*.

There is nothing. No such agency exists.

He dials the number on the Pierre Bolton card.

A not-in-service recording plays.

He searches the database for Everett Smith based out of Calgary and Pincher Creek. A criminal record for violent offences displays.

He calls Everett's number. It goes to voicemail. The greeting is by a rodeo-style announcer who, with a *Hee Haw Y'all,* suggests that he leave a message.

He calls Joyce back at the CGIS and reviews the leads he's obtained. He talks about Pierre Bolton, who is likely an also-known-as, and Everett Smith, who is a for-sure. Smith is probably somewhere down in southern Alberta, riding a horse in a bunch of cows. He asks her to search records on Jackson Horvath to see if there has been any investigation for pedophilia.

Lars goes over the tasks he assigns her. First, she is to go to the telecom companies to find where Everett Smith's phone might be pinging. Then the next step would be with car rental and fleet suppliers who rent black Malibus, to find one that has been damaged with dents in the front fender and the side-view mirror knocked off.

She's got it.

Dodi rushes out of Estelle's hospital room, leaving Nikki behind keeping watch. Approaching the nurses' station, she asks, "Can I get a meeting with Dr. Marsh?"

"He's back over on the unit. He only consults here on medical in the mornings."

"Can I get a message over to him to come? Something is happening with Estelle."

"Medically?"

"Psychiatrically, she's starting to come out of her unresponsive state."

"Here, I'll get you the extension to the ward. You can leave a message for him."

Dodi does.

Dodi then heads toward a small sitting area at the end of the corridor. She takes out her phone to call. "Leanne? Dodi here . . . Better, showing some signs of improvement . . . Yeah, a relief . . . she's starting to recognize me, like with more than a hand squeeze, with her eyes . . . Leanne, I have a question for you . . . that portrait you did of Estelle, the one with the book, you know the one you had out when I came yesterday evening? . . . In that picture, there was a book, I remember something about Stella and books . . . yeah, *Bookish Stella,* that's it, is that an actual book? . . . you wrote it and illustrated it? . . . Wow, yes . . . do you have a copy of the book? . . . Could you bring it? . . . and the painting too . . . yeah, down to the hospital . . ."

Nikki emerges from the room. She looks at Dodi, then mouths the words, *Who is it?*

Dodi mouths back—*Leanne.*

Nikki makes a gesture to indicate that she wants to speak with her.

"Wait a minute. Nikki is here, she wants to talk to you."

"Hi Leanne . . . yeah, I sat with her . . . listen, do you know where the car is, our car? . . . That would make sense, if she drove there . . . can you take me out to get it? . . . it'll be easier if . . . yeah, okay . . . sure, yes, I heard her ask . . . Okay, I'll meet you at the front of the hospital, bring those up to Dodi for Estelle, and then we can go . . . twenty minutes, sure . . . Thanks."

The two women stare at each other, uneasy about the presence of the other in the life of the woman they both love, the woman gradually returning to connection on the hospital bed.

Arriving at Nose Hill Depression and Anxiety Clinic, Leanne and Nikki see the police crime scene tape enveloping the entrance to the clinic. It is also contains Jackson's Lexus and Estelle's Honda. A gaggle of camera and sound men stand just outside the tape at the rear of the cars. Jason Gilbert from *Global News* is there with a middle-aged woman.

Jason nods and begins, camera rolling. "I'm standing outside the scene of a gruesome murder that took place last evening. Dr. Jackson Horvath, eminent Calgary psychiatrist, was found dead in his clinic here up in Country Hills. With me is Dr. Monica Lebresque, a colleague of Dr. Jackson. She wishes to speak to the patients of the clinic. Dr. Lebresque . . ."

"Thanks. We're deeply saddened and shocked to hear of the death of our colleague and friend. We are also concerned for the well-being of all the patients at our clinic. We've set up a temporary office in the North West Community Health Centre. The phone number for the clinic has been transferred there. My colleagues—Dr. Amir Alimessha, and Dr. Eric Johannsen—and I are there to respond to calls from our own patients and those of Dr. Horvath. We expect that our office here will be closed today, perhaps for the week. We encourage our patients to contact their family doctor or the hospital emergency department if they require immediate care."

"Will you be contacting Dr. Horvath's patients directly?" Jason asks.

"Our receptionist will put calls out cancelling his appointments. If his patients wish to speak to one of us, we will call them back. "

"And before we go, can you speak of Dr. Horvath, the legacy he leaves?"

Dr. Lebresque tears up, swallows. "He was a great man. A leader. We will dearly miss him."

"Thank you, Dr. Lebresque."

Nikki and Leanne stare at them, dealing again with a finality they had not expected.

Nikki approaches a police officer standing guard outside. "That's my car. Can I take it?" She asks, pointing to Estelle's Honda.

"I'm afraid not, ma'am."

"It's my car, see . . ." Nikki takes the key fob out of her purse and unlocks the doors of the Honda. Its headlights flash at the officer.

"I see. It's currently being held as a part of an investigation." His eyes flash with an expression of *it sucks to be you.*

Officers in baggy blue coveralls emerge from the door of the clinic. They take evidence cases to their vehicle.

"Well, it looks like it's wrapping up now. You can take down the tape, and I'll take the car out of here," Nikki asserts.

"I'm afraid not, ma'am."

A flatbed tow truck pulls up in the parking lot. One of the forensic officers goes over to the driver and points out the two vehicles to be taken away.

Dr. Aaron Marsh gently opens the door to Estelle's room. The hospital bed has been articulated so that Estelle is sitting up. Her eyes are open, but her face is still blank. Dodi sits beside her, reading a children's book, holding it so that the pictures are in front of Estelle. Dr. Marsh stands, quietly assessing and appreciating the scene in front of him. Entering the room, he catches sight of an oil painting facing the bed. It sits on the eraser tray of a whiteboard that announces, *Today is Monday, June 26. My name is Rochelle. I am your nurse for today. Your doctors are Dr. Wesley and Dr. Marsh. You have no tests scheduled today. You are allowed to have only two visitors at a time, family members or close friends only. Have a great day!* The oil painting is uncannily similar to the scene on the bed. Patient Estelle Caylie has the same book in front of her, *Bookish Stella*.

He smiles and takes a deep breath. He goes over to Estelle and takes her pulse. In doing so, he checks the rigidity of her peripheral musculature. "Hi, Estelle. I'm Dr. Marsh."

She deflects her eyes to look at him, makes no sign of greeting or recognition, then looks back to Dodi.

"You were reading. Can you continue?" Dr. Marsh settles back with a smile.

Not letting Dodi begin again, Estelle grabs the book, props it up in front of her, and in a childlike voice rhymes off the gentle chorus while her finger follows the words on the page. *"And just what colour will her jumpsuit be? Pinkle or bluey, greenish or yella? To know the colour will surely help me. Oh, help me find my bookish Stella."*

A subtle, brief smile teases the corners of Estelle's mouth.

Dr. Marsh motions Dodi toward the door. They leave together.

"Well, that's quite remarkable compared to this morning."

"Yes, yes indeed."

"Sometimes, these psychotic breaks due to shock can be quite brief. The issue, of course, is whether there is an underlying functional psychosis. The episode might be the tip of the iceberg. I'm encouraged, but still—"

"I don't think it's psychosis," Dodi says respectfully but firmly.

"This morning, when I assessed her, she was still in a catatonic state. From the look of her, that is easing."

"She's sitting up now."

"In the bed, but yes. Is she speaking yet? This morning, her verbal utterances were word salad. Excited gibberish."

"No, not speaking yet, but I don't think that was word salad we were hearing this morning."

"Her verbalizations were completely non-contextual to the questions that I asked. Rhyming words. Grammatically fragmented."

"You were hearing Dr. Seuss."

"Dr. Who?"

"Dr. Seuss. *The Cat in the Hat, Green Eggs and Ham.* That Dr. Seuss." A smile breaks across Dr. Marsh's face, a smile at the incongruity of it all.

"You know, we have no Dr. Seuss on staff here at Riverview Hospital."

"Well, I bet you do. In pediatrics, probably."

He pauses, feeling respect for this family member who seems to be making a connection with his patient. "Okay, Dr. . . ."

"Marseilles."

"Dr. Marseilles. Tell me why our catatonic patient is reciting Dr. Seuss."

"It's not catatonia at all. It's a severe regressive state. She's back in childhood. Dissociated."

"You psychologists! You keep coming up with pathologies that can't be medicated." Dr. Marsh's tone is taunting, jocular. A rapport is building between them.

"When she came in, in the fetal position—it was a deep infantile regression. She was speaking then but only angry, incoherent words, words spoken to her, not her own, like echolalia, repeating over and over. Through the night, the fear response passed, and the muscular rigidity relaxed. Now, she's rebuilding herself. As I've cuddled her and reassured her, she's started coming forward more like a preschooler, a little girl. It's happening slowly. It's as if her mind is trying to return to her, return through the developmental stages."

"Interesting. That book, the one you were reading?"

"Let me go and get it."

Dodi goes back in the room, sees Estelle sleeping peacefully in the bed. She slides the book from her hands and hastily retrieves the painting, too.

"This is her, her as a child. The author of the book is her Aunt Leanne. She did the illustrations, too. On the book's front cover is Estelle as a child reading the book, reading the book her aunt wrote about her. She was called Stella back then. In the painting, Leanne has the same book but shows Estelle as she is now."

"Now that is interesting. Look at her. The puzzled look. Gosh, her aunt is talented."

"So this makes sense now. The shock of the trauma, her father brutally murdered right in front of her. And, that's not all. A week ago her brother was murdered too. She profoundly regressed. But she's coming back."

"Is she conversational, responding to the present? I heard her read, but it was more like a recitation of a familiar story."

"Not yet—not speaking, but she is responding to me, looking at me. And for a brief moment, the child goes out of her eyes, and I think she is seeing me as an adult. We were lovers. We're still close. I think she's recognizing me for the adult relationship she has with me. Then she goes back to the child."

"I've never seen a case like this."

"Me neither. Well, that's not quite true. Down in Missouri, we had a number of young adults from a cult brought in when the police raided. There was some severe regression there. Not this profound, though."

"Well, we have no idea . . ."

"No." Dodi looks at him grimly.

Dr. Marsh looks at her, working out care plans and prognosis in his mind. "If this is what you say and given the improvement that we have seen in just a half day, I suspect she will spontaneously come out of it with your support."

"I'm concerned about something, though. She's at the stage of a preschooler now. Affect is positive. She cuddles in with the books as if she feels safe. But . . ."

"But?"

"But if there is childhood trauma, trauma subsequent to the developmental stage she is in now . . ."

"Abreaction?"

"Yes, and depending on the trauma, there could be quite a severe emotional and behavioural reaction to the repressed memory of that trauma."

"Do you have any reason to suspect?"

"The fact that her dissociative state is so. . . so persistent. Yes, normally, if there was no childhood trauma, we wouldn't see this degree of dissociation to an adult shock."

"What do you suggest?"

"Well, I'm building safety for her. The books, the companionship. I'm sure that she's hearing my voice. She's responding affectively, if not verbally. If there are severely traumatic Adverse Childhood Experiences, I could work her through them. I could use clinical hypnotherapy."

"I'm not comfortable with this. You're talking about performing an intrusive clinical procedure with someone you have a close personal relationship with."

"Do you have anyone else on staff who could . . . ?"

Dr. Marsh and Dodi look up to see Leanne walking down the hall.

"Auntie Leanne," Dodi greets her with relief.

Dr. Marsh turns and looks at her. "Leanne? I'm Dr. Marsh, psychiatrist. You must be the artist?" He glances from her face to the author's name on the cover of the book Dodi is holding.

"Yes, Estelle is my niece. I adopted her when she was a child."

"Hope you did a good job. Dr. Marseilles here has a hunch that she is going to be going all the way through that again."

He turns to Dodi. "Don't. Just be a friend, a family member. Let's see how this naturally resolves. I'm on shift until seven. I'll check back before I go."

Leanne looks intensely at Dodi and says, "We don't know where Nali is."

Dodi looks back and says, "Who is Nali?"

With that, the three look up and see Detective Lars Jonsson coming back down the hall.

An hour or so later, by the time Lars finally makes it back to the conference room at the CGIS, both Staff Sergeant Danton and Inspector Grant are meeting with Joyce. Lars comes in to hear discussions already underway—overtime and staff resource deployment. He's glad he's missed that part.

"So bring us up to date, Detective Jonsson." The inspector settles him under a piercing gaze.

"Well, I've just been to the hospital. According to what we have from the notes taken at the scene and forensics, we think an Estelle Caylie there is a witness. She's the daughter of the deceased. She's still not able to be interviewed. I met with her doctor, a psychiatrist." Lars consults his notebook. "A Dr. Marsh. There's improvement, but she's still uncommunicative, presumably still in shock. We continue to have a uniform posted at her door.

"I have concerns about Estelle's spouse, Nikki Blaser. Horvath's daughter-in-law. When I asked about her whereabouts when Horvath was attacked, she gave an alibi that turns out to be bogus.

"And now, since earlier today, I also have two other suspects. They were seen arguing outside a residence. The first is a Mr. Everett Smith, father of Jackson Horvath's granddaughter, Emma . . . Emma is it?" He looks at his notes again. "Jemma. Apparently, they were arguing about the possibility that Horvath is, er . . . was, a pedophile—"

Joyce breaks in. "I've done a search of both CPIC and our own database. There's nothing to indicate that Horvath was. I have a call in to Children Services to see if they have anything on their databases."

Lars continues. "This Everett Smith apparently has a temper and a criminal record for assault. He was last seen yesterday, leaving his parents' Calgary home in a fit of anger. To be clear about the timelines here—Everett left his parents' home hours before Horvath was killed. They aren't an alibi for him at the time of the murder. His parents indicated he was on his way to his job as a cattle hand down in the Pincher Creek area."

Joyce adds a further report on the progress of the investigation. "We've just started to verify Everett's whereabouts and timing of travel. We are in the process of accessing telecom data to determine where Everett Smith's phone is. We're also going to access text messages from his phone and the meta-data on his calls."

The inspector turns back to Lars. "And the other suspect?"

"Can I?" Joyce asks.

"Go ahead," Lars says.

"Everett Smith's parents, Jean and Jerry Fitzgerald, had a business card for the person arguing with their son. They gave that card to Lars—it named a Pierre Bolton. The Fitzgeralds report the argument took place in front of a late-model black Malibu outside the home. In the argument, Everett took the boots to Bolton's car. Lars, here, suggested that we canvas car rental and fleet services. So, I got in touch with all of those companies. Several rent out Malibus. It's apparently quite a popular car on the rental circuit. When I mentioned the dented front fender, Hertz Rentals downtown said they had one returned this morning with damage. I put in for the warrant but went down to check it out even before we had the warrant in hand."

"And?"

Lars sits up in his chair. He hasn't heard this part.

Joyce lays a photocopy of a driver's licence on the table. "The vehicle was returned by . . . no mystery here . . . a Pierre Bolton. He's a resident of Chicago, Illinois. The manager of the car rental was quite cooperative. He had heard of Dr. Jackson Horvath's death, had even been his patient at one point. Wanted to help out however he could."

"So did your investigations turn up any further information on this Pierre Bolton?"

"He's not in any of our databases. I was just going to canvas the hotels near the car rental, figured that if he was from Chicago and turned in a car in downtown Calgary, perhaps he's staying in a hotel here."

"Good idea." A restive silence settles over the conference.

Lars goes to speak but Staff Sergeant Danton interjects before he has a chance to do so. "We have some preliminary forensics."

"Go ahead," the inspector says.

"First of all, we have an approximate time of death for the victim: yesterday, between five and six pm. And the officers have completed the investigation at the crime scene. They still have the blood spatter analysis from the photos to do and are sending away blood for DNA. It's likely that blood is just the victim's, this Dr. Horvath. They've impounded the two vehicles that were out in front. Those vehicles are registered to the victim and Estelle Caylie, who was found collapsed at the scene—"

The inspector looks to Detective Jonsson. "But who you haven't been able to interview yet."

"No, not yet. She's in the hospital, in shock and uncommunicative."

"Go on." The inspector looks back to Danton.

"Well, it looks like in addition to Estelle Caylie and the victim, there were at least two other people in the room. There's a distinct blood spatter shadow standing right beside where Estelle Caylie was collapsed on the floor. So the perpetrator is thought to be the fourth person in the room. There were chaotic shoeprints in the blood that we have photographed also. From the shoeprint size and shape, most likely a male. There were multiple blows and stab wounds to the victim that created a very complex scene."

"So are you thinking that these two suspects, what were their names . . ."

"Pierre Bolton and Everett Smith."

"Yes, that one or other of them, or both, could've been in the room, as well as the deceased's daughter—"

"—Estelle Caylie. Yes, could very well be."

"Are either capable of murder? Do either of them have a motive?"

"Well, if Horvath is a pedophile, then the former son-in-law, the father of Horvath's granddaughter, would definitely have a motive."

"That's this Everett, right?"

"Yes. And he's likely to be physically capable. He's a cowboy, so probably fit and strong. He's also described as having a temper and has a record for violent assault."

"What about this Pierre Bolton?"

"There's something sketchy about him. He gave Everett Smith's parents a business card with a fake agency name. He posed as an investigator for the safety of their granddaughter. He was the one who insinuated that Horvath was a pedophile."

"You mentioned that the woman found at the scene—"

"Estelle Caylie,"

"Yes, Caylie, could she have been the perpetrator?"

"She was in shock when the police arrived and covered in blood, presumably the victim's blood. She is his daughter, raised by her aunt. If, as has been suggested, this Horvath was a pedophile, she could've been a victim of incest, would have motive. Or, maybe she suspected Horvath of doing something to her own daughter. But, of course, we think that Caylie had already collapsed on the floor at that time of the attack.

"And if not her, then maybe her partner, who is this Nikki Blaser, a second mother to the little girl."

"Didn't you mention that she gave a bogus alibi? Do you think she would be capable of a violent murder?"

"Nikki Blaser, yes. But the style of killing—multiple blows, sufficient to break the wooden shafts on really old golf clubs and then stab wounds with a sizable knife. That doesn't seem like a woman's way to kill. And the shoeprints were most likely male. Setting that aside, I guess that this Blaser, if she somehow had found out about incest against her partner . . ."

"Didn't you mention that they have a child, their own little girl?" The inspector asks.

"Yes."

"So if Horvath is a pedophile it's possible he sexually assaulted their daughter. If so they both would certainly have motive against him. The rage that they felt might motivate such a violent assault, more than we might normally expect for a woman."

"Remember though, we have no real evidence that Horvath was a pedophile. And by the way," Joyce pulls a binder out of the evidence bag she had brought into the room, "This was recovered from Estelle Caylie's car. It was lying on the back seat but open to a particular page." Joyce places it open on the table in front of the staff sergeant and inspector. Lars looks on curiously.

"I've just taken a cursory look. It appears to be written by Estelle's brother, GJ. It has worksheets and writings from being in rehab. Where it was open to . . . well, it looks like a letter of amends, like from AA. He's taking responsibility for sexually abusing his sister in childhood. GJ sexually abused Estelle Caylie."

A hush settles over the room. Finally, the inspector speaks. "GJ . . . Caylie . . . For some reason, that rings a bell."

"Should do," Staff Sergeant Danton interjects. "Gerald Jonathan Caylie was killed in the Starbucks incident just over a week ago."

Nali rouses herself. For the first time since pulling herself from the unconsciousness of her injury, her eyes immediately focus, clear of the blur and
double vision she had fought earlier in the day.

She takes in the claustrophobic angles of the A-frame cabin. The sofa where
she's been lying looks out through patio doors. The sky is a brilliant azure with
billowy clouds lit to salmon hues.

Four cans of ginger ale sit on an end table beside her. All are open, all
only partially consumed. A large bottle of Extra Strength Tylenol is there,
too—her sustenance in recovery. Her mouth feels fuzzy. Her saliva is thick
with the drink's remnant sugars, now rancid between her teeth. She is thirsty,
profoundly thirsty. She feels a desperate need to brush her teeth.

As she rouses herself, a familiar nausea creeps at her gut causing her tummy
to heave.

Jimmy Murphy stands at the railing of the deck, having a smoke, looking
out away from her.

Nali stumbles to her feet, finds her bearings and walks weakly to the bathroom. Sitting on the toilet, she feels relieved—relieved of the pressure in her
bladder, relieved of the unsteadiness of her legs and feet and the resolve it
has taken to walk there, relieved of being in Jimmy's sight. She searches the
drawers of the vanity for a toothbrush and finds one still in its packaging. She
struggles to release it, her fingers fumbling to find their coordination. A clean
feeling washes through her as she brushes the stench off her teeth.

Looking in the mirror, she is struck by the sight of the tattoo—the curl of
the cobra up her chest and around her neck, the magic of the tongue beneath
her right jawline. It embraces her. It empowers her. It enables her.

Then she looks down at her clothing—a light denim jacket, a navy shell,
jeans—all splattered in blood. Lifting her jacket to her nose, she smells the
blood's stale, metallic dryness there.

Nali looks at her hair. Her purse had been left on the counter, its comb
protruding. Nali tugs at tangles that pull at her scalp. Her hair is dank, lifeless,
and deflated. As the comb goes to the back of her head, the sharp pain of

the wound catches her. She dampens a washcloth and daubs at it. The bright crimson of fresh bleeding accompanies the flecks of blood. Touching it, the headache returns.

Nali winces with the pain.

There's an open window high above the toilet, between the vanity and tub. Nali awkwardly climbs on the closed lid of the toilet. Steadying herself on the windowsill, she peers out. The tremble of an aspen grove greets her. It is darkening, dense. A damp, cool breeze blows through it. She leans on the windowsill, breathes in the clean, pure air, air ripe with the ozone smell of a thunderstorm nearby. Nali leans and thinks.

With deliberate and exhausting effort, Nali forces herself to remember back through the day. She places each awakening, ginger ale and Tylenol, as stepping stones back to her arrival with Jimmy Murphy at this cabin. She steps back further to the memory of being in the backseat of his car, the sun streaming in. Dawn, and now dusk. A day has passed.

And before that, nothing. Nothing to tell her how she fell into Jimmy's grasp or how she got the gaping wound on the back of her head and the blinding headache that has weakened her. Yesterday is blank. Slowly, a haze of her life rebuilds to remember awakening on her day off and then waiting for her kid sister, Estelle, urgently coming to pick her up.

That is there. She is here. There's nothing in-between.

In the empty space she places Jimmy Murphy, the creep of him, places him within her tortured circumstance as her captor.

Slowly, it occurs to her that she must engage with him.

Gathering strength she walks from the bathroom, walks as steadily and resolutely as she can. She opens the patio door and takes her place, leaning against the deck railing.

"I feel gross. I need to have a shower."

"Sure, go ahead." Jimmy turns to look at her, "How's the head?"

"Still pretty painful. No funny business, eh?"

"I'll be a perfect gentleman. After all, we are starting something here, you and me together. Let's get off on the right foot."

She looks at him, at the absurdity of it.

"My clothes, they need to be washed."

"I was planning on doing a wash tomorrow. I'll throw them in with mine."

"Blood on them."

"Yeah, I guess. You hit your head pretty bad." Jimmy looks at the back of her head. "Still bleeding a bit."

"Until then? Until we do the wash?"

"Oh." Jimmy pauses. "There's my mom's stuff, in her bedroom. Old lady stuff, though."

Nali winces.

"Tell you what. I'll get out a clean pair of boxers and a T-shirt for you. That should keep you covered until we do the wash. I'll go and get that now."

Jimmy leaves. Nali watches a train cross the trestle bridge. The noise of it penetrates the trees, echoes in the valley. She remembers Jimmy said something about a town on the other side of the hill. She will watch for its lights tonight, make that a destination. The salmon in the eastern clouds is turning to ruby red, the azure in the sky to indigo. The entire sky overhead is ablaze.

On the way to the bathroom, she checks out Jimmy's mom's room. It smells stale in there. The furnishings are old, decent. Tatted doilies are placed underneath jewellery boxes. A flowered, pink housecoat is hanging in the closet, its synthetic fabric pilled. It will cover her. Depending on just how pervy Jimmy Murphy is, it will probably be a sexual turnoff between him and her. Jimmy's mom has a small two-piece bath off her bedroom. Nali slips off her clothes there and gently washes her underclothing using lingerie soap she finds underneath in the vanity, laying them on a towel to dry. Nali puts on the dowdy housecoat with the sash pulled tight, picks up her clothes, and heads to the main bathroom to shower.

Life is returning to her, and with it a sense of abject terror of her situation.

After her shower, Nali takes her place beside Jimmy. The tattered housecoat covers his boxer shorts and T-shirt. They feel grossly perverted to her but somehow add an extra layer of modesty. The sky has darkened and stars are emerging. Pocket thunderstorms are erupting to the south. The scene flashes with sheet lightning. A ragged slash traverses from cloud to ground and the constant rumble of thunder breaks into a high-pitched crack.

They watch yet another train cross the trestle bridge. Its light illuminates a short section of track in front of it. The rumble and mournful whistle add to the soundscape.

"Feeling better?" Jimmy asks, his gaze deflecting down the length of her.

Nali's years of experience judging the leers of men tell her to be cautious. She decides not to bite at the sexualization of his stare—to be straightforward but ready to take defensive action if needed. Given her weakened state and being on his home turf, it makes no sense to confront as that just might escalate him.

"Yes. Tired, still a bit weak and shaky. Still feel like I might puke."

"The headache."

"The Tylenol is knocking it down. Thanks for putting it out."

"Beautiful here, eh?"

"Yeah. Jimmy, what are your intentions?"

"For tomorrow? Tomorrow, I think I'll bring Mom out, out from the nursing home. She'll want to meet you. She's heard lots about you."

"You know, Jimmy, I'm not here willingly."

"Yeah, I know. For now. But give it time. This place will grow on you. A relief from the city."

"But if I don't want to be here?"

"We all face things we don't want to deal with. And we deal with them. I certainly did—your rejection of me as a teen, watching you dance for other men at the club. But now it'll be different. You'll see soon enough that you are free out here. I've enough money from the sale of the family land, enough that we can live here in this beautiful place for the rest of our lives. You and me."

"But if I don't want to?"

Jimmy turns and looks at her. There is an edge to his jaw, visible as the lightning briefly flashes. "Look, Anna. Your brother got me in a peck of trouble back in Calgary. You introduced me to him years ago. Then you left us both to our devices. Well, I dealt with that. I did time, his time, came back and put an end to it all. And what I know now . . ."

"What do you know?" Nali's eyes are getting tired. The brain fuzz is coming back.

"Enough!" Jimmy turns from her, turns to go back into the cabin. "You ungrateful bitch! I saved you. Appreciate it. Appreciate me. You'll thank me for this. Just give it time."

Jimmy turns in disgust and goes back inside the A-frame. Nali moves to the other end of the deck, looks back out over the valley. Reflected in a low bank of clouds, she sees the dull light of town, a town just over the hills.

CHAPTER NINETEEN

Tuesday

Leanne sits gently at the side of the spare room bed. "Dodi . . . Dodi . . ."
When they left the hospital the night before, Estelle was content. She related to Dodi and then Leanne—related in a childlike way, innocent and grateful. She was speaking but still in phrases from children's books. There was no reference to the trauma that had brought her into the hospital, that horror Leanne and Dodi had stumbled upon twenty-four hours before. Occasionally, there'd be a flash of fear across Estelle's face. Occasionally, the storm clouds of temper would appear. Then she would calm, almost eerily so. She could say their names—Leanne was Auntie, and Dodi was Dodi. When Auntie and Dodi left the hospital, a nurse was at Estelle's side, providing her with nighttime sedation. They had come a long way with her.

Arriving back at 113 Durham Lane, Dodi showered and unpacked her suitcase, settling in. Leanne checked in with Nikki—found that she and Jemma were doing okay at the condo. She updated Nikki that Estelle was coming around and decided not to mention the key role that Dodi was playing in her recovery. She called April and gave her the update. As Estelle's car was impounded, they still couldn't come for her. April understood. And when April observed that little Harry had now lost both a father and a grandfather, Leanne commiserated. Again it hit home with her—she had lost a brother and GJ, whom she'd raised as a son. Finally, Leanne sent desperate text messages to Nali, messages that languish unanswered.

And now it is morning. "Dodi . . . Dodi . . ."

Dodi rouses, having caught a few solid hours. An urgency creeps into Leanne's awakening of her.

"Dodi, the hospital called. Estelle had a bad night. They want you there as soon as possible."

When Nali wakes on the sofa, the A-frame is bathed in light. She hears the gentle rhythm of Jimmy's snoring in the loft above the kitchen.

The headache that gripped her through the previous day is losing its grasp—not yet gone, but at least down to a dull roar. Her eyes are clear when they open, her vision no longer doubled. She is able to make her way toward the bathroom without dizziness. As she passes the kitchen, she sees it is 8:07 on the microwave clock.

Catching her own image in a mirror, she orients to the Bryan Adams T-shirt she is wearing, the one telling her to *GET UP*.

She is.

Nali looks out through the patio doors, across the deck to the valley below. It rained heavily through the night and there's still the sound of water dripping. Now, the sky is clear. She stands considering what to do, then turns back into the cabin and begins.

Nali had noticed a patio door off Jimmy's mother's bedroom the night before. Looking now, she sees it exits out onto a small deck surrounded by trees. She could escape from there, and Jimmy wouldn't see her leave.

Reassured by Jimmy's snores, she begins to collect what she'll need.

Going into the small laundry room at the back of the A-frame, Nali trades in his T-shirt and boxers for her own clothing, clothing splattered in blood. Jimmy's sweaty, blood-splattered clothing is there, too. She picks it up with a sense of disgust. Her stomach heaves as the scene from the day before comes back to her—the memory of his brutal attack on her father is clear now. As much as Jimmy Murphy was an annoyance when he was harassing her, now she sees him for the monster he has turned out to be. Presence of mind, the clarity that she had honed at the gentlemen's club, comes back to her. While some men are just pathetic, others are dangerous—knowing the difference is essential for survival. She knows now.

Deliberately, Nali picks up Jimmy's blood spattered T-shirt from the day before and finds a plastic grocery bag to put the disgusting thing into. In the pocket of Jimmy's jeans she notices a hunter's knife, the kind that the handle can contain the blade with a swivel and a snap. It's covered with blood. Nali searches the kitchen and finds a box of Ziplocs. Carefully, she turns one inside out and picks up the closed knife with the inside of the bag. She turns the bag back onto itself and zips it shut. On a hook in the entranceway she finds a small backpack. She stuffs his shirt and the carefully preserved knife into it.

The refrigerator has a couple of bottles of water, the cupboard some cereal bars. She stuffs those into the backpack as well. She brushes her teeth, taking comfort in the normalcy of the action.

On the desk in the kitchen she finds a lime green pad of Post-it notes. She writes—*If we are going to make this work here, Jimmy, I need a proper bed to sleep in.* Then a second note—*So last night I took your mom's room.* And another—*Please let me sleep in tomorrow. I am recovering from an injury.* Finally—*We will talk tomorrow when I get up.*

Nali places the notes on the outside of the door to Jimmy's mother's bedroom, closing it from inside. She stuffs pillows and blankets into the bed in the form of a sleeping body, dishevels the sheets and covers.

She slips out the patio door. Behind the A frame is Jimmy's Camaro. Looking inside she sees her cellphone on the front passenger seat—tantalizingly just a few feet away, inaccessible as all the car doors are locked. Nali heads up the winding road tunnelling back through the trees.

"So, the situation is this," Dr. Marsh begins. "Through the night, she had two agitated awakenings—like a child's night terrors. The first one passed and she went back to sleep. Dr. Isaac had to intervene with the second one. He was nervous to do so but did add in a dose of alprazolam—nervous because there was already temazepam on board.

"But this morning, she is fearful. I keep remembering what you said, Dodi—can I call you Dodi?—about the chance of early-life trauma predisposing her to severe dissociation. I can't help but think in looking at her that she might be avoiding reliving that childhood trauma by staying stuck in this child-like state.

"So I've decided that we will try the hypnosis." He pauses for clarity, for emphasis. "*I* will try the hypnosis. I'm trained to do so. I don't want you doing it, Dodi, being a close friend. But may I ask that you be present? If there is trauma and I am unable to calm her hypnotically, perhaps you could do so with your physical presence."

"Certainly."

"I'd really like to record a video of the hypnosis. I must admit that I'm apprehensive. A colleague was falsely accused by a patient he'd hypnotized who had a history of childhood sexual abuse. And there is the issue of consent. For obvious reasons, Estelle is not able to consent—to either the hypnosis itself or the video recording."

Dr. Marsh turns to Leanne. "You were listed as next of kin on the hospital admission form. Would you give consent?"

Leanne looks hesitant. "It really should be her wife, Nikki Blaser. She's at home taking care of their daughter."

"I met Nikki yesterday."

"Yes. I can phone her. Would that do?"

"There'll be forms to sign. I'll make notation of verbal consent from Nikki and you signing on her behalf."

Dr. Marsh pauses, looks back to Dodi. "This might be messy, given her severely dissociated state already."

"Yeah, you won't need to do an induction or deepening. Establishing authoritative connection or even just a place of curious engagement should be all you need to do."

"I'll do a light induction, just to establish a presence in her mind. Then, depending on what she abreacts to, I'll follow the lead of her mind. Do we have any idea what we might uncover?"

Dodi shakes her head. Estelle had been guarded in talking about her childhood while they lived together in graduate school. Dodi always wondered what might be back there, had a sense of certainty that something was.

Leanne looks more fearful. She knows the Horvath/Caylie family story.

"Can I go in and see her now?" Dodi asks.

"Sure." Dr. Marsh motions Leanne back toward the nursing station. "Let's get those forms faxed over from my office, and we will get you to sign. I have to check in on the other ward. Let's walk over there together and you can fill me in on Estelle's childhood. We will do the hypnosis when I come back."

The gravel road behind the A-frame is sloppy with the deluge of the night before. Arriving at the top of the hill, Nali finds herself in a farmyard. A couple of men are busying themselves with a tractor and an enormous spraying apparatus. She watches them for a long time, waiting for them to clear away onto the farm task of the day. Living this close, these men would know Jimmy. At this point, her trust in men has pretty well been shattered.

Nali walks back down the lane toward the cabin and decides she'll make her way on her own—down onto the valley floor, up the hill to the town that awaits at the other side of the rise. The slope is slippery. She's soon soaked with the wet of the trees.

The river at the bottom of the valley is five or six metres wide. She takes off her shoes and rolls up the legs of her jeans, stepping in the muck to make her crossing. The water smells foul—foul from the runoff of a commercial hog operation upstream, foul from pesticides and fertilizer sprayed on crops but washed off into the river by the heavy rains the night before. The foot she places into the murky water searches for a firm place in the bottom's slime. Sliding with the uncertain footing, she oozes halfway up her calf in the muck. She almost topples over—one foot in, the other still on the bank, dizzy with the unbalance of it all. With the dizziness, the headache roars back in full force and she feels bile rise in her throat. The yuck of the clay bottom releases more of its stench. As she pulls her foot out of the mud she finds a leech attached to her calf.

She can't do it, can't put her feet back in there.

The trestle bridge is overhead. A train passes over, its burden borne by the steel beams stalwart under its weight. The screaming of metal on metal and the rattle of the swaying cars are deafening. As the sound fades, she becomes aware of the war games pounding again in the military base just a couple of kilometres away. Repeated thuds of mortar fire rumble in the distance.

She'll have to cross the valley on that trestle bridge above.

When Dodi enters the room, a huge smile breaks across Estelle's face. It's still a naïve, childlike smile—more like how a besotted grade one student would greet her wonderful teacher. But it is a smile. Dodi feels emotional harmony with the child Estelle, a remnant of their playfulness and shared delight with infant Jemma those years ago. A breakfast tray sits on the bedside table. Dodi notices that some of the applesauce has been eaten, a few bites of toast. The glass of orange juice is now only half full. The plastic tub of honey has had its silvery top torn back, and a small plastic spoon coated with toast crumbs is stuck back into it.

"Good morning!" Dodi greets.

Estelle quickly reaches for *Bookish Stella*, as it sits on the nightstand. She holds it firmly in her grasp. The catatonic flaccidity has gone. They settle in together. She recites the entire book as Dodi turns the pages, her child voice loud and clear.

Then a look of abject fear crosses her face. Dr. Marsh has come into the room. Dodi reaches out and holds her hand. Estelle clutches it, panicky.

"Good morning, Estelle. You may remember me. I'm Dr. Marsh, the psychiatrist, from yesterday. I was to see you here in the hospital." He places a cellphone against the box of tissues on the hospital tray. A small red light on the screen blinks that it is recording.

Estelle stares back suspiciously.

"I'd like to speak with you a few minutes—would that be okay?" He waits for Estelle to reply and gets a tentative nod of acquiescence. He takes a deep breath. "We're going to have a special sort of conversation today, one that will help us help you. Is that okay?"

Again Estelle nods.

"To start this conversation off, for a few minutes, you just need to listen, listen to the sound of my voice. Can you do that?"

Estelle nods, and her eyes close.

"Thank you for being willing to listen as I talk. For you to listen, to really listen, might be hard, but you can listen, and in listening, you will feel safe, and you will feel relaxed." Dr. Marsh's voice takes on a gentle, swaying rhythm, almost as if he is reading a children's story.

"In listening, you will find that you remember. And sometimes, in remembering, you will forget to listen, but you will listen instead to what you remember. You will remember things from a long, long time ago. You will remember things from just a few days ago. You will remember . . ."

Estelle softens into Dodi, who now sits on the bed beside her. Estelle reaches out her hand and places it in Dodi's. She leans in, cuddling. Her face is set on that of Dr. Marsh. Her eyes blink open and are now staring blankly.

"And some things that you remember will be fun. And some things you remember might be scary or sad. And whatever they are, you can remember because you are safe here, safe with Dodi, safe with me, your doctor."

Suddenly, a look of terror crosses Estelle's face. Tears form in her eyes. Her body starts to tremble. Her brows form low over her eyes. Her upper lips curls in, her chin sets resolute. Dodi feels Estelle's heart suddenly race. The monitor behind the bed tracking her vitals goes into alarm, beeping plaintively, lights flashing. She stares daggers at the male presence in the room.

Slowly, Dr. Marsh goes around behind Dodi and flips a switch on the front of the vitals monitor, silencing it. He goes to the door and intercepts the nurse who had rushed to the room. Dodi takes Estelle into her arms and speaks soothingly to her.

When Dr. Marsh comes back to the bedside, Estelle looks at him warily. Her face flashes a hundred feelings in a half second. He is held in place by the look. Dodi catches his eye and mouths *Back off.* He does and stands aside, hidden from Estelle's sight by the curtain around the bed.

Dodi speaks. "Stella, Stella dear. I have you. You are safe . . . That's it . . . you are safe . . . I have you . . . I will keep you safe. The man is going to stay over there." Dodi's voice has taken on the same slow and gentle rhythm. Her words are unhurried, clearly articulated, and softly spoken.

Estelle relaxes. Dodi shifts back away from Estelle—no longer at her side holding her but sitting down the bed so she can look at Estelle's face to read the play of emotions there. She turns and adjusts the camera by the tissue box so that it captures Estelle's face full on. Then she deliberately reaches her left hand to hold Estelle's right hand.

"And we were remembering . . . remembering . . . remembering can be like watching TV. We can watch a program for a while, and then if we need to, we can switch the channel to watch something else. Some programs are just for the grownups, but kids sometimes watch them too . . . and some programs are like reading a favourite book . . ."

"Pippi Longstocking?" child Stella asks.

"Yes, Pippi Longstocking . . . or Dr. Seuss . . . you can watch whatever you want . . . and sometimes grownups want to you watch something with them . . . and that is okay, too.

"We're going to play a fun pretend game. You can feel my hand, but I want you to pretend that my hand is the remote control of the TV you are watching. You have the remote. Not your daddy, not your Auntie Leanne. But you. And you can change the channel when you need to do so. You can change it by moving your fingers. Can you move your fingers to change the channel on the TV, on your remembering? . . . That's so good. . . you are good at this game."

Estelle is smiling.

"How old are you, Stella?"

"I am five." Dodi looks at Estelle's face. It is peaceful, playful.

"By magic, I am going to ask you to fly through time to when you are six. Can you do that?"

"I am six. Go to school."

Then Estelle's face clouds.

"Let's just stay there. Can you tell me what you are feeling?"

"Scared. Really scared."

"Okay, then. Remember, I am with you. You're safe with me. And when you need to change the channel on your remembering, you can do so. Do you remember how to do so?"

Stella nods.

"Can you tell me where you are?"

"On the ceiling."

"On the ceiling? Okay. What's it like up there?"

"Cold, but that's okay. The woodstove is on."

"Can you tell me more? Listen . . . listen. . . what do you hear?"

"The rain, the rain on the windows. And the wind. And the ocean. It's scary out there."

"And what do you taste in your mouth?"

"Nothin.'"

"And what do you smell?"

Estelle sniffs a bit. Her face screws up.

"You're smelling something, Stella. Can you tell me what it is?"

"Bad breath. Yuck!"

"Yuck. Is there someone else there with you?"

Estelle nods.

"Up on the ceiling with you?"

Estelle shakes her head.

"Down below?"

Estelle nods.

"Okay, Stella. You are so good at this. But remember you can change the channel, can change it anytime you want."

Estelle nods.

Dodi takes stock. She realizes she must proceed really carefully. What she asks must be asked with complete neutrality, not leading in any way. Memories come back but are malleable, can be distorted. She can't lead here, only follow. She takes a quick glance over at the phone's video camera. It is still recording.

"I want you to listen really carefully, listen. Is it one person with you, or more?" When Dodi said *one*, Estelle shook her head, but when she said *more*, Estelle nodded. "Are the people with you saying anything?"

Estelle, in her Stella voice, adopts a mocking tone. "Do it, GJ. Do it... You are such a wimp, GJ. Can't you do it? Do it to her."

Dodi swallows hard.

Estelle gags, as though something has touched the roof of her mouth. Her eyes dart with confusion, then a tear escapes.

"Remember ... you are safe ..."

Estelle deliberately pushes her index finger into Dodi's hand. Her face relaxes.

"That's really good, Stella. You remembered ..."

Estelle sits. Her breath comes in gasps. After a minute or so, she asks, "Can I go back?"

"Only if you wish."

"I want to see. I want to tell you."

"You go back when you are ready."

Estelle speaks with a hollow child voice. "Daddy is here, and he stinks. And Anna, too. And GJ. I am lying there. They make GJ pull down my pyjama bottoms. Then Anna pulls down his. They are laughing. Laughing at GJ. I can't breathe. Down there on the rug, I can't breathe. I can breathe up here on the ceiling. Not down there. Now GJ is on top of me. He's crying. He can't breathe either. They are laughing.

"Then Daddy falls. And everyone is mad."

Estelle's eyes dart back and forth. Her stomach is heaving, as if she might be sick. Then she stills. "That's all."

Dodi sees that the tension is gone from Estelle. She speaks comfortingly to her. "Thank you, Stella, you have done really well to tell me all of this."

Dodi pauses. Her eyes connect in a different way with the patient on the bed.

"And thank you, Estelle. Your wise and gracious subconscious mind has shared its memories. Your deepest mind, in its wisdom, will know if your conscious mind can handle this memory after you come out of this hypnosis. When you alert, you will remember in your conscious mind just what you need to remember to be able to return to us as the adult Estelle."

A determined look overtakes Estelle. Her eyes narrow, her jaw sets. She deliberately pushes her index finger into Dodi's hand. She begins to vibrate. Dodi feels Estelle's hand go clammy in her own.

"Estelle, Stella, you've changed the channel... what do you see?" Dodi asks.

"Father."

"You see your father?"

"He has a golf club, and he's swinging it."

Dodi hears the voice, not of child Stella, but of adult Estelle. "Take your time, Estelle... Let's do this slowly. Remember, I'm here with you, and you can change the channel whenever you need to... Where are you and your father?"

"In his office, on the North Hill."

"Are you safe there?"

"I'm on the ceiling again."

"Okay, that is okay. You tell me from the ceiling what is going on. Do you know why your father is swinging a golf club?"

"Because he has a knife."

"Who has a knife?"

Estelle goes silent but her eyes dart back and forth. Her clammy hand reaches out for Dodi's.

"Take a deep breath, Estelle. I am here with you, take a deep breath."

Estelle's body calms, but her eyes still flash.

"Is there anyone else in the room with you and your father?"

"I'm not in the room. I'm on the ceiling."

"Who else is there with you?"

"No one. No one is on the ceiling with me. Just me."

"You are doing really well, Estelle. Really well. Some things are hard to remember. I'm with you through this. You're safe with me, but the memory is scary. The memory can't hurt you anymore. It's just a memory. You can tell the memory, and it doesn't need to be just inside of you any longer. I can be with you when you tell it. Remember, if you need to, you can switch channels."

"I don't want to switch channels. Stop saying that!"

"Okay, Estelle. Stay and watch. When you're ready, tell me more of what you see."

Estelle takes on another voice, a coarse and sarcastic voice. "Oh, GJ you're so weak. Just do it. Don't wimp out, GJ. He went after you with a club. Be a man, GJ. You can hit him, too. Hit him hard. Do it GJ. Let him have it. Oh good, GJ, you have a knife. Use your knife on him, GJ. Do it."

Dodi lets the words reverberate in the room. Still she holds Estelle's hands. Her own mind is reeling.

Estelle speaks again. "Stab him, GJ. Stab him with your knife. It's not little. Put it in him."

Estelle's voice changes, a different feminine voice now, urgent. "Estelle, that's not GJ. That's Jimmy, Jimmy Murphy. Stop! Stop, Jimmy!"

Estelle curls into a fetal position on the bed.

Dr. Marsh emerges from behind the curtain. He takes a quick look at the monitor and then mouths, *Alert her. Bring her out of trance.* Dodi nods.

"Okay, Estelle. I am with you. This is Dodi. You are safe. In a few minutes, I am going to count, count upward from one to three. When I reach three you will be able to open your eyes, and you will be fully awake and alert.

"But first, before we start counting, I want you to know that you have done good work. You are now relieved of holding your painful memories alone. You will remember all that you need to remember from the work that you have done here, all that you need to remember for you to return to us as adult Estelle.

"And so, I'm going to say the number one. As you hear the number one, your body is able to relax. You can rest comfortably on the bed. One. You are safe here. I am with you. I, Dodi, am with you."

Estelle straightens out on the bed, her jaw unclenches, then clenches, and then unclenches again. Her brow smooths.

"That is excellent. In a few minutes, I will say the number two for you. Not yet, but soon. And when you hear the number two, you will see through your mind's eye the hospital room we are in. You may have trouble remembering that room, but you have seen it, and you are excellent at remembering. You don't need to see it yet. Other scenes may still be passing through your eyes, scenes from the remembering work that you have done so excellently here. The remembering work that you have done will allow you to return to us as the adult Estelle. You will still have work to do on those memories, work to do in your conscious mind, work to do with me, with Dr. Marsh here. But you can do that work when you are more ready."

Dodi watches for abreaction to the name Dr. Marsh. She sees no reaction from Estelle. Her face is calm.

"Two."

Dodi sees Estelle's eyes dart under her eyelids.

"Very good. With your eyes still closed, I want you to remember everything about the room. There are flowers on the windowsill. Kindly Dr. Marsh is here with you. Just outside the door is Auntie Leanne. I am with you. You are hearing my voice now as my voice, as Dodi's voice, southern drawl and all. And you will remember the love and concern that you have from your dear Nikki. She is not here yet today but will come soon, will come when you are ready, only when you are ready. And you are loved by your Auntie Leanne. You have always said that Leanne is your rock. You are loved. Loved by so many people. Especially, loved by that darling little girl Jemma. Just let the images of all the people who love you come to mind while your eyes are closed."

Dodi watches a smile curl at the edges of Estelle's mouth. Her face softens.

"And when I reach number three, I am not there yet, but when I do, your eyes will open. We have turned down the lights here, so it is not too bright for you. You will see Aunt Leanne's painting hanging on the wall. *Bookish Stella* is right beside you on the bed. You will see me, Dodi, here with you. Your body will continue to feel very relaxed. You will remember everything from this experience of remembering that you need to remember to return to us as the adult Estelle."

Dr. Marsh goes over to the light switch, dims the lights in the room, comes back, and stands in the corner behind Dodi.

"Three."

Estelle's eyes blink open. She takes in the full presence of Dodi with her—reaches out for a hug, then retreats from the hug with a loving smile to Dodi. Estelle nods to Dr. Marsh, says a weak *Hi* to him.

"Now, take your time, Estelle. Take your time. You've been hypnotized. You'll remember what that is from our training together. You needed to be hypnotized because you have been through a horrible trauma and dissociated. But you are back now. Take your time, and if you wish to speak of what has happened to you, what you remember now, you can do so."

"Father has been hurt, has been hurt really badly. Jimmy did it to him, Jimmy Murphy. Where's Nali? Nali was there, too. And . . ."

A look of horror crosses Estelle's face.

"Oh my God. Where is Nali?" She breaks into tears—conscious, fully aware, tears. "Jimmy hit her, dragged her out of the room after he killed Father."

Dr. Marsh quietly picks up the iPhone from the bedside table. He puts his hand on Dodi's shoulder. "I'm going to leave the two of you alone for a few minutes, to have some time together. I have a call to make. If it's okay, I'm going to send Aunt Leanne in, too."

"Give us a few minutes first, okay?" Dodi asks.

Dr. Marsh nods and leaves.

Dodi stares into Estelle's eyes, sees in them the adult Estelle, the Estelle she post-hypnotically suggested could return.

"I want to see Jemma," Estelle states.

"Sure, soon, really soon."

Dodi hesitates. "I want to ask you first about what else you remember from the hypnosis. You described the scene with your father and Jimmy. What else do you remember?"

Estelle looks puzzled. Silent tears flow down her cheeks. Dodi reaches out to her, holds her hand.

"I remember I thought it was GJ there attacking Father. And . . ."

Estelle starts to sob. Dodi waits patiently.

"And I encouraged him to do it. I told him to stab Father with his knife. It was like all the brutality Father had inflicted on GJ over the years, that it was payback time. But it wasn't GJ. It was Jimmy. And I urged him on."

Estelle looks up at Dodi as if to beg forgiveness. "I told Jimmy to kill my father."

Dodi reaches her hand out to hold Estelle's. "It's okay, Estelle, okay. You survived; you've come back to us to tell us what happened."

After a few moments Dodi queries Estelle further. "And anything else? Do you remember anything else, say from further back in your life?"

Estelle's face shifts from horror to confusion, from confusion to emptiness. Slowly, she shakes her head. Nothing else to comes into her conscious mind.

Lars Jonsson stands looking out over the large holding corrals of the Bar J feedlot. He had come with some apprehension, knowing of Everett Smith's violent past.

He feels an odd sense of being out of time, in the wrong place. On the way down, he'd received a call from Joyce. She found where Pierre Bolton had been staying—the Hilton Garden Inn, Downtown Calgary. Bolton checked out yesterday soon after he'd returned the dented black Malibu to Hertz Rental Car. Already, one of Lars' prime suspects was in the wind. In reviewing the hotel records, Joyce found that Bolton requested and paid for an additional space in the underground parking. He'd registered another vehicle with its make, model, and licence number—an older model Subaru Impreza. In running the licence plate, she found it registered to Calgary Rent-a-Wreck. Efficient as ever, she'd just talked to the franchise owners to ascertain that Bolton had rented it. The office was disorganized, had no idea when it was due back. It looks most likely that Chicago Bolton is gone in that aging Subaru. Joyce has advised Traffic and the RCMP to watch for the vehicle and retain the driver for questioning if it is found.

So that leaves Everett, Everett in a stinking feedlot. Everett—oh, and that Nikki, too. Nikki Blaser, who was supposedly in Fort Mac when she was actually in Red Deer, easy driving distance to get back to Calgary about the time that Horvath was killed. She'd been cagey in talking to him about where she was. And then, more recently, he'd been advised that Blaser had tried to reclaim the Caylie car, claim it before forensics had a chance to go over it.

Now standing at the staging area of the feedlot, Lars views the mass of cattle in constant, rolling motion. A posse of riders is marshalling a hundred or more head toward the compound. Beside Lars stands Quin Jacobs, feedlot owner. He's a man of few words but of intense eyes, watching the operation before him.

The roll of the land and the movement of the cattle toward Lars creates a sense of waves—dense brown waves, raw energy organized into movement by the cowhands. The sound of the lowing is growing ever more intense, and the smell is piercing. Even the ground trembles when enough cattle break into a run. The hands are pushing them forward into ever-narrowing spaces. Concentrating them, creating agitation.

"Everett Smith, I'm Detective Lars Jonsson. I'm investigating the death of Jackson Horvath. I have a few questions for you."

Everett stands uncomfortably in the small, filthy, crowded office of the feedlot operation with the police detective. The shocked look on his face in hearing the news passes quickly, then a sly smile emerges.

"Horvath you say. Dead? You don't say."

"Do you know anything about that?"

"Can't say that I do."

"What can you tell me about Horvath—how you know him, what your relationship with him was like?"

Everett's eyes dart, he shifts on his feet. "No friend of mine. Can't stand him really."

"How so?"

"Horvath? Estelle's father? Well, he's done everything he can to try to keep my daughter from me. Wouldn't even let me into the hospital room down in the States when Jemma was born. Got every high-priced lawyer he could to keep me from getting custody. I had to fight to even get access visits. It would've killed my mother if she couldn't see her only granddaughter. It got really ugly."

"So you feel animosity toward him then?"

Everett's hands clench repeatedly into tight fists. Jonsson glances at the movement. Everett starts to speak, then holds back.

"You were going to say something?"

"Forget it, no concern now that he's dead."

"What?"

Everett doesn't speak. His eyes look toward the window.

"Are you acquainted with a Pierre Bolton?"

Still no reply.

"Apparently, you met him at your parents' place last Friday."

Everett walks over to the window, looks out at the yard watching the various hands and tasks being performed, readying the setup for when he would be back. Jonsson notices the tension ease within him while he is turned away.

Looking back at the detective, the firm line to Everett's mouth has returned. "That Pierre? Well, I don't trust him. I talked to him again Sunday morning. He was all about getting me going. Lighting a fire under my ass about Horvath. Something didn't ring true to me. But he sure got me riled."

"What? What didn't ring true?"

"That pedophile business, especially when he was over at my parents' place. I had never thought it, not until that Pierre started to hint all around it . . . made it real obvious . . . right under my nose . . . if it's true."

"So what did you do with that, with what Bolton was telling you?"

"Took the boots to his car. That's what I did. There, I confess. Quin's been working with me on that, to own up to what I do when I lose it. Arrest me if you have to, I've been through this before."

"That's not what I'm here about. Tell me, where were you Sunday evening between the hours of five and seven?"

"Down here, I came down on Sunday."

"What time?"

"Sunday morning, after that Pierre guy was back at me on the phone, going on about Horvath, really pushing it about my daughter."

"So what did you do then?"

"Me? Well, like Quin taught me, I took a moment . . . I was boiling mad, but I took that moment to try to think it through. Realized I needed to get in touch with Quin down here. Quin has been working with me, working on my temper. I called him."

"You called here?"

"Yeah. Quin could hear it in my voice, hear how pissed I was. Told me to get right back down here—immediately."

Just then, Lars gets a call on his phone. He picks up to hear his sergeant update him.

The detective turns back to Everett. "I just got word from the hospital. Caylie is able to talk now. The doctor says she can tell what she saw as a witness to the murder. What would you say, Everett, if I were to tell you we have an eyewitness to the murder, one who can identify who the perpetrator was? And what if the person they identify is you? You said you were pretty mad with what Bolton had said, maybe you decided you had to deal with Horvath yourself. Will that witness identify that it was you who killed Jackson Horvath?"

"Look man. Not me. I booted that Pierre guy's car. That's the extent of it."

"So I ask again, between the hours of five p.m. and seven p.m., the day before yesterday, where would you've been?"

"Like I said, over at the Black Creek."

"Do you have any witnesses who could confirm that?"

"Yeah."

"Who?"

"You met him. Quin. When I called him he said he'd trailer up a couple of horses and we meet over there, go riding in the rangeland. So that's what we did."

Everett strides toward the door. "We're done here, right?"

"Wait. Wait right there. You have named Quin as a witness to your whereabouts. I'll need to speak to him before you can collude with him."

Everett walks out, flipping a middle finger at the detective. Watching him go, Lars contents himself that the cowboy is not going over to Quin but to where his horse waits patiently on the other side of the yard.

Quin comes up to the detective, seems to have something to say.

Everett mounts up and is gone.

"Can you let me know what time Everett got down here last Sunday?" Jonsson asks.

"Oh, that'd be about noon. Actually, not here. When he called, I could tell he was really riled. Snortin' like a racehorse, could hear it over the phone. So I suggested we meet at Black Creek. I'd trailer up the horses and meet him over there. Nothing like it, eh? Range country on a horse. We rode until the sun started to dip. Suppered up when we got back."

Jonsson makes notes on the time frame.

"You know, he's a great hand, good with horses and with the cattle. Lousy with people, though. But he's learning, learning to control the temper, to back off when he needs to. He's like a son to me, like the son I never had. Just might take over the feedlot one day. Lord willing."

Lars pounds his fist on the dash of the unmarked car. The interior has grown hot with the morning sun.

Lars is convinced of the alibi that Quin Jacobs provided. Unfortunately, it contradicts the likelihood that Everett was involved in the death of Jackson Horvath. All would have fit together in terms of character and motive for Everett to have been the one. The alibi negates that. Lars is left with Pierre Bolton, impostor and agitator—and Nikki Blaser, who has lied about her alibi. Considering that preliminary forensics suggest there were two others in the room with Estelle and her father, Lars struggles to figure what connection there might be between those two, Blaser and Bolton.

Perhaps soon it will all make sense. Estelle Caylie is talking. Frustrated, he's more than a two-hour drive away.

Nali clambers up the bank farther south from the A-frame so she's hidden, arriving at the terminus of the bridge. Military jets scrape the sky in circles overhead—circles that have her at the centre as if they are watching her escape. Another train passes just a few metres away. Its length goes on forever as it rumbles past. A hundred or more cars. At least. She looks down the length of the bridge and figures she can make it before another one comes. Hopes so, anyway. Nali steps out onto the lofty passage.

The bridge has a single track held high in the air by steel girders. Beside the track, on both sides, are metal walkways. Their surfaces are perforated, allowing rainwater to drain through. The holes provide a visual of the ground falling away beneath as Nali takes a few steps from the concrete embankment at the south end. Metal handrails beside the walkway are held up by thin metal posts every three metres or so. Nali's first few steps leave her feeling perilous, exposed. It brings back a memory—on the coast as a child, her dad encouraging her to cross a swinging suspension bridge, losing her footing and feeling as though she's going to fall. Quickly, Nali abandons the walkway to walk between the rails, stepping from one tie to the next.

The creosote-laden railway ties warm in the summer sun, the top surface becoming oily slick. Taking one step and then another, she feels for the awkward spacing of the ties, out of rhythm with a natural stride. She watches the placement of her feet. In doing so, the farther she gets from the terminus of the bridge, the farther the ground falls off in the distance below her. Soon she can't look over the sides without feeling the vertigo of the height. She settles into a pace and makes her way fifty metres or so across the bridge.

Then she senses vibration on the rails, vibration translated into the ties beneath her feet. Another train is coming. She listens carefully to determine if it's from behind or ahead of her, then decides she must make for the closest end of the bridge. Fighting her vertigo, Nali propels herself back to where she began, throws herself onto the deep grasses as the train passes.

Notice comes into the Wainwright RCMP detachment from Central Alberta dispatch in Red Deer. A call came in from CN Transit Control—a woman spotted on the Fabyan Trestle Bridge. CN will hold trains at both the Wainwright and Irma lay-bys until the bridge is cleared.

Constable Aaron Shelby sighs. The last such call was a suicidal teen walking on the bridge with earbuds in. But at 9:30 in the morning, with high school classes and exams done for the year, it's unlikely that this is a youth. Aaron signals to Sergeant Wilson that he will go.

Access to the north end of the trestle is about ten kilometres out of town. When Constable Shelby pulls in, he sees two other pickup trucks parked on a gravelled area near the north terminus of the bridge.

Gus Bellak in a western plaid shirt and jeans, has taken his 308 from the gun rack in the back of his truck. He's steadying it on the door frame of his truck so that he can look through the powerful scope on top of the rifle. "Over there, at the south end. You can see her now." He looks at the officer, then down at his rifle. "By the way, my Remmy is unchambered. Just using the scope."

Constable Shelby nods and looks through the scope. He can detect the frightened face of a woman wearing a backpack, picking her way across the bridge. She's about a third of the way.

"I suspect she'll make it between the trains. You can arrest her at this end," Gus muses.

"Sometimes, they just get into the middle and jump. One of them waited for the train in the middle and did himself in that way. Story was told that the engineer, in seeing someone in the middle of the bridge, braked the train. That didn't work out well—for anyone."

Military jets still rasp the sky overhead, drowning out the sound of the mortar fire from the base exercise. As Gus and Constable Shelby look up at them, they hear the loud, high-pitched *pock* of a rifle, the sound echoing in the valley. They watch the distant figure hit the deck of the bridge. Through the scope of Gus' rifle, they can see her lying prone between the rails.

On her stomach with the smell of the tarry surface in her face, Nali feels something wet against her back. She reaches around to touch, to check for blood. Her hand comes back wet with water. She realizes a bullet had pierced the backpack she wore and drained one of the water bottles.

The loud *ping* of another bullet ricochets off the track rail a few feet away.

Amid all the noise of jets and mortar rounds, in the lull between shots, she hears Jimmy Murphy curse her name in a coarse yell from the deck of the A-frame.

Another shot rings out.

Nali lies between the rails, partially shielded from the danger in the air above. She's concerned that the longer she lies there, she'll be stuck between the rails beneath a train passing overhead. She can imagine the horror of what that would be. She can't go back so she crawls forward, not lifting her body any more than absolutely necessary. She moves forward, one painful motion after another on her belly, continuing to make her way across the kilometre span to the other side. The cobra embracing her torso keeps her sleek and low in the slither.

Then another ricochet off one of the rails.

Constable Shelby radios back to Sergeant Wilson about the shots fired. He and Gus have figured from the sounds of the pocks and pings that the shots are originating from the other side of the valley. Most likely the Murphy place—they've had trouble with Jimmy before, a little fast and loose with that rifle of his. Shelby can't determine if the woman on the bridge is wounded or just frightened, keeping herself low and slowly working her way to safety.

When Wilson arrives, shots continue to ring out over the valley. Civilian calls are streaming in through the RCMP dispatch to the local detachment, it not being hunting season and all. Shelby asks Gus to keep his eye on the woman on the rail bridge deck. The two officers concur—sniper fire at a fleeing woman lying in the middle of the trestle. They make calls. A request for the RCMP Emergency Response Team indicates that it'll take about two hours for tactical backup to arrive from Edmonton. Vermilion detachment can send down an officer to assist, could be here in about half an hour. The military police are unable to assist as they are tasked out to the exercise with their own investigation to conduct.

Wilson and Shelby decide they will take Vermilion for now and wait anxiously as the woman crawls inch by inch across the bridge.

A call comes in from the base commander. He has ascertained from the commanding officer for Summer Ex Steadfast that a chopper can be spared— *Would it be useful?*

Wilson takes a megaphone and a carbine from the hatch of the police SUV. The A-frame is visible from a rise above the parking lot. Using the scope on top of the rifle he scans the building, seeing Jimmy on its deck. He places a call to the commanding officer of the RCMP ERT in Edmonton to brief him on the situation, decisions are made. Wilson will go the long way around to the other side of the valley, wait for the Vermilion support, and then approach the Murphy place from the west. Shelby will keep him apprised by radio of what he sees from this vantage point.

An ambulance is dispatched to the parking area to await the woman or her recovered body.

Inch by inch, Nali crawls the remaining length of the trestle. When she lifts her body too far off the surface of the rail ties, shots ring out. Jimmy Murphy has exchanged his swear words for catcalls. At least he is enjoying this. The sun's heat on the surface tar of the ties burns her hands.

A military chopper briefly hovers over her head. She hears rifle shots, and suddenly the chopper banks and heads back to the south. She hears Jimmy yell, *Yahoo*.

The air is still. She crawls. Her mind has brilliant clarity now, and with it an understanding of the events of the last few days—the horror of her father's brutal murder, the chill of being with this Jimmy she had once thought just a nuisance, and now the terror of him shooting at her. Determined, she presses on.

Then she hears the police megaphone. It warns the shooter to put down his rifle, advises that a police tactical unit has been called. She waits and then lifts herself slightly off the bridge deck. There is no further shot. In relief to her cramped legs and arms, she comes to a kneeling position. Still no shot. She stumbles to her feet and begins the long walk to the other side.

By happenstance Detective Jonsson rides the same hospital elevator with Nikki and Jemma, also on their way to see Estelle. Jemma is excited and immediately talks about going to see her Momma-Stelle. He wonders as to the wisdom of bringing a child to see the obviously psychiatrically ill woman. Estelle had been completely unresponsive on the previous day when he had been at the hospital. He watches a tense and angry Nikki trying to contain the happily excited child.

Lars tries to establish eye contact with Nikki. She deflects his gaze. He remains suspicious, given her bogus alibi about being all the way up north when she was less than two hours' drive away when Jackson Horvath was killed. He sizes her up—the bulky, broad shoulders, a tough cowgirl stance. He now realizes she looks sturdy enough to get into an altercation, to use golf clubs as a weapon—and certainly strong enough to break them and stab with them. Lars is concerned about Nikki going in to see Estelle before he has a chance to interview her. Nikki's look back at him suggests distrust, resentment of him for his presence there. She kneels down to Jemma who has announced her tummy feels funny with the movement of the elevator. He formulates a plan to keep Nikki from going into Estelle—soon, they'll reach the fifth floor.

They walk the corridor together to the place where Constable Philman stands at Estelle's door.

Jonsson shows his badge and speaks to the uniformed officer. "Constable, please detain Ms. Blaser here for questioning on my authority as the investigating officer." He stoops down to Jemma and says, "Little girl, would you like to see your mommy?"

Jemma dances with excitement as he holds her hand. They walk together into the hospital room.

The fury, the abject rage, on Nikki's face does not go unnoticed by the detective.

Lars waits out the joyous reunion of Jemma with her Momma-Stelle. There are lots of stories about harmonicas and ukuleles, and about her Momma-Nik coming home even before she was supposed to. Jemma has drawn a picture for her Momma-Stelle. Estelle proudly places it on her hospital tray.

Finally, Lars intervenes, speaking to Estelle. "I'm Detective Lars Jonsson. I'm investigating the death of your father, Jackson Horvath."

"Jemma," Estelle calls her daughter over. "Jemma, I need to talk with this man. He's a policeman. Who brought you? Auntie Leanne, Momma-Nik?"

"Momma-Nik."

"Jemma, can you go and be with Momma-Nik while I talk with him?"

"Okay, Momma-Stelle. I'll draw you another picture."

"I'd like that."

Jemma skips out of the room, a picture of joy and contentment.

Estelle looks at the detective. "It has come back to me, what I saw when Father was killed."

"Go on."

"It was Nali and me there. We went to see Father. It's coming back to me since Dodi did the hypnosis with me."

"Wait a minute. You were hypnotized?"

"Yes, that's what brought me out of it."

"By Dodi?"

"Yes."

Immediately, the detective tries to sort the significance of what he's being told. Just yesterday, he'd seen Dodi and Nikki Blaser together at the hospital. At that time, Nikki looked to be fuming angry, Dodi not confronting it but accepting of her. Could they have been colluding? Now he hears that Dodi has hypnotized Estelle, perhaps implanting a false story that will take the implication away from Nikki if Nikki is indeed the killer. Now Nikki had tried to get to Estelle herself, perhaps to be reassured that the false story has been told.

"And so what did you come to remember under the hypnosis done by this Dodi, your former lover?"

"When we, Nali and me, were talking to my father about his abuse during our childhood, a man came in. He had a knife. Father picked up a golf club from the bag in the corner to get the man to back off. When he swung the club, the man caught it and used it to beat Father. When he had Father going down, he broke one club after another over my father and really went at him with the knife."

"And this was a man, you are sure of that, that it was a man? Not a woman, a woman you may know?"

"Yes."

"Did you know the man?"

"I didn't. But Nali did. She whispered to me that it was Jimmy Murphy. I had thought it was GJ, actually, but it couldn't have been. GJ is dead. Nali told me it was Jimmy Murphy—at least that's what I remember from the hypnosis Dodi did with me."

"Nali is?"

"Nali is my sister. Annalise. She was Anna when we were growing up."

"Did you know this Jimmy Murphy? Had you ever met him before—to be able to recognize him yourself?"

"He was at the funeral, the funeral for GJ. I remember that now. Nali had told me who he was because I hadn't remembered him from back when we were kids. I didn't have much to do with him back then, I was too young. He was friends with both GJ and Nali, Anna back then."

"So, he was at the funeral. Did he speak to your father there?"

"Not that I remember."

"We know there is a connection between this Jimmy Murphy and your brother, what about with your father, was there any connection there?"

Estelle stares back blankly.

"I'm not so sure here, Ms. Caylie. You name this Jimmy Murphy after you've been hypnotized. It could be a false, implanted memory. I want you to think carefully. To your knowledge did anyone ever threaten to kill your father?"

"Not that I recall." Then Estelle goes pale. She mouths the name *Nikki* silently, the chaos of their fight the night before GJ's funeral coming to mind. It's just too horrid to even think that it could've been her.

"You were going to say something?" Lars had detected the change in her.

Estelle closes her eyes, sinks back onto the bed. "I'm tired now. It's been a shock. Can that be enough for today?"

"Yes, we are sorting this out, sorting out just who did this to your father. I will be back. Thank you for your time. Recover."

When Lars emerges from Estelle's room, he receives a call from Joyce.

Apparently, a potential suspect in the death of Jackson Horvath has been apprehended in Wainwright, Alberta—yes, a Jimmy Murphy. Murphy had taken hostage another witness to the killing, a Nali Freeman. Jimmy Murphy had also tried to kill this Nali earlier in the day. He's currently being questioned by Wainwright RCMP. Nali asked that someone gets word to Estelle and Leanne Caylie that she's okay. Wainwright RCMP also have in their possession a bloody shirt and a blood-covered hunting knife. Nali Freeman indicates that these belonged to Jimmy Murphy. When she escaped from him, she took these with her as proof of what he'd done. More details to come as they are available.

CHAPTER TWENTY

Wednesday

Dr. Marsh had ordered Estelle to stay in hospital at least one more night. The awakening terrors of the previous night concerned him. He was particularly worried about possible somnambulism and a small child being back at home. If she were to have a good night, he would allow her to go home the next day. He would prefer she'd stay a week or so on the psych ward for observation and a trial on medication that could prevent a subsequent psychotic break. Estelle, with Dodi at her side, refused. She needed to be home.

Throughout the evening Nikki had been calling the police about the car. Finally, the detective relented, saying it could be released. Nikki and Gordon went down to get it.

Around ten Nali called from Wainwright. The hospital there would release her in the morning, could someone come to get her? Gordon headed off about midnight for the five-hour drive. He was pleased to find that Cactus Corner Truck Stop in Hanna was on his route. He thought it would make a good title for a blues song and patted the emergency harmonica in his jacket pocket to make sure he had it with him.

Through the night, Leanne prepared a welcome home banner to greet Estelle when she got out of the hospital. Made of craft paper taken off a roll and running long enough to span the arch between the living room and Gordon's studio, it reads *Welcome Home Estelle*. In the bottom right corner is the phrase *signed... Your family*. Leanne drew several cartoon likenesses of

Jemma—sitting on the chair made by the *H,* bursting from the letters *o.* The *Y* is drawn as Jemma with her arms raised in joy. Around the words, Leanne placed likenesses of herself and Gordon, of April and Harry. At the end, she has Estelle with her arm around Nikki's waist. Dodi stands respectfully behind. Leanne didn't put colour into the drawing, but carefully designed the shapes like a colouring book. When Jemma got there in the morning, they'd finish it together.

The next morning when Nikki and Jemma come over they settle together into colouring the welcome banner. Soon after Nikki gets a call from Estelle.

"Hi…that's awesome, home today!…I got the car back so I can come and get you…oh?…Dodi?…Okay I guess, I'll stay here with Jemma…we're colouring, but I would really rather…okay…yah…I will see you when you get here then…"

Nikki waves Leanne over, Dodi follows. "Estelle comes home today, later this morning. I guess you are supposed to go, Dodi. The doctor wants to speak to you."

"Do you want to come, too?" Dodi looks at Nikki.

"Momma-Nik, can you stay with me? We haven't finished colouring yet."

Leanne's phone rings. "Oh, hi Merrill…we just heard, coming home today…great…sure, give us a while to get her here."

Nikki resigns herself to settle back at the table colouring with Jemma, who is determined to get it all done before her Momma-Stelle makes it back. Leanne asks if she can take Estelle's car over to get April and Harry before Dodi leaves for the hospital—she's sure they'd want to be here too when Estelle comes home.

Coming in with Dodi, Estelle takes one look at the banner and breaks into tears. Her knees buckle and she leans back on Dodi. Leanne rushes over and embraces her. The three women cry together. It is a release. As much as Estelle had come back to her mind in the hospital, she needs yet to come back to her heart. Her heart feels the loss of two members of her family. She needs the hugs of these two women who had been there for her through this all.

Jemma rushes over from the breakfast nook where she has been reading with Nikki, wraps her arms around her Momma-Stelle's legs. Estelle crouches to embrace her daughter. Nikki stands off to the side, Estelle turns to her and motions her into the group hug too.

April comes over, toddler Harry on her hip. "Sister," she says. She puts an arm around Estelle to join the hug.

Boxes of crackers and packages of plastic-wrapped, individual portions of cheese adorn the table. Leanne has pulled cans of frozen fruit juice from the freezer and a large bottle of ginger ale. She has set them beside a punch bowl but hasn't got around to putting them together yet. Estelle collapses onto a kitchen chair and asks for a coffee. She looks wan. Her ordeal and the two days in the hospital bed have taken a lot out of her.

The doorbell rings.

Merrill enters. He has a large vase with eighteen roses, stems still in their water tubes. Around the neck of each rose, just below the flower, is a carefully attached ribbon with a name on it. He presents the vase to Estelle with an explanation that everyone at ReClaiming Ourselves Inc. sends their love. Estelle looks at one of the ribbons. It has the name Charlie on one side and the words *I believe in your capacity to heal* on the other—the same words Estelle has spoken over and over again to the clientele at the agency.

Leanne clears a place for the vase of roses on the table and goes about making the punch. She introduces Merrill to Dodi, and the two start talking shop—about his graduate school program and the practicum he's doing with Estelle, and about her role as clinical psychologist in a busy emergency and psychiatric acute care ward in a Missouri hospital.

Jemma is on her Momma-Stelle's lap as they sit under the banner.

On the way back from Wainwright, Nali insisted that Gordon first take her back to her place, to shower and change. When they arrived there, she handed him a can of Febreze to spray the stink inside his car from her transit there in blood-soaked, creosote-stained clothes. Weakened from the last two days, the tattoo of the cobra holds her upright. At the back of her neck, a large gauze still covers the stitches she received at the Wainwright hospital.

When they arrive at 113 Durham Lane, Gordon stands back for her to go in first. Estelle stands to greet her.

The sisters embrace. There are so many words for them to speak together that they can't even begin. They hold hands. In Nali's eyes are decades of concern for the well-being of her kid sister. Within Estelle's eyes is the relief of coming home to sisterhood.

In the silence between them, Gordon walks into his studio, takes out his emergency harmonica from the Mickie pocket of his denim jacket and begins to softly play the *Cactus Corner Truck Stop Blues*. Its melody trembles, sacred. Leanne silences him with a dirty look.

Nikki clears her throat. All eyes go to her.

"Well, it seems somewhat anticlimactic, with what has happened to Estelle and Nali and all, but I do have an announcement to make that I think is very relevant. This morning I received a call from AltaWindTech. I've been hired on as a driver and installation assistant for wind turbines here in southern Alberta. No more departures for two weeks in Fort Mac. On this job, I can be home every night."

Estelle stands and goes over to Nikki. She takes both of Nikki's hands in her own. Jemma winds herself between their legs and hugs them together.

"Thanks, Nikki. Bad things happen when you go away, I guess. I know it's important for you to be here to protect me." Estelle makes eye contact briefly with Nikki. There's genuine appreciation in her eyes. With all that has happened, maybe she does need protection. And there's Jemma, too—Nikki protects and plays with Jemma. Jemma needs them both.

But Dodi is standing just off to the side, and Estelle's eyes deflect to hers. There's a profound sense of longing, longing for the security and love that she felt in connection to Dodi in the hospital. She knows Nikki could never love her in that way—reactive, protective Nikki. The two loves are so different.

"No more bad things. Okay?" Nikki's statement has a sense of command to it. It brings Estelle's eyes back to her.

"Okay. When did all this job thing happen? I didn't know anything about it." Estelle struggles to bring her mind back, a mind so caught in so much over the last few days.

"My interview was Monday morning. It killed me not to come home Sunday night when Leanne texted me and told me you were unconscious and in the hospital. But I decided I needed to get this job. The interview was at eight a.m. in Red Deer. That's where AltaWindTech head office is. So I figured—it being just a few hours different in coming home and you being safe in the hospital and all—I'd go to the interview, get back to Calgary as soon as I could after. They called me this morning to tell me I have the job."

Leanne interrupts. "But I picked you up at the airport, like you'd flown down from Fort Mac."

"In case I didn't get the job, I didn't want anyone to know that I had tried for it, had gone to Red Deer rather than all the way north. If it hadn't been for what happened to Estelle, after the Monday morning interview I was going to hop a plane and be back in Fort Mac for my shift Monday night. But, of course, I needed to get back here. So I rented a car and dropped it off at the airport for you to pick me up there as if I had flown in from Fort Mac."

There's an awkward silence around the room. Nikki continues. "Then, today, I hear I got the job. It all comes out okay in the end."

Estelle stares emptily at Nikki. Monday was absent for her, absent in recall of anything except for a vague awareness of Dodi's presence with her when she needed the silent, steady love of another. Dodi was with her, and Nikki was putting on a ruse about a job interview.

It's awkward. Nikki reads that awkwardness, stares intently at Estelle. Finally, she says, "I'm sorry that I didn't come sooner." Her voice now sounds regretful.

"You came and you aren't going away so far away anymore," Estelle replies, her voice flat.

Then Estelle feels waves of emotion washing over her, waves still too powerful to resist. There's love. But there's pain and regret and grief and disappointment and a hundred other feelings, too.

And still, there is that empty space within, the space that haunts with the sound of the wind and the lash of the rain—that sucking space that threatens to pull her under. It is like a tide coming in, a tide that could deposit a swimmer roughly back onto the beach to be pulled to safety by a loving hand—or a riptide, so powerful with its undertow, that could take that swimmer helplessly back out to sea.

EPILOGUE

Three letters arrive at the Nose Hill Depression and Anxiety Clinic, one for each of the psychiatrists. Monica opens hers. It is obviously a form letter.

Dear Dr. Lebresque,

Your participation in the 47th Canadian Congress of Community Psychiatry recently held in Vancouver was most appreciated. Conference organizers hope that it was a valuable time of learning and connection for you,

We are deeply saddened to announce the death of one of our presenters. Dr. Jackson Horvath was killed in his Calgary office just twelve days following his inspiring presentation to us entitled, The Gift of Health. *We all mourn the death of this highly respected member of our nationwide community of psychiatrists.*

Dr. Horvath's presentation provided insight into a different approach to community psychiatry and presented pre-liminary data on the effectiveness of that approach. We are delighted to announce that his work will become the focus of further research seeking to validate and extend his findings. We anticipate that with this research, Dr. Horvath's legacy as an innovator and excellent clinician will be preserved.

In the future, you may be approached by Mr. Pierre Bolton, who has been assigned the role of managing director for this research project as sponsored by the Consortium of Pharmaceutical Treatment and Research Initiatives. *We encourage all of our members to work together with Mr. Bolton in the development of this research initiative.*

We join with you in your sadness at the loss of one of our members.

Sincerely yours,
Dr. Samuel Smithson, FCPP
Conference Organizer

CPSIA information can be obtained
at www.ICGtesting.com
Printed in the USA
BVHW080112301221
624251BV00006B/81/J